ISBN 978-1-331-29621-8
PIBN 10170490

FB &c Ltd, Dalton House, 60 Windsor Avenue, London, SW19 2RR.
Company number 08720141. Registered in England and Wales.

For support please visit www.forgottenbooks.com

MARIELLA; OF OUT-WEST

The Co.

MARIELLA; OF OUT-WEST

BY

ELLA HIGGINSON

AUTHOR OF "FROM THE LAND OF THE SNOW-PEARLS," "A FOREST ORCHID," "WHEN THE BIRDS GO NORTH AGAIN," ETC.

"IN men whom men condemn as ill
I find so much of goodness still;
In men whom men pronounce divine
I find so much of sin and blot—
I hesitate to draw a line
Between the two, where God has not."

—JOAQUIN MILLER.

New York
THE MACMILLAN COMPANY
LONDON: MACMILLAN & CO., LTD.
1902

Set up and electrotyped October, 1902.

Norwood Press
J. S. Cushing & Co. — Berwick & Smith
Norwood Mass. U.S.A.

To my Niece

IVY MORGAN

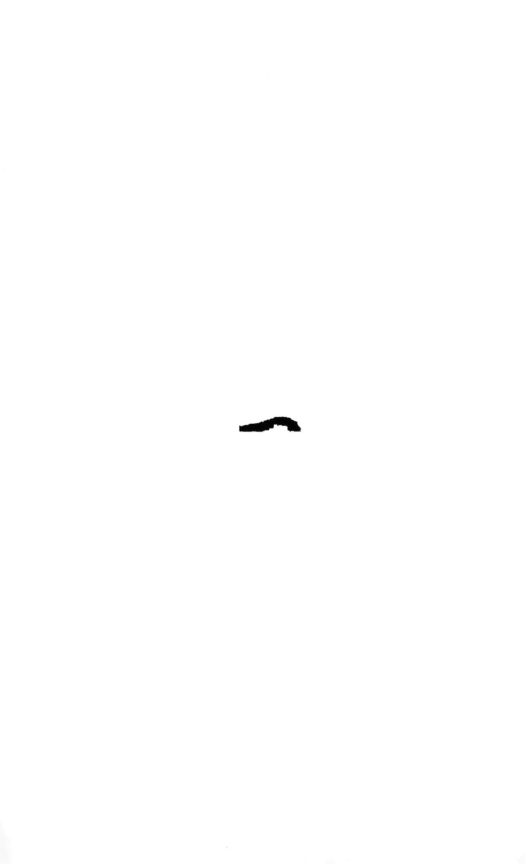

PREFACE

An isolated ranch on Puget Sound. A hillside that swung like a cloud of blended gold and rose and green between the blue of the sky and the deeper blue of the sea. A big orchard whose trees had taken on long downward curves beneath the heaviness of their fruitage. Under these trees, in the brightest hour of the brightest day, twilight, dim and fragrant. Butterflies drifting brilliantly here and there, or sinking to rest under the lifted tents of their wings. The goldness and the languor of autumn hovering over everything; and a stillness, broken only by a low wind, lingering and elusive; a wind that breathed out the very heartbreak of the year. Mist-fragments, pink as fields of oleander bloom, loitering across the water and purpling as they settled into the hollows of the hills on the islands, — where the smooth madrones shone redly among the dark firs and cedars. North, east, and south the unbroken forest, climbing and darkening as it climbed; and at the far horizon the snow-mountains, glimmering, misty and beautiful, through the autumnal splendor. To the west the wide sweep of undulating sea which ebbs and flows, under its opaline lights, on the northwesternmost shores of the mystical and misunderstood land, — the land of forest and plain and desert; of deep-flowing, majestic rivers and vast spaces swimming from snow-mountain to snow-mountain, — the land which is vaguely known to the rest of the world as "Out-West."

MARIELLA; OF OUT-WEST

MARIELLA

PART I

CHAPTER I

Mrs. Palmer came up through the orchard with long strides.

"Mariella! Mariella! Come an' help me bin the apples."

"Oh, mother!"

"Don't you 'Oh, mother' *me!* Lay there 'n the sun an' smell o' them yellow roses. I'd think you'd be ashamed!"

The child rose slowly from the deep clover in which she had been lying. She was a little, slender thing. She had startled eyes and a sensitive mouth. Blue veins ran through her temples and wrists. Her pink calico dress was too short and gave her a look of awkwardness.

There was a big bunch of late yellow roses in her hands.

"Oh, mother! Are they binnin' apples to-day?"

"Yes, they're a-binnin' apples to-day. Is there any law agen it? You do beat all! You act so! What makes you act so? Does anything ail you?"

"Oh, I just can't go down there 'n the fruit-house an' bin apples all day. I can't. It makes me ache all over."

"It — makes — you — ache — all — over?" repeated Mrs. Palmer, slowly.

She put her arms akimbo and laughed with a kind of good-natured contempt.

"It makes you ache all over, aigh? Well, what do you suppose it makes me do — to stand a-stoopin' from floor to box, an' box to bin, all day — if it makes you ache all over to set down comf'terble on an apple-box an' put 'em into the bins after they're all sorted over?"

"I can't! Oh, I just can't! It makes me sick!"

"Well, you've got to; that's all."

The child flung her roses from her and cast herself, face downward now, in the clover again and sobbed.

"Now, see here, Mariella," said her mother, sternly; "you've got to help bin them apples, an' that's all there is about it. You needn't to act the lady so. We ain't in the lady-raisin' business. For pity's sake! Are you any better 'n your mother, I want to know? I'd be ashamed o' myself — to go a-puttin' everything off on my mother so! Get up now, an' come on."

After a moment the little girl arose and followed her mother silently down the hill through the orchard to the fruit-house. She seemed to not lift her feet high enough; they dragged. She was pale and trembling.

"See how them little russet pears are a-fallin'," said her mother, cheerfully. "An' them Glory Mundys, too. Your father'll have to hump himself to get 'em all in. They've hung on lots later 'n usual this year. You can eat russet pears all the time you're a-binnin' apples, Mariella," she added, encouragingly.

She was the kind of woman that is always generous to the subjected. But Mariella made no reply.

The fruit-house stood alone at the foot of the hill. There was an upstairs in which the hired men slept. The lower floor was one large room. There was a door at each end, and both were propped open with smooth stones. Long tables occupied the centre of the room.

The sides were lined with bins as high as one could reach.

Mariella sat upon an apple-box and transferred apples with deft touches from a box at her side into the bin in front of her.

She made no complaints; but after a glance at her pale face and folded lips her mother felt the necessity of cheerful speech.

"I'd think you'd be glad to handle them pretty red Bald'ins," she said, being entirely without tact. "If they were marbles or balls, you'd play with 'em all day. They wouldn't make you ache all over then, I'll be bound."

The child set her lips a little closer, but made no reply.

"Come now," continued her mother, encouragingly; "what is it aches you so — a-handlin' pretty red apples? I just want to know."

"I don't know," said Mariella, briefly.

"Well, try an' think. You said it made you ache all over."

"It doesn't always; but some days" — she shivered suddenly — "I *can't* work. It makes me sick!"

Mrs. Palmer laughed — a mellow, exasperating laugh.

"I guess it won't make you so terrible sick. It won't get you out of work to go to puttin' on airs, either, over farm work. You was born on a farm, an' you're liable to stay on a farm an' do farm work for the rest o' your life. Set up straighter."

Mariella lifted her figure from its listless stoop.

"I notice you don't turn sick over eatin' some nice apple-sauce, or some apple-butter, or Brown Betty. I notice that. You can eat Brown Betty with thick cream on seven times a week, I'll be bound! But a little work makes you ache like the ague. I don't want to hear any more about it, now."

Mariella was silent.

"I don't want any more to-do about it — now!"

"I'm not makin' any to-do."

"It's a pity you ain't! You ain't a-makin' it with your tongue, I'll allow, but you're a-makin' it with your *looks*. I'd just as lieve you'd make it with your tongue. I do' know but I'd liever."

Mariella went on with her work. She never looked at her mother. Sometimes she glanced past her out of the open door and sighed. The sunlight lay so yellow on the hill, it seemed as if she could smell it; and once she thought she smelled hazel-nuts.

Her heart leaped at the thought; but immediately it sank, and she sighed again.

"Good grieve!" exclaimed her mother. "You sigh like they say them new people from Mizzoura do. They say they are so shiftless they sigh every time they get up out of a chair."

"What's shiftless?" asked Mariella, with a show of interest.

Mrs. Palmer stood in a ruminating attitude.

"For pity's sake," she said, at last; her face was red. "Don't you know what shiftless means? Dumby!"

"I wouldn't asked if I knew."

"W'y, when a man's shiftless, he — he — oh, he don't clean off the porches an' paths after a snow-storm; he waits for 'em to *melt* clean. He lets doors drag on the hinges rather 'n shave 'em off a little; an' he — he — ties his horses' breechin's up with bale-rope. That's what shiftless is."

"What do shiftless women do?"

Mrs. Palmer sorted apples for a full minute.

"Well, I can tell you one thing," she said, then, slowly, "there ain't a shiftless hair in my head. Not a one!"

"Well, what do they do?"

"W'y, for one thing, they look like all-fire around home. They never have their hair smooth at work, an' they have spots on their clo's. Like as not, they take the corners of their kitchen aprons to pick up hot fryin'-pans. I expect they'd rather burn fat up than to try it out an' make nice drippin's."

Her eyes were caught by the bunch of roses lying beside Mariella on the floor.

"I wouldn't be surprised," she added, "if they'd rather lay 'n the clover an' smell o' yellow roses than to bin apples to help their mother along."

Mariella laughed for the first time.

"I did know a woman once," continued Mrs. Palmer, after a pause, "who was so shiftless she used to run a thread around the holes in her husband's socks an' draw em' together 'n a hard lump rather 'n darn 'em. They say he swore wicked."

At noon they stopped work for an hour. Mariella arose with stiff and aching limbs. She slipped away through the orchard and flung herself down in the tall clover under a tree, sinking her face into the hollow of her arms.

But in a few moments her mother's voice, loud and harsh, came ringing after her.

"Hoo-oo-hoo! Mariella! Hoo-oo-hoo! Mariella! You Ma-ri-ella! Where are you at?"

The child sat up.

"I'm down here under the Bald'in tree."

"Well, what on earth are you a-doin' there? Come an' git your dinner. We ain't got any time to set under Bald'in trees in apple-getherin' time."

"I don't want any dinner."

"You don't want any dinner, aigh?" Her mother came down through the ferns with long strides. "Now, see here, Mariella! You stop a-actin' the fool an' come to your dinner."

"I don't want any," repeated Mariella, sullenly.

"Yes, you do, too. You needn't to cut up so just because you have to bin apples. It won't git you out of doin' it. Come on, now."

She stooped and grasped one of the small wrists and pulled the child to her feet.

"I'll show you how you tell me you don't want things!"

Mariella gave her one look of the helpless hate that is sometimes seen in a dog's eyes.

"You can make me go to the house," she said; "but you *can't* make me eat when I don't want to."

"*Mule!*" cried her mother, furiously. She pulled her along up the hill and pushed her into the hot kitchen. She was careful, however, not to pinch her wrist nor do violence to her body in any way. She was of that large class of mothers that are called "indulgent" because their hurts are always of the spirit and never of the flesh.

A burst of laughter from the hired men greeted Mariella's scarlet-faced entrance.

"Hey, little gal!" cried one, chucking her under the chin with an unclean finger. "You got *pulled* up to your dinner, didn't you? Pretty soon you'll have to be hoisted up on a pulley, like the pigs, won't you?"

Without an instant's hesitation she struck him in the breast, as he barred her way, with all the strength of her poor little arm and closed hand. "Yes, *fool!*" she flamed out passionately, and sped past him through the house and up to her tiny room in the attic, whose door she bolted before flinging herself on the bed.

Her mother looked after her in despair. "I never see such a disposition in all my born days," she said, helplessly. "Set up. Dinner's on the table, an' we ain't got any time runnin' to waste to-day." She sat down heavily at one end of the table. Mr. Palmer twisted into his chair at the opposite end. He was as small and thin as his wife was large and buxom. He wore a faded flannel shirt and blue overalls, with suspenders of an indescribable color.

The table was spread with a red cloth and laid with the commonest of thick earthenware, iron knives, and three-tined forks; but the dishes were almost aggressively clean; they fairly shone with cleanness, and the knives and forks were polished white.

"I do abominate a nicked dish," Mrs. Palmer frequently declared. "I can stand anything but that, most. It makes me squeamish."

The spoons were of pewter and were polished so that they were like little hollowed mirrors.

In the centre of the table stood the pride of Mrs. Palmer's heart — a big fat caster, silver-plated, stuffed out with bottles like a horse with hay.

The dinner consisted of fried ham and eggs, gravy, and baked potatoes. At one end of the table was a thick, wobbly custard pie; there was also a dish of apple-sauce freckled over with nutmeg. The hired men sat around the table, clean-faced, but odorous of perspiration. The hired girl came in with her sleeves rolled to the elbow, and slipped, laughing, into a chair beside one of the men. A conscious scarlet swept over her face, bringing out all her heavy freckles.

"Pitch in," said Mr. Palmer, heartily. All helped themselves, reaching across the table for anything desired. Pepper-boxes were hammered on the bottoms, and little cones of salt were chinked off the knives with the forks. There was a cheerful crunching of food and a guzzling of coffee, which was poured into the saucers.

Suddenly the man who had chucked Mariella under the chin burst out laughing. "That little gal's got a spirit," he said, admiringly.

A twinkle came into Mr. Palmer's eyes. "She has so. Guess you won't chuck her under the chin ag'in soon, Gus. 'Fool,' aigh?"

The men roared.

"She'd ought to be tanned for that," said Mrs. Palmer, in an ominous tone. "She flares up like sheet lightnin' at nothin'. I don't see where she gits her temper at."

She gave her husband a look.

"Oh, don't you?" said her husband. The hired girl tittered.

"No, I don't. I did intend to let her off this afternoon, she's such a weakly thing; but now, I'll make her bin apples till suppertime."

"You'll have fun a-gittin' her out o' the attic," said her husband.

"I'll git her."

But, notwithstanding her boast, when the men had scraped their chairs back from the table and tramped out through the kitchen, Mrs. Palmer did not know just how to set to work to get Mariella out of the attic. She stood around, rubbing her chin, and ruminating.

"I guess I'll git the hammer an' pound on her door. She'll think I'm a-goin' to smash it in. She'll open it up fast enough, I bet."

But when she was almost at the stair-door, it was quietly opened, and Mariella entered the dining-room. All the scarlet and fury were gone out of her face.

After her first start of surprise, Mrs. Palmer slipped the hammer guiltily into the folds of her dress.

"Oh, here you be, aigh? High time, you sulky little piece! Come on now an' step spry. I expect you'd like somethin' to eat, but you'll wait till suppertime to pay you for your smart-Ellickness. Step spry."

Mariella walked silently behind her mother. At another time she would have felt the soft beauty of the noon that burned down upon her; but now she was conscious only of her own suffering.

At the last moment she was saved. One of the hired men, taking a look at her face, said to her father, "I wouldn't make that little gal work to-day, if I was you."

"Her mother's doin' the makin'," responded Mr. Palmer, grimly.

"Well, I wouldn't let her. That little gal ain't fit to work."

"What's the matter of her?"

"Matter of her? I do' know. Look at her! She's about ready to drop in her tracks. She wa'n't able to set here an' work this mornin'; an' then Gus had to pester her — pore little peakid thing!"

"She's peakid," admitted Mr. Palmer, dryly, "but she can keep her end o' the line up. She's sheet lightnin'. Say, ma!"

"Aigh?"

"You let Mariella off to-day; Hoover thinks she looks sick."

Mrs. Palmer looked at the child, who was, indeed, ghastly.

"She ain't any more sick 'n I am," she said. "She hates work like rattlesnakes."

But she took the child by the arm and led her to the door.

"Now go an' play with your *hen!*" she said, contemptuously. "You ain't worth a pinch o' salt."

CHAPTER II

THE following day being the seventh of the week, the Palmer family arose with Sunday faces and Sunday manners. Mrs. Palmer moved on tiptoe, and reproved the hired girl when she dropped a tin lid. "I'd be ashamed to go a-makin' so much noise on a Sunday," she said. "You'd try the soul out of a saint hisself! Have you got the coffee on? It's a wonder. Carry the breakfast in, an' look out you don't spill the gravy. There, look at you! Can't you step easy? *Pigeon-toe!*"

The big platter was filled with ham instead of bacon, as on other mornings; there was a dish of marmalade in the centre of the table; and at each end was a cold pumpkin-pie, with narrow strips of golden pastry making a checker-board on top.

It was a cold, bare dining-room, into which Mariella always came shrinking. The walls and the ceiling and the floor had once been painted a dull drab. There were drab calico curtains hanging limply and somewhat skimpily over the two small windows. There was not a picture, not an ornament, not a flower. There was not even a braided rag mat on the floor.

Out in the kitchen the fire in the cooking-stove kept up a musical crackling, as if it felt that the whole burden of making cheer depended upon itself. The teakettle took the hint, and pushed a long white funnel of steam out toward the dining-room, singing away right merrily; and the hired girl had slid the front "draught" open with the toasting-fork, revealing tiny scarlet isinglass windows. With the big, gold-colored cat stretched luxuriously under the stove, the kitchen presented a cosey and tempting appearance. The little girl looked yearningly through the open door.

"I want to eat out in the kitchen," she whispered, standing awkwardly beside her mother's chair.

"What's that, Petty?" Mrs. Palmer had on her Sunday affection, too. "Eat out in the kitchen? Well, eat there, then; I don't care — but, good grieve! What for?"

"I'm cold."

"Cold? Well, why don't you put on your thick underclo's? Pass up your plate to your father. He'll fill it up for you. You don't deserve a mouthful, though," she added suddenly, having been born with a soul for nagging, "after the way you acted up yesterday."

Two or three of the men laughed. Mr. Palmer crossed his knife and fork on his plate, and looked at his wife contemptuously. "Well, you are a bright one," he said. "Can't you let the young one alone, now she's behavin' herself? I never see your eq'al fer naggin'! You'd nag a saint into his grave!"

Mrs. Palmer flung up her head. Her face was red. Her mouth curled with angry scorn. "You'd ought to talk!" she cried, shrilly. "You'd ought to talk, hadn't you? It's a lot you know about governin' childern! Whip 'em one day an' kiss 'em the next! Nice raisin' she'd git if it wa'n't fer me. You'd ought to talk — *you!*"

The men exchanged winks and joked in undertones — coarse, full-mouthed undertones. It was understood throughout the neighborhood that the Palmers didn't "live happy," and never a meal passed without a quarrel, save now and then a Sunday dinner. When guests were present the battle waged silently, but just as surely, although on such occasions the only weapons used were threatening glances and indescribable tones.

Mariella took her plate and slipped out to the kitchen table, where she ate her breakfast in peace. What good noises the fire made, she thought, with a sense of warmth and comfort stealing through her little thin body. She thrilled with pleasure when the cat came and rubbed his head caressingly against her. "Do you love me, Mose?" she whispered. "Oh, Mose," — she gathered him up to her breast with a sudden, convulsive movement, — "I wish — oh, I *wish* — you could say yes!"

She started guiltily as the door opened and her mother came bouncing in for some hot biscuits.

"What's the matter now, miss? You look guilty. I'll be bound you're up to somethin' the minute my back's turned. Oh, I see! Nursin' the cat right while you're a-eatin' your breakfast! That's a pretty thing to do. A body 'u'd think I never teached you anything. Cat's hairs a-flyin' into everything! Put him down — er I'll give you a whack you'll remember." Then, recollecting of a sudden that it was the Sabbath, she added, piously, "D' you know your catachism?"

"No," said the child, sullenly.

"*No?* Don't you 'no' *me*, miss. 'No' what?"

"No, ma'am."

"Well. That's more like it. You take an' learn it, then, as soon's you're through, an' I'll hear you."

She piled the biscuits into a pyramid on the plate, and returned to the dining-room. At once her high-pitched voice arose in hot and bitter dispute with her husband.

Mariella leaned her elbows upon the table, and pressed her palms over her ears, so she could not hear. Her gaze went out the window; out to the blue stretch of sea, with the beautiful mists rising from it and burning with opaline lights as they caught the mounting sun. Far to the west, across those miles of water, the majestic Olympian range of snow-peaks stood out in splendid fire. She was shaken with the longing to get away from the sordid, coarse tumult of her daily life; to go drifting with that cloud of silvery sea-birds that sank one moment to the cool hollows of the sea, and the next arose, throbbing, to the sunlight with a shower of liquid jewels flashing from wings and breasts — to go drifting with them out to the wide and terrible ocean.

She was only fourteen years old; but the quarrelling of her parents always gave her the feeling that she must flee away — anywhere to escape hearing it. Many a time she had fled far into the orchard and hidden her shocked face in her arms, deep in the ferns. When she dared not run away, she held her hands tightly over her ears. She did this now; but the shock of loud voices came to her.

At last she stole to the door on her tiptoes, and closed it softly.

When the men had gone out to the barnyard to attend to the Sunday feeding of various animals, and the hired girl was washing the dishes with a great clatter thereof, Mrs. Palmer sat down by the big, black fireplace in the sitting-room, and opened the little catechism. She had a consciously solemn look.

"Now, then," she said, clearing up her throat, "you ready, Petty?"

Mariella sank upon a low stool, sticking her thin legs out to the fire.

"Mercy, child, don't set so awk'ard! Draw your legs in, an' don't stick your elbows out so. They're as sharp as razors. An' I'd hide my legs as much as I could, if I was you. They're as thin as pipe-stems." The child blushed so deeply that the tears came into her eyes. "No wonder the boys laff at you an' pester you."

"I *hate* 'em!" burst out Mariella, passionately. "*Little devils!*"

"Chu, chu, chu!" cried her mother, in a fine rage. "What d' you mean by usin' sech language? On a Sunday, too! I'll —"

"You say it yourself. You know you do. You call some of the neighbors devils every day."

"I'll punish you fer this to-morrow," cried Mrs. Palmer, furiously. "I'll show you how to talk to your mother! I'd whip you now within an inch o' your life if it wa'n't a Sunday. You little heifer, you! You ever call anybody a devil ag'in!"

"I'll call anybody a devil that laughs at my legs," said the child, sticking them out, with a proud defiance, farther than they had been before. "I'll do it, if you whip me till I can't stand up."

Mrs. Palmer was seized with a sudden spell of coughing, and pretended she did not hear. It was a spell with which Mariella was well acquainted. It came on conveniently whenever her mother was defeated. She sat quietly waiting for it to run through its graded paroxysms.

"Well, now," said Mrs. Palmer, recovering at last, "I'll choke to death yet with that cough. It must be a specie of bronsheetis. Now, then, we'll see 'f you know your catachism. What — is — your — name?"

"Mariella."

"Who — gave — you — this — name?"

"My sponsors in baptism. What's a sponsor?" added the child, suddenly.

"Your sponsors is your par'nts," replied her mother, with dignity.

"Well, what's baptism?"

"My land, don't you know that? I wish it wa'n't so fur to a Sunday-school. W'y, the minister puts water on your head an' says what your name is — that's babtism."

Mariella twisted around on the stool, so she could look at her mother. Her eyes were large with wonder. "Did any minister do that to me?"

"Er — hum — no," said Mrs. Palmer, reluctantly. "We never had you babtised."

"It's a wonder the teacher never told us what it meant. We've had it in our reading and spelling." Then she added, with a change of tone, "Well, if I wasn't baptized, it's silly to ask me that question. It isn't true to answer what the book says. I won't do it."

Mrs. Palmer realized that she was getting into deep waters. She went on slowly and laboriously with the questions. She had no education, and could barely read by spelling out the more difficult words silently before attempting to pronounce them. The child went as laboriously through the tiresome answers. The long tangle of words about the articles of the Christian faith, and renouncing the works of the devil, the pomps and vanities of this wicked world, the sinful lusts of the flesh, the salvation through Jesus Christ — it all meant absolutely nothing at all to her, and she knew her mother could not explain it. But suddenly she stopped and drew her brows together.

"What does it mean by saying that Christ was conceived by the Holy Ghost?"

"It means that the Holy Ghost was his father," said Mrs. Palmer, firmly.

"Mother!" cried Mariella, reproachfully. "A ghost is a dead person that comes back and scares us — you told me so yourself!"

"My land!" said poor Mrs. Palmer, desperately. "You're offul dumb. I never see anybody so dumb." Her face was scarlet. "You can't seem to understand anything."

Mariella stood up. There was a dull red on her own face. "That's all I learned," she said, briefly. "And I don't see any sense in learning that. I don't know what a word of it means. I wish it was grammar. I'd rather learn grammar than *eat*."

"You can't expect to understand catachism till you git older," said her mother, encouragingly.

"Then, what's the use in learning a thing till you *can* understand it?" She was leaving the room with short, impatient steps, but at the door she paused.

"Maybe I am dumb," she said, with bitter remembrance, "but I can learn grammar, and spelling, and geography. And *I'll bet*" — this was one of her mother's favorite expressions — "that the minister himself don't understand how a *ghost* can be anybody's father!"

She went out, banging the door behind her. Mrs. Palmer sank back in her chair and closed the catechism with a snap. She was laughing, guiltily, but with keen enjoyment. "I'll bet he don't, neither!" she whispered to herself. "She hit the nail on the head that time."

CHAPTER III

One big apple tree far from the house was Mariella's confessional. She went to it in her passionate longings, her vain rages, her gray despairs. Its long slender branches sank in graceful curves and rested their tips upon the earth. She was compelled to turn them carefully aside before she could enter the perfumed twilight underneath.

Here she told everything to the silence. And here on that particular Sunday noon she was lying, face downward in the grass, wondering about the Holy Ghost, when her mother's voice, pitched in a cautious key, aroused her.

"Mariella! Where are you at?"

She sprang to her feet and slipped out from her little chapel. She had kept it, so far, sacred from all eyes. She ran along the path away from it now, as a mother bird leads artfully away from her nest.

"Here, mother — here."

"Oh! W'y, who d' you s'pose has come to dinner an' spend the day? *Them Mallorys!* With all their childern. A hull wagonful of 'em! It makes me want to swear. I would, if it wa'n't a Sunday."

"Is it any worse to swear on Sunday than any other day?"

"Oh, of course. What makes you ac' the dunce so? You don't seem to have good sense. You ask sech fool questions! I want that you should come in an' keep all them childern out o' mischief."

"I hate visiting folks," said the little girl, bitterly. "What makes them come? Why can't they stay at home? Sit around an' say 'yes, ma'am' and 'no, ma'am'!"

"Well, it wouldn't hurt you if you was a little politer, like them little girls. Their ma makes 'em toe the mark. They walk jest so, an' set down jest so, an' fold their hands in their laps, as nice as you please. It won't hurt you none to take pattern after 'em. Come on, now. You can take 'em out to see the little pigs. I sha'n't have 'em goin' a-pigeon-toein' all over the house. I can't see what they want to come a-visitin' for on Sunday. They must be pushed. Work an' slave all day now to git up a nice dinner. That's all they come fer. 'Offul glad to see you!'" She mimicked her guest's tone. "'Ain't see you fer a coon's age. We jest said to ourselves that we'd up an' come to spend a Sunday with you, an' have a reel good visit!' Jest as if I didn't know they come fer their dinner! She's got on a black alpaco dress," she added, in a different tone. "It's made new fashion; one o' them polonay things, all looped up in the back. I bet it ain't paid fer! I'd like to have a black alpaco. I wish your father wa'n't so all-fired close."

The visitors had brought their chairs out on the pleasant porch. Mrs. Palmer's face assumed an amiable expression as she came around the corner of the house. "Out here 'n the cool?" she said. "That's right. Make yourselves to home. I've b'en after Petty. She's always a-slyin' off somewhere in the orchud. Come an' speak to Mis' Mall'ry."

Mrs. Mallory was very thin. Her shoulders fell forward toward her flat chest; her shoulder-blades stood out sharply. Her movements were precise and ladylike. She never crossed her knees nor put her arms akimbo.

She held her elbows close to her sides and kept her hands folded nervously in her lap. She had ridden two miles in a spring-wagon, but there was not a crease in the crisp alpaca dress. She had turned the skirt inside out, before getting into the wagon, and held it firmly around her waist.

"Well, Mariella? W'y, what a thin little girl! Nothing to you! Well, I'll declare!" She commenced laughing, as if at a great joke; tiny wrinkles ran in all directions away from her mouth and eyes. "What a funny little girl! You're so thin. And where'd you get so many freckles?"

Mariella stood awkwardly before her, scarlet-faced. She was filled with sudden, silent hate. "I don't know," she said, unsmiling.

"W'y, Isaphene hasn't got a one — not a one! She always puts on her bonnet when she goes out to play. I expect you know a little girl that doesn't do that — don't you, now? A little girl with lots of freckles on her face — aigh?"

"Here come the men," put in Mrs. Palmer, hurriedly. She had seen danger-signals in Mariella's eyes. "They've been a-puttin' up the horses. Well, Mr. Mall'ry?" She blushed and smiled coquettishly as she gave that gentleman a large hand. "Ain't this nice weather fer fall? Have a chair. Pa, you get thet little green one, will you, from the settin'-room — w'y, the one with the rawhide bottom. Don't ac' so dumb. You know which one I mean jest as well as I do. We ain't got so terrible many."

Mr. Mallory was large and handsome, and knew it. Mrs. Palmer, in all the pomp of her comfortable flesh and high spirits, had wondered many times how he ever happened to take a notion to "Mis' Mall'ry — little, dried-up, stoop-over bundle o' bones!" She always

wound up the thought with — "Well, everybody to his taste." And then she smiled.

"I declare," she frequently said, "I do enjoy to joke back and forth with Mr. Mall'ry. There's so much fun in him, an' I guess he don't have much to liven him up at home, poor man! Some women freeze a man up so! He does seem to have a good time when he comes here."

So she "joked back and forth" with him; and at times this joking was not of the finest kind. Often Mariella turned a wondering look toward the loud laughter, and marvelled at her mother's flushed face and the way she threw her large hand out at Mr. Mallory, and cried, "Oh, now, *you!*"

But what woe would have betided Mr. Palmer had he thus openly attempted any gallantries with Mrs. Mallory. He sat with one thin leg crossed over the other, and his foot working regularly up and down. There was a blush of bashful misery across his eyes. He had the nervous manner of a new deacon who is expected to make his first prayer at the weekly prayer-meeting.

He and Mrs. Mallory conversed solemnly about the crops, and about a new seed-drill which he had recently purchased, with a spring-seat, and about the proper mode of curing ham.

Once something was said that caused both to laugh out in innocent and hearty enjoyment. Mrs. Palmer broke down in the middle of a sentence, and turned sharply.

"So that-a," she said, lamely. "So — that-a — w'y, whatever 's so funny over there, Mis' Mall'ry. I didn't ketch the joke."

Mrs. Mallory took advantage of her inning. "Oh, nothing much," she said, with a thin smile. Then she looked at Mr. Palmer and laughed again — this time with significance. Mr. Palmer responded, but it was in a somewhat sickly fashion. He knew that he would suffer for it later on.

After that the conversation became more general.

Mariella sat out in the clover with the baby in her lap. The immaculate, unfreckled Isaphene sat beside her with folded hands, her dress spread out stiffly to prevent wrinkles. Two or three smaller Mallorys were sitting up primly in the grass. They were not above getting into mischief. They were merely making acquaintance with their surroundings and awaiting large opportunities.

Mariella had a look of suffering on her face. As a rule she loved babies, but not a Mallory baby. She hated all children with fat legs and no freckles. Most of all she hated the spotless Isaphene, with her smooth curls and perpetual smile of friendliness; her unwrinkled dress and her white chip hat which she had worn all summer without getting so much as a fly-speck on it; her pretty legs — which she never "braided" as Mariella did hers — and her well-behaved elbows which never got out at right angles to her plump little body.

As Mariella devoured her with her eyes, and listened with a kind of fierce patience to her small talk about her dolls and her dresses and her new organ, a black thought came into her mind and stayed there. O, that it were spring, and the Maydukes hung red and juicy in the big tree above them, and she might climb the tall ladder and entice her unsuspecting guest up behind her, and then turn and squeeze a big cherry, drop after drop, drop after drop, upon that chaste chip hat!

It was a horrible, a sinful thought; and she repulsed it with shudders. But it returned. She tried to think of something else. She told herself that there were no cherries; that the stains would never come out; that she was wicked, and God would never love her again for thinking of such a thing; she talked about the

new pigs, dwelling upon the "little white runt" with the black tail; about the bumblebees that would climb down into the crimson hollyhocks; about the little russet pears that lay so thick under the trees that you couldn't step for them; she even gave her finger to the baby and tried to force herself to kiss him — and failed. And when her strength gave out, lo, there was the same thought, just as black and just as firmly fixed in her mind as before.

She got up suddenly, almost rolling the baby out of her lap. "Do you like currants?" she asked. Her eyes glowed at Isaphene out of a pale, frightened face. Her heart hammered her throat as she awaited the answer.

"What is it?" said Isaphene, in her thin, polite tone.

"Do you like currants?"

"What is it?"

"I say, do you like currants? *Currants!* Do you like currants?"

"I like 'em in spring."

"There's some on the vines now. Great big, juicy ones. Don't you want some?"

"I don't mind." Isaphene arose daintily. "Mother says they ain't got any flavor when they hang on so. What makes 'em hang on so? She says they never hung on so in Ioway."

"I don't know. Here, they're down this way. You sit on the clover, and I'll pick some and drop them down to you."

The unsuspecting guest obeyed, lifting her dress precisely as her mother would have done. Mariella, torn in that eternal conflict between right and wrong which makes us all kin, stood over her. The currants were in her hand. The juice was in the currants, waiting to be squeezed out by those firm fingers — and oh, the soft whiteness of the hated hat! And yet —

[illegible] "Mariella," [illegible]

[illegible] guess.

[illegible]

"[illegible]," said Mrs. Mallory, [illegible]

[illegible] What have you been [illegible]?"

"Picking currants," said Isaphene. Mariella walked behind her, white-faced. "Mother, what makes 'em hang on so? They don't taste as good as they do in the spring."

"I don't know. Why, for the land's sake! What have you got onto your Sunday hat? Come right here to me an' let me see! As I live an' breathe, it's a great big currant stain! Why, how did you get that onto you, you careless child, you?"

"I don't know," said Isaphene. She took off the hat and looked at it with tears. "Mariella, how did I get it onto my hat — my pretty hat?"

The lie scorched its way out. "I don't know, either," said Mariella. "You must 'a' got your hat under a ripe bunch."

"I guess she must of," said Mrs. Palmer. "What was you two a-doin', anyhow? You must of been on a regular high."

"No, ma'am," trembled Isaphene; "we wasn't on a high, was we, Mariella?"

"Well, if you hadn't been so avoracious," said Mrs. Mallory, who prided herself upon her vocabulary, "you wouldn't have got your hat ruined. Now, you'll start in an' tew an' tew, an' keep a-tewing! What did you want to be so avoracious for, eating currants at this time o' year? Now, set right down, an' don't keep a-wiggling round like the Wandering Jew. I'd be ashamed!"

The little girls sat down again in the clover, one weeping, the other pale and silent. The hat lay in Isaphene's lap, and presently Mariella reached out a trembling hand and drew it to her. "Don't you think anything would take it out?" she whispered. "I'd do *anything* to get it out."

"That's a nice little girl," spoke up Mrs. Mallory, kindly. "That's reel clever in you, Mariella. But you better let it alone. It's too late to undo a thing after it's once done."

"I don't believe it!" cried Mariella, passionately. "I'll bet I can undo anything if I try hard enough."

"Well," said Mrs. Mallory, with a sigh, "I'll guarantee you can't. You go through life, a-trying to undo things you've done, an' you'll get awful sick of it. But you let the hat alone, or you'll just make it worse; besides, it ain't your fault. I'm only dreading the way Isaphene 'll tew an' tew over it."

"—struck it when I bought that little three-year-ol' filly," Mr. Mallory was saying, in a confidential undertone. He was leaning back in a big wooden rocker. His handsome legs were stretched out comfortably. With a graceful, regular movement of one large hand he pushed his black hair up in loose waves. The palm of the other hand he twisted round and round on the great wooden button on the arm of his chair. His brow silently spelled out in its own peculiar letters the word "egoist;" and just as silently, just as surely, the lower part of his face spelled out "voluptuary." "Broke her just as easy. She ain't got a bit o' sense. No spir't. Just let me put the bridle an' saddle on, an' went wherever I told her. She ain't much to look at, but she's going to be a *bird* for work. I always advise young men" — he spoke in a lower tone, laughing — "to pick out a wife as they would an unbroke filly — good an' plain, without any spir't an' not hurt with sense. They're the ones for work an' wear. This new filly o' mine, if I whip her, stands an' takes it, patient as; an' if I pet her, just follows me all over an' rubs her nose agen me. Some men always pick out a filly for show — one with a high head an' a flash 'n the corner o' her eye, an' a thin nostrul with a curl out at the edge, with her ears pointed together and a spring in her ankles — an' a dooce of a dance she leads 'em! Every other man 'n the county swells up with jealousy when they drive by with a stepper like that — but the man driving sech a filly 's always got his hands full, always in hot water. She's just the thing for peert occasions, but no, thank you, for every-day use."

It was small wonder that a man blessed with such large views should consider himself wasted on Puget Sound. Mr. Palmer squirmed in his chair as he listened, and tugged with nervous fingers at his scanty beard. He was guiltily conscious that Mrs. Palmer had led him a deuce of a dance, and that all the neighbors were aware of it and gossiped about it behind their backs. Her voice, pitched in a loud and friendly key, came to him across the porch.

"I like a man of fine large freseek myself," she was saying, with the air of a connoisseur. "Prehaps it's because I'm large that I do admire to see large men." Mr. Mallory looked over at her and smiled with self-satisfaction. "Well, if you'll excuse me, I'll go an' see about dinner. If I didn't" — she lowered her voice — "it never 'd be started. If I kep' that girl ten years she wouldn't have enough gum'tion to start dinner without bein' told when."

"I never see one that would," said Mrs. Mallory. The wrinkles ran away from her nose and eyes again. "Such a time 's I had with my girl last winter when I was sick so long with pneumony o' the lungs. I guess Mr. Mallory didn't get much to eat. An' such a time with the children! Into mischief from daylight till dark. They'd get on a regular train, an' train, an' train, an' keep a-training. An' such cooking! I guess Mr. Mallory didn't get much to eat."

"I want to know," said Mrs. Palmer, politely. "Was you sick long?"

"Was I sick long?" Mrs. Mallory drew a long breath. "W'y, d' you mean to say you don't recollect that long fit o' sickness I had — pneumony o' the lungs? It held on so — "

"The doctor said he never see a fever hold on so 's the one I had a year ago," interrupted Mrs. Palmer, firmly. "It held on an' held on! He said it were the only case on record of a fever a-holdin' on so — "

"Well, mine held on so that they thought I'd never get over it. I just *existed* on wine an' egg beat up together — "

"I drunk ninety-six bottles o' porter, a-gettin' my strength back to where it was." Mrs. Palmer swelled out, proud as a peacock. Her voice was deep. There was a crow down in her throat. "The bottles are all out 'n the fruit-house, set up 'n a row agen the wall — "

"First I took port wine till I got sick of it, an' then sherry; an' then I tried angelica — "

"Wine ain't as strengthenin' 's porter. I took ninety-six bottles. Well, I'll have to see to dinner — "

"Now, you won't go to fussing, will you?" said Mrs. Mallory, pleadingly. "I'll feel condemned if you do. We didn't think o' staying to dinner, did we, Mr. Mallory? An' we won't, either, if you're going to the least fuss. Well, then . . . "

At five o'clock the Mallorys, large and small, climbed into the spring-wagon over the wheels. Mrs. Mallory gathered her dress skirt up carefully around her waist, revealing a strip of white petticoat. The Palmers all stood around, deploring their early departure — all save Mariella, who was pale and silent. She was conscious of nothing but the crimson stain on Isaphene's white hat.

"I feel condemned," Mrs. Mallory said, over her shoulder, as the horses started slowly. "You went to such a fuss over the dinner. But it was unsurpassed. Oh, I meant to get your rule for floating-isle. Now, come an' spend Sunday with us!"

Mrs. Palmer's cordial assurance that they would was drowned in the rattle of the wagon. "Hunh," she added, amiably, as they turned back to the house, "if we did, much of a dinner we'd get! Boiled beans an' cabbage, like 's not. Floatin'-isle! I'll give *her* my rule — in a horn! She'd make it for the minister, an' starve us on bread-puddin'. *I'll* give it to her — in a horn!"

"I thought you liked her," said Mariella. "You kissed her."

Mrs. Palmer reddened.

"Yes, I kissed her," she said, with bitterness. "I had to. She acted so clever to me, a-tellin' what a good dinner she'd had, an' a-askin' for my rule for this an' that. I had to. I'd just as live kiss a clothes-pin!"

"I wouldn't kiss anybody I didn't like," said Mariella.

"Yes, you would, too, if they offered to. I'd see that you did."

"What makes you keep saying that?" cried Mariella, passionately. She turned upon her mother with flashing eyes. "You *know* you can't make me do a thing like that. Suppose that old Methodist preacher with the gold tooth offered to kiss me! You *know* you couldn't make me kiss him! I'd die first."

"Oh, you heifer!" cried her mother. "Just you wait till to-morrow!"

At nine o'clock that night, Mariella went groping up the dark and steep stairway. But the attic itself was flooded mistily with moonlight. It was a long, narrow room; the roof sloped on both sides to the floor. There was a large window at each end.

The moon had just climbed the crest of the hill behind the house; the firs stood, dark and slim, against it. All its splendid soft fire was burning through the attic's eastern window.

Mariella forgot the hurts and the miseries of the day as she went stumbling toward it. She sank upon her knees.

She had no thought of the unwelcome Mallorys. She forgot her parents' quarrelling and the work she detested.

For a little while she was utterly happy in the peace and the soft beauty of the moonlight, although unconscious of the reason of her happiness. She heard the faint sweet shiver of the sea far down the hill. A star fell slanting across the east.

Then from somewhere below came the sound of a closing door. A bolt slipped into its sheath. She remembered suddenly; and, hastily undressing, she slipped into bed. The dark seemed studded with stars of currant-red; and all night long, when she had fallen into a feverish sleep, they went starting across her dreams.

CHAPTER IV

The following morning Mariella went stepping along the road to the little log schoolhouse. Her face was paler and more thoughtful than usual. Her air of scornful independence was gone. She was unusually silent and her eyes held a troubled look; but she set her heels down, as she walked, with her customary decision.

The teacher, a grave young man of twenty-four, walked beside her. Her home was two miles from the school. The road led through the dense forest for a mile and then sloped down to the beach. There were wild animals in the forest; and sometimes a high tide set danger upon the beach way. Mariella scorned danger, and openly defied her parents when they forbade her going alone. "Beasts never touch anybody but cowards," she said, disdainfully. "And suppose the tide did cut me off? Couldn't I climb up the rocks and wait?"

"Yes, you'd look pretty," said her mother. "Settin' up there till mornin', mebbe, an' we couldn't get to you any way on earth. You'd look pretty!"

"I'm not afraid," said the child, proudly. So she went alone; but more than once she had heard the dry crackling of twigs which told her that a bear was near; and several times she had raced with the tide until her frail strength was exhausted.

Then the teacher went to board at her nearest neighbor's, and told her quietly that she must always wait for him. "I do not wish you to go alone either way again," he said, simply.

The teacher was the only one whom Mariella unquestioningly obeyed. She loved him. His wish was a command.

For two years he had been her daily companion to and from school. Often, too, he came in the evening to read or study with her. The mysteries of figures were deeper than the mysteries of the Bible to her. The mere mention of the word "fraction" sent an ache to her head and a blur to her vision. She was so far ahead of other scholars in all the other studies and so far behind in mathematics that her teacher was frequently in despair.

"Mariella's as sharp as a new steel trap," her father would say, with a twinkle in his eyes, "in grammar an' g'ography, an' oh, *everything* but just arifmetic. She's perfectly dumb in arifmetic. She can parse — I never see her beat! *I* never learned to parse. I only had three months' schoolin' a year back in New Jersey, so I never got to parsin'. It always took me all winter to get up to where I'd been when I quit off the winter before. But you'd ought to see her fill up a blackboard with all them little squares j'ined together, an' put *words* in 'em, an' parse — rattle off a lingo about subject an' preducate! An' *spell!* W'y, she could spell 'tic-douloureux' when she wa'n't but six year old. An' she can read a ghost story so's you can feel the ghost goin' right through you, or a story about some beggar so's you'll *almost* put your hand in your pocket — but she can't do a sum in fractions! I bet my last two-bits she can name the Presidents of the United States right down without a break, but can't say the multification-table backwards. The teacher says she just looks at her other lessons an' knows 'em by heart."

The teacher carried the child along in her arithmetic unblushingly. He had recognized her unusual gifts, and was determined that her failure in mathematics should not discourage her.

During the troubles arising over the settlement of the boundary between British Columbia and the United States during the fifties, San Juan Island was the most important of those in dispute. On this island dwelt the "historic pig" which started the trouble; and oddly enough, he did not start the trouble until he was dead. It was the killing of this innocent pig and the consequent threats of the agents of the Hudson Bay Company which caused General Harney to place a company of soldiers upon this island for the protection of the American inhabitants. Three British war vessels were placed broadside to the American camp, and their captains demanded that the soldiers should immediately vacate the island. General Harney, on the contrary, sent reënforcements.

Ten miles from the American camp, on a noble and picturesque bluff descending in deep, wide terraces to Puget Sound, was located the British fort, afterwards famous as Old English Camp. Here still remain the officers' houses, the terraces and arbors; the stone steps and ivy-covered trees; the macadamized roads leading out into the country. But the old parade-ground is now only a meadow of hay.

After the settlement of the boundary had given the island to the United States, English Camp was purchased by an Englishman and converted into farms. Here, a few years previous, was born the child who afterward became Mariella's pale and thoughtful teacher. Of humble parentage, the son of a pioneer father and mother whose early education — so far as the education of books goes — had been neglected, he would have grown up in ignorance had it not been for the Englishman who came to live for several years upon the island, alone with his son — a youth near the age of Gilmer

Leaming. The boys became companions, and the stern, silent Englishman taught them together, carrying them into studies far beyond their years.

Gilmer's mother had died while he was very young. When he was seventeen his father died. Two years later the Englishman left the island with his son, suddenly and quietly, as he had come. Why they went, or why they had dwelt there so many years, Gilmer never knew. He owed them everything; that was all he cared to know. His will was strong and the Englishman had taught him self-control. His glance did not fall, his lips did not tremble, boy though he was, when he told those two, who made all his life, good-by.

"I owe you everything, sir," he said; his face was white. "You have made it possible for me to go out into the world alone, and hold my head up before men and say, 'I am one of you,' by the noble right of knowledge. Without you I should have been forever a blind creature crying for light which I could not find. I cannot repay you now; but if I ever can — "

He stopped. The man's face — the face of the man who had taught him self-control — had quivered strongly. He reached for Gilmer's hand, and pressed it hard and long. Then he turned away, and the two boys fell upon each other's necks and embraced silently and without any outbreak of emotion.

But all that day and half that moonlit night Gilmer Leaming sat on the rocks high above the bay, and looked out across the straits to the ocean.

It was a boy who went out to sit alone on the windy headland; but it was a man who walked home slowly under the morning stars.

This was the young man who was Mariella's teacher and daily companion. He had discerned at once that she was an unusual child. She drew him to her uncon-

sciously. He remembered how he had often felt the superior intellect of the Englishman reaching out to him, like a sudden glow from a search-light, and the quick lighting of the stern face when that was discovered which proved that he was not working in vain. So was Mariella now tried. Not once did she fail to respond promptly and with alert interest. Soon she grew out of the uncouth speech to which she had been accustomed always. Sometimes, in a sudden rage, she would burst out into strong language — the fierce expressions of close kinship to oaths which her mother used whenever in a temper — but a glance from Leaming checked her, and she would stand, scarlet-faced and silent, before him.

As they walked along silently that morning they came of a sudden upon a handsome youth who had reached their road from a side trail. He was waiting for them. He was about eighteen years old. His face reddened as they approached.

Mr. Leaming looked at him in frank surprise.

"Good morning, Mahlon."

"Good morning."

He looked at Mariella, and smiled a conscious greeting.

"I thought I'd come around this way," he said, walking along beside Mariella. "It's a good deal farther; but I thought I would."

"We are glad of your company. This was turning out to be one of our silent mornings."

The lad reached out slyly from his pocket, and slipped a big red apple under Mariella's shawl. His fingers got tangled up in the fringes and the folds of the shawl, and he was compelled to give her arm a little surreptitious rap with the apple. He was in terror lest the teacher should discover his hand under Mariella's shawl.

"What is it?" asked Mariella, turning to him.

He gave her an appealing look and another sharp rap with the apple.

The color flew to her face. She reached quickly under the shawl, and took the apple. He withdrew his hand with a sigh of relief.

"How's your mother?" asked Mariella, hastily.

"She's just as usual."

"How's her rheumatism?"

"It's just as usual."

They walked a short way without speaking then. Mariella held the apple tightly in one hand, and with the other she held the shawl over it. There were bright red spots in her cheeks.

"It must be a mile farther for you to come this way, Mahlon," said Mr. Leaming, presently.

"It's full that," agreed Mahlon; "but I thought I would," he added, stubbornly.

Mariella glanced shyly at him from under her hat. His kind dark eyes looked back at her reassuringly. There was something frank and honest and trustworthy in his look.

They came presently to a large root that stretched across the road. Mr. Leaming always helped Mariella over it, and was preparing to do so now, when the boy stepped quickly to her side and, taking hold of her arm, almost lifted her over it.

"Do you know your arithmetic?" he asked, rapidly, in a low tone.

"I've only got one example," she whispered back, wretchedly.

"I've got every one," he said, proudly; he drew up his shoulders. "I'll do 'em all on paper an' roll 'em up in a little wad an' throw 'em over to you. You watch when I cough *hard*, as if I had consumption."

They had reached the turn in the road where the descent to the beach began. They stood still. Through the fine gray fretwork of the trees, bared over night by the wind, they saw Puget Sound breaking blue and beautiful beneath them. There was a rosary of pearls around each tiny wave.

Mahlon made a sudden movement forward.

"I guess I'll climb down an' pick some asters," he said. "I see some hanging over the side of the cliff."

Leaming looked at his watch. "There isn't much time, Mahlon," he said. "Better leave them for another day."

"I guess I'll pick 'em now," replied the boy, going right on.

Leaming looked after him and smiled.

"There is no one quite so stubborn as Mahlon, I am sure," he said, with decision.

"I think he's nice." Mariella lifted her chin.

"He is nice," agreed Mr. Leaming, "but stubborn. He is stubborn with every one but you. I have never seen him act stubborn with you about anything."

"I never did anything to make him want to be stubborn," said Mariella, looking after the boy with wistful eyes. Then she added, "They say he's just as good as gold to his mother."

The teacher paused.

"Then we'll wait for him," he said, smiling, "stubborn or not stubborn. I was going to punish him by going on and leaving him."

The little girl's eyes shone at him gratefully. The boy soon climbed back with his hands full of great lavender asters. His face fairly glowed toward Mariella. He forgot the teacher.

"Ain't they beauties? They're all for your desk, Mariella. I won't give a one to another girl — not a one! I'll carry 'em for you."

"I wouldn't want 'em if you gave some to any other girl," bragged Mariella, proudly, with her head high.

"Well, I don't mean to," insisted Mahlon.

"I wouldn't have 'em if you did." Her eyes flashed at him. "I wouldn't have one of 'em."

"I tell you I don't mean to," said the boy, earnestly. "I hadn't give a thought to such a thing."

"If you hadn't give a thought to it, you wouldn't have mentioned it. There ain't a boy in school but what knows better'n to give his flowers to me if he means to give one to any other girl."

"I know better, too," said Mahlon; his face was sober, but his voice was gentle. Mr. Leaming had walked on, leaving them to settle their quarrel. "I know better, too, Mariella. I only said it to — to — "

"To what?"

Mahlon's feet dragged a little; the lavender asters hung, heads downward, in his hand.

"Why, to — to make you smile at me, an' speak soft. I thought maybe you would."

Mariella's proud spirit melted at once. She moved a little closer to him, utilizing a rut in the road as an excuse. She smiled up into his face sweetly and guiltily. "Oh, was that it?" she said.

"Yes, that was it," he replied, decisively. "I'd do anything you said, if you'd smile at me."

"Well, then," said Mariella, and her little air of ownership took the sting from her words, "I wouldn't put my hands in my pockets."

He was unconsciously walking along with his right hand in his pocket. He drew it out at once, coloring.

"What would you do with 'em?" he asked, half in humor, half in embarrassment.

"Oh," said Mariella, "I'd keep 'em where I could help folks over roots!"

Then, at once, she lifted her voice. "Mr. Leaming, don't walk so fast. I can't keep up."

CHAPTER V

One Sunday morning Mr. Palmer was "blacking" his boots in the kitchen.

"You let 'em go so," his wife had declared with scorn, "they're actually foxey. All wrinkled up! I'd be ashamed! You'd let 'em go till Christmas if I'd keep still. Here the minister come an' stayed all night, an' a-settin' in the other room, a-waitin' to go to church — an' you a-lazin' around with your boots all foxey. I never see your beat!"

Mr. Palmer sat on a low stool. His left hand and arm were thrust into a boot. In his right hand was a brush. The little tuft of bristles on its back was worn off on a sharp slant to the wood. He was laboriously digging dry sand with the handle out of the groove between the sole and the upper. His head was leaned to one side. The thin bunch of whiskers on his chin stuck out at right angles to his chin. His brows were drawn fiercely together. His jaws were set.

"He praised the ham we had for supper last night," said Mrs. Palmer, in a propitiatory tone. "He said it was smoked just right an' fried just right."

There were three things that Mr. Palmer had all his life resisted with a noble determination — the polishing of his boots, the shaving of his upper lip, and the wearing of a white shirt. In these three he could be conquered only by the most persistent nagging on the part of Mrs. Palmer.

At his wife's last words his face relaxed somewhat. "Aigh?" he said, with unwilling curiosity.

"I say he praised up the ham. Where's your ears at? He said it was smoked just right an' fried just right. He proved it by the way he eat."

A twinkle came into his eyes. His lips — the upper one blue from the recent visit of the razor — unclosed reluctantly. His whiskers dropped stiffly with his chin.

"Talk low," he said.

"Well, ain't I talkin' low? My land! Talk low yourself. You ac' as if I hollered. He's got Mariella up in a corner, a-talkin Sunday school an' Hebrew childern into her. I bet she answers him sassy — "

"*Talk low.*"

"Well, ain't I talkin' low? Good grieve! He can't hear anything when he gits to ridin' his Sunday-school horse. You do aggravate a body so with your 'talk low,' 'talk low.' Just as if I hollered!"

A bedroom opened into the kitchen. Mrs. Palmer walked into it with a high and bitter step. From the mysterious depths of a green box she brought forth a white shirt and some fresh underwear of her husband's. After examining these with the critical eye of a careful housewife, to make sure that they were mended, she spread them out on the bed. Then she returned to the kitchen.

"Now, pa," she said, mildly, stooping to conquer, "you get an' dress yourself. I've got your clean shirt an' things all laid out on the bed."

Mr. Palmer set his lips together. "I don't propose to put on a white shirt to-day."

"Yes, you do, too. It's all laid out." She spoke calmly.

"Well, I don't." He commenced drumming fiercely on the table with his broad fingers. "I don't propose to, I say. What do I want of a white shirt? Aigh? I'll wear that gray flannel."

"Yes, you'd look pretty in that gray flannel! *At church!* With the minister a-ridin' along in the wagon with us, an' everybody a-lookin' at us. You'd look pretty. I must say!"

"Well, I'd just as live look pretty as not. I don't propose to put on a white shirt." He glared at her. "I say I don't propose to."

"Well, I say you do. What ails you? I don't see what gits into you. You're as stubborn 's a mule. You'd go to church a-lookin' like Moses an' all his wives if I'd let you. The minister —"

"Oh, damn the minister!" cried out Mr. Palmer, furiously.

A sudden smile of reluctant humor came upon Mrs. Palmer's face. She turned upon her husband in triumph. "*Talk low,*" she said.

Mr. Palmer saw the joke, but failed to appreciate it.

"I didn't catch what you said about the minister, pa. What-a-say?"

Mr. Palmer made no reply. He stared sullenly at the boot he was drawing on. His wife regarded him steadily. "What-a-say?"

He mumbled something and stood up, still tugging at the boot.

"Don't forget to pull down your pant-leg. There. I didn't hear what you said about the minister. Why don't you speak up?"

He gave her a fierce look. "I said *damn* the minister."

Mrs. Palmer laughed exasperatingly. "Oh, he's a Prespyterian. You can't damn a Prespyterian. It's already done, or it ain't done, with a Prespyterian; an' that settles it. I wouldn't waste my breath so. I'd go in, if I was you, an' put on my white shirt. It's all laid out on the bed," she added, encouragingly. "I bet Mis' Mall'ry don't have such a time to get a white shirt on him! I bet—"

"God A'mighty!" shouted Mr. Palmer. He shot out of the kitchen and into the bedroom as if borne along on a cyclone.

He disrobed in silence. He got himself into his clean underwear. He clutched the white shirt and flung it over his head. It rattled crisply. His face emerged, purple and perspiring, from its immaculate depths. He buttoned the wrist-bands with difficulty. Then he bowed his head bitterly and commenced a desperate struggle with the collar button. Five minutes later he gave the shirt a jerk that tore it down to the hem, and flung open the door.

"Come an' button this *thing!*" he said, with a hiss. "I wish you had to put it on an' button it at the back of your own neck—damn stiff board of a thing!"

In the "other" room the minister had drawn Mariella between his knees and had his arm around her. Her face was pale with hate.

"Now, then," he said; his spectacles shone at her. "Can you tell me the story of Samuel?"

"No, sir."

"What, what? Can't tell me the story of Samuel? Oh, yes, you can, if you'll just try to remember. Don't be scared."

"I'm not *scared.*" Mariella smiled. It was a smile

the minister did not quite like. "But I don't know a thing about Samuel. Was he in the Bible?"

"Yes, he was in the Bible." Mr. Myers, the reverend, gave a sigh of collapse. "He was a good and saintly child. He was so good that God spoke to him and called him by name while he was very young."

"He — *what?*" cried the little girl. Her large eyes were set sternly upon the minister. "God *spoke* to Samuel — to a child?"

"Yes." The minister colored under those steady eyes. "The Lord — er — frequently spoke to people. That was in the old days, you know, the Bible days."

"Spoke to them?" She was almost breathless. "Talked to them?"

"Yes, oh, yes."

"And does He now?"

"Why, no — not exactly — "

"Why doesn't He?"

"Because He — He — "

The minister had a severe coughing attack. Mariella, having had experience with coughing attacks, looked more suspicious than sympathetic.

"The times are changed," concluded Mr. Myers. "The Lord is with us all the time, but He doesn't speak to us as He did to the good people in the — er — Bible days."

"Why doesn't He?"

"Well — the people in those days were very good. They were — hum — prophets, and walked with the — hum — Lord. They prayed day and night."

"Who heard the Lord speak to Samuel?"

"No one. Samuel told Eli."

"Did Eli believe him?"

"Oh, yes. Eli had faith. He believed that God can do anything."

"If I told you that God spoke to me, would you believe it?"

There was a silence. Then the minister bobbed up like a cork. "We're getting in too deep, little girl," he said, fixing a wise gaze on a morning-glory that bloomed in the wall-paper. "You're too little to understand these things."

"Can anybody as young as I am understand them?"

"No; I think not."

"Then what makes you talk about them? What makes you? Why don't you wait till we can understand them? If you didn't believe me if I told you that, you don't believe the Lord can do anything."

"You're a very ignorant child," said the minister; his face was red. "Let us kneel down and pray to the Lord to lead you out of your ignorance."

"I won't do it!" cried Mariella, furiously. She broke away from between his knees and faced him passionately. "I know how to pray for myself. I don't get up in the pulpit and say the same prayer over every Sunday. You never pray without putting in that about *enabling us to press forward to the mark of the prize of the high calling!* Mother says you always get it in somewhere. I'd laugh if I couldn't pray without saying the same thing over and over every Sunday. Maybe I am ignorant," she added, bitterly, her eyes flaming at him, "but I guess I know some things that you don't know. Do you know when the blue-birds come? Do you know where the humming-birds build their nests? Do you know a blue jay's nest from a woodpecker's? If a tame canary got out with a lot of wild ones, could you point it out from the others? Do you know a wild orchid from a tiger-lily before it blooms? *Do you know it from anything? There!*"

She had spluttered it all out. Shaking her head at

him in helpless rage and resentment, she turned to flee away from him before he could speak, and ran almost into the arms of the teacher, who stood in the doorway with stern eyes set upon her.

"Mariella," he said; and at his look and tone her face trembled. She burst into violent weeping, clinging to him and hiding her face on his breast.

"He said I was ignorant," she sobbed, her breast struggling fearfully before each word. "I hate him. He doesn't know anything. He's an old, ignorant fool himself. I know — things he — doesn't know. And it's a *lie* — what he says about Samuel — you know it is! If I told him God spoke to me he wouldn't believe me!"

The young man's face had softened. He drew her gently out upon the porch. "Go out into the orchard, dear," he whispered. "I'll come as soon as they go to church." Then he went back and faced the preacher. "Sir," he said, calmly, "don't you know any better than to begin subjects that you cannot explain to a child of Mariella's understanding?"

"She is the most ignorant child I ever knew," said the minister, haughtily.

"I beg your pardon," returned Leaming, warmly; "she is nothing of the kind. She is educated far beyond her age in all things save the Bible. The Bible is not for children. It is too much for most people of mature years and thought. Why not teach children to love and worship God through the sunshine and the flowers, the birds and the woods; through love and truth and kind hearts toward their neighbors; and leave the Bible with all its sublime beauty and divine mystery for them to read when they are old enough to interpret it for themselves — as they read Homer or Milton?"

Mr. Myers gasped out — "Young man!" He fairly shook. His face was gray. "This is — hum — blasphemy. I never heard anything to — hum — equal it. I am not surprised at that child's astonishing ignorance. I am not even surprised at her ungovernable temper — "

"Oh, nonsense," interrupted Leaming. "You should use a little more love and common sense in managing children, and a little less religion."

"What's all this about?" asked Mrs. Palmer, softly. She came in with her Sunday air. She had on her best black gown, and was laboriously working on her black kid gloves. The ends of the fingers had worn thin and shiny. Her hat was coquettish enough for a girl of eighteen. It turned up on one side; a bright red rose rested against her dark hair. Her shawl was an orange-red Paisley, and it had required six months' manœuvring to inveigle it out of Mr. Palmer. Surely, therefore, her flaunting carriage, whenever she wore it, might be pardoned. "You look all het up, Mr. Leaming. You must of walked over fast. People complected like you color up so when they walk fast. You look all het up. You goin' along to meetin' with us in the wagon?"

"No, thank you," said Leaming, politely. "I'll stay with Mariella."

"Well, do try to keep her out of mischief. She does act so. I don't see what gets into her. I struggled an' struggled to get her to meetin' an' Sunday-school with us," she added, with an apologetic glance at the minister, "but she can't be drug to. I don't see what gets into her. There go the Mall'rys by. See how nice Isaphene sets up alongside the other childern, without a speck on her clean dress. I don't see why Mariella can't be like her. Let's go on, an' keep 'em company."

Her unspoken thought was that Mrs. Mallory would begrudge her the minister's company. So she hurried that coughing gentleman and her reluctant husband out to the wagon. Lightnings were still playing in Mr.

Palmer's eyes. His wife knew that the last mutterings of thunder, not loud but deep, were still lingering; but she kept a cheerful front. Did she not have on the war-paint of victory — the Paisley shawl?

When they were settled in the wagon, the minister asked, between jolts, "Do you think that young man is a nice companion for your child?"

"Oh, yes," said Mrs. Palmer, "I guess so. She don't have much company, she's such a funny child."

"He — he was expressing some most — hum — remarkable views when you came in."

"Was he?" Mrs. Palmer laughed amiably. "Well, that's what made him look all het up so. He was havin' a tew, was he? May I ask, what was it about?"

"He doesn't think children ought to study the Bible, or — or — "

Mr. Myers choked. His face was purple. Mrs. Palmer commenced her easy, mellow laugh.

"Oh, I know he's funny about some things." Her face was eloquent with enjoyment. "Mr. Leaming's great fun with his idys. He says — "

She stopped abruptly. It had suddenly been borne in upon her that she was revealing secrets of a doubtful nature to a preacher. Her face settled into decorous lines.

"Is Mis' Graham goin' to have her baby christened to-day?" she asked, solemnly.

Mr. Myers did not know. If his soul were lost because of it, he did not care. He was thin and delicate, and the jolts of the wagon over a corduroy road caused his soul to wax bitter within him. It was five miles around the Bay to the town where his church and his home were. He wondered in dumb anguish why it had not been predestined that he should have reached the Mallorys at supper-time in his round of country calls. *They* had cushions on their seats. *Their* horses lifted up their feet.

Mrs. Palmer glanced sidewise at him.

"I guess what the teacher said to him is a-wranglin' an' a-wranglin' in him," she thought, with repressed exultation. "He looks peakid."

They passed a farm with a fine young orchard baring itself around the house. The grass beneath the trees was covered with soft yellow leaves.

"Mr. Rice done well with his grape-vines," spoke up Mr. Palmer, so suddenly that the horses gave little leaps as if at the stroke of a whip.

"Well, he nearly killed himself with his grapes," said Mrs. Palmer, firmly. "Appendiktis," she added, with a glance of explanation, to the minister. "Hadn't you heard? Oh, he's a Methodist. That's so. Yes, they had three doctors an' the minister for two days an' nights. The neighbors all come in their teams an' stood around in the house an' yard, an' talked as low. It was a great deal to prepare for so many to eat, but Mis' Rice said it was a reel pleasure. It was appendiktis. From eatin' one o' his own grape seeds. I always take 'em out myself."

Mr. Myers was uncommunicative as to what his grape-eating habits were. After recovering her balance from a severe jolt, Mrs. Palmer added, "It does seem as if it wouldn't of been so hard to bear if it hadn't of been a seed out of one of his own grapes that he'd worked so hard over. The whole neighborhood 's been watchin' him an' his grapes for three years! An' then to have one o' the very first ones turn around an' serve him so!"

There was another silence, broken by two more jolts.

"I suppose it was ordered that way, though," said Mrs. Palmer, with a pious after-thought that took on a little Presbyterian flavor out of compliment to the occasion.

"Where was that young man educated?" asked the minister, suddenly.

"It's still a-wranglin'," thought Mrs. Palmer, with a quick mental chuckle. "Well," she said, "some Englishman over on San Juan Island teached him till he was about nineteen. Then he picked up an' went off east som'ers to some big university or other; stayed five year, an' then come back here an' went right to teachin' in the woods. You'd think he'd be stuck up, after goin' to sech a big university — but he ain't. He says Mariella's offul bright."

"She's as smart 's a steel trap," spoke up Mr. Palmer, suddenly, and the horses leaped again.

They now approached the outskirts of the town. Here and there was a white or a yellow house, with a two-plank walk running along one side of the street. Puget Sound's great "boom" had not yet come, and there was a stillness, as of waiting, in the very atmosphere of the towns.

Gradually the houses grew sociably closer together. A few people were going to church, walking stiffly and looking uncomfortable in their best clothes. Two women, talking over a side fence, turned at the sound of wheels and stood silently looking. Cows with bells and the placid countenances of those who enjoy undisputed possession walked firmly along the middle of the road. Mr. Palmer turned aside for them without the faintest hesitation. "Fine beef, that," he would cry out, now and then, eying some unusual specimen of cowhood with the air of a connoisseur.

Then they got down into the heart of the town. Mrs. Palmer sat erect. The red Paisley fell in even, dignified folds from her broad shoulders. She held herself with an air of importance. Was not the minister with her? And was not all the church-going town on the street looking at her? The sidewalks were the regular width now. Occasionally there was a lamp-post, with a battered, smoky lamp on top. The stores had square fronts. Their sides and backs were of rough boards. First there would be a general merchandise store; then two vacant lots; then a tin-shop; a drug store with red and green things in the windows, and a druggist in his shirt-sleeves and a doctor with a busy air standing out in front; two vacant lots; a saloon with a fir tree growing in the window; a bake-shop with sticks of striped candy in big glass jars to tempt young country eyes and stomachs; one vacant lot; a livery stable with family rooms overhead; a restaurant with girls smiling out the windows, their hands on their hips; then more vacant lots and more square-fronted business houses; and at last, in a quiet space with maples and firs growing about, the Presbyterian church.

Several conveyances were scattered under the trees. Women were standing in twos and threes talking over their recipes or the latest gossip, with repressed enthusiasm. They looked askance at Mrs. Palmer when she bore down upon them with Mr. Myers. They took it hard that their pleasure should be thus broken in upon; but Mr. Myers paused to shake each warmly by the hand, and inquire after the family's welfare. "I boil mine in milk," Mrs. Deane was saying with decision as she turned to find herself face to face with the minister. "Water's best," said a stubborn voice behind her, and she dared not contradict. She went into church with anything but a proper spirit.

CHAPTER VI

THE recent winds had bared Mariella's apple tree. She stood among the torn, russet ferns, a little blown figure with a piteous face. Leaming came to her, smiling tenderly.

"Forget it, little maid," he said, taking her hand and leading her along with him through the orchard. "After a thing is done it can't be undone. He was wrong and he hurt you, but it was through ignorance. He was really trying to be good to you, as he sees goodness, so you must forgive him and forget all about it. Where do you think we are going?"

He was swinging a basket in his hand. The child looked. "Mushrooming?" she cried. Her face lighted eagerly. "Oh, I'm so glad! Won't it be fun? And mother tried to make me go to church! And *Sunday-school!* I wouldn't."

Then her face grew grave. "What did he mean about God speaking to Samuel?" she asked soberly.

They had reached the orchard fence. Beyond lay the forest. A mile farther on was a deserted ranch that had long been cleared. There the mushrooms sprang up after windless rains and heavy fogs. Leaming sat down on the lowest step of the stile that led over the fence. He drew the child to him.

"Mariella," he said, "I don't want you to think about such things until you are old enough to understand them. You love nature, and nature is God. You cannot love and study birds and flowers, mountains and seas, without loving and growing into familiar companionship with God."

Then his fine face softened. He arose and, taking her hand, led her over the stile. They walked on together then, slowly, through the woods. His eyes, bent upon the ground, were deep with thought.

"Little maid," he said gently, "try to think more kindly of Mr. Myers. He is trying to do right, and it is so hard to say the right word and so easy to say the wrong one. . . . Do you see that woodpecker—how steadily he flies? He is the same color as the month, mottled, brownish gray, the lifeless gray of the branches when the leaves are fallen. But see the beautiful red streak that the under side of his wing leaves shining along the air! That is a poem, Mariella, and although you may not be able to understand it now, it is sweeter to think about when you have gone to bed than the story of Samuel."

"And now," he added, in a lighter tone, "let us forget all about it. We are after sunlight and mushrooms today; and yonder is the old ranch."

Years before some one had taken up a timber claim, built his little log cabin, and done the amount of clearing required by law; then he had gone away and left the embryo ranch for the years to make valuable. Neglected fruit trees grew here and there in the clearing.

As they came nearer and obtained a first unobstructed view of the low level land, Mariella uttered a sudden cry of delight and darted forward like a bird. "Oh, see them! See them!" she cried out, in a very ecstasy.

It was indeed a beautiful sight—a little level, open space walled in by the dark forest. The short grass was still green. A few sturdy thistle stalks stood, torn and ragged, in defiant and dusty beauty. There were fragments, too, of russet ferns; and there were smooth, dark-veined stones. Everywhere the mushrooms had put up their tiny silver-gray tents with their delicate salmon-tinted linings. Some were flat, like dainty umbrellas. Others folded down long and close over the stem, almost touching the turf; and the inside coloring of these was tinted like a sea-shell — deepening from pearl on to faintest lavender, rose, and violet; and in the older ones even to purplish black. And so soft, so velvety, so elusive, that they seemed like ethereal things that might vanish if one closed the eyes for but a second.

There was a deep stillness upon the small field, and an odor, agreeable and not quite describable, of the earth and of moisture, of resting trees and of dying ferns.

Mariella sped fleetly in among them, and, kneeling down, commenced drawing them with the gentlest care off their pale stems. She turned each over, quickly and deftly, to examine the coloring. She was silent now of sheer delight. She breathed quickly. The blood throbbed, rich and red, in her cheeks. Occasionally she glanced up at Leaming, who held the basket for her, and smiled at him. He smiled in sympathy. His enjoyment was as keen and as unaffected as hers. Nothing could exceed the gentleness with which she transferred the mushrooms from her palms to the basket, letting them roll softly down her fingers that they might suffer no bruise.

"Oh, Mariella," said Leaming, suddenly, "it is a real fairy circle!"

She gave him the swift, asking look which always meant that she did not understand.

"When they have a circular growth," he explained, smiling, "it is a fairy circle, and the fairies dance inside the ring on moonlit nights and sleep in these tiny tents. This delicious, but uncanny, odor is the fairies' breath."

They both laughed at this bit of poetical nonsense;

but it was wistful, half-sad laughter, the child — and perhaps the man, too — wishing that it were true and that they might steal there some night and behold the fairies in high revel, until, worn-out, they should vanish into their tents and sink to dreams in velvet couches.

When the basket was full and rounded over, so that there was not space for another, no matter how tiny, the field was still full of them. "How can we go and leave them?" said Mariella, disconsolately.

"You have more than you can possibly use," said Leaming.

She gave him a swift, reproachful glance. "It isn't that," she said, in an injured tone. "I *want* them. I don't want to leave them here. They will all be gone to-morrow. There's only to-day for them."

She gave him the basket which he had bidden her take that she might know how light it was with all its fairy load. She gave a long, regretful look behind her before turning into the homeward path.

"Let's go home by the cut-off path," she said, presently, in the decisive tone of one who has only to express a wish to have it carried out. "That new house is finished and some people have just moved in." She laughed. "They're from Missouri."

"We might stop and make their acquaintance," said Leaming. "They have a daughter about your age who is coming to school. She will not dread the first day so much if she knows you."

"I don't want her to go to school with us," said Mariella, with quick jealousy.

"I think she will, Mariella."

"I don't want her to." She spoke passionately; her face was flushed; tears stood in her eyes. "I won't go if she does!"

"Why?"

She was silent.

"Why, Mariella?"

"I don't want her to." Her voice broke; her face was quivering with emotion. "I don't want to go with you, if somebody else goes, too. I want to go all alone with you. I don't have — anybody — but you; and I want all of you, or I don't want you at all!"

Leaming took her hand. He was deeply touched. He could not reprove her. "Mariella," he began, but at that moment a little girl came running across to them from the new house. She was waving her hands to them, and crying out in a shrill voice: "My ma's got a spell! My ma's got a spell!"

They hastened to meet her, turning off the path.

"What is it you are saying?" called Leaming.

"Oh, my ma's got a spell. She's terrible bad. She thinks it's her last spell. There ain't nobody with her but auntie. Can't you hurry up?"

Leaming and Mariella went with her. The house gleamed through the trees in all the rich yellow of new, unpainted fir. The front door stood open. They hurried across the porch and into the house. In the big "front room" a middle-aged woman lay upon a carpet lounge, with a bandage around her head. A pale, worn-looking woman a few years younger stood over her. She had cloths and bottles in her hands. She was bathing the sufferer's brow. Upon the abrupt entrance of unexpected visitors she raised her head and stood looking at them in dull surprise.

"Keep a-rubbin'," commanded a gasping voice from the pillow. She obeyed instantly. It jarred upon Leaming. It seemed like the patient devotion of a faithful dog.

"Can I help you?" he asked kindly. "Shall I go for a doctor, or — or any one?"

The sick woman opened her eyes, looked at him, and closed them again.

"I'd a great deal drether have a neighbor woman," she said faintly. "Doctors can't do *me* no good. We've spent a fortune on 'em. I've got the worst case on record." There was a note of triumph in her voice. "I feel as if this was my last spell. I'd a great deal drether have a neighbor woman 'n a doctor."

"Mother'll be home from church," cried Mariella. "I'll go after her."

She flashed out before Leaming could prevent her. She sped in a wild, light way that reminded him of the frightened flight of a bird. He looked after her, half smiled, and returned to the lounge.

"She has 'em terrible often," said the woman. "The doctors can't do her any good. She seems to have 'em harder an' harder. We never expect her to get through 'em any more."

"She is your sister, isn't she?"

"Yes, sir. Her husband went a-fishin' an' she didn't want him to go. She wanted he should put down the rag carpet. But no, he would go a-fishin', whuther or no; an' soon 's he was gone, she up an' went right into this —"

"Keep a-rubbin'."

"— spell."

"Auntie," spoke up the weak voice from the pillows, "if this should be my last spell, you see that everything is done proper. We're strangers, an' I don't want any remarks about us after I'm gone an' can't answer back. Silas never was beknown to answer anybody back but me, an' it was years an' years before he ever answered me. I've always said I'd like a nice funeral. I'd a great deal drether have that after I'm dead 'n a three-ply carpet while I'm alive. I never could get things out of Silas, but he always did promise me a nice funeral."

"Yes, yes, sister," said the auntie. Tears were running down her wrinkled face. "I'll do everything. Don't talk about it."

"When I feel this spell a-comin' on, I thinks, says I, well, it'll be my very last spell. Semia!"

The little girl, sobbing silently, came to her mother's side.

"You'll be a good little girl, if your ma never gets over this, won't you? Your auntie 'll stay right here an' raise you. She's took care o' me through a spell or two a week all my life. She don't know much o' anything except to take care o' folks. She's never sick herself. She don't let anybody wait on her if she is."

Leaming's face was a study. "How often does she have these spells?" he asked the weeping auntie.

"Two or three times a week. She never misses a week."

"How long has she been having them?"

"Ever since she was a girl."

"And have you taken care of her all her life?"

"Oh, yes, sir. There wa'n't anybody else. We set up at least two nights a week with her."

"What do the doctors say about it?"

"They don't say much."

"Do they think it is serious?"

"I — they don't say much."

"Well, did you ever ask them if it was dangerous?"

"Yes, sir. They didn't say much."

"What's the matter here?" Mrs. Palmer came in, crimson-faced, panting. Mariella followed her, large-eyed, white as death. "Where is she sick at?"

"I do' know," said auntie. "It's one o' her spells."

"Spells! *Spells?* Well, what kind o' spells?"

"I do' know. She's had 'em all her life. But she thinks this is her last one."

"What makes her think so? Can she talk?"

"Oh, yes," said Leaming, confidently. "She can talk."

Mrs. Palmer leaned over the lounge. "Where you feel bad?"

The sick woman opened her eyes. "Hey?"

"I say, where you feel bad?"

The sick woman looked at her sister and closed her eyes.

"It's a spell," said the sister, gently but firmly. "There ain't any other name. The doctors never called it anything else. Many a time our old doctor 'n Mizzoura has come in an' set down an' wiped his forehead all over with his silk han'kacher, an' said: 'Well, Mis' Pollard, you've got another spell, hain't you? You pretty bad off?'"

"Well, what did he *do* for her?" interrupted Mrs. Palmer, impatiently. "That's the main thing."

"W'y, I do' know 's he ever done much. I guess there wa'n't no hope for her right from the start, poor, sufferin' soul!"

"Well, I guess she'll come out o' this spell all right side up," said Mrs. Palmer. She gave a sniff. "I've see hysterics lots o' times, an' it looks just like this. Got any mustard in the house?"

The sick woman gave a gasp. She straightened out suddenly. Gray hues spread over her face. Her eyes rolled upward and set themselves on the ceiling. One arm fell stiffly over the edge of the lounge and hung there.

"Fer the land's sake!" cried out the auntie. "She's a-goin'! An' he ain't to home! After all the spells he's see her through!" She threw her apron over her head. "Oh, Semy, your ma, your ma! She's a-goin'!"

"Yes, I guess she is," said Mrs. Palmer, with a routed air. She stood back on her heels. Some of the red went out of her face.

Leaming, too, grew pale. This was surely Death; and he and Death had looked into each other's eyes only two or three times.

Suddenly he remembered Mariella. He turned quickly, meaning to take her away. But he stood still instead, unable to move or speak. Mariella was gliding in among the watchers by the bed. Her eyes were uplifted. There was a strange exaltation in her bearing. Her face shone. It was as if she looked into the very eyes of God.

She sank upon her knees and put one arm up around the other child's waist and drew her down beside her. There was no awkwardness in her movements now. She was absolutely unconscious of herself. For a moment she knelt so in silence, with that rapt look in her eyes. It seemed to Leaming, who scarcely breathed as he watched her, that the shining upon her face was not of the earth. Suddenly she smiled and spoke, as if to some one in the room, so sure did she seem of being heard. "God," she said, softly; "*God*—if she dies" —she hesitated as if for words. Then the smile grew in her eyes. "If she dies—*be good to her*—and to the little girl!"

A moment longer she knelt. Then, trembling strangely, Leaming lifted her and led her from the room. "I'll take her home," he said, in answer to Mrs. Palmer's awed look.

"I'll stay all night," she whispered back sternly. "I" —she followed them to the door—"I wish it 'u'd be so's you could stay all night at our house, an' kind o' see after Mariella." She lowered her voice. "What do you suppose ailded her? I never see her act so. I never see the beat of her, anyhow. Where do you suppose she ever heard anybody pray that way? I'll be switched if she ever heard me!"

"I'll stay at the house all night," said Leaming.

He was turning away when she stopped him. She leaned toward him with a mysterious air. "You tell Mr. Parmer to oil up the wagon. It ain't fit to ride to a funeral in — a-squeakin' so!"

Leaming walked home beside Mariella in silence. He held her hand in one of his, and carried the mushrooms in the other.

The child's simple prayer in that solemn moment had shaken him strangely. He had heard many prayers by high ministers of God, — earnest, eloquent, impassioned prayers, — but never had he heard any one speak directly *to* God; never had he seen upturned, praying eyes that seemed to be holding God's own eyes within them. As a rule, praying eyes are closed — as if to see far away; and praying voices have a sound as of one speaking at a great distance from the one spoken to. It was the first pure, simple, spontaneous prayer he had ever heard.

But the new neighbor did not die. Early the next morning Mrs. Palmer came home, in a state of mind. The family was just sitting down to breakfast, Leaming with them. She had a pale, sleepless look. She took off her things and sat down silently. For some moments no one dared ask any questions. Then Mr. Palmer screwed up his courage.

"When's the funeral?" he asked solemnly, looking into his coffee cup. His tone was gentle. On really great occasions, like the present, he and Mrs. Palmer had even been known to be affectionate.

"Funeral!" cried Mrs. Palmer, furiously. "Yes, you'd ought to talk funeral! W'y, she's up an' gettin' breakfast! As well as anybody! After me an' that poor weak-kneed, walked-over *auntie* a-settin' there all night, a-talkin' low if we so much as talked at all, an'

expectin' her to die every minute! Up an' gettin' breakfast!"

"Pass me somethin' to eat," she added helplessly. "I'll see if I can eat my mad off. I never was so mad in my life. To think that a woman could fool me that way! She's fooled that auntie her whole lifetime. Kept her a-dancin' attendance on them harrowin' death-bed scenes. I held a lookin'-glass over her face to see if she was still a-breathin', an' she was; so I got a sharp mustard-plaster an' was just about to put it on her chest, when she opens her eyes an' looks right at me, an' says out, cold and spiteful — 'You put that onto me, if you dar'! Greasy thing!' I liked to drop dead."

"Oiled up the wagon an' washed off its curtains all for nothin'," said Mr. Palmer, regretfully. "Are they Prespyterians or Methodists?"

"I don't know what they are," said Mrs. Palmer, bitterly, "an' I don't care. They're from Mizzoura; that's enough. I know one thing. They won't fool me there with their spells an' their 'she's a-dyin's' again in a hurry."

Mr. Palmer laughed.

"The little girl is a-comin' to step along to school with you an' Mariella," Mrs. Palmer added, after a moment, to Leaming. "She ain't a bad child. She's got it in her to make a beauty after a while."

Leaming glanced at Mariella. Her face burned; the tears came into her eyes, but she was too proud to let one fall. She would not shrink from his questioning look. Her lips trembled, but her eyes met his resolutely.

Breakfast was eaten in silence; but when Mrs. Palmer arose from the table she pushed her chair back with a violence that indicated a lingering of her anger.

"Such a ruination of Sunday!" she exclaimed. "A-settin' up all Sunday night with a case o' hysterics! An' now have to face the wash-tub!"

CHAPTER VII

Semia came the next day to accompany Mariella to school. Mariella did not dislike her; when they were alone together, she enjoyed her company; but when Mr. Leaming talked to Semia in his kind, impartial way, Mariella was torn with jealousy. The teacher had always seemed to belong to her more than to any of the other scholars, because he spent so much more time in her society.

Whenever he talked to Semia or walked beside her, Mariella withdrew in proud and bitter silence and walked alone. Leaming understood the ache of her little wild heart, but he could not entirely ease it. He could not withhold kindness from the strange child, to please Mariella.

As time passed, however, the little girls gradually became good friends, and Leaming wisely left them to themselves as much as possible on the way to and from school.

At noon one day, between a hard-boiled egg and a piece of bread-and-butter, Mariella asked suddenly of Semia, "How's your mother?"

"Sick," said Semia. She looked out across the water

with a deep look in her eyes. Her face gloomed over suddenly.

"What — again?"

Semia nodded her head.

A puzzled look went over Mariella's face. "What *makes* her get sick so much?"

Semia's eyes came back and looked into her companion's. There was a soul shining bare in them, but neither knew. "I don't know," she said helplessly. "Pa went off deer-hunting and she just up an' got sick. She got awful sick. I never see her so sick. Auntie an' me set up all night an' took turns fanning her. I fanned while auntie got breakfast an' washed the dishes, an' now — well, I guess poor auntie's been fanning ever since."

Mariella let go of her breath with a great relief. "Maybe she won't live so dreadful long," she said encouragingly.

To her surprise her companion burst into tears, and sobbed out, "That's a pretty thing to say."

"Why, what's the matter with it? If I had spells like that two or three days out of a week, an' somebody had to set and fan me, I'd a good sight rather die. I'd a good sight rather. I wouldn't mind having the spells so bad as I'd mind having somebody set and fan me. Every time you want to go to Sunday-school, you have to fan; every time you want to come over and see me, you have to fan; every time you want to do anything, you have to fan. It's fan — fan — fan — till I'd think you'd turn into a pa'm-leaf an' shake yourself at her!"

There was silence on Semia's part — an ominous one, as it proved to be. She drew several hurried breaths; then she fairly flung out these words, with flaming eyes: "You're a mean thing! I'd rather have my ma than your'n! Any day!"

Mariella laughed. She criticised her mother constantly in her own mind, and defied her; but she would not allow any one else to cast a slur upon her. "Oh, I guess not," she remarked scornfully. "She don't have spells three days in the week."

"No," said Semia, "maybe she don't." Her eyes narrowed suddenly by the closing up of the lids; her face worked with the conflict within her. "Maybe — she — don't; but anyhow" — she hesitated, and then burst out, like a fury — "anyhow — *Mr. Mallory don't come to see my ma!*"

She did not wait to witness her triumph. Terrified by the gratification of her evil impulse, she seized her dinner bucket and ran to the schoolhouse, leaving Mariella sitting alone on the rocks above the sound.

Mariella was pale with rage and something else. The words had struck her like a blow. That an insult was intended by insinuation for her mother she understood perfectly; but she was in the dark as to its nature. She felt instinctively — nay, she knew by that fine perception which a sensitive child possesses — that there was some mystery about it; it was something altogether out of the ordinary. Semia had flung out the words with a startled and shocked face — shocked at her own audacity; and because she was shocked, reasoned the shrewd Mariella, there was something shameful about the insinuation. It was as if Semia had said, "My ma doesn't steal!"

Little fury that she was, she would have rushed after the fleeing child and shaken the truth out of her, had she not, from some inexplicable reason, shrunk uncontrollably from learning it — from hearing it put into plain words in Semia's thin, tantalizing tone; also because she suspected that Semia knew no more than she did; it was something she had gathered vaguely from her elders.

She sat staring out over the water under frowning brows. Certainly Mr. Mallory did visit at her home. Why shouldn't he? What was wrong with him? Did he drink, gamble, steal? Did he brand cattle that didn't belong to him? Had he ever — Mariella shuddered hard — been a smuggler and murdered a Chinaman and thrown him into the sound when the officers were after him? These were all the sins she knew. He was her favorite of "that Mallory tribe," as her mother always spoke of the family. "Oh, there comes the Mall'ry tribe!" Mrs. Palmer would exclaim, in a tone of scornful resignation. "See 'em hurry — as if they'd been sent for!"

Mariella would not willingly believe any ill of Mr. Mallory. Mrs. Mallory now, or Isaphene — Her thought flashed back to the cherry stain and stopped there. She threw her head down upon her knees, and burst into passionate sobbing.

Here the teacher found her. He sat down beside her and put his arm around her as usual. She clung to him, and buried her tear-wet face in his breast.

"I won't walk home with her any more," she sobbed vehemently. "Never! If you want to walk home with her, you can walk with her alone! I'll g-go on behind or ahead! I — won't walk with a s-sow! I hate the sight of her!"

"Mariella!"

"Oh, of course, you'll scold me and take her part! I didn't do a thing. I was trying to be good to her, and help her out. I told her maybe her mother wouldn't live so dreadful l-long. I thought that would help her to bear her burdens." She uttered these words with a tone and air so like her mother's that Learning smiled; but fortunately for him, she did not see. "You know I didn't want her to come with us to school — you know it!"

She drew away, but Learning held her closely. He stroked her shaking hands soothingly. "I only let her come with us at last because you begged me. I did it to p-please you. And now you like her best! You take her part! You can have her, if you want her! I don't want you! I hate her! But you can have her, if you want her!"

Learning did not speak again. He held her quietly and firmly, with strange patience, smoothing her hair with delicate touches, drawing his fingers across her beating, blue-veined temples, straightening out and caressing her slender fingers, drawn up with nerves. When her passion of convulsive weeping and reproach had spent itself, he lifted her quietly, wiped her tears away with his own handkerchief, — as he had done many a time, — and looked tenderly and sadly into her eyes.

"I forgive you," he said, "although you do not ask me. But oh, my own little one! What will you do without me? Who will take care of you when I am no longer with you? Who will bear these outbursts and help you through them, and be patient, and love you still? Mariella, my heart aches for you. When I am away from you, it always will be aching for you. Remember that, whenever you can. You will not always be able to remember it at the very beginning of such an outburst, but you will after a little; and as soon as you remember it, you will be able to control yourself. . . . Now, come. Here is our friend, the woodpecker, flashing the red lining of his wing at us."

So he led her back to the schoolhouse, making her forget her trouble and the ache in her heart by pointing out the marvellous things of nature to her.

Mariella walked home that evening fifty yards behind Learning and Semia, who flaunted along beside him in an undisguised triumph that was agony to Mariella's jealous soul. Gall though this triumph was, she would not allow Semia's thin figure out of her sight; when the way was straight she walked slowly far behind, but when a bend in the path or a bit of forest hid them, she ran, panting, desperate, like a little wild animal, until her burning eyes were again upon them.

Her hands were clenched, her temples throbbed, her back ached, every nerve was drawn, tense; she was sick, sick, of jealousy and hate. At intervals an awful sob swelled up from her breast and shook itself through her throat and lips; and with it she uttered audibly each time, without intention, but in fact always startled when it stung her hearing, the one word, "sow!"

It was one of her mother's words. Scarcely a day passed that Mrs. Palmer did not call some woman of the neighborhood by that name. She did not employ the word vindictively, nor in a rage, — there were terrible words in her vocabulary reserved for that, — but more as an expression of utter contempt. Sometimes, even, she used it in a spirit of good-natured badinage.

Mariella loathed the word. She shrank always when she heard it from her mother's lips. Because she did loathe it so, because it suggested such low and repulsive things to her, it seemed now the only one strong enough to relieve her feeling toward Semia. She was conscious of her own ignominy; she sank lower, and realized her own disgrace more keenly, with each utterance of the loathed word; but she could suppress the utterance no more than she could conquer her passion of hate.

When they came to the place where Semia's path turned off, Leaming sat down on a log and waited. Mariella approached him, trembling. He held out his hands to her, moved deeply by the storm of suffering in her face. For the first time she would not come to him.

She struggled a moment, and then cast herself full length on her face among the russet ferns. Convulsive, shuddering sobs tore themselves from her. Sorely distressed, Leaming tried to comfort her, but she would not be comforted. He talked to her gently and kindly, trying to convince her that Semia could not have hurt her, could not have triumphed over her, if she herself had not permitted it. But she met him, full front, with an argument whose truth staggered him into silence. "She couldn't have hurt me if you hadn't let her! You walked with her instead of me. She couldn't have, if you hadn't let her!"

He finally got her home; but she left him at the gate, stubborn and unrelenting.

CHAPTER VIII

THE next day was Saturday.

"Now, Mariella," said her mother, after breakfast, "step spry. There's lots of work. You wash the dishes up; an' then you stand an' stir the apple-butter, so's it won't stick or splatter all over the stove. I abominate blacking the stove. For pity's sake! don't stand stooped over so! Why can't you hold yourself up straight like Isaphene Mall'ry? Even Semia holds herself better 'n you do. What makes you try a body so? You do try a body so!"

"I'd rather be stooped over than to be like Semia!—or Isaphene either, for that matter."

"Well, now, don't get sassy. They're both nicer-lookin' than you are. They know what to do with their hands an' feet, an' they've both got better legs. Semia's got rill pretty legs."

Mariella looked at her mother and laughed full in her face, wickedly. She knew it was wicked, but she didn't care. It felt good to be wicked. She was thinking of white hats and scarlet currant stains. She wondered if Semia would have a white hat.

"What are you a-laughin' at? Impudent heifer! I'll give you your walkin' chalk, if you don't look out. I'll teach you to laugh at your mother!"

Mariella looked steadily at her mother. "What's the matter with Mr. Mallory?" she asked.

"Mr. Mall'ry?" repeated her mother.

"Mr. Mall'ry?" echoed her father's voice, from the

doorway. "I come back to get some bale-rope. It's up in the antic. What about Mr. Mall'ry? Anything wrong with him?"

Mrs. Palmer had sunk limply into a chair. Her face was a dull crimson. There were even splashes of crimson down on her neck. She gathered a huge wooden bowl, filled with butter, fresh from the churn, into her lap, and commenced working it vigorously with a ladle.

"Pfew!" she said. "This kitchen's awful hot. I'm all het up. Pa, you want Mariella to run up in the antic an' find your bale-rope? She can let the dishes stand."

"What about Mr. Mall'ry?" repeated Mr. Palmer, standing as still as if planted. "Haigh?"

"The teacher says Mariella's a-doin' fine," put in Mrs. Palmer, approaching her husband's weak spot with caution. She was working away at the butter for dear life. Her head was turned on one side in an attempt at ease of bearing, but her heart was hammering. She cast one fearful glance at Mariella. "He says she's a-beatin' 'em all. Head of her class in everythin', an' a-takin' so many head-marks he can't keep track of 'em. Now, if she'd only hold herself like somethin'," she concluded, with an admiring and encouraging look at her daughter.

"She holds herself all right," said Mr. Palmer, ready, as usual, to take up the other side, whatever it might be. "I don't like a stick. You stoop over all you want, Mariella, an' be a tomboy, too." He cleared his throat.

"What about—"

"Semia's ma's got another spell!" announced Mrs. Palmer, trying to hold her husband's eye. "An' him a-deer-huntin'. Loon! He goes off up in the mountains an' stays in a cabin without any door, or window,

or chimbly in it, an' eats cold victuals an' freezes solid at night — an' never so much as *sees* a deer's tail — they ain't got so terrible much tail to see!" she interjected, smiling, with a desperate attempt at humor. "An' all the time he's gone she's a-havin' spells, one after the other, as fast as she can have 'em. Mariella, you got them dishes done? Mercy, child! You're as slow as molasses on a January mornin'."

"If I stand here all day, an' don't so much as *smell* bale-rope," said Mr. Palmer, firmly, "I'm a-goin' to find out what Mariella meant about Mr. Mall'ry. Mariella, you speak up."

Mariella was puzzled. The insinuation had appeared to refer to her mother only, and her father's sudden and unexpected return had embarrassed her. To betray her mother had been no part of her plan; and, young as she was, she understood perfectly that her question concerning Mr. Mallory had thrown her mother into a panic of fear, which she was endeavoring to conceal. There are no eyes to equal those of small, shrewd children for reading the faces, and underlying motives, of their elders.

"I didn't mean anything," she said, calmly enough. She had been reared in an atmosphere of deception and falsehood. Catechism in hand, her mother would solemnly talk for an hour on the unpardonable sin of telling a lie; and then, perhaps, closing the book and rising, would say: "Oh, Mariella, if your pa should ask you how much my hat cost, tell him three dollars. It cost five, but I don't want him to know it. He'd jaw."

Mariella loathed a lie; but thanks to her daily associations, when the occasion arose, she arose to the occasion.

"I didn't mean anything," she said, feeling a kind of bitter scorn of herself; it was so easy to get out of a hard situation by lying; anybody could do that — even a dumb-head like Isaphene, who couldn't bound Italy.

"Then what made you ask what was the matter with him?"

She hesitated a second. Then she laughed out scornfully. How easy it was! "Oh, he's so — funny!" she explained, looking around at her father, as if to invite him to join in the laugh at Mr. Mallory's expense. "He thinks he's so good-lookin'. He always puts his hand up to his face, and — oh, looks as if he thought everybody was saying, 'Oh, what a pretty man!' So I just wondered what was the matter with him to make him act so funny."

Mr. Palmer's eyes twinkled. He crossed the kitchen, chuckling, and patted Mariella on the back. "I'll get the bale-rope," he said, and went out, still chuckling.

"Mariella," said her mother, after a little while, "I'm a-goin' to town, Monday, if the team goes for shorts. What color new dress would you like?"

"I'd like a pale green," said Mariella, demurely.

"Well. My land, stir the apple-butter, child! It's a-splutterin'. I can't see what makes apple-butter splutter so. Oh, here's your father. Find the bale-rope?"

"Yes. Mariella, you come out an' let the bars down for me."

At the bars he stood still, looking straight ahead of him. "You need any new things?" he asked stiffly. "Any hats or shawls, or things?"

"I need a hat."

"What color you want on it?"

"Pale green," said Mariella. "And pink."

He patted her on the back. "You're as smart as a steel trap," he said; and went away, chuckling, as if at the joke of his life.

Mariella laughed scornfully again as she turned back to the house. What a disgrace to be bad. It was so easy. Mariella scorned easy things.

She returned to the long-handled stirring.

Mrs. Palmer squeezed the butter from one side of the wooden bowl to the other, and back again. She was an excellent and conscientious housekeeper. She understood all branches of work that the wife of a pioneer rancher in the Northwest is expected to understand.

She was one of the finest housekeepers in the neighborhood. She knew the best way of doing everything. It was a pleasure to watch her working tiny blue veins out of the butter, working with short light movements of her strong arm until the grain of the golden mass was fine, holding her head on one side, breathing heavily, and watching her work with the air of one who knows when better is perfect.

"That Mis' Mall'ry!" she frequently declared with scorn; "I wouldn't eat her butter. She's too lazy to work the *whey* out of it!"

Mariella, stirring the apple-butter round and round in the great brass kettle, whose inside always shone like burnished gold, watched her mother with unconscious pleasure and admiration. Mrs. Palmer, looking up suddenly, met her full gaze. She colored. Her eyes fell.

"Oh, Petty," she said, with a fine affection and a finer indifference, "what was it you was a-goin' to ask about Mr. Mall'ry?"

"Oh, nothing. That is — why, is he a nice man?"

Mrs. Palmer tasted the butter to gain time.

"W'y, yes, of course. Why?"

"Is there any harm in his coming here?"

The butter required salt; more salt; it had to be tasted several times.

"W'y, what a silly idy! Of course, there's no harm in his comin' here. My-O! If you ask such fool questions in front of your father or any one, I'll whale you."

"I ain't likely to." Mariella smiled — the smile her mother didn't like. "I didn't ask before pa because anybody could see you didn't want I should."

"That's a good girl," said Mrs. Palmer, hurriedly. "It didn't make any difference; only if you never ask questions before anybody, I'll never whale you. But what makes you ask such fool questions, anyhow?"

"I just wanted to know," said the child, boldly. "Just so's if his coming here *isn't* wrong and some one should happen to think it is," she looked her mother full in the eyes again, "I could *slap* 'em. That's all."

"Oh, there's old Speckle again, a-makin' three-corner tracks all over the porch!" cried Mrs. Palmer, mentally blessing the hen as she hurried out to shake her draperies at her.

CHAPTER IX

SUNDAY afternoon Learning was wandering through the forest, as he usually did on that day, when he came suddenly upon a man whom he knew to be Mr. Pollard. He was about fifty-five years old. He wore a cheap pepper-and-salt suit of clothes; under it a flannel shirt of an indescribable color. His figure was spare, his chest was slightly sunken, his legs were thin, his brown hair was turning gray. His eyes were blue, and had a dreamy, far-away look in them. A thin grayish beard reached to his chest. His elbows were on his knees; his chin was in his hands; he was a picture of reflection.

He put on the friendly, wagging air of a dog as Learning approached. "You're the teacher," he said. "I know you when I see you. I'm Semy's father. Set down a spell."

Learning sat down. "I'm glad to know you, Mr. Pollard," he said, in his sincere and simple way. "I've always missed you, somehow. I thought you were off in the mountains after deer."

"I was," said Mr. Pollard. "I just got home last night. Mari', she took a turrable spell. Semy says she's been a-spellin' ever sence I went away. I got home late last night. I slipped around an' peeped in the window, an' they was all a-poppin' corn around the fireplace an' havin' a good time. I was as hungry as a bear, an' tired; but I was so durn afraid if I went in she'd up an' have a spell that I sneaked back to the barn an' crawled into a haymow an' slept there. I'd do anything on this earth to get away from them spells. Anything but get a three-ply carpet. She set her soul on havin' a three-ply carpet once when I didn't have enough change to buy a gunny sack, an' she pestered, an' pestered, an' kept a-pesterin' tell I got my dander up an' swore I never *would* get one! I'll be durn if I ever do! But Lord-A'mighty! Them three-ply carpet spells!" He picked up a stick and commenced chewing it. "The one you see her in wa'n't a circumstance to one of her three-ply carpeters! It wa'n't a circumstance. There ain't any tellin' what they're like! There ain't enough words in the diction*ary* to describe 'em. . . . She has the fishin' spell, an' the deer-huntin' spell, an' the grouse or duck-huntin' spell, an' a lot of other 'ns — but nary a one can hold a candle to the three-ply carpeter. She don't have 'em so often, for we kind o' patched it up with a handsome fun'ral. She's bent on that. So I promised her one if she'd let up on the carpet. So she has. But what do you think?" His blue eyes twinkled suddenly. "Once she took a *fun'ral* spell! Yes, sir. You'd think that 'u'd be the last one she'd take, but she did. She got it into that head of her'n that I mightn't keep my word, so she went right off into a fun'ral spell. She couldn't be *drug* out of it till I offered to prove that I'd keep my word any day she'd set. . . . Well, when I went to the house this mornin', she was a-gettin' breakfast as chipper *as*. I went in an' I says, 'Well, Mari', you a-gettin' breakfast? — an' I'm durn if she didn't go right into a comin'-home spell quicker 'n scat. . . . Well, after breakfast I just lit out. I eat first. I didn't know when I'd get another meal. An' here I set like a bump on this here log."

"It must be very hard on her sister," remarked Leaming, "taking care of her through so many attacks."

"Auntie? Yes, it is. She ain't got three idys above takin' care o' Mari', an' a-carryin' out her wishes when she dies, an' before she dies. Auntie's had a turrable hard life," added Mr. Pollard, with a reminiscent look. "Their ma was dreadful bad off for years — creepin' paralysis — an' after Mari' an' me got married, auntie had to take care o' her mother day an' night. She had to set up nights an' work days. Waited on her mother like a baby. Fed her with a spoon. Combed her an' carried her fresh drinks, an' rubbed her. Just like she's done, ever sence her mother died, for Mari'. I guess she's got so's she can work in her sleep! . . . Well, auntie was engaged to the most promising farmer in Mizzoura. He kep' a-urgin' her an' a-urgin' her; but no, sir-ee! She wouldn't leave her mother without anybody to take care of her, an' she wouldn't put her mother on him; so she says, 'Oh, Perry, you'll have to wait.' 'Wait!' says he, with the durndest look of disgust I ever see; 'Wait! For creepin' paralysis!' I was in the room. They didn't mind me. They never had a chance to be alone. I'm sorrier for that than for anything in my whole life — that I didn't help 'em to be alone now an' then; I believe they'd a-patched it up, somehow. But auntie, she got as gray as ashes all at once; she'll never be any grayer the day she's dead. She commenced to trimble awful — hands, an' mouth, an' throat, her mouth most o' all. I've never see such trimblin', an' I've never forgot it. I bet I'll see it after she's dead. She trimbled a long time before she could say a word. Finally she says, 'Oh, Perry, — if you — love me, you can — wait! You will — wait — if — you — love me.' Well, sir, the words jest *jerked* out of her throat, as if every one hurt her clear through. But bein' a man, he thought he'd make her give in. 'There's a plenty girls that won't ask me to wait!' he hisses out at her; 'an' if you loved me, I reckon you wouldn't. Now, it's come to this pass. You choose between creepin' paralysis an' me, an' you choose 'n a hurry. You go to church next Sunday, if you choose me; an' if you choose creepin' paralysis, you stay at home. Then I'll know, an' there needn't be any more words about it.' With that he ups an' offs. . . . I never felt so sorry fer anybody 'n my life as I did for that girl. You wouldn't reckon so now, but she was as pretty as a peach on the sunny side. Her cheeks was like wild roses, an' she was always ready to run her feet off for anybody that hollered 'fetch here,' or 'fetch there.' . . . But that week," Mr. Pollard commenced chewing a fresh stick, "she went around, gray-faced an' trimblin'. The old lady, she just seemed hell-bent on bein' sicker 'n usual an' takin' more waitin' on; an' she kep' a-glarin' at auntie an' a-sayin': 'What's the matter with you? Haigh? What ails you, haigh? You look so! What makes you look so? You look as if you'd be'n drawed through a knot-hole! Lost anything?' Well, when Sunday come she was so sick we couldn't any of us go to church. But when the bells commenced to ring, I see auntie turn just like a dead woman; an' she let all holts go an' set right down. She give me one look, an' her eyes said just as plain as any words, 'Don't you tell 'em anything about it.' 'I won't,' says I, right out loud. 'Then you needn't!' snapped Mari', madder 'n scat; an' it turned out she'd been askin' me to rub her ma's hands, an' I hadn't heard a word for starin' at auntie. 'You just laze around,' says Mari', 'an' go a-jacketty-pinchin' around in the woods an' won't do a thing I want you should!' Well, sir. Auntie, she can't bear to hear church bells to this day. It's been twenty year, an' over, but just let the wind bring the sound of 'em from town an' she gets up as if she'd been shot an' goes out the room a little while. . . . Well, along that afternoon we heard wheels an' horse's feet, an' we all upt an' looked out the window, an' I'm durn if there didn't go auntie's beau an' that Sal Hargood, big as life! Sal's head up in the air! Even the horse a-steppin' high. 'Good land!' hollers out Mari', till I wanted to eat her. 'Look a-there! If there don't go Perry Rynearson an' Sal Hargood, you may shoot me dead! A-buggy-ridin'! As close as he is! What's got into him? Why didn't he ask you? I'd show him, if I was you!' An' you bet your last dollar she would of!" interjected Mr. Pollard, grinning and winking one eye, humorously. "But auntie, she never said a word. She ain't said a word to this day. Perry, he never come a-near her again. He begun goin' with Sal Hargood; an' in about three months he ups an' marries her; an' if you'll believe me, I'm durn if the old lady didn't die next day. She always was con*tra*ry; but I never see the beat of that! Now, only think. One day wouldn't have made any difference to the old lady, one way or the other; but just think of the difference it made to Perry an' auntie! Don't it just beat you all hollow? Perry, he come to the house the morning of the funeral, an' he called me out to the barn, an' he looked *awful*. 'My God,' he says, 'but I'm sorry I acted up the way I did about the old lady's creepin' paralysis! I feel all broke up; an' I — I —' he looked at me an' his face quivered all over — 'I'd give anything I got — yes, sir, my whole farm! if it 'ad happened last week, yes, two days ago! Don't you tell any old gossip-fool — '" Mr. Pollard winked and chewed hard on the stick. "He meant Mari'," he said, grinning at Leaming. "'Don't you tell any old gossip-fool that I said that, but you tell *her*. Will you?' I nodded and shook hands. He gripped my hand hard. 'You tell her I'm sorrier 'n I ever was for anything in my life. And I'll be sorry as long as I live.' Then he walked off, just as fast as he could go. He must of regretted to miss the funeral, too; there hadn't been one thereabouts for quite a spell. The old lady had a big one. Mari' nudged me to look back at the bend an' count the teams as they come up the hill. There was sixty; an' Mrs. Brown, her sister, come a-horseback. . . . Well, sir, when I told auntie what Perry said, she stood an' looked like a chalk woman on a blackboard, an' she didn't say a word. She never opened her head. I expected she'd holler out he ought to be ashamed o' hisself, to talk that way, an' him just married; but not her. She never opened her head. She ain't to this day. She's got a little gold ring on he give her; she never sent it back to him. It's wore away most to nothin'. She's a-gettin' so thin, I expect it'll drop off. Some people think there's a joke some'ers about bein' an old maid; but they don't joke auntie more'n once—if I'm around. Some nice men of took a notion to her off an' on, but, Jerusalem overtakers! she freezes 'em up at one settin', till you'd think they'd never thaw out! That's the only thing I ever see in auntie to laugh at."

"She must have taken a great deal of Semia's care upon herself," ventured Leaming.

"Semy? Say. It used to hurt me down deep—the way she mothered that girl when she was little! Rocked her to sleep every night in her arms, an' sung 'Wave, willow, murmur, water' to her—till the young one got so big she couldn't hold her any longer. Then she'd go off an' put her to bed, an' lay down along-side o' her till she went to sleep; an' then—*by gosh!*—set up an' fan Mari' half the night, turnin' with me. Semy ust to wouldn't let her out o' her sight. An' then they talk about old maids not bein' much account." Mr. Pollard looked up at Leaming suddenly from under his slouching hat-brim. "I reckon that's about enough of auntie? I reckon I've tired your ears out?"

"On the contrary," replied Leaming, who was deeply touched by the story, "I have been greatly interested. It is one of the most pathetic real stories I ever heard. I am glad you appreciate her."

"Auntie an' me understand each other," he replied briefly. "Along about sundown, if Mari' gets over her spell, so's it gets safe, I'll see a white rag a-flyin' out the kitchen window; then I'll go home. If it don't get safe, I'll sneak into the barn about dark, an' I'll find auntie's been an' foddered the stock down, an' left a good supper an' some hot coffee. I'll sleep there all night. . . . You thinkin' about gettin' married?"

Leaming smiled — that smile, at once amused and tender, that so often lent a rare beauty to his face. "No," he said.

"I was only goin' to say, if you are, to inquire into spells. I ain't a-sayin' a word agen Mari'" — Leaming smiled again, involuntarily — "not a *word;* she's a first-rate wife an' mother — when she ain't in a spell. But my father ust to always say, 'You might just as well fall in love with a girl that's got money, while you're a-fallin', an' I'm durn if it don't apply just as even to spells, only turned back'ards; you might just as well fall in love with a girl that don't have spells. You can always tell. Mari' didn't have any spells before we was married, but she give warnin's. I didn't know a warnin' then, when I see it; but I know 'em now. One Sunday soon after we was engaged I went a-fishin'. I'm durn but I do like to go a-fishin'! I never ketch any fish, but I always think I'm a-goin' to; an' there ain't any fun I know like settin' under a maple or a ba'm-o'-Gilead, an' a-holdin' a pole in your hand, an' just a-smellin' things *grow* an' *bloom.* In the evenin' I went to take Mari' to church. She was a-settin' in the parlor in a stiff-back chair. 'Well, Mari',' I says, 'I come to take you to church.' She just *glared* at me. 'Where you been?' she hisses out. I felt seventeen chills go up an' down my spine. 'A-fishin',' I says, kind o' feeble. 'A-fishin',' she hisses. 'Instid o' comin' to set the afternoon with me! I've set here this blessed afternoon, expectin' you! An' you a-fishin'! You can go to church alone! I ain't the kind to set around, a-waitin' for somebody that's gone a-fishin'!' Well, I can't begin to remember all she said, but I felt awful. I coaxed an' hummed an' ha'd, an' coaxed ha'f the night, but she wouldn't give in till I went to talkin' *ring* to her. I hadn't got her a ring yet. She got as sweet as honey. . . . I reckon the only way to get a woman out of a spell is to talk *present* to her; the only trouble is, she'll go to havin' spells too often. You got to draw the line som'ers. I drew it on the three-ply carpet. That wasn't a real spell she had that time — but it was a warnin', a solemn warnin'! An' there was others," he added, with a deep and significant look — as if he might tell if he would.

"I think I see a white cloth flying from your kitchen window," ventured Leaming.

Mr. Pollard got up quickly and looked. "So it is," he exclaimed, looking as pleased as a child. "I guess I'd best scoot home right away. Mari' goes into a spell quicker 'n scat, an' she comes out the same way. Come over an' see us. I'm glad I met you. I enjoy to hear you talk."

CHAPTER X

"I'M a-goin' over to Mis' Proudfoot's," said Mrs. Palmer to Mariella one Sunday afternoon. "If you want to come along of me, hurry up an' git ready. I'm a-goin' to set the afternoon, so I want to get an early start."

Mariella ran up to the attic and got herself hastily into her prettiest pink calico dress. Over it she slipped a white apron that tied on the shoulders in soft bows. She brushed her brown hair quickly around her finger in long curls, and tied them in a cluster at the back of her head with a pink ribbon. On them she set her white hat with the wreath of pink roses around the crown. Then she went down-stairs.

"Well, good land!" exclaimed her mother. She stood still in the middle of the floor and looked at the child. "Are you gone crazy? What you dressed up so fer?"

"Why — to — go to Mrs. Proudfoot's," faltered Mariella; her face was as pink as her dress.

"To go to Mis' Proudfoot's!" mimicked her mother. "To go to Queen Victory's! I'd be ashamed to dress all up so an' be so vain — to go to Mis' Proudfoot's! I'll take the starch out o' you. You get an' put on your pink calico with the *dots*, an' your pink sunbonnet. Here you've got three pink calicos — the one with the dots an' the one with the bars an' the one with the vines; an' you've gone an' put on the one with the *vines!* To go to Mis' Proudfoot's! That's a pretty piece of business! I'll make you haul in your horns!"

"I won't go, if I can't wear wear this dress an' my hat," said Mariella, sitting down.

"Yes, you will go, too — now!"

"I say I won't."

"I say you will, too — now. Go an' change your dress."

"I won't budge," said Mariella, turning pale. "I wouldn't go if you turned black in the face trying to make me."

Mrs. Palmer coughed long and hard. She went around the room, coughing, and looking for her handkerchief-bag and cotton gloves.

"Well, I'll declare!" she exclaimed suddenly, with a glance at the clock. "It's after one a'ready. We'll have to set right out. I'm all out of Kansas-starter, an' Mis' Proudfoot's is better 'n any other but mine. Well, come on. You ain't got time to change your dress, or I'd make you."

She walked out, and on through the orchard. She walked with short, high steps. She carried her bag on one bended arm, and swung the other to and fro with a rock of her body as she walked.

Mariella walked patiently behind her. Having gained her point, she was cheerful and good-natured. Her eyes glanced alertly into every tree for birds.

"That Mahlon Proudfoot," said her mother, sweeping the yellow leaves behind her in clouds with her skirts, "he's so stubborn, they say, he'd ought to be named Mahlon Stubbornfoot. He's so stubborn that if he'd accidentally crook his finger, he'd let it stay crooked rather 'n uncrook it."

"He never's stubborn to me," said Mariella. Her head was up and her cheeks were red. "An' I don't believe he's stubborn to his mother."

"Well, they do say he most carries his mother on two

chips," confessed Mrs. Palmer, unwillingly. "Well, talk about the old Harry!" she added suddenly, in a cautious tone.

Mariella put her head to one side and looked past her mother. Mahlon Proudfoot was sitting beside the road on a log, with his dog at his feet. His gun was between his knees. He had seen them and his face was flushed.

"Well, Mahlon," said Mrs. Palmer. "You out huntin'?"

"I've been. I got six quail. You goin' to see mother?"

"Yes, we're on the way."

"You stay to supper, an' mother'll cook the quail. Mariella an' I can pick 'em while you an' mother visit. I'll walk home with you after supper."

"Well, we'll see."

Mrs. Palmer walked on, and Mahlon flung his gun over his shoulder and walked beside Mariella. The path was narrow, and he stumbled along in the grass outside. Mariella gave him one brief sweet look, then she turned her attention to the dog. "Nice Fanny! Nice old Fan!" she kept saying, as the dog leaped and fawned upon her.

Mahlon opened his hunting-bag. "See here," he said proudly.

Mariella gave one look.

"It's a shame to kill the pretty innocent things!" she flashed out at him. "It's kill, kill, kill! You're never happy unless you're killing something."

A guilty red stain went across the boy's brow. He closed the bag.

"Oh, hear her talk!" said Mrs. Palmer. "Talk's cheap. You wait. She can eat more fried quail than any hired man we got. Don't you mind what she says, Mahlon."

Mahlon put out his free hand and touched Mariella's arm timidly. "That's a joke," he said very low, smiling, when she looked at him. "Anybody a-smoothin' my feelin's because they think you've hurt 'em 's a joke—even when it's your mother."

Mariella smiled gratefully at him.

"Aigh?" called out Mrs. Palmer. "What-a-say, Mahlon? Why don't you talk out so's I can hear?"

"I was a-sayin'," spoke up Mahlon, red but bold, "that I didn't think myself it was just right to be a-killin' things all the time, but I don't see how we can live without it."

It was only a mile to the Proudfoots'. Mrs. Palmer walked fast, and they soon turned a bend in the path that brought them in sight of the ranch. The house, the encircling fences, the barns, and all the outbuildings, which taken together seemed almost a "settlement," were unpainted; they had worn through the years to that soft rain-washed and wind-beaten tint that is warmer than gray and paler than lavender, yet has a suggestion of both at a distance. No paint can beautify like the slow, passing touch of years; no stonework can mellow to such beauty as wood so touched and retouched.

Through nature's marvellous taste for harmony the shingled roof had deepened to a darker, richer gray; a great Mayduke cherry tree spread its long branches all over the roof of one porch which ran along the entire side of the low house; a long grape arbor extended from the porch to the gate; the fences wound in and out around the buildings in silver lines.

Mahlon Proudfoot was a lonely lad. He had no companions, and he was deeply attached to his mother and to his home. Always, before reaching the bend which brought him in sight of the ranch lying a little below, on the slope that stopped only when it reached the sound, he walked faster, and something came into his throat that had to be swallowed down. But to-day Mariella was talking, and he did not think of it until Mrs. Palmer cried out heartily: "Here we are! Not more 'n a hundred yards further! My-O! If your mother ain't got her chores all done up, an 's settin' out on the porch, a-readin'!"

At the gate a slim stalk of hollyhocks stood up straight and tall, starred with belated pink bloom.

"Well, look at that!" Mrs. Palmer pointed a crooked finger at it. "See that tom-fool thing, will you? What's it a-bloomin' now for, I'd like to know."

"It didn't bloom in June," said Mahlon, apologetically. Then he turned and looked a second time at the slender shaft of pink. It came to him that Mariella looked like a pink hollyhock — she was as pink and sweet, and she had the same look of still pride. He wanted to tell her, as they walked down the shadowy arbor behind her mother. He cleared his throat and said, "Mariella"; but when she gave him her sweet, grave look, the words he wanted would not come. "We'll pick the quail, won't we?" he faltered out; and she assented cheerfully.

"What you doing these days?" he asked, after a moment's silence.

"Binning apples!" she replied, promptly, with a scornful laugh. "I bin apples Saturdays and evenings after school. I wonder I don't bin apples on Sundays! That wouldn't be any worse than killing quail, though," she added, flashing a glance at him out of the corners of her eyes.

"Mother don't like to have me hunt on Sunday," confessed the boy; "but it's so lonesome to sit around all day. Wish I could come over to your house!" he added; but he hung down his head and shuffled his feet along through the yellow leaves after he said it.

"And here's Mariella, too," his mother said just then, having welcomed Mrs. Palmer; "come here, my dear, an' kiss me. Well, what a little sweet, pink girl she is to-day, ain't she, Mahlon?" The boy blushed with pride and the little girl with pleasure. Mariella loved Mrs. Proudfoot; she never made any remarks about thin legs, but always found something comforting to say.

She sat down near Mrs. Palmer and drew the child into the curve of her arm.

"I wish I had a little girl," she said, smoothing Mariella's curls after taking off her hat.

"You'd soon send Mariella home, if you had her," said Mrs. Palmer; "she ain't worth a pinch o' salt to work."

"Oh, little girls her age oughtn't to work; she works at school."

"Well, I got up at three o'clock when I was her age an' milked ten cows before breakfast," said Mrs. Palmer, triumphantly.

Mrs. Proudfoot was not impressed. "I want to know," she said politely. "Now, you must take off your things an' stay to supper. Mr. Palmer's away, ain't he?"

"Yes, he's gone to Tacoma. Everything's a-jumpin' down there. Villard's drove the last spike an' we've got a railroad at last. Pa went down to buy a lot while they're cheap. I wish some o' their boom 'u'd trickle down this way! Not much danger, I guess."

"If it did," spoke up Mariella quickly, "they'd go an' burn all our trees down. Mr. Leaming said so."

"Well, supposin' they did, dumby? What's trees for, in the name o' all? You an' Mr. Leaming!"

"All is, I'd like to see 'em try to cut down my big cedar! Or my maple!"

"Oh, you talk so! You an' your cedars an' your maples!"

"Well, I'd shoot 'em with pa's rifle, if they tried it!"

"I'd aim while you pulled the trigger," said Mahlon, laughing, but with the kindest of glances at her.

"He went yesterday," said Mrs. Palmer, rocking comfortably, "an' he won't be home before early to-morrow mornin' on the *Idaho*. W'y, I declare!" Her face took on anxious lines. "Is this Mr. Proudfoot a-comin'? W'y, I thought he was away."

"Why, so it is," declared Mrs. Proudfoot. "It's your father, Mahlon."

She and her son exchanged uneasy glances. Mrs. Palmer's face colored, and Mariella's eyes grew large with fright.

Mr. Proudfoot came slowly down the arbor. He was an old man. He was held in awe by the whole neighborhood. It was well known that visitors were welcome with him only under the most favorable conditions. Mrs. Palmer put on a bold front.

"Why, father," faltered Mrs. Proudfoot, "we wa'n't expectin' you."

"So I see."

"How are you, Mr. Proudfoot?" said Mrs. Palmer, getting up out of her chair to shake hands.

Mr. Proudfoot did not see her outstretched hand.

"I'm torrable, ma'am," he said, and with a scowl at Mariella he went on into the house.

"He's tired," said his wife, in a cheerful tone which did not go well with her pale face. "Excuse me, an' I'll go in an' find his slippers."

She followed him through the sitting-room into the bedroom. "You tired, father?"

"Yes, I'm tired, father!" He mimicked her tone. "How long they been here?"

"Just a little while."

He raised his voice.

"How long they goin' to stay?"

"Oh, father, talk low; *please* talk low. I asked 'em to supper. I didn't know you'd come home tired."

"You didn't know I'd come home tired, aigh? You thought I'd come home fresh, I suppose! You thought I'd come home dancin' a Highland fling, I suppose! Well, I'll go out an' set down an' *look* at 'em'. I guess they'll soon conclude they're wanted at home."

"Now, see here, father, don't you dast to do it. I won't have you a-lookin' anybody away from here again. It's my home just as much as it's yours, an' I won't have you do it. I won't have my company treated that way. The whole neighborhood talks about your just a-settin' *a-lookin'* at people till they up an' go home."

"Oh, it does, does it?" The old man thrust his feet into his slippers, with his head on one side. He chuckled wickedly.

"I never ordered anybody out o' the house yet," he boasted. "Where's my cane?"

"You might just as well order 'em out as to *look* 'em out, every speck. Mis' Hanna, she couldn't stand it but half an hour. She got so nervous she could pretty near fly. She up an' went home. She told Mis' Risley she'd 'a' gone clear out o' her head in five minutes more — just from your lookin' at her so!"

"They can't a one say I ever ordered 'em out," boasted the old man, chuckling. "Not a one."

He got his cane and started for the porch. His slippers were too loose, and they shuffled along on the floor, as he went with a stiff-jointed, sliding movement. Mariella heard the shuffle and the regular pound of the cane on the floor. She looked at her mother in large-eyed suspense.

"Hadn't we better go?" she whispered.

"Not by a jugful," replied her mother, bravely. "I ain't afraid of anybody's tongue on earth."

But his tongue was a weapon Mr. Proudfoot seldom used. Tongues were fool things for women, in his estimation. He sat down opposite Mrs. Palmer and folded his hands on his cane; then he rested his chin on his hands; and when he was quite settled to his liking, he fixed his eyes on Mrs. Palmer. They were black, piercing eyes, set deep under shaggy brows.

Mrs. Palmer returned the look, but she soon felt her eyes waver. She kept talking to Mrs. Proudfoot, at first quite cheerfully. She tried not to look at the old man, but her glance wandered to him against her will. His eyes always met hers steadily.

Mrs. Palmer had heard that he looked unwelcome guests out of his house. She summoned all her courage; but presently it went oozing, bit by bit, out of her finger-ends. She managed to keep up a desultory conversation with Mrs. Proudfoot; but between sentences she usually was compelled to let her eyes turn to Mr. Proudfoot, whereupon she would straightway fall to saying, "So — that — a —" several times before she could remember the words she desired.

At last Mahlon arose, and, beckoning to Mariella to follow him, moved down the porch toward the kitchen.

Mr. Proudfoot twisted around in his chair.

"Where you two a-slyin' off to?" he growled, in a deep voice.

"We're a-goin' to pick the quail for supper."

"You set down."

Mahlon stood still.

"You hear me? You set down."

Mahlon stood up very tall and straight. He looked big and splendid to Mariella. His eyes flashed at his father.

"Now, see here, father. You heard me say we were a-goin' to pick the quail. You know if I say I'll do a thing, I'll do it. There ain't a bit o' use in your wastin' your breath. Come on, Mariella."

"You stay where you be," commanded the old man, fiercely. Mariella looked at her mother.

"Now, father," pleaded Mrs. Proudfoot, "don't you say another word. Please, father. You remember what I told you."

"Mariella," said Mrs. Palmer, in a deep voice, feeling herself reënforced as it were, "you go on with Mahlon, if you want to. Run along." Then she turned a withering look upon Mr. Proudfoot. "You must be pushed," she hissed out at him.

The old man spluttered and fumed; his face was scarlet.

"You talkin' to *me?*" he almost squealed.

"Yes, I'm talkin' to you. I say you must be pushed!" She fairly rocked her head at him in her rage. "*Pushed!* I say you must be pushed! You think you can look everybody 'n the neighborhood out o' your house; but you'll git fooled this time. Mis' Proudfoot an' Mahlon both asked us to stay to supper, an' we're goin' to stay, look or no look, hiss or no hiss. You can look till doomsday, but you can't look a hole through *me!*"

The old man jumped up, choking with helpless fury.

"I wouldn't set down at a table with you," he cried out. "I wouldn't —"

He stopped suddenly, remembering his boast that he had never ordered any one out of his house. He had been sliding away, but he stood still now, and set his eyes at her in one of his most terrible looks.

Mrs. Palmer shook her head at him like a fighting and daring hen. "Proudfoot!" she cried out, tauntingly. "*Proudfoot!* You'd ought to be called Proudfoot! Shufflefoot's more like it! You'll find out you can't look a hole through me."

The old man went shuffling and thumping away on his stiff-jointed, sliding run. His face was purple. His lips babbled wildly, but no words came from them.

"My mercy!" said Mrs. Proudfoot, looking after him, with a pale face, almost unconscious of Mrs. Palmer's presence. "If he should have a stroke! If he should have a stroke! He was as purple as a starfish. I always feel to regret crossin' father —"

"That's just what ails him," said Mrs. Palmer. "You feel to regret crossin' him till he'd ketch cold an' die of pneumony of the lungs if you'd cross him once good an' hard."

Mrs. Palmer and Mariella stayed to supper. Mariella sat beside Mahlon and felt safe and happy. He gave her all the wish-bones, and broke them with her, she getting the long end every time. Mahlon looked stern, save when he smiled at her. His mother was pale and anxious; but Mrs. Palmer kept a brave countenance. Outside, Mr. Proudfoot shuffled back and forth on the porch, glaring in at Mrs. Palmer as he passed the window. His eyes were sometimes red and other times green — like a cat's in the dark; his lips babbled continuously, but not a word could be understood.

They did not remain long after supper. As dusk approached, Mrs. Palmer felt her courage retreating. But she held her shoulders the higher for that.

"I declare," she said cordially, "we've had a beautiful time. Your quail were fried to a T, an' your quince marmylade was perfect. I'm obliged for the Kansas-starter. I don't know what I'd of done. Them Pollards' ain't fit to use — I guess their'n is Mizzoura-starter, which accounts for it's never startin'. Now do come an' stay to dinner" — she paused and fumbled with her glove; then she added — "you and Mr. Proudfoot an' Mahlon."

She walked along silently behind Mahlon and Mariella. At the gate she glanced back. She drew a long breath of relief, and, taking her handkerchief out of her bag, wiped her face and neck. She laughed, with a kind of grim and reluctant humor.

"Pfew!" she said to herself. "I never worked so hard in my life. I'd rather milk fifteen cows an' wean the ca'ves! But this is the first time I've gave way to perspiration since it begun. My, but it is a relief to give way to perspiration. I wouldn't do it to humor him, an' let him see I was scared of him — old Hatefulfoot! — but it is a relief, let 'em say what they will. I'll just walk slow, an' perspire it all out. . . . Well, all is," she added conclusively, "I bet he never gits another chance at me. I come off best this time, but I'd rather milk fifteen cows — cows that wouldn t 'so' when I told 'em to. Old Devilfoot!"

The hired men had done up all the Sunday chores and gone away for the night when Mrs. Palmer and Mariella returned. The hired girl was gone home, the house was empty.

Mrs. Palmer made a fire in the kitchen stove and stirred up some corn-meal mush.

"It'll fry nice for breakfast," she said.

She stood over it, stirring rapidly with a long spoon in her right hand, the yellow meal sifting finely all the time out of her left hand. Mariella stood watching her.

"What made Mr. Mallory talk so low when he met us on the road home?"

"I didn't know as he talked so low."

"Well, he did. Mahlon and I couldn't hear a word he said to you."

"Oh, you beat all! Go on to bed now. You do ask more fool questions. It seems to me you ain't got any gum'tion. Go on to bed now."

CHAPTER XI

Mariella went to the stair-door and stumbled up in the dark, sliding her hands along the walls. Her mother came to the foot of the stairs.

"Oh, Mariella," she called, in her most affectionate tone, "you goin' right up?"

"Yes." Mariella stumbled on without stopping.

"What are you goin' to do up there?"

"Nothin'."

"Well, you goin' right to bed?"

"Yes."

"You got a drink with you?"

"Don't want none."

"You might want one 'n the night. Mercy, child! Don't be a snappin' turtle. I'll set a drink here on the stair steps, so's if you want it, it'll be right here. Well, good night."

"Good night."

"Oh, Mariella."

"Hunh?"

"Don't 'hunh' me!"

"Ma'am?"

"Your window open?"

"Unh-hunh — yes, ma'am."

"Shut it, will you? The wind might come up 'n the night, an' bang things around. You'd ketch cold too. Hear?"

For answer Mariella went stumbling down to the window. She closed it with a loud noise, and instantly slid it up again as high as it had been before, and slipped the stick that held it up in place. She heard her mother close the stair-door and go away. She sat down on the floor beside the open window.

She was breathless with amazement at her own act. When she had put her hands on the window to lower it, she had not been conscious of any intention to lift it again. It was as if the window had lifted itself and had got the stick under it, somehow. Her mother's peculiar nervousness and solicitude had betrayed her. The child was seized with the certainty that something unusual — something in which she was not to share — was occurring or about to occur. Her mother did not wish her to go down-stairs for a drink of water, and she desired the window closed.

"She must think I'm green," muttered the child, in her mother's language, which she always spoke when off guard, "not to see through her! She never brings me drinks unless I'm sick. Maybe it's a surprise party! She acts just like she did the night the Mallorys got one up on pa, and she knew about it. She went tiptoeing around from window to door, and door to window."

At that moment she heard a faint step on the path beneath her window. The path led through the orchard to the front door. Just at first she was frightened and drew back. Then the front door was opened cautiously; not so cautiously, however, that its customary brief squeak did not accompany its opening. Mariella leaned out suddenly then, but she was too late. Some one had entered from the outer darkness. She caught a glimpse of a large, dark figure. A narrow beam of light was streaming across the porch and the grass, clear to the row of currant bushes. There was another faint squeak; then the beam withdrew, and all was darkness and silence.

Mariella set her lips together. She unlaced and drew off her copper-toed shoes. She stood up and stole with

limber, stealthy movements toward the stairway. She moved on her toes. Her shoulders were drawn up. Her arms swung bonelessly at her sides, a little in advance of her body. Her head was bent forward. Her steps were long and noiseless. She felt as if she were a mass of boneless flesh, propelled not by her own will or desire, but by some unknown power. Once or twice a board creaked, and she stood still, with red lights shaking before her eyes. She wanted to make her way down-stairs unheard. It was a silly wish to be working so desperately for. But Mariella never did anything by halves. Her reaching the stairs undetected could scarcely have been of more importance had her life depended upon it.

She reached them and descended noiselessly. She put her hand on the knob — it turned without sound; she held it firmly, so it could not click, and pushed the door. It did not move. It was locked on the outside.

After a while Mariella returned to the window, and huddled down again on the floor. The brilliant Orion was rising in the east. Sirius was still tangled in the dark firs on the crest of the hill. The child knew nothing of astronomy; but the most beautiful of the planets and constellations were familiar to her, from long and loving watches. She looked nightly for the three brilliant stars in Orion's belt; she knew that down below would be a splendid, changeful star. They were all stars to her.

The "dipper" was the only constellation she knew by name. Her mother had pointed it out to her one cold winter's night. She had gone out to the pump to get water, and had called: "Oh, here's the dipper! Mariella, come an' see the dipper."

"The *what*," said the child, coming out.

"The dipper. W'y, up 'n the sky, dumby! Look-ee there!"

She pointed it out, also the North Star.

"What makes you call it the dipper?" Mariella had then asked contemptuously.

"W'y, that's the name. The books an' grammars all call it that."

"How silly! To call anything as beautiful as a star, or, a lot of stars, a *dipper!* ugly tin thing!" Mariella had replied, going in without waiting for any more lessons in astronomy.

To-night the stars appealed to her more powerfully than usual.

She had forgotten the mystery below when, about ten o'clock, she was startled by the faint creak of the front door. She leaned out quickly. A man was stepping stealthily across the porch. He was a large man. The narrow strip of light was again streaming across the porch and across the yard to the currant bushes. At the steps the man looked back into the room, and smiled. The light struck full on his face. Mariella never forgot the smile on that face. She drew back; her heart was beating to suffocation. She had recognized him.

When Mariella went down-stairs the following morning, the men had breakfasted and were already out in the orchards with their blue-bedded, creaking wagons, gathering apples. Mr. Palmer had returned, and he and Mrs. Palmer were in the midst of a violent quarrel.

"Well, I know somebody was here," Mr. Palmer was saying as the child entered, "because the orchud bars wa'n't the way I left 'em. There was a man's tracks in the soft ground; he'd had on high-heel boots."

"The preacher wears high-heel boots," said Mrs. Palmer, attempting humor, although there was no appreciation of it in her face. "Sundays," she added. "Oh, here's Mariella! Why don't you ask Mariella? Mariella, your pa thinks there was comp'ny here last night."

Mariella looked at her mother and smiled. It was a smile that brought that lady's heart up into her throat. It took some of the fine color out of her face, too. "You tell him there wa'n't anybody here. He don't see fit to believe me. I do enjoy to see the day your pa don't believe my solemn word! I told him solemn there wa'n't a soul here."

Mariella looked full at her father, without faltering. "There wasn't anybody here," she said.

"Oh, ho, Miss Steel Trap! How d' you know? Did you stay up till bedtime?"

"Yes, I stayed upstairs."

"Would you of see if anybody had come?"

"Yes."

"Oh, ho. Where was you?"

"Sitting by the window."

"Window open?"

"Yes."

"Mariella," said her mother, piously, "don't tell a lie, not even to make your mother's word good. My word's good." Mariella tittered. "Didn't you shut the window when I told you to, for fear you'd ketch cold?"

Mariella looked at her mother, and laughed contemptuously. "Yes, but I opened it again."

"When, child?" Mrs. Palmer's face was a study in purple.

"Right away. Before you locked the door."

"Locked — the — door!" stammered Mrs. Palmer. "I didn't lock the door."

"Didn't you?" said Mariella, indifferently. "Then it just locked itself. It does sometimes, only it was unlocked this morning."

"You must be mistaken about it's bein' locked." Mrs. Palmer was pulling herself together with difficulty. "Well, pa, I guess you'll take Mariella's word about nobody a-bein' here, if you won't take mine. I'd like to know who'd come! The preacher at church!"

She was going out into the kitchen with some dishes as she spoke. She gave her husband an injured look. It was intercepted half-way by Mariella—who returned the look, and smiled.

CHAPTER XII

When Mariella was gone to school, Mrs. Palmer did some thinking. She was bending over the wash-tub on the back porch. She considered Clary, the hired girl, "mighty fiddlin' stuff" when it came to washing. She either got too much bluing in the clothes or not enough. Then, all the towels and all the tea-towels and bread cloths, which were made out of ravelled flour-sacks, should have been always spread out carefully over the currant and gooseberry bushes to bleach; this Clary could not be driven to do. As Mrs. Palmer was rather under Clary's thumb, hired girls being, as she frequently declared, scarcer than hen's teeth, she decided to do the washing herself.

Mrs. Palmer was a real laundress. She loved the work. Instead of wearing an old torn dress and coming forth on wash-day with untidy hair, as slatterns do, she always put on a neat calico dress and a big apron, checked black and white so finely that the effect was lavender. Her hair was always neatly combed, and her sleeves, rolled above the elbows, revealed plump, well-formed arms. Her waist was simply bound at the neck, without a disfiguring collar, and edged with narrow, crocheted lace of Mariella's making on long winter evenings. Mrs. Palmer's neck was fair. Her movements were alert and vigorous, her face full of animation; in a word, this was Mrs. Palmer at her best — the careful, neat housekeeper, the cheerful mistress, the solicitous mother, neighbor, and wife. Alas! that wash-days only came once a week.

It was a pleasure to see her washing the linen. She did not huddle all over the tub; she held her back straight naturally, and bent forward from the waist. With light movements of her powerful arms she spread piece after piece of linen on the bluish, accordeon-pleated zinc of the wash-board, and rubbed over it carefully the great bar of yellow soap; then up and down she rubbed the piece itself — three times and then into the soapy water it went with a splash, three times again, and then into the water — over and over until all stains were removed. Then into the big bright boiler on the stove it went for a boiling; afterward it was lifted on, and twisted around a clean bleached broom-stick, and held suspended above the boiler until the soap-suds had dripped from it, when it was lowered into a tub of clear water, wrung, and then put through another tub of clear water; last of all it was plunged quickly into the tub of bluing water.

When there was no danger of being invited to assist, Mariella loved to watch her mother washing. She liked the regular, rhythmic rubbing, and the soft splash into the water; she liked the bluing and the making of the starch; she liked the white folds curling around her mother's arm, and the rainbow-tinted flecks of bubbled foam scattered over her apron; most of all, she liked the long line of neatly hung clothes, and the clean, pleasant smell of their drying in the sun.

On this particular Monday morning Mrs. Palmer was not taking as cheerful pleasure as usual in her laundry work. If her thoughts, as she bent over the big tub, had been put into words, they would have been something like this: "Well, don't that beat you! She slipped down there an' found that door locked, and she knows I locked it! She put that window down when I told her, an' then she put it up again, right off, an' *set* by it. I bet my soul she saw through the drink, an' the window, too. I bet my soul she knows somebody was here! But she wouldn't tell on me! Lord Almighty — if she had!" Mrs. Palmer paled through all the steam that enveloped her like a cloud and freshened her as a bath of dew freshens flowers. "Well, she didn't — but, my soul! The way she laughed when I told her she mustn't lie! It almost made my teeth chatter in my head! If her pa wa'n't too terrible dumb, he'd of see there was something up the way she laughed. It wa'n't a natural laugh. I never see her beat. She sees right through everybody an' everything. It does my soul good, the way she sees through the sky-pilot, as Mr. Hoover calls him. An' pa — she sees right through *him*, as if he was a strip of isinglass. He's almost as thin as isinglass — My-*O!* But I don't propose to have her a-seein' through me, not by a jugful! The worst of it is — I don't believe I'll ever dare to shake her again. I believe she knows she's got the dead-wood on me. I can't do anything with her if I can't shake her. I'll get her a new dress."

Mrs. Palmer stopped washing suddenly and straightened up. She stood a long time, thinking deeply. From time to time she gathered up a handful of foam and let it fall in flecks, like beaten cream, back into the tub. Finally she stripped all the foam off her arms and then wiped them on a towel.

She went around to the front of the house with the porch broom in her hand. Under a pretence of sweeping, but looking over-pale for the exertion, she peered along the edge of the porch with her eyelids wrinkled together, and a strained look in her eyes. When she had finished the porch she began sweeping the narrow path from side to side. She swept slowly and calmly, as if challenging the whole world to look, clear on out through the orchard to the bars.

"You must be pushed," said her husband's voice suddenly, from under a near-by tree.

She started violently. "That you? My-O! You give me a turn. What-a-say?"

"W'y, I say you must be pushed. Sweepin' the *path!* On a wash-day! You must be pushed. What ails you?"

"I don't know as anything ails me. What ails you?"

"Nothin' ails me. I was a-comin' back to the house, when I see you a-sweepin' the path off. On a wash-day! It looked so funny I thought somethin' must ail you."

Mrs. Palmer faced him now, defiant and at her ease; one hand held the broom; the other was spread out, thumb up, on her generous hip. A slow, tantalizing smile went over her face. "'D you come back for bale-rope?" she asked.

A dull red flamed across Mr. Palmer's brow and eyes, paling off toward the lower part of his face. This was a sure indication that he was at once furious and helpless.

"No, I didn't come back for bale-rope!" he hissed out.

"Oh, I was just goin' to say," — Mrs. Palmer laughed again, — "there wa'n't any more. It's all gone. You took it all the other mornin' when you come back so all of a sudden — as if *you* was pushed! What ailded you?"

"Maybe you'll find out yet what ailded me!" said Mr. Palmer, fiercely. "Maybe you'll find out. A-jacketty-pinchin' around out here, sweepin' *paths* — on a wash-day! A-sweepin' out *high-heeled tracks* — that's what you're a-doin'! You think I ain't got any eyes 'n my head — "

"Eyes!" interrupted Mrs. Palmer, laughing now without restraint. "Oh, no; I know you've got eyes.

But high-heeled tracks! Good grieve! You do act so! I can't see what ails you. For the land's sake! Don't you know *stilt* tracks when you see 'em yet? You're awful dumb."

"*Stilt* tracks?" Mr. Palmer looked dazed.

"Yes, pa, stilt tracks. Mr. Harrison's boy was over here yesterday on his stilts. I reckon some o' his tracks went right into boot-heel tracks — an' you went an' thought it was a high-heel track. You must think the preacher had lots to do, a-comin' here after church was out! If he'd of come, I'd of put him up all night — a preacher that way."

Mr. Palmer removed his hat, and, taking out of it an old silk handkerchief of an indescribable color, wiped the perspiration from his brow. He had a silly look. "I've see stilt tracks afore," he remarked, "but I never see any that fitted right into heel tracks the way them did."

"You'll see a lot before you die that you never see before," replied Mrs. Palmer, with good-humored contempt. "Which apples the men a-getherin'?"

"The blue pearmains, an' the yallow pippins."

"Hunh? Fallin' off?"

"Terrible."

"I never see their beat for lateness. It's an awful late season. We had the apples all in the fruit-house a month earlier 'n this last year. When you goin' to make the cider?"

"I do' know," he said. He had a shamed, routed look. "Soon 's we get the apples all stored in, an' sort 'em over."

"It's high time. Well, I got the path all swep' off. You comin' on to the house?" she questioned sociably. "Oh, what was it you said you was a-comin' back all of a sudden so for?"

"I didn't say."

"Oh. Well, what was it you was a-comin' for?"

Mr. Palmer turned and gave her a look of helpless rage. His blue eyes blazed at her. His face went red and white in streaks. He stuck his thumbs into his palms and shut his fingers down over them hard.

"Gunny-sacks," he hissed out at her between his teeth. "God A'mighty—*gunny-sacks!*"

"Oh," said Mrs. Palmer, blandly. Her husband flung himself around and went on toward the house, down the newly swept path. He stepped short and high. Mrs. Palmer walked behind him, her face wrinkled up with noiseless laughter. Once a little sound of mirth escaped her lips unexpectedly. "Haigh?" she exclaimed instantly, as if he had spoken; but he walked right on, with his chin up. Mrs. Palmer made short apologetic dabs here and there, to the right and to the left, with her broom.

"There, your wash-water's all cold!" hissed Mr. Palmer, passing the porch.

"Plenty more where it come from," replied his wife, cheerfully.

When he came back from the barn with his arms full of the gunny-sacks he did not want, his face was dark with helpless fury. She straightened up, and, leaning the wash-board over on its stomach, slushed a sheet up and down in the water behind it. He gave her one look. She returned it. She was shaking with laughter.

"Heavy?" she asked. This time no words came from his lips in reply; he only hissed, speech being quite beyond him.

When he had passed on and was entirely out of sight, Mrs. Palmer crossed the porch and looked into a square, wavy mirror that hung upon the wall. The humor which had served her so well in allaying suspicion had all gone out of her face; only the pallor of fright remained. She looked long into her own eyes.

"You're a pretty smart woman," she said slowly, and with some admiration. "You ought to of had an education; but you're a pretty smart woman without it. I bet my soul you could learn the multification-table backwards in no time! *Stilt* tracks! My land! There ain't another woman on the face o' the earth would of thought of stilt tracks. All is, them heels 'll come off o' them boots!" She rubbed her face with her fingers, grooved white from washing, to bring some color back. Then she said slowly, going back to the tubs: "I bet a picayune I never sweep another path off again on a wash-day! Excuses like stilts don't come to the same body more 'n once in a lifetime."

Clary appeared suddenly in the door. "Mis' Parmer," she said loudly, as if doubtful of that lady's hearing, "Mr. Mall'ry's come."

Mrs. Palmer started violently. "How?" she faltered.

"W'y, I say Mr. Mall'ry's come. He's in the parlor. I took him in. He wanted he should see you just a minute. I wanted he should go out in the orchud an' see Mr. Parmer, but he wanted he should see you just a minute. I put up the window shades, an' took his hat an' set it on the table," she added, in a lower tone, looking at her mistress for a word of praise.

But Mrs. Palmer did not even hear. She was wiping her hands and arms; her hands shook strangely. She pulled down her sleeves and fastened them. "How did he come?" she asked, with a fine carelessness. "Which way?"

"Up from the water. He come in a sail-boat."

Mrs. Palmer breathed again.

"Pin in these ends of my hair, will you? I look like

all-fire. I wish people wouldn't come of a wash-day. I expect Mis' Mall'ry's sent him for some Kansas-starter — she always bakes a-Tuesday. I'm all het up, washing. Do I look like all-fire?"

"You don't look so terrible bad," replied Clary, with cold cheer. "But I've see you look lots better."

Mrs. Palmer's feathers drooped.

"I wish I didn't get all het up so, washing." She looked in the mirror, and started reluctantly for the parlor.

"You don't look so terrible bad," repeated Clary, putting a little more warmth into her assurance.

Mrs. Palmer went on slowly. She smoothed down her sleeves and pulled out the bows of her apron strings as she went. She had on her old shoes. They creaked, so she went on her tip-toes.

In ten minutes she returned. Clary looked at her with breathless curiosity. "He gone?"

"Unh-hunh?"

"He went terrible sudden. Did he come after Kansas-starter?"

"No, she'd got some."

Clary meditated. "Maybe he was just going along by?"

"Maybe he was."

"Did he go out in the orchud to see the men?"

"I do' know. The apple-sauce made?"

"I'm makin' it. It's terrible odd for a man to go a-visitin' on Monday forenoons, ain't it?"

The humor of this appealed to Mrs. Palmer. She laughed suddenly.

"I expect it is." Whenever the humor of a difficult situation presented itself to Mrs. Palmer with sufficient force to make her laugh, she was saved.

"Maybe he come to borrow the harrow," suggested

Clary, her mind flying wildly from one need of a man to another.

"Clary," said Mrs. Palmer, confidentially, "you mustn't tell a soul Mr. Mall'ry's been here. You mustn't tell Mariella nor her pa, nor a *soul*. I'm — I'm — thinkin' of gettin' my life insured," she looked impressively at the girl, "an' I'd want it to be a terrible surprise to 'em both."

"Oh, my!" said Clary, letting out deep breathings of awe. "How much?"

Mrs. Palmer turned her head to one side and looked modest, as if deploring admiration. "A thousand dollars," she said, with solemnity. "You must never tell a soul."

"I never will," breathed Clary. "It'll come in awful handy when — "

She stopped, and coughed politely. "Sho-o-o!" she cried, shaking her apron at a hen, to cover her confusion.

"My mercy! Don't scare No-tail so's she hurts herself, or Mariella 'll have a duck-fit."

Clary faced around; her eyes were big. "W'y, is Mr. Mall'ry an agent? I didn't know he was an agent."

Mrs. Palmer hesitated a moment, and then, at her wit's end, went into a violent spell of coughing. She coughed long and hard. She coughed Clary's question down three times. When she finally came out of the paroxysm, she said hastily: "Now, don't let's talk any more. I'll never get that washin' out. You put some cinnamon in your apple-sauce, an' set it away to cool. Then you take an' make the starch for me. Don't fool any more time. We'll just pick up some scriddlin's for dinner."

She was bending over the tub again, and chuckling to herself over having disposed of Clary's curiosity, when that young person appeared in the doorway.

She held the pan of apple-sauce in her hand. In the other was a long-handled tin spoon, with which she was stirring the cinnamon into the sauce.

"Say! Mis' Parmer! Well, say! Did you ever see such high-heel boots as he had on? What makes him wear such high heels? And on a Monday forenoon! He must be pushed. Maybe he was a-goin' somewheres, though."

Mrs. Palmer's face had turned to the crimson-purple of a starfish.

"Look a-here!" she exclaimed sternly. "Don't let me ever hear you a-criticisin' anybody's clo's! Never again. An' don't you ever let me hear the word high-heel boots out of your mouth again. Never! If you ever tell a livin' soul Mr. Mall'ry had on high-heel boots, I'll send you a-pikin' home, with your duds."

"I didn't think it was any crime." Clary was beginning to cry. "I just thought it was terrible strange — on a Monday morning."

"Well, don't think." Then she changed her tone. "Clary, if you'll be a good girl, an' not cry, an' never speak Mr. Mall'ry's name before a soul, I'll — I'll give you that buff calico to make yourself a dress. But Mr. Mall'ry 'll be comin' here so much about that insurance I expect I'll get sick of hearin' his very name. Don't ever let me hear his name out of you. That's a good girl. I'll give you that buff calico."

"You're awful clever," said Clary, with feeling. "I declare, you're awful clever to me, Mis' Parmer. I'll have it made with a V neck and flowin' sleeves," she added proudly.

"That'll be nice. Go on now an' don't fool any more time."

Clary turned away, beating the sauce hard. She took three steps; then she paused. "Maybe he was on his way to town," she said. "It was terrible odd."

CHAPTER XIII

It was evening at the Mallorys'. The family was gathered together in the sitting-room. It was a big room, and would have been a cheerful one but for its painful neatness and precision. Everything that was capable of shining shone. The chairs were ranged evenly around the sides of the room. There was a bright fire on the hearth, which was well swept. A crane swung across the fireplace. The andirons were polished, as were the shovel and tongs, standing each in its corner. A table in the centre of the room held books and papers and a coal-oil lamp, whose chimney had not a blur.

Mr. Mallory was leaning back in a big chair, reading the weekly paper. He looked handsome and very comfortable. Mrs. Mallory sat opposite, upright, thin, unattractive. Her hair was drawn plainly away from her face, accenting the sharpness of her features. She was sewing on white muslin. Isaphene sat between them, reading. The smaller children were playing "doll" in a quiet corner.

Mrs. Mallory looked at Isaphene over her sewing. "You learnin' that piece to speak?"

"Yes, ma'am."

"Let's hear how much you've learned."

Isaphene handed over the book with a sigh. She began at once:—

"From the Cascades' frozen gorges—"

"Stand up," commanded her mother, sternly. Isaphene stood up, meekly, and bowed — a short, bobby bow.

"Leaping like a child at play —"

"Here, stand straight. There. Now put your heels together an' your toes this way." Mrs. Mallory arose, held her dress high in front, and illustrated. Isaphene imitated faithfully.

"Winding, widening thro' the valley,
Bright Willamette glides away.
Onward ever — "

"There, there! Hold your shoulders back! More yet!"

"Onward ever, lovely river,
Softly calling to the sea!
Time that scars us,
Maims and mars us,
Leaves no track or trench on thee."

"That ain't bad. Don't run your words all together so. Don't hold your hands so stiff. When you say 'onward ever, lovely river,' make a gesture." Mrs. Mallory made a solemn, soaring movement with her thin arm. Isaphene imitated, following the soaring of her own arm with bewildered eyes.

"There, that's it," said her mother, with admiration. "You did that real graceful. I'm glad you ain't all arms an' legs, like Mariella Palmer! I don't know, though, but what I'd as live be all arms an' legs as to be all flesh, like her mother." She raised her voice, that her husband might hear. The paper rustled a little in his hands.

"I declare, of the two, I'd rather be a *leetle* too thin than to have so much flesh to carry around. She's always a-complainin' of gettin' het up so. No wonder! All that flesh to carry around! She's no more shape! She thinks she is, though."

"She makes good floatin'-island," said Isaphene, with reminiscent eyes.

"She does so," said her mother, cordially. "An' a pretty sum it costs to make it that way. Eggs! My mercy! She puts a dozen in, I expect; an' them forty cents a dozen now. I'd like to see your father if I'd cook so extravagant. I'd like to see him. He wouldn't think floatin'-island was so good then. It's easy to be a good cook, if you just cut an' slash into butter, an' eggs, an' cream. She's no housekeeper when it comes to savin'. She fries in butter half the time. . . . Well, go on. What you waitin' for?"

> "Spring's green witchery is weaving
>   Braid and border for thy side,
> Onward ever —"

"There, that don't come in there."

> "Spring's green witchery is —"

"Oh, don't go clear back to the beginnin'! You'll be sayin' the title over next."

> "Hither poetry would dream —"

"Oh, goodness me!" Mrs. Mallory flung the reader down on the table contemptuously. "You don't half know it. You'll study it twenty minutes before you go to bed. Do you know the 'Prize Banner Quickstep' yet?"

"Yes'm."

"Well, go an' play it. Be careful when you open the organ; you're so careless. Pull that flute stop out slow. Now, hold on! Screw your stool up higher; always have it high enough so's your elbows are even with the keys. I'd enjoy to see a daughter of mine set hunched over the way Jemima Watson does, a-playin' in church. I'd enjoy to see that! Now."

Isaphene played with rigid fingers the "Prize Banner Quickstep." She sat erect and stiff, her shoulders even, her elbows held in close to her waist, her chin level. Her eyes were set painfully upon the music. She did not make a mistake, but hammered every note out sharp and hard, without expression.

Mrs. Mallory sat with equal stiffness in her chair, regarding her daughter. Her face was wrinkled up around her eyes. Her thin lips were closed tightly and drawn down at the corners, tracing a narrow line across her face in the shape of a new moon. Not until the last note was sounded and Isaphene folded her hands in her lap, after an apologetic cough, awaiting praise or blame, did the muscles of Mrs. Mallory's face relax. Then she breathed her delight out and in with deep breathings.

"You know *that*," she said, with a crow of triumph in her throat. "I enjoy to hear a daughter of mine play like that. That's a terrible difficult piece to learn in such a short time. I'd enjoy to watch Mis' Parmer's face the first time she hears you play that piece — I'd enjoy to watch her. They're always a-talkin' about that Mariella a-bein' so smart. Look at her. All skin an' bone! She holds her elbows every which way for Sunday. She'd look pretty at an organ, I must say. . . . Can you play 'General Percifer F. Smith's Grand March' yet?" she added, with tremblings of doubtful awe in her tone.

"I'll see."

She played the piece through without a mistake. Her mother glowed at her, and even her father lowered his paper and looked over it at this brilliant performance, caressing his full cheek with one hand.

"Well, I never see the way she improves," announced Mrs. Mallory, looking at her husband. "She ain't been no time a-learnin' that piece; an' she don't know a one that's similiar to it — not a one. All the runs an' trills are different, an' had to be learned a-special. . . . Can you sing 'Gypsy's Warning'?"

Isaphene took a sheet of music from a neatly arranged pile on the organ, played the prelude, and began the song in a weak treble: —

"Do not trust him, gentle lady,
  Tho' his voice be low and sweet,
Heed not him who kneels before thee,
  Gently pleading at thy feet."

"That's too low," interrupted Mrs. Mallory, sternly; "pitch it higher."

Isaphene pitched it higher.

"Now thy life is in its morning,
  Cloud not thou thy happy lot;
Listen to the gypsy's warning,
  Gentle lady, trust him not;
Listen to the gypsy's warning,
  Gentle lady, trust him not."

"That's terrible sad," said Mrs. Mallory, when the song was concluded. "Sing that last verse over; you listen," she added, to her husband.

Isaphene sang: —

"Lady, once there lived a maiden,
  Young and sweet, and like thee fair,
But he wooed and wooed and won her,
  Filled her gentle heart with care;
Then he heeded not her weeping,
  Nor cared he her life to save;
Soon she perished — now she's sleeping
  In the cold and silent grave;
Soon she perished — now she's sleeping
  In the cold and silent grave."

"Don't that beat you? Where'd she get her voice from, I'd like to know."

"I sung some when I was younger," said Mr. Mallory, modestly.

"You didn't set the well afire. I sung some too; but we didn't either of us carry a toon that way. Where'd she get her voice from? She'd ought to be encouraged."

"Well, encourage her."

"When she learns a piece like 'General Percifer F.' in such a short time, an' plays it without a mistake, we'd ought to buy her something."

Mr. Mallory resumed his reading at once.

"I say we'd ought to buy her something. She wants some ear-bobs the worst way. A pair of ear-bobs would encourage her to do her — her utmost endeavor."

Mr. Mallory held the paper high and read on.

"She'd like a pair we saw the other day. They're round, kind of crusted gold, with a pearl in the centre and a black stripe around the pearl; and there's a little gold drop danglin' down underneath. They're real gold" — Mrs. Mallory was warming to the occasion, encouraged by the silence behind the newspaper — "anybody can see that with half an eye. Isaphene 'u'd like 'em. They'd encourage her up, I know."

She stopped to draw breath. She expected a reply; but none came.

"Eben, you hear? Why don't you answer me up? You want I should select 'em out next time I go to town?"

Still there was no reply. A certain kind of woman can live with one man fifty years without learning to recognize a sign when she looks it squarely in the face. Mrs. Mallory was that kind of woman. Not receiving a reply, she added, with a petulant inflection, "Eben! Hear?"

The newspaper quivered and came down. Mr. Mallory glared at his wife. His face was white with anger. He was not handsome now. "I hear." His voice shook.

"No, I don't want you should 'select 'em out'" — he mimicked her tone — "the next time you go to town, nor the last time. Buy, buy, buy! It's all a woman can find fit to talk about! You'd drive a man insane with your encouragin's here an' your encouragin's there! I don't want to hear any more about it. It's a pity if you can't encourage a twelve-year-old without forever a-buyin' her somethin'."

"My land!" stammered out Mrs. Mallory. "You needn't get worked up so. What's a pair of ear-bobs? They only cost five dollars."

"Only cost five dollars, aigh? What's a pair of ear-bobs? A pair of ear-bobs is a pair of ear-bobs! My Lord! Why don't you say *five hells?* That's what you'd drive a man to, with your buyin' here an' your buyin' there; an' your only costin' this and your only costin' that!"

"Oh, if you're goin' to swear," said Mrs. Mallory, weeping, "all about a little thing like a pair of ear-bobs! A body'd think I'd asked you to give her a *farm* to encourage her!"

"It 'u'd amount to a farm. It's a pair of ear-bobs here, an' a pair o' shoes there, an' a petticoat som'ers else —"

A sudden ray of humor glimmered across Mrs. Mallory's face, like a rainbow across a storm. "Well, we can't wear everything in the same place," she said.

"I don't want to hear any more of your encouragin's an' your buyin's! You understand? It's come to a pretty pass! A man can't set foot 'n the house without your hollerin' at him for money! If it ain't somethin' to eat, it's somethin' to wear; an' if it ain't somethin' to wear, it's somethin' to act the fool over in your ears. It's come to a pretty pass! I don't want to ever hear ear-bobs out o' you again. You'll drive me to the poor-house yet!"

"Oh, I guess not," said Mrs. Mallory, contemptuously. "Not as long as you can buy seed-drills, an' harrows, an' rakes, an' ploughs — all with spring-seats on 'em! I guess you won't go to the poor-house as long as you can make yourself so comfortable. I never see a man yet that thought his own buyin's 'u'd send him to the poor-house; it's always his wife's! Isaphene, you get an' study that 'Beautiful Willamette' piece over again; I'll make a lady out of you, ear-bobs or no ear-bobs. I'd be ashamed to not encourage a child that nobody else can hold a candle to — an' then set up lazy on a spring-seat! I'd be condemned! I'd —"

Mr. Mallory arose heavily, and crushed the paper down on the table.

"I'd rather be condemned any day than to get your tongue started," he said, in a desperate tone, going off to bed.

CHAPTER XIV

"WHY, for pity's sake," said Mrs. Mallory, "you don't rub your cake of cleaning soap right on the woodwork, do you?"

She was sitting erect on a straight chair in Mrs. Palmer's kitchen. She had come early one January afternoon. "Mr. Mallory was goin' right by to town," she explained cordially, "so I thought I'd come an' visit."

"Well, do," said Mrs. Palmer, without warmth. "I'm rill glad; but my work ain't all done up yet, so I'll have to invite you into the kitchen till I get through. Clary's home. She has to go every so often, rain or shine."

So they had gone into the warm and pleasant kitchen. Mrs. Palmer turned around now and looked at her guest.

"What's it for?" she asked briefly.

"Why, I wouldn't say it was for rubbin' right on to woodwork."

"Why not?"

"It seems to me it must be terrible wasteful."

There was a silence, then Mrs. Palmer said slowly, "What do you use it for?"

"Oh, just a little on the dish-cloth to polish my nicest things up. I don't use a cake in six months."

"Hunh." There was another silence. "What do you clean your woodwork with?"

"Oh, I powder up some Bath brick. It's better an'

quicker, an' it costs ten times less. I clean all my pans an' kettles with it, too."

Mrs. Palmer went on rubbing the white cake of cleaning soap on her table. "I thought it was to use, myself," she said. "I'd call a cake in six months no more use 'n a hen's teeth to clean with."

"Oh, it's nice if you can afford it," said Mrs. Mallory, in a thin tone that went far; her lips seemed to get thinner as she spoke, and her nose sharper because of the wrinkles that suddenly ran away from it. "I can't afford much wastefulness myself. If I wasn't equinomical I couldn't have more 'n three new dresses a year."

Mrs. Palmer felt her face grow red. It had been two years since she had had a new dress of any material better than calico. She rubbed the table hard. She would have liked to rub the whole cake of cleaning soap away, right before Mrs. Mallory's eyes. Three new dresses a year!

"If I wasn't equinomical," repeated Mrs. Mallory, with her short, exasperating laugh, "I expect I'd have to go to the neighbors' attired in calico."

"Well, I'm savin'," announced Mrs. Palmer, in a deep bass, "but I ain't so savin' that I don't use enough cleanin' soap to keep things clean."

Mrs. Mallory smoothed out the folds of her dress skirt.

"This is my third best black alpaco. My new one is as pretty! It fairly glimmers. It makes me think of moonlight."

Mrs. Palmer looked around at her now and smiled scornfully. "*Black* moonlight?" she asked briefly.

A little pink splashed delicately across Mrs. Mallory's face. Even her blushes were ladylike. "*Fine* black goods," she said coldly, "always have a kind of a gleamy look. It's just like moonlight. Common wool stuffs don't have it. I never buy an alpaco that don't look gleamy." She coughed thinly. "I wouldn't feel to afford 'em gleamy if I wasn't equinomical."

"Well," said Mrs. Palmer, slowly, "I'm savin'; but, I swan, I won't squeeze a nickel if I never get anything gleamy. There's some things we don't do here out West. If a thing costs twenty cents an' I throw down a two-bit piece, I don't wait for no nickel change. I notice that. Everybody comes out here from New England sooner or later, but we come sooner, an' we got some o' the picayunishness took out o' us. I drether," she spoke out fiercely, walking around the big kitchen with short, high steps, and rattling pans and things for emphasis, "I drether go with one dress for six year than to be picayunish. Scrimp, scrimp, scrimp! I know people that wouldn't put twelve eggs in floatin' isle to save the minister's soul. No wonder he's so bent on comin' here to dinner. I expect gleamy dresses ain't so terrible good to eat! About as good as bread puddin' with one egg in it, I expect!"

Mrs. Mallory looked a little frightened. "You are a beautiful cook," she declared, in a conciliatory tone. "That's universally preceded. Everybody precedes that. Your rules are always in demand. I hear only the other day your Kansas-starter was unsurpassed."

"Hunh," said Mrs. Palmer.

"Yes, I did. Your puddin's, too."

"Well, I ain't afraid to put cream an' butter an' eggs into my cookin' if I do say it myself," bragged Mrs. Palmer.

Mrs. Mallory was making tatting. She held her work high, and made short, jabbing movements into her left hand, with the shuttle held stiffly in her right.

"No, indeed," she said, with cordial warmth, "your

cookin' is unsurpassed. Mr. Mallory fairly declares by your floatin' isle."

A little pleased red came to Mrs. Palmer's face. Her movements became less vigorous. "I hope he won't get caught in a storm comin' from town," she said. She drew a chair near her guest and sat down more sociably. "That's a rill pretty pattern," she said, narrowing her eyes at the tatting.

"Yes, it is so; it's a five-leaf clover."

"Mariella does all our tattin'."

"Isaphene don't have time; she spends so much time on her practisin'," said Mrs. Mallory, overcoming her fright and beginning to brag again. "She can play 'General Percifer F. Smith's Grand March.'"

"Mariella can learn anything an' have plenty of time left for tattin'," said Mrs. Palmer, who was always on the watch for the waving of a red rag. "She don't spend much time a-practisin' anything she wants to learn."

"I didn't know she was so quick with her sums."

"Well, they're one thing she ain't so terrible quick with," confessed Mrs. Palmer, with bitter reluctance. "Tom-fool things! I can't see any sense in 'em myself."

There were danger signals in her face again. Mrs. Mallory recognized them, and shied away from them.

"What have you got to say about Mr. Leaming's doin's?" she inquired; her tone invited gossip.

Mrs. Palmer set her lips together.

"It's a sin an' a shame!" she declared, "for him to up an' leave right 'n the middle of a term this way just because that old Englishman he calls his — his —"

"Factotum?" suggested Mrs. Mallory, undaunted.

"Well, then, factotum — just because he teached him an' was good to him when he was a boy! Now he's wrote he's a-dyin', an' he wants Leaming to hike right over there all the way to England, an' he ups an' offs, as if he was pushed! I never see the beat!"

"His factotum's rich, ain't he?"

"Yes, he's rich; but his son 'll get it all. I don't believe in skuropin' all over the earth unless there's somethin' to be got out of it."

"He got a teacher to take his place?"

"Yes, he telegrafted right down to Seattle an' Tacoma, an' he got one. It's a wonder he did, too; pneumony o' the lungs is terrible brief up there this weather, they say."

"It's brief enough here. Like as not a new teacher 'll have a hard row to hoe with Mahlon Proudfoot. He's so stubborn."

Mrs. Palmer laughed. "I expect. I know he's stubborn. He gets it honest, though. His father's the stubbornest man on the sound. He's one o' the oldest settlers round here. The old pioneers tell on him that he's so stubborn that he set down on a live coal o' fire once, an' was so stubborn he just set still an' let it burn. Mule-head!"

"I expect Mariella 'll miss the teacher," hazarded Mrs. Mallory.

"She's pickin' now," reflected Mrs. Palmer, shrewdly. "Well, let her pick. I'd just as lieve she'd know."

"She will so," she admitted candidly. "I don't know what to do with her; she's most cried her eyes out a'ready. He come around last night an' took her out for a walk, an' told her. We were all eatin' supper when she come home — all except her pa — an' I told her to set down an' eat, but she wouldn't; she'd been cryin'. The hands teased her. Gus said her eyes was like boiled gooseberries, an' Hoover, he said her sweetheart was a-goin' to England. She was terrible sassy to 'em." Mrs. Palmer paused, as if remembering. "She was sassy to me too," she said more slowly.

Mrs. Mallory sent the shuttle to and fro with little short emphatic jabs. "That's one thing about Isaphene. She never is sassy. She's always polite."

"I don't mind a girl bein' sassy," said Mrs. Palmer, holding her head high. "I brought Mariella up that way. It shows a girl has got some spunk in her. Anything but skim-milk!"

"Isaphene never is," insisted Mrs. Mallory. "I want her to be a lady. I mean to send her to a seminary. Well, I declare! If he hasn't returned a'ready!" She waved her thin hand across the window; her husband had just driven up to the gate.

"He's just like a child about me. He's perfectly devoted to me."

"He is?" said Mrs. Palmer; her face was eloquent with exclamations.

"My, yes. He hardly lets me out o' his sight. He humors me high an' low. Once a lover, always a lover."

"Pfew! but it is warm in here!" Mrs. Palmer's face was crimson. "Come again soon. I'm sorry he come for you so sudden."

She went out on the porch with her guest, making conversation in a difficult way, until her humor came to her aid. Then she laughed out suddenly.

"You tell Mr. Mall'ry I think he's as smart as a steel trap," said she, still laughing. "I always did think he was smart; but I didn't know as he was so *terrible* smart."

"What's he so smart about?" Mrs. Mallory's face took on a thin, suspicious look.

But Mrs. Palmer had already said good-by and was going back into the house. The wind blew her skirts about her stout ankles.

"I'd like to know what she thinks he's so smart about," reflected Mrs. Mallory, going to the gate. She had a feeling that there was a joke somewhere.

Mrs. Palmer had not faithfully reported the scene of the evening before with Mariella. When the child returned from her walk with Leaming she sped through the dining-room like a wraith. The family was at supper.

"Here, you Mariella!" cried her mother. "Where you been? Come here an' eat your supper."

"I don't want any."

"Come an' eat some, anyhow. Look round here. Why, good grieve! What's got into you? You look like you'd been drawed through a knot-hole! What ails you?"

"Nothing."

"Nothin', aigh? With eyes like boiled gooseberries! What ails you?"

Mariella was silent. She stood looking steadily at her mother. There were devils in her eyes.

"Come an' eat your supper now. Hear?

"I don't want any."

"Ho, ho!" cried out Gus, chuckling coarsely. "The teacher's a-goin' to England to-morrow. It's a-makin' his little sweetheart sick."

The child flashed around on him, as he spoke. "Shut up!" she cried instantly. "You old ignorant fool!"

The other men roared. Her mother flushed scarlet. "I'll punish you for that. Come an' eat your supper."

"I don't want any."

"Come an' eat, anyhow."

Mariella did not move.

"Where you been? You've got to tell."

Mariella did not speak.

Mrs. Palmer arose in a threatening manner. "You little heifer! You answer me when I ask you questions. Where you been?"

Mariella laughed in her mother's face.

"I've been looking for *high-heel tracks!*" she said, and went on upstairs, banging the door behind her.

She threw herself on the bed in the dark, without undressing, and lay there, face downward, all night.

PART II

CHAPTER XV

It seemed to Mariella that there had never been a time when she and Mahlon Proudfoot had not been sweethearts. She was sixteen when they became acknowledged ones. It happened one April night, when they were coming home from a candy-pull at the Mallorys'. They walked along through the soft darkness without talking. They walked slowly, although it was eleven o'clock. There was some low marshy land along one side of the narrow path, and there the frogs were murmuring in a deep, sweet chorus that seemed to set the air into vibrations. The fragrance thrown out by saps in their upward flow through the veins of firs was heavy about them. On the hill where the young alders grew a bird poured out beautiful notes of drowsy rapture. It seemed to the girl, stepping lightly along beside her boy sweetheart, that the very atmosphere was charged with something wonderful and mysterious, something that made her heart beat loud in her throat and the veins in her wrists feel big. She had pulses all over her, and every one was beating fast. The world about her trembled with ecstasy.

They came at last to a little creek that went shivering and laughing over the stones; a shadbush in its last bloom hovered over it like a dreamy cloud, and right under it Mahlon Proudfoot stood still and drew her suddenly and with compelling tenderness into his arms.

Mariella trembled, but she did not draw away from him. She let him hold her close to him, and lift up her face and kiss her with the startled, unbelieving passion of a first kiss. Waves of rapture flowed over them with little shocks of delight.

"Put your arms around my neck," whispered the young man; and Mariella obeyed him; her little hot, red cheek touched his. "Your breath is like voylets," he whispered, crushing his lips down upon hers again. "Oh, Mariella, Mariella! how is it I never kissed you before!"

After a while they walked on, he keeping his arm strongly about her and almost lifting her over the stones. There was a light in the kitchen. He stopped among the lilacs and kissed her again, shivering in sheer amazed joy. "Your breath is like lilocks," he whispered. "Oh, Mariella, I love you! I—love—you!" The words seemed to shake against his teeth. "You know I'm poor, an' I don't know how soon we can get married. It may be a long time. Promise me you'll wait. Promise me you'll never marry anybody else."

Mariella, smoothing his hair with pulses big in her palms, whispered back: "I'll never marry anybody but you. I'll wait for you. I promise."

Her mother sat by the kitchen table, sewing. She looked up at the girl, wrinkling her eyes suspiciously.

"Pretty time o' night to get home from a candy-pull with a boy," she exclaimed fiercely. "I'd think Mahlon Proudfoot 'u'd be ashamed."

"It wasn't his fault," said Mariella, proudly. "I walked as slowly as he did. It's a nice night. I wanted to walk slow."

"It's a pretty note if you can't get home earlier 'n this from a candy-pull. Skuropin' around! Your father went to bed, but I thinks, says I, well—I'll set up the whole durin' time till she gets back, if it's ten-eleven, eleven-twelve o'clock!"

"You needn't sit up for me," said Mariella, coming in out of the shadows. Her face was burning. She tried to keep it turned from her mother. "I can take care of myself."

"Turn round here," commanded her mother, sternly. The girl faced her defiantly. "Mariella Parmer, what ails you!"

"Nothing ails me that I know of."

"Nothin' ails you, aigh? With a face as red as fire and your eyes shinin' out like a cat's in the dark. You tell me what ails you."

"I told you," said Mariella, wearily. All the rapture and ecstasy went suddenly out of her, and a chill fell upon her. "Nothing ails me. Anybody's face would be red coming in out of the wind."

"Wind? Hunh! You must think I'm from Mizzoura! There ain't any wind; there ain't been a snuff o' wind to-night. You may be as smart as a steel trap, but you can't fool this old hen."

Mariella's lip curled. "Why don't you let me be?" she cried fiercely. "I haven't done anything wrong. If I stayed out till morning with Mahlon Proudfoot, there wouldn't be any harm in it. Why can't you let me be?"

"Wouldn't be any harm in it, aigh!" cried out Mrs. Palmer, in a great voice. "You let me ketch you a-stayin' out till mornin' with Mahlon Proudfoot or Mahlon anybody else! That's pretty talk to your mother. Such goin'-ons among young upshoots I never see in my born days. All is, you let me hear any more talk about you an' Mahlon Proudfoot a-stayin' out till eleven or twelve o'clock this way. You're sixteen years old, but I'd tan you within an inch o' your life. In a minute!"

"If you did," said Mariella, standing still with a white face and speaking down in her throat, "I'd leave home the same day."

"You'd leave home the same day, would you?" mimicked her mother. "You'd play hob, wouldn't you? You think you're some pum'kins, don't you? I've hear folks talk about uppin' an' offin' before now, but I notice they don't up an' off so terrible fast. I notice that. Where'd you up an' off to so all of a sudden?" she cried out in fierce derision. "You'd go a-teeterin' over to Mis' Proudfoot's, I bet! That's where you'd go. You'd teeter around first on one foot an' then on the other, a-waitin' for 'em to take you in. You ain't got any more pride 'an to run after that Mahlon Stubbornfoot, I bet! About the time that old devil of a father o' his'n come a-shufflin' after you, a-stampin' his cane an' a-glarin' at you out o' his eyebrows to see how much you eat, I bet you'd get into a teeter all over." Mariella shuddered and turned her white face away from her mother. "Lord knows we're as poor as Job's turkey, but I guess they're as poor as Job's pullet. You'd feather your nest."

"I don't care if they are poor," flashed out Mariella. "That's no disgrace. There isn't one boy in a thousand that would work the way Mahlon works to pay off that mortgage and keep a home for his mother. He had to stop school when he was eighteen and go to clearing land and planting crops — when he wanted to go to the university in Seattle. He told me — "

She stopped abruptly, and stood there, trembling all over with passion and rage. Her arms hung down at her sides. Her thumbs were pressed hard into her palms, and her fingers were stiffened down over them, holding them as in a vise. Her mother stood up, too, facing her. Both were borne along on great tides of passion that lifted them out of themselves. It was as if they had no bodies, and their bare souls cried out and grappled with each other.

"He told you what?" hissed Mrs. Palmer; her face was convulsed. "You tell me what he told you."

"He told me —" the girl's lip quivered and her voice broke — "that he *prayed* that something would turn up so he could go to the university."

"Well, all is — he's a tom-fool."

"It is a terrible thing," went on the girl, as if she had not heard, "for a *man* to cry; but it seems to me a more terrible one for a man to pray."

"He's a tom-fool, I tell you; he's a tom-fool."

"He went way out in the deep forest; he didn't want his mother to know how bad he felt about it; and he went down on his knees and prayed out loud to God to make some way for him to go —"

"An' did He?" put in Mrs. Palmer, her curiosity getting the better of her rage.

"And it never did a bit of good! Here he's been ever since tied down with his face to the earth, working to save his home, and bearing the insults of his father every day. He never had much schooling, anyhow — only five months a year! And he's just starving for an education. He sits up in his attic and reads and studies till after midnight, and then gets up at four o'clock to milk and fodder and pay off mortgages! And you sneer at him! You ought to be ashamed!"

"Now look at here!" cried Mrs. Palmer, wildly. "You look at here! You tell me I ought to be ashamed, an' I'll send you a-pikin' over there."

"If you ever say another word against him, I'll go without your sending me. I'll go out in the field and work with him."

"I'll say as many words agen him as I want to. You

talk like a pullet!" cried Mrs. Palmer, helpless in her fury. "You ain't any more sense 'an a pullet has teeth. Well, all is —"

Then, for almost the first time in her life, speech failed her. She caught up her sewing and went out of the kitchen with a wild rush and a sweep of calico draperies. But she whispered to herself as she went, in a scared way: "I bet in my soul she would! She's just dar' devil enough to do it. I swan, she just takes the starch clean out o' me sometimes, when she gets that blue blaze in her eyes an' talks up to me. She gets it honest. I'm glad enough she's got the spirit to talk up to me. She's the only one does. It 'u'd be kind of lonesome if nobody did."

Mariella stood for a full minute after her mother had rushed out of the room, without moving. Her eyes were full of misery and her face was still pale. Then she gave herself a little shake. "I'm not going to be wretched to-night, anyhow," said she to herself, resolutely.

She extinguished the lamp on the kitchen table and went upstairs in the dark. She made her way straight to the window and looked out. A mile down the sound, away from the town, through a straight opening that had been cleared through the forest years before for a road, was Mahlon Proudfoot's home. When a light was shining in the gable window of his attic, it was clearly visible from hers. There was no light now; but when she had lighted her little lamp and turned back to look once more, the light was there, shining a tender message across the darkness to her. She had often watched for Mahlon's light, but this was the first time it had ever seemed to flash back an answer to hers.

Mahlon Proudfoot went stumbling home in the darkness. He was so happy that he had a dazed feeling. He

could not see the road; it seemed to sway out from under him as he stepped, and then fly back to meet him. When he looked up the stars appeared to be falling toward him through a blue blur that had red lights woven through it. His heart felt big, and it was beating hard against his side; he heard it beat. He had an odd feeling, as if pulses were being drawn back and forth in his head; there was a regular vibration in his ears.

A great exaltation had possession of him. He stepped out strongly, after his first uncertain pace, holding his shoulders high and thrown back proudly. His thought was burning with the girl who had just promised so sweetly and seriously to wait until he could marry her. He remembered the light in the kitchen, and wondered if her mother had reproached her for the lateness of the hour. He blamed himself. "I oughtn't to have kept her out so," he thought remorsefully. "Little delicate thing! But her lips were so sweet" — he shivered again in keen remembrance — "a man couldn't stop kissing her."

He was twenty-two, and it was the first time he had thought of himself as a man. "If her mother abuses her now —" He drew himself up again with a kind of fierceness.

Then other thoughts came to crush down his joy and exaltation. He remembered his mother's hard and bitter life, through which she had managed, somehow, to hold fast her sweetness; he remembered how she had toiled, and how his wife must toil after her; he had a vision of Mariella, bending like a wind-blown flower before the labor that would be his wife's lot. He thought of his lost education, whose very hope was like a dream now; the mortgage and taxes that must be paid; the almost unbearable fiendishness of his father.

At sight of his home he stood still. The old choke

sprang thick in his throat, and sharp needles of pain stung his eyeballs through and through. He threw his arms out against a tree that stood beside him, and laid his head down upon them, with a groan of passionate misery.

"Oh, Mariella, Mariella!" he cried. "I love you — oh, God! I love you! And what have I to give you? What hope have I of ever deserving you or being able to make you happy? But I want you — I want you!"

There was a light in his kitchen, too, and when he went in he found his mother sitting there alone, waiting for him. He saw, with a new pang, how old and gray she looked in the dim light. He went to her and, stooping over her, kissed her wrinkled cheek. "Up yet, mother?" he said cheerfully.

"I was waitin' for you. I couldn't go to sleep. Your father was so mad. You hadn't ought to stay so late, Mahlon, when you know it makes him so mad."

"I don't care if it does make him mad," cried Mahlon, fiercely, but he kept his hand on his mother's hair. "He's got to stop meddling with me. I am a man now, and I won't stand it."

His mother commenced crying silently, with her hand over her face. Mahlon put his arms around her and leaned his face down against hers. "Oh, mother," he groaned, "don't cry; don't make it harder for me. I do the best I can, but I *can't* take any more from him. He's ruined your life, and now he's doing his best to ruin mine."

"Don't talk so about your father, son. He can't help his disposition. He used to try to, when he was young an' he see how it hurt me. But he couldn't; he was born that way."

"I wish you had left him when you were young!"

"Hush," commanded Mrs. Proudfoot, in a tone as stern as she ever used to Mahlon. "I don't want to hear any talk about leavin'. In my day, when people got married it was for better or worse; if it happened to be for worse, they put a good face on it an' kept still. They didn't go around publishin' their misery an' leavin' their husbands an' takin' new ones. I don't want any more such talk. If I can stand it, I guess you can."

"I guess I can," admitted Mahlon, conscience-stricken, "but oh, mother! I'm young and life is all before me. I want to get something out of it."

"So did I once," said his mother; then her chin trembled suddenly. "He wasn't always so, Mahlon," she said, after a moment, in a different tone. "Or, at least, it didn't seem so bad. He worshipped the ground I trod on, an' he couldn't bear me out of his sight. He wouldn't let me *look* at another man. He was tall an' straight, an' I never saw a young man so handsome. I didn't mind at all while he was only ugly about young men, for I didn't want to look at anybody but him, an' it was easy to coax him back into a good humor; an' then he'd be so sorry an' beg me to forgive him, an' promise to never be ugly to me again. He offered to promise of himself. It was only after we grew older that it seemed to get such a hold on him. He took to gettin' ugly about everything. I couldn't please him at all. His ugliness just seemed to come out an' be chronic."

"He's like a snake that gets so mad it eats itself up," cried Mahlon, bitterly.

"Hush! I won't hear such talk. That's a pretty way

to talk about your father. I tell you he can't help it. He was born that way."

Mahlon stooped down and kissed her again. "You're an angel, mother," he said tenderly, "and I'm a brute to ever complain."

His mother veered around instantly. "You're not; I won't have you talk so. I know how tryin' your father is, an' how hard it is for you. I know all about what a hard life you have an' what you give up." Mahlon thought that perhaps she did not know all that he gave up. "All is," concluded his mother, "I knew him when he was younger, an' all the happiness I get out of life is in rememberin' him as he used to be."

That seemed a cold comfort to Mahlon. He kissed his mother, with the old choke in his throat.

"Come and go to bed now," he said gently. "And don't get up early; I'll get my own breakfast."

"Well, then. The pancake batter is all ready to thin up; an' I'll set the skillet here on the stove-hearth. You know where the turner hangs?"

"Yes, mother." He stood a moment watching her with eyes that were grave with thought; then he turned silently and went up to his attic.

He went to the window and saw Mariella's light. He set his own lamp on the table near the window. "Maybe she'll see it," he thought for the first time. "It'll answer hers."

When she confessed later that she had seen it, not that night only, but many others, he said at once, in a voice shaken with emotion: "I'll set my light in the window, if only for a few minutes, every night, Mariella, as long as we live apart. Then you'll know I'm always thinking of you; if I wasn't, I'd forget the light."

"I'll set mine in the window, too," Mariella promised with tender eyes; it seemed to her the most beautiful and poetic idea in the world — sweeter than the amethyst ring which Mahlon longed to put upon her hand, but which he could not afford. "I'll set it there," she whispered, with her lips on his cheek, "as long as I love you; and that will be —"

"Forever," whispered Mahlon, kissing her.

CHAPTER XVI

For three years Mariella's love story ran along smoothly and sweetly. She had a pony, and rode to and from school over in the town morning and evening. Mahlon groaned sometimes at his work when he saw her ride by, fair and dainty.

"She's getting so much education," he would cry out bitterly, to himself, "pretty soon she'll take up with some town fellow who knows more than I do. I don't know anything but work and slave here in the dirt!"

Then he would grow hot with shame, and bend his back again over his plough. "God knows I want her to learn all she can. I don't want she should be dumb because I have to be. I know she'll be true to me — only sometimes it just feels as if somebody'd stepped over my grave when I see her riding by. There can't a man look at her without wanting her!"

But Mariella remained true. There were little parties around the neighborhood, and Mahlon always accompanied her. The nights when he walked home with her alone under the stars, and the evenings when he came to sit for an hour or two with her in the parlor or out in the dim grape-arbor, made up his heaven.

There was nothing else for him aside from his work. He shared none of the country pastimes of other young men; he never went to the town to loaf in the saloon or the back room of the cigar-store. His hours were filled with work and his heart with Mariella. His thought

went to her constantly as straight and clear as the light he set nightly in his window for her to see.

He never noticed any other girl. Semia Pollard had grown into a soft pink-and-white prettiness which she emphasized with many ruffles and airs. She came often to see his mother, and frequently remained to supper. She was almost the only person in the neighborhood who could not be looked away by his father. She returned the old man's look, laughing and dauntless, her eyes dancing with fun. When he laid his knife and fork on his plate and glared at her because she had helped herself airily to butter, she smiled at him sweetly, and at once helped herself to some more.

Mahlon enjoyed her defiance of his father; but when her smiles were turned upon himself, he was as cold as icicles.

"Semy's here again," said his mother, one evening, when he was washing his face and hands at the sink on the back porch.

"I wish she wouldn't stay to supper," he replied, plunging his brown face into the basin of water.

"She comes to see you, Mahlon," said his mother timidly. "That's the reason she stays so."

Mahlon lifted his head, and gave his mother a long, stern look. "She needn't to," he said briefly. "If I wanted to see her, I've got sense enough to find a way to see her. I know where she lives."

"Don't talk so loud, Mahlon, and don't get worked up so," remonstrated his mother. "It seems as if it was natural for some girls to run after young men. They don't seem to be able to help it. There was that Sal Hargous," — her eyes took a far-off, reminiscent look, — "she run after your father — "

"I wish she'd got him!" burst out Mahlon, passionately. "I wish she had him now!"

"You hush," commanded his mother, reproachfully "You talk nice about your father, don't you? I'd be ashamed. Your father never looked at a girl but me an' all the girls after him, Sal Hargous the worst o all — trollop!"

The thought of all the girls after his father was too much for Mahlon's gravity. He cared too much for hi mother to laugh, so he lowered his head and scrubbe his hands vigorously. "All is," he said, after a moment, in a stubborn tone, "if she comes to see me she needn't to. I don't want to have anything to do with her, and I won't."

"It gets dark so early," said his mother, her though leaping ahead to all sorts of possibilities, "like as not if she lingers an' lingers, you'll have to take her home."

"Like as not I won't!" cried Mahlon, furiously.

"Don't talk so loud; she'll hear you. You'll have to if she lingers. She may linger. I've known girls to linger. Sal Har—"

"Let her linger!" Mahlon slushed the water out o the pan with a great splash, and strode across the porcl to the long roller-towel, giving it a violent jerk to bring down a clean place. "She can linger till doomsday before I'll walk home with her! She can—"

"Mahlon Proudfoot!"

—"Linger like the lingering consumption or the creeping paralysis before—"

His mother gave a little terrified scream.

"What's the matter?" asked a soft voice, and there stood Semia.

"You startled me," faltered Mrs. Proudfoot, in an agitated way.

"What was Mahlon making such a to-do about What ails him?"

"Why, he's tired, 's all," Mrs. Proudfoot assured her hastily.

"Well, good evening, Mahlon," said Semia, coming out on the porch and looking at him with appealing eyes. "Why don't you speak to me?"

"Good evening," responded Mahlon, coldly, emerging from the folds of the towel with a shining face. He gave her a chill, unsmiling look, and, turning away to the little wavy mirror hanging on the wall, began combing his hair. His lip curled as he tried to imagine Mariella forcing herself upon a young man, even himself, during his toilet.

"You tired?"

"Yes, I'm always tired at night."

"What you been doing to-day?"

"I've been ploughing."

She came closer and stood in a coquettish attitude, with her hands on her pretty hips. She turned her head a little to one side, and looked at him with her eyelids drawn slightly together.

"Mahlon!"

"Well?"

"You turn round here and look at me."

He turned and gave her a long, cold look. "Well?" he said again.

"What ails you?"

"Nothing ails me as I know of."

"Yes, there does something ail you, too. You mad at me?"

"No."

She swung from side to side on her heels. "I believe you are. What makes you treat me so? I never get mad at you. I never treat you cool."

"You can if you want to," said Mahlon, unflinching.

"I don't want to. I never do want to. I wouldn't do anything to hurt your feelings for all the world."

Thinking the matter might as well be settled there

and then, Mahlon suddenly decided upon heroic measures. "Oh, pshaw!" he said, in a slighting tone; "you couldn't hurt my feelings if you tried."

It seemed to him a brutal thing to say, even to one whom his mother called a pushing girl. He felt his knees tremble as he said it; he was glad his mother had gone in to put the supper on the table.

To his amazement, instead of being offended, Semia came closer by several steps.

"Oh, Mahlon," she said, in a soft, inviting voice, "couldn't I? I'm so glad. It's nice in you to say so."

He turned and stared at her, not realizing at first that she had misunderstood him. But as he looked a dull red grew slowly across his face. He felt rather than saw the invitation in her eyes. There seemed to be an impulse of her body toward him. She made him think of a full-blown flower, reaching to be gathered. He almost shuddered, so violent was his sudden aversion.

"Supper's all on the table an' gettin' cooled off," announced Mrs. Proudfoot, appearing at the door. "Come in an' set up. Your father is all at the table."

Mahlon obeyed the summons with a sigh of relief. Semia floated along before him in her light dimity draperies. Her dress was made with many ruffles, all edged with coarse lace. The neck was cut low, with a frill of lace around it. She had a fair, full neck, as different from Mariella's slender one as a peony is different from a lily.

As they took their places at the table and the lamplight fell upon her, Mahlon gave her a long, searching look. When his eyes reached her neck, bared boldly and intentionally, full of voluptuous curves, without at all understanding why, he was seized with strong repulsion. It was like the uncontrollable shudder of disgust that shook him when his plough cast up a serpent to slide and coil across the gleaming share.

"Good evening, Mr. Proudfoot," said Semia, gayly, to the old man, who was already settled in his big chair at the table. He glared at her and hissed unintelligibly. His eyes were like little balls of green fire.

"What-a-say?" said Semia, radiantly. "Oh, you're glad I came to supper? Thank you; I'm glad, too. Mrs. Proudfoot cooks such good things. And she does make the best butter! I eat three times as much as I do at home. How's your rheumatism to-day?"

The old man snarled.

Semia lifted her eyebrows. "Oh, that's good," she said cheerfully. "I'm glad to hear you say you're better. Mother's having a yellow-leghorn spell. She's tired of ordinary chickens, and nothing but yellow-leghorns will do. She's had three yellow-leghorn spells already," she concluded, laughing across the table at Mahlon.

The old man's sharp eyes caught her look.

"Ho, ho," he chuckled out, unexpectedly, "you're castin' sheep's-eyes at Mahlon, be you? Ho, ho! That makes my side ache. I won't sleep to-night for thinkin' o' that. Ho, ho! no wonder our butter tastes so good you eat near a pound every time you come!" He chuckled again, in fiendish delight. He could not look this young person out of his house, but maybe he could talk her out. "You hurry up, Mahlon; don't be too shy. Don't hold back too bashful. It's nice to have a pretty girl come a-courtin', an' it saves a long walk for you when you're tired; but it's terrible expensive when butter's forty cents a pound an' the courtin' seems to increase the girl's appetite for butter —"

"You old fiend you!" flashed out Semia, with a scarlet face and blazing eyes. "Mahlon Proudfoot, why don't you make him keep still — you know I don't come here to see you!"

"Of course I know it," returned Mahlon, looking at

her steadily, but growing pale instead of red. "Of course I know a girl never 'd think of going to a young man's home if she cared anything for him — unless he cared for her and asked her to." He caught his breath after this speech; he could not meet the eyes blazing at him across the table. His mother fumbled the cups and saucers with trembling fingers; her eyes were downcast.

"Don't pay any attention to him," continued Mahlon, desperately. "Nobody pays any attention to him."

There was silence then around the table. The old man sat with his head hanging over on one side, chuckling down in his throat. Mrs. Proudfoot still fumbled cups and saucers, as if for her life. Semia sat perfectly still. The scarlet remained in her face, the fire in her eyes.

After a few moments the supper went on as usual. Semia convinced herself that Mahlon had not meant anything. It was only his awkward way of reassuring her. She was not one to acknowledge defeat. There must be a mistake somewhere. She had never encouraged any other young man. She had always liked Mahlon, and had felt sure that it would be easy enough to take him away from Mariella when he once understood that he might have Semia. Semia was content to wait; and she did not scorn stooping to win.

She purposely dallied long over supper. Mrs. Proudfoot cast anxious glances out the window at the gathering March dusk. Mahlon's face darkened ominously. The old man sat watching her and chuckling wickedly.

"You'll have to churn to-morrow," he cried out once to his wife. "Good Lord, 'd you ever see her beat?"

Whereupon Semia calmly helped herself to more butter and another biscuit, making his jaw fall in sheer amazement at her audacity.

When they finally arose from the table, Semia glanced out the window for the first time, and gave a little scream.

"Oh, it's gone dark," she cried, "and me a good half-mile from home. I'll be scared out of my wits. Mrs. Proudfoot, where's my hat? I can't even wait to help you with the dishes."

"My, no; I don't want any help. Your hat's in the settin'-room on the lounge — up on the head of it."

Mrs. Proudfoot followed Mahlon through the kitchen and out on the porch.

"You Mahlon! Where you slyin' off to? That's a pretty way to act up! I won't have a son of mine act up so about a neighbor girl. You take an' walk home with her."

Mahlon groaned. "Oh, mother, I'd just as lieve walk home with a snake!"

"Well, if you would just as lieve walk home with a snake, she can't go through them dark woods alone."

"You take the lantern and go with her, mother, and I'll follow along behind."

"That 'u'd be a great note, I must say. That sounds nice for a young man twenty-five years old, I must say."

"Well, here I am, all ready," announced Semia, coming out into the darkness. "I can't stop to say good-by. It's as black as black cats."

"Mahlon's findin' his hat to go with you; just wait a minute," said Mrs. Proudfoot, firmly. "You mustn't go alone."

"Why, the idea —"

"You found your hat, Mahlon?"

Mahlon came forward into the light with his hat in his hand. His face was pale and his lips were set together. He knew that tone of his mother's voice; she employed it seldom, but he had never disobeyed it.

"Oh, you've found it, have you?" said his mother, sternly. "Well, Mahlon 'll walk home with you, Semia.

It ain't safe for you to go through them woods alone after dark. Well . . . good night."

"Good night," said Semia, gathering up her skirts in one hand with a graceful bend of her body at the waist. "I've had the best time! But mother will be having a tew. She tews if I so much as crook my finger."

Then they went on their way. Mahlon walked fast, with great strides. He held his head high. He walked so stiffly that his legs seemed scarcely to bend.

He went striding along beside Semia trembling with rage. He knew she would tell Mariella the next day at school; and he would have no opportunity until Sunday to explain it to Mariella. Perhaps, then, she would not believe him. He could see the grave, sweet glance that would search his eyes for the truth. To show him that she did not care, she might even permit Henry Bonning to ride home with her from town on his big chestnut mare.

Mahlon almost groaned.

Presently he became aware that Semia was walking closer to him. Her ruffles fluttered around his knees; he heard her breathing fast in her effort to keep up with him.

"Mercy, Mahlon, don't walk so fast. I can't keep up with you," said Semia.

"I have to walk fast," said Mahlon, fiercely. "I've got something to do when I get home."

He had seized a lantern from its place on the wall and lighted it with a kind of savage joy. No young man, he reasoned, would carry a lantern taking a girl home, if he cared a row of pins for her. He swung it now in his right hand, and his lips curled in grim humor as he watched a dozen shadows of his legs dancing along beside him. He could not imagine himself doing anything so ridiculous with Mariella at his side.

"Oh, don't have things to do when you take me home," wheedled Semia, softly. She stumbled and caught hold of his arm. "There, look at me — I nearly fell!" she exclaimed, holding fast to his arm. "I am so clumsy; I can't walk after dark. Don't hurry so, Mahlon."

"I have to hurry."

She clung closer to him as they neared her home. He almost pulled her along.

At the gate he paused. "I'll wait here and hold the lantern," he said coldly, opening the gate. "Good night."

She turned and leaned over the gate, after she had passed inside, and took his left hand suddenly in both her own.

"You're a great big cross thing," she said tenderly, "but I believe it's all because you're bashful. I bet you was just as wild to come with me as I was to have you. Wasn't you?"

He stood like a tall, red-faced fool, trying to get his hand from hers, but she held it firmly. "Wasn't you?" she repeated softly.

"I don't know as I was," he said distinctly. His hand lay stiff now in hers.

"Well, I know," she said, taking heart, being one of those maidens who cannot read signs aright. "I know that the more you think of a girl down in your heart, the colder you'll be to her, just to try her affection and patience. You'll be downright mean to her, and you won't even meet her half-way. You're so proud, you want to humble her and be sure she loves you before you ever let her know you love her. Now, ain't I right?"

Mahlon drew a long breath. The lantern hung motionless in his hand. A strong odor of kerosene mounted to assail their senses. His eyes glowed back at her through the half-light.

"I don't know as you're right," he said slowly and cruelly; "I don't know as I'm like that. I wa'n't like that with Mariella. I never made her meet me half-way, or a third-way. I was glad to go the whole way, and sit and wait patient till she'd smile at me. She's the only girl I ever loved. I loved her when she was a little girl in short dresses. I've loved her six years. I love her now, and I'll love her as long as I live. I don't know anything about any other girl, and I don't want to. I don't know whether any other girl's eyes are blue or green or black. I just know the color of Mariella's. I ain't had a thought or a dream in six years that didn't have Mariella in it and all through it. So I don't know as you're right about me — anyways, not where Mariella is concerned. . . . I'm going to see her to-night; that's what I'm in such a hurry for. Good night."

He drew his hand away. It was moist and trembling with nervous shame.

Semia drew herself up like a snake, and away from him.

"I'll tell you one thing, Mahlon Proudfoot," she said, in a shaking voice. "She'll never be true to you. You just mark my words. I say she'll never be true to you. She'll set her cap higher'n you. You just mark my words!"

She turned and flaunted down the path. Mahlon looked after her, holding the lantern high, until she disappeared in the house; then he, too, turned and went home.

A chill, as of some evil, had fallen upon him. He paused at the sink on the porch and spat in a passion of rage upon the hand Semia had fondled. Then he stooped and washed it with soap.

"It's a lie! It's a lie!" he kept saying bitterly, in his throat. "Snake! If she was a man I'd knock her

down! It's a lie — but if it wasn't a lie, —" he shuddered strongly, — "I'd rather go on loving her —"

But a sob came up into his throat then that seemed to choke the very thought from him. He went blindly through the kitchen and upstairs.

CHAPTER XVII

MAHLON was troubled no more by Semia Pollard; but in the following year another and more serious trouble arose for him.

He was twenty-six years old and Mariella was twenty. The mortgage was not paid, and he could not as yet see his way clear to marrying; but as spring was well advanced and the evenings growing long, he decided to begin his long-planned cottage and do the work himself slowly after his day's work was done. Building a home for Mariella could never cause him weariness. The driving of nails and the sawing of boards would be music in his ears.

He wanted the cottage on the most sightly location on the whole ranch, and he would have Mariella herself select the exact spot; but he did not know how to manage it. His mother and Mariella's parents had long known how it was with the young people, but old Mr. Proudfoot had no suspicion of it.

No one dared to tell him. His own wife turned white and lost her breath at the mere mention of it. Mahlon had often wondered if it would be wicked to wish that his father would die. "I suppose it would be," he always groaned afterward to himself. "But he's only a misery to himself as well as us. He's so mean he don't take a minute's comfort for fear somebody 'll eat five cents' worth."

He never permitted himself to give the wish entrance; it hovered outside the door of his heart day and night, awaiting admittance. He was constantly starting to find it there, and dreading that he might some day be surprised off-guard and let it in.

He did not know how to take Mariella all over the place without his father's finding it out and suspecting the reason of the visit. The old man never went away from home, and he was always shuffling around, stamping his cane, and peering out with narrow, inquisitive eyes from under his great, hanging brows. Mahlon knew that Mariella — proud and high-spirited though she was — fell into a panic at the thought of meeting his father.

But it had to be managed; and finally his mother arranged it.

"Mr. Parmer's away," she said, "an' we'll ask Mis' Parmer an' Mariella to Sunday dinner. After early dinner you an' Mariella wander off. Your father 'll be kept so busy tryin' to look Mis' Parmer home that he won't notice you're gone."

Mahlon smiled reluctantly. "It 'll be awful hard on Mrs. Palmer."

"I guess she can stand it. It won't be so terrible easy on me. Mothers have to stand things for their children; they get used to it."

A few moments before the unwilling guests were expected Mr. Proudfoot passed through the dining-room and saw the table arranged for company. He had complained early in the day of feeling ill, and had been lying down. Mahlon's heart beat high with hope that his illness would continue; and Mrs. Proudfoot had not mentioned that company was coming.

"If he don't see the table all set," she reasoned, "he'll natur'lly think they come unexpected. It won't be any harm to let him think so."

She made him comfortable on the bed, propped up

with pillows. She spread an immaculate log-cabin quilt over him.

"Now, don't you move all day, father," she said. "You'll be better off to stay right in bed. I'll bring you a drink whenever you want one; an' I'll fetch your dinner right in on a tray. Then you won't get the smell o' the victuals an' make you sick."

But in her eagerness to keep him in bed she was too solicitous. She came too frequently to inquire as to his wants and desires, always admonishing him to remain in bed.

It was not until two o'clock that the truth suddenly flashed upon him. He flung the quilt from him and staggered out upon the floor, reaching for his cane. "There's somethin' up!" he ejaculated. "There's somethin' up. I ain't anybody's fool! They can't pull any wool over my eyes. She's too durn polite an' clever all at once. I'll just slip out an' see for myself what's up."

He went shuffling out, sniffing and peering about him suspiciously. Everything was as usual until he reached the dining-room. There he stood still and gazed. In a moment he pounded loudly on the floor with his stick.

Poor Mrs. Proudfoot's heart sank when she heard that sound in the dining-room. She came in from the kitchen, and her face was pale, although she had been cooking.

"Why, father," she faltered, "you up?"

"Yes, I'm up," he squealed. "You look at here. You just look at here! What does this here table mean?"

"What here table, father? I don't know what you mean."

"Yes, you do, too, know what I mean. Who's comin' here to eat?"

"Why, Mis' Parmer an' Mariella are. Didn't I tell you?"

"Didn't you tell me?" he mimicked. "No, you didn't tell me. You even tried your bluest to keep me in bed so's I wouldn't know."

He went shuffling on into the kitchen, and went around the stove and table, lifting covers and peering into pans.

"Now, father," pleaded Mrs. Proudfoot, quaking.

"Now, mother," he mimicked.

"Don't go to uncovering things so, father. It's the ruination of potatoes to uncover 'em when they're boiling."

"Oh, it is, is it?" He jerked the cover clear off, and stood holding it and leering at her like an animal; drops of steam dropped from the lid upon the floor.

"Well, it doesn't ruin 'em exactly," said Mrs. Proudfoot, with a regular masterpiece of diplomacy. "It just *wastes* 'em. They boil down about half."

Mr. Proudfoot jammed the lid down upon the pan.

"Why didn't you tell me? Think I want potatoes boilin' away about half? Think I've got things runnin' to waste that way? . . . Aigh?"

He rasped the cover off another pan that stood on the table. Mrs. Proudfoot turned paler. Her knees refused to bear her weight, and she sank helplessly upon a chair.

The pan held a Brown Betty, all ready for the oven. She had made it with unusual care, having heard Mrs. Palmer declare it to be Mariella's favorite pudding. "Little mink!" Mrs. Palmer had concluded, proudly. "You'd ought to see her waste butter on the top layer! She puts butter on every layer, but she just spreads it *thick* on the top one."

For once Mrs. Proudfoot had spread butter with a reckless hand all through the pudding, and especially upon the top layer. "He's sick in bed," was her unspoken, and almost unconscious, thought. "He'll never know it. I may as well have it good an' rich this once."

"[illegible]" he asked.

"It's a Brown Betty, father."

"A Brown Betty, hey! A brown devil you'll think [illegible] with it. What's all this butter [illegible] for?"

"[illegible] a Brown Betty, father. If the butter [illegible] the sugar an' cinnamon, it [illegible]"

"[illegible] Brown Betty, or Red Betty, or Blue [illegible] a Betty, without [illegible] We'll see how *she* [illegible]"

[illegible] the pieces [illegible] into a dish. [illegible] from the [illegible] the arms of Mahlon, who [illegible]

[illegible] putting his [illegible] matter? Is father [illegible]

[illegible] his shoulder and began [illegible] Mahlon — your father! your [illegible]

[illegible]

[illegible] at the Brown Betty!"

[illegible]

[illegible] the Brown Betty! Oh, [illegible] unless there's a [illegible] sugar. I never do put so [illegible] Mariella's favorite puddin', [illegible]

[illegible]

"Do you mean father's taking off the butter you put on?"

"Yes, he is. He got up an' come out when I wa'n't expectin' him. If I'd only got it in the oven! But he see the butter all over the top, an' it seemed to make him crazy. It seems to me sometimes" — she burst out into wilder sobbing — "as if he must be *marked* for butter. It seems to me as if he couldn't act so if he wa'n't."

Mahlon put her gently aside and strode into the kitchen. "Father!" he cried out. "You look at here!"

The old man turned around. His head was trembling and jerking with rage.

"You let things be and go back to bed! If mother wants butter on top of that pudding, I'll see that she has it there. I earn it."

"I'll Brown Betty her!" chuckled the old man. "She'll keep me in bed, a-bein' so clever an' a-now-you-fatherin' me! I ain't anybody's fool. She'll have company a-eatin' us out of house an' home! *I'll* show her! Just let me get my eyes on 'em."

"Oh, Mahlon!" cried his mother, in a stifled voice. "They're comin'. They're right here. You go an' meet 'em, so's I can get my eyes cooled off."

Mahlon hastened away after a warning look at his father. One glance at Mariella's sweet and radiant face made him forget all his troubles. She was all in white, and he wondered how she could have such happy eyes with the dread of meeting his father in her heart. Then he saw with a kind of angry surprise that Mrs. Palmer's face wore an expression of cheerful relief. She even moved with a certain exultation.

He ushered them into the sitting-room and offered them chairs with embarrassed awkwardness. "Mother 'll be in, in a minute," he said, flushing self-consciously. "Have some chairs."

Then his eyes went seeking Mariella's and found them. He felt his face redden more deeply at her glance of shy joy. How could she be so easy and saucy? He expected every instant to hear the fierce thumping of his father's stick. It was a sound that always stopped his heart for a few beats and then sent the blood flying to his ears. It seemed to him that he had known and dreaded the sound all his life, and that he would hear it after his father was in his grave.

Mrs. Proudfoot came in, apologizing gently. Her eyelids were faintly red, but the redness showed only when she glanced sidewise, and she avoided this as much as possible. "Why, Mahlon, son," she chided gently, "you didn't take their hats. For pity's sake! You make me feel so. When a mother hasn't a daughter to do such little things, she expects her son to take right a-hold 'n' 'tend to them for her. When you get married your wife 'll think I never taught you anything."

She stood stiffly before her visitors, possessing herself of their capes, hats, and gloves, which she ranged neatly over her left arm.

"You let Mahlon alone," flashed out Mariella, with a little air of ownership and protection which made Mahlon thrill and the two mothers smile at each other. "I don't think men should take visitors' hats and wraps — "

"We are plenty able to take off our own things, I guess," bragged in Mrs. Palmer, cheerfully. "I guess we could take 'em off an' lay 'em on the lounge without botherin' Mahlon. Now, Mis' Proudfoot, I don't know what I'll do to you if you've went to a great fuss over dinner."

"Oh, no, I haven't," assured Mrs. Proudfoot, thinking of the Brown Betty.

"Well, if you have," said Mrs. Palmer, with threatening playfulness, "I don't know what I'll do to you. You'll see. I'll pound you, if you have!"

"Well, I haven't." Mrs. Proudfoot was wondering where her guests had become possessed of such amazing cheer and good spirits. "I could take it all out of 'em in a hurry if I'd let 'em see him tearin' that Brown Betty to pieces," she reflected, with grim triumph.

Both she and Mahlon grew more bewildered as the moments passed and their guests showed no signs of uneasiness. Never before had even the brave Mrs. Palmer sat in that room save on the edge of her chair, like a clumsy bird poised for flight, and with her eyes fixed apprehensively first on one door, then on another. But now she sat well back in her chair, with an air of such marked comfort that it suggested relief. Her large hands were folded in her lap, as if she had come to stay long and have a good and gossipy time. Mariella, too, had settled down into her chair with her elbow on its arm, and her soft cheek in her hand. Mrs. Proudfoot and Mahlon, with their ears strained for a sound of thumping in the kitchen, envied their guests.

"You promised us a Brown Betty," said Mrs. Palmer, rocking to and fro, "an' we wondered comin' along if you made it like Mariella does."

"Maybe you didn't make one, after all," said Mariella, with quick politeness.

"Ye-es — I made one," faltered out Mrs. Proudfoot, with a shudder. "I don't know as it will be as good as Mariella's. How do you make yours, Mariella?"

Mariella flashed a soft glance at Mahlon. Her cheek burned against her hand. It seemed almost like keeping house. "Well," she said, laughing gayly, "first you butter your pudding-dish; then you crumble in a layer of bread crumbs, then one of thin sliced apple; then plenty of cinnamon and brown sugar — a large handful — and flecks of butter all over the sugar; then another layer of bread crumbs, sliced apple, cinnamon, sugar, and butter; so on till the dish is full; put bread-crumbs and ever so much butter on top; eat warm, not hot, with thick cream, after baking slowly nearly an hour. There" — she drew a long breath, proudly — "*that's* the way to make a Brown Betty."

"Why, I made mine just so," said Mrs. Proudfoot, who had been following the recipe closely. Then her face fell. "I don't know as it'll turn out all right, though. Sometimes, somethin' happens to it after it's all made."

Mahlon looked at his mother and smiled against his will.

"Oh, it will be good if you made it that way," said Mariella, confidently. "It — "

She stopped abruptly; her face grew very pale. A loud and long thumping had sounded in the kitchen.

"Why — what is that?" stammered out Mrs. Palmer. She, too, turned pale. She sat bolt upright for an instant, then went sliding forward to the front edge of the chair, which was her customary place when at the Proudfoots'.

"It's only father," said Mrs. Proudfoot, trying to speak easily; and not one in the room was conscious of the deep humor in the "only."

"Oh!" said Mrs. Palmer. Her face had lost all its rich color, her manner all its ease; her eyes were very large. "W'y, I thought — that is, I hoped — I mean we met Henry Bonning on the way over, an' he said Mr. Proudfoot was sick in bed. He said he was certain he wouldn't be able to get up to-day."

"He has been sick all day," said Mrs. Proudfoot, hopelessly. "He just got up before you come in the gate."

"Oh," said Mrs. Palmer, in an indescribable tone;

then, after a long silence, she added, in a voice that refused to utter more than two words, "I'm glad."

After another long silence, she added suddenly, with a start — "I mean I'm glad he's better — of course."

"Yes, he's out in the kitchen," said Mrs. Proudfoot. "I guess by the thumping he wants to see me. If you'll excuse me —"

"Oh, certainly."

Mrs. Proudfoot got as far as the door; then she paused. "I don't know," she said slowly, to Mahlon, with a significant look, "but you an' Mariella had best go an' take your walk right now, before your father gets all worked up. It may be your only chance."

CHAPTER XVIII

MARIELLA sprang up eagerly and put on her hat. She was still pale with fear. It seemed as if she could not breathe until she got into the open air.

"I'm so disappointed!" she burst out, walking rapidly and casting apprehensive glances back over her shoulder toward the house. "Our hearts came up like feathers when Henry Bonning told us he was sick in bed. Mother said it was a clear case of Providence; but now —" she shuddered — "I'm afraid to go back to the house. And we might have had such a happy day."

Mahlon reached out and folded her delicate hand in his big, brown palm. "Don't worry about it now," he said, tenderly. "It'll be time enough when we go back. Don't let's worry about anything now. We don't have so many hours together that we can afford to waste 'em; an' the Lord only knows how soon we'll have less."

His voice was bitter; the words sounded like a prophecy. Mariella drew closer to him and leaned her burning cheek against his arm. "Oh, hush!" she whispered, shaken with a great tenderness.

Mahlon put both arms around her and drew her close to him, and held her there silently. Neither the young man nor the girl ever forgot that hour. Their pulses throbbed deep and slow, with a passion that seemed like holiness. The spring sweetness was all about them. The silver buds were on the firs, and their fragrance was shaken loose on the still air. From a near pond the frogs jarred the air with their shrill clamor. Wake-robins spread their white or lavender leaves around every stump and tree, and the wild currant shrubs were motionless clouds of rosy bloom.

They were in a grove of half-grown firs and alders, on a noble headland that jutted out over the sea. "It is here," said Mahlon, at last, "that I thought you might like the house."

He turned her face to the sea; it seemed to be moving to them with long, slow-flinging waves. Her gaze went far out to the purple islands and the silvery shimmer of sea-birds in flight; then still farther, to the white mountains strung upon the horizon. "It is the place," she said softly.

After a while he said hesitatingly, "It will not be much of a house, you know, dear—"

"I know," she assured him quickly, pressing her cheek closer to his breast.

"And it may be long before it is finished, and longer before we can live in it together. I had planned to have the parlor look out on the bay, and the dining-room on this side,"—he was speaking diffidently—"and the kitchen here; and the bedroom here."

There was a quality in his voice that shook the girl's heart. She looked up at him through a sudden mist of tears. It was as if he had spoken aloud in a dream that would never come true. His voice sounded sad and unreal to her. He had planned it all out in his heart so many times; he had stood alone so often on that spot and said to himself, "There will be a window here for her to look out to the sea, and one here for her to look down to the town;" he had seen it so often in his dreams, a soft gray cottage standing among the evergreens,—that it had, indeed, grown to be a dream to him, a dream that was with him day and night.

"It is just as I want it," said the girl, sweetly; "I might have left it all with you."

"I wanted you to come; I wanted you to stand right on the spot and be sure it was the best place. And besides —"

His throat choked suddenly, and he could not go on. Mariella waited a moment, caressing his big-veined wrist with her soft, slow fingers. It was almost the only caress she ever gave him voluntarily. It had grown so dear to him that he awoke sometimes at night with the certainty that her hand was stilling his pulses.

"Besides what, Mahlon?" she said after a while.

"Why, I wanted to say something to you. I wanted to say" — his throat choked again, but he went on with an effort — "that it might be a long time before the house is finished, but it is *your house*, Mariella, from the time the first nail is driven. It is yours. It never will be any other woman's as long as I live. Even if you — even if we — if something happened to separate us, or you — were taken away from me in any way, — why, it would always be your house. I wanted to tell you that. Every time you look down this way you will be able to see it, and I want you to say to yourself, 'It is my house, it is my home; and it is the dearest thing on earth to him, except me.'"

She still looked up at him, but she could not see him. His face was a blur through her tears. "I will," she promised, in a trembling voice. "I'll not forget. Don't say another word about it, Mahlon. I'll never forget. I'll think of it every time I look down this way — and that is all the time," she added, laughing quickly through her tears.

"Don't laugh," he entreated, in a voice that was hoarse with emotion. "Don't laugh about anything just now, Mariella. Oh, my dear," he burst out, in a passion so real and so deep that all his awkwardness and self-consciousness fell from him, "you do not know what you are to me. You are just like heaven to me. It seems to me as if I didn't have any thought but you. I follow the plough and I follow the harrow, and think of you; I fell trees and I burn thickets, and I think of you; I see a wild flower, or I see a star fall, or I hear a bird sing, and think of you; I go to my window first thing in the morning and last thing at night, and think of you; and I dream of you — I believe I dream of you every night."

Mariella could not reply; she stroked his wrist silently, and her tears fell down upon it.

"I want to tell you another thing," he went on, more slowly. "I trust you. I never have a doubt of you. I've got an ugly temper, and I'd go mad with jealousy if I once thought I had cause; but I ain't hunting cause. I trust you. . . . That's all," he added suddenly, in a different tone; "let's go back to the house. It's all settled, and I'll drive the first nail a week from to-morrow."

They went back through the orchard. Mariella walked in the narrow path, and Mahlon stumbled along in the ferns and tangles of blackberry vines.

Old Mr. Proudfoot and Mrs. Palmer sat alone in the sitting-room, glaring at each other. Mrs. Palmer was red but defiant. Her eyes were narrowed like a serpent's, but their basilisk gaze had not affected Mr. Proudfoot. He had the best of it.

He turned his attention at once to the young people. "Where you been?" he growled.

"Keep still, father," said Mahlon, sternly. "Mariella, here's a chair."

The old man turned to her. "See here, missy! You tell me where you've been a-slyin' around with my son. Nice girls don't go a-slyin' round through the orchard with young men."

"Father!" threatened Mahlon, furiously. "If you don't keep still—"

"He'd best keep still," cried out Mrs. Palmer, in a great voice; her face had grown purple. "Old devil possessed, you! You'd best talk about my girl a-slyin' anywheres. I'll let you know she ain't one o' the slyin' kind."

"Oh, she ain't, aigh!" chuckled the old man, wagging his head from side to side. "She ain't, aigh! What does she come a-settin' her cap at my son for, then? Just like that trollop of a Semy Pollard!"

"Oh, you talk about my girl a-runnin' after your son, will you?" Mrs. Palmer was beside herself with rage. "You talk! You!—with your son almost a-livin' at my house!—"

"Mrs. Palmer!" warned Mahlon; he was very white.

"—an a-followin' my daughter like her shadow—"

"Oh, mother!" entreated Mariella, in terror.

"—an' a-askin' us over here to let her pick a place for them to build their house on! You talk! You old butter-miser, you! They're all afraid to tell you but me! I ain't afraid of you!"

The old man's head was shaking from side to side, as if he had palsy. "What's this?" he hissed out. "What's this woman a-sayin'?"

"She's saying the truth," said Mahlon, suddenly standing up. "I'm going to marry Mariella, and we've been picking out a place to build a house. You keep still, I tell you! If you don't—"

"He, he, he!" cackled the old man. "*Marry* her! He, he, he! You've lost your gum'tion, if you ever had any. Men don't marry girls that go a-slyin' around, a-settin' their caps at 'em the way she's been a-doin'—"

"*Father!*" Mahlon almost roared. They all turned, suddenly aware that Mr. Palmer was standing in the

doorway. His face was white; his eyes, flaming out of it, looked like Mariella's; he gave an impression of greater height than usual.

"I've heard every word," he said briefly; there was an ominous calm in his voice. "My daughter don't sly after any young man, an' I won't let even an old man like you say so. Mahlon Proudfoot, you make your father take that back, or you can't come under my roof again."

White as death, Mahlon looked at Mariella. His eyelids trembled. He felt his heart tremble within him.

"It's no use," he said hoarsely. "You don't know him. He never took anything back in his life. Don't say it, Mr. Palmer. I ain't to blame for havin' such a father."

The old man had quivered down into a chair, and sat with his hands folded on his cane, wagging his head from side to side and chuckling fiendishly.

"I say it again," said Mr. Palmer, calmly. "I ain't quick to fly up, but when I do fly up, I stay flew up. That's all. You make him take it back."

"God help me," said Mahlon, in a low voice. "I can't."

"Well, if you don't think any more of my daughter than to let any man alive talk that way about her, — right in her presence, too! — you don't deserve her, an' you shan't have her. You can make him take it back, or run him off the ranch, I guess."

Mahlon shuddered terribly. "I can't — I can't," he uttered helplessly. "He's my father. It 'u'd kill my mother."

Mariella moved quickly across the room and clasped her hands around Mahlon's arm, leaning her cheek against him, right before them all. Mahlon threw his other arm around her and leaned his face down to hers with a sob.

"Father!" she cried, and her eyes flashed their fire out fiercely. "You keep still. I don't care what he says. Everybody knows what he is. I wouldn't notice him. Mahlon can't make him take it back, and he can't turn him out of doors. Mahlon isn't to blame."

"That's so," put in Mrs. Palmer, who had been cooling off. "Stubborn old loon!"

The old man pointed a crooked finger at Mariella.

"Look at there!" he squealed out. "Look at there! She don't sly around, aigh? She don't traipse after an' set her cap after young men, aigh? I'd like to see any young man get away from a girl like that. You'll tell my son he can't come under your roof, aigh? You keep your girl at home —"

"*Father!*"

"Oh, you 'father' him!" screamed Mrs. Palmer. "Much good your 'fatherin'' him does! He's possessed with a thousand devils! I wouldn't belittle myself a-noticin' him any more than if he was the dirt under my feet! I —"

"Look out there!" cried Mrs. Proudfoot, in a thin but angry voice; she was teetering wildly in the doorway, between the dining-room and the sitting-room. "Don't you stand there an' abuse my husband right to my face. I won't have it! I say I won't have it!"

Her voice died away in a fluttering scream. Mariella and Mahlon looked at each other. Their faces were stern with despair. Mariella released herself gently. "We might just as well go," she said dully. "There isn't a thing to be done."

Mahlon's lips trembled. "You'll be true to me?" he said, almost inaudibly.

"Yes, Mahlon," said Mariella, "I will."

"You know I'll be true to you," he said; and then they turned away from each other, blindly, and Mariella was conscious after several moments that she was following her parents homeward through the woods. Mr. Palmer walked with short, stiff steps. His arms hung rigidly at his sides; his thumbs were thrust into his palms. He had made the supreme effort of his life to stand on his dignity. Mrs. Palmer struggled along at his side. She held her dress up high on one side and the tail of it swept and lashed the innocent ferns at the roadside, like the tail of an enraged whale. She and Mr. Palmer did not keep step when they walked; their shoulders rolled together at every other step.

"Onery old mule!" Mrs. Palmer kept exclaiming, in deep chest tones that uncoiled themselves like the whistle of a siren. "Old Stubbornfoot! *I'll* show him! He'll walk over me! An' even Mis' Proudfoot a-twitterin' there in the door, scared out of her life of him, an' then takin' the old mule's part! With her 'look at here,' an' her 'look at there,' an' her 'I won't have its'! Well, all is—"

In this guise had the deepest trouble of Mahlon's life come to him. As he stood at his window that night, watching for Mariella's light, he was in such despair that he could only turn helplessly from side to side, like a dumb beast in torture. His whole life seemed, as he looked back, to have been one of disappointment and struggle and trouble. And this was the climax. He had lost Mariella! Lost her? A groan burst from him, and he fell on his knees by the window and laid his head down on his arms.

"Oh, Mariella, Mariella!" he cried out. "I have not lost you! I can't lose you while we love one another and are true. God forgive me if I ever forget for more than a minute the happiness you have been to me all these years! I wouldn't change lives with any man I ever knew — not even Leaming with all his education and his goin' to England — if I had to give you up to do it."

He lifted his head and, looking, saw Mariella's light shining in a clear path to him, as if for her thoughts to cross upon.

Mariella at her window could not see his light for tears. Her father had followed her to the stair door.

"You just listen here, Mariella. Mahlon Proudfoot don't put his head under my roof again, an' you don't put your head under his. I don't set my foot down often, but when I do, it stays set."

"You hear what your father says?" cried her mother, pressing after her. "Turn around here an' answer up. You can't have another thing to do with Mahlon Proudfoot. If you do, I'll turn you out o' the house! You don't meet him anywhere, either. You hear? I'll show that old father o' his! His mother a-teeterin' around there, too, like a scared Jenny Wren, a-talkin' up to me! If Mahlon Proudfoot can't take your part — "

"Oh, *hush!*" cried Mariella, desperately; and she slammed the door and fled up the steep stairs to the attic.

A year passed. Mariella had graduated at the private grammar-school in the little town around the bay. Mahlon saw her no more riding by on her pony. Once or twice he had seen her at sociables; but Mariella, afraid that the meeting would be reported to her parents, would grant him but few words. He managed to ask her, in a shaken voice that hurt her for days afterward, if she still loved him and was true to him. She gave him the desired assurance with her eyes and a low, steady "Yes."

At first the parting had been very hard for Mariella.

She had wept many nights, and had listened, expecting to hear his footsteps. She had felt sure that he would brave her parents' displeasure and come. But Mahlon had no thought of such a step. He could not marry her until the mortgage was paid; but he could be true to her and wait, and while he waited he could build the house. He arose early in the mornings to work, and, in spite of his father's furious opposition, he worked late in the evenings. He scarcely took time to eat his supper, his mother gently complained.

Mariella was as loyal as he. She never gave the slightest encouragement to any of the young men of the neighborhood, although there was, as her mother frequently declared, "a plenty of 'em danglin' after her." But as the year wore away and her school work engrossed her more and more, her separation from Mahlon gradually became more bearable. Not seeing him, he no longer filled her mind and heart to the exclusion of everything else. She became interested in other things.

She thought of him many times a day, but more vaguely, as one thinks of a friend who has gone far away. She could no longer feel his presence at will, as she had been able to do at first. She could no longer close her eyes and see the tenderness of his look or hear the passion-cadence of his voice that had once thrilled her through. But she never forgot to watch for his light, nor to set her own in the window for him.

Mariella would have fiercely resented the faintest suggestion on her mother's part that she was forgetting Mahlon Proudfoot. Her mother was too shrewd to make such a suggestion. She contented herself with sneering at the Proudfoots on every possible occasion. "They're just on a par with them Mizzoura Pollards! Shiftless 's no name for it. Mahlon Proudfoot 'll never make his salt. You'll see."

Mariella bore such taunts in defiant silence; but at times when she was alone her own heart sank at the thought of the future. "Go an' marry him!" her mother had cried once, in fierce rage. "Go an' fry potatoes for him the rest of your life!" Ever afterward Mariella had visions of herself stooping over Mahlon's stove, and turning slices of potatoes over in hot drippings with a knife.

"Well, why shouldn't I?" she would cry out, angry with herself for shrinking from the vision. "Am I any better than Mahlon? Can't I work for him the way he works for me?"

But all the time Mariella's soul was yearning for something different. Farm work was repulsive to her. She wished to teach school. "I won't hear to it," her mother would cry. "You don't have to! Teach school!"

"I'd rather teach school than do farm work," said Mariella.

"Well, you won't. I won't hear to it. You'll stay at home an' go in company. I don't want any more talk about it."

PART III

CHAPTER XIX

THE year of 1888 was an eventful one for the Puget Sound country. It marked the beginning of the great boom which has become a part of the history of the state. Wherever the railroad made an unusually graceful curve a town sprang up in a night — no one ever asked why; he was satisfied that it *was* there.

One day a well-dressed, quiet-mannered man approached Mr. Palmer when he was ploughing, and offered him five thousand dollars for his "ranch." After a consultation with Mrs. Palmer, the offer was accepted. The purchase did not include the house, orchard, barns, and other outbuildings, nor the ten acres of land surrounding them. Mr. Palmer and his neighbors considered it a marvellous stroke of fortune for at least three days. Then they changed their minds.

The quiet, well-dressed man was the agent of the railroad company, which at once founded a city — or "started a town" — whose business centre was only one mile from Mr. Palmer's front door. It was announced that this was eventually to be the terminus of a great transcontinental railroad. The adjoining ranches had been purchased in the same quiet way. The railroad owned almost the entire town site.

Then came the building of the town. The company built roundhouses, wharves, a city hall, a hotel, and several stores to rent. For a week or two business lots sold for one thousand dollars each for inside lots, and fifteen hundred dollars for corners. In less than a month the same lots were worth from thirty-five hundred to five thousand dollars. The mail-boat — the old dingy *Idaho* — came struggling down from Seattle daily instead of three times a week. Daily, also, came the *Eliza Anderson* and the *George E. Starr* — spelled *Geo.* for brevity's sake, brevity being supposed in the West to stand with godliness and cleanliness as a triplet.

A wharf was built a mile out over the tide-lands to deep water. Hundreds of men were set to work clearing the timber off the town site. The ring of the axes beating into noble trees, the buzzing of saws, and the steady chime of the carpenters' hammers united with the scream of the little sawmill — which had been hastily thrown together — to make the discordant music dear to the soul of the "boomer."

Fires blazed day and night. Often great trees burned standing, limb by limb, the flames creeping upward slowly, their heat drying the saps out of the limb above before they leaped up to seize it; thus to the very tip they climbed, turning the firs into tapering torches against the sky. There were few to bemoan the sacrifice of the beautiful. "Damn nature; give us a town!" was the motto of the boomer. When a tree fell and the flames died out of it without consuming it, numerous holes were augured into its prostrate body and fires were kindled in its heart. One who has seen a tree burning in this manner at night — with the scarlet jets of flame pumping steadily and high out of these holes and licking the dark like parched tongues — will forget neither the beauty of it nor the pity of it.

All was energy, excitement, speculation. Money was plentiful, and it was spent royally. Those who had no money purchased luxuries with their wits. Before the town was a month old, Mrs. Laramier, the gay young wife of a gay young speculator, expecting the suite of rooms they had rented to be completed when promised, sent out invitations to a tea. The carpenters drove the last nail at dark the day before the tea. Mrs. Laramier was undaunted. She summoned all the gentlemen of her acquaintance. Such a moving in, and setting to rights, of furniture as there was that day! Fine curtains were draped over the unwashed windows. The unpapered walls were hung with sea-green silk. Hundreds of yards of pearl and palest rose ribbons were festooned over the ceilings. Rich rugs almost concealed the hastily swept floors. In one room the tea-table was daintily laid in silk and lace, cut glass and china. The rooms were darkened and the candles lighted. At the appointed hour the hostess, fresh and radiant in her pretty white gown, was receiving her guests. It was winter; but the drawing-room was a dream of spring.

It was the first social function in the new town of Kulshan. It was a brilliant success. "Mrs. Laramier's tea" took a notable place in the history of the town.

The one long business street was a thing to dream about. The buildings were all wooden; now and then one was "veneered" over to imitate brick. They were one or two stories in height. The upper stories were used for residences, even livery stables being utilized in this manner. Residences were also partitioned off in the rear of stores and even banks. There was a little strip of sidewalk here, and a little strip there. Between strips the pedestrian descended two or three steps into the soft mud of what had been a potato field. After a few steps he climbed back patiently, or profanely, according to temperament, to the dignity of another brief wooden elevation. The buildings were painted blue, green, red, yellow. Those of one story only were adorned with high square fronts — to give them a two-story look.

Hideous red telephone poles, with outstretched arms, were already staggering drunkenly down the street. Every other building contained a saloon, or a variety theatre, or both. At noon daily, yellow band wagons, drawn by yellow horses, went up and down the town. The wagons were trimmed with white; the horses had white manes and tails; the members of the band discoursing enchanting strains wore yellow and white uniforms. Following closely in carriages were the actresses who danced nightly in the variety theatres. They were dressed in yellow gowns trimmed with white fur; their hair was yellow; long white plumes swept from yellow hats down over their shoulders. Violins, accordeons, and revolvers made original and stirring melody in the saloons from dark to daylight.

The tide-land "jumpers" were staking off lots along the water-front, hastily, as the territory was on the point of being admitted into the Union. Day and night the steady, rhythmic *b*-r-r-rr, *b*-r-r-rr, of the pile-driver beat through the medley of discordant sounds that for a time made life a nightmare to all save the boomer of corner lots. This "boomer" himself has, like the cowboy, the stage-driver, and the tough character of the mining-camp, passed on; he is no more. As picturesque as they, — and as necessary, — he filled his place, which was an important one at the time. He has outlived his day; but fourteen years ago he was a fascinating figure in the West. He had the ear of railroad kings. There was a vague supposition that one could make a fortune if one were a mind-reader, and could penetrate the mysteries of the boomer's mind. Well-dressed, alive with nervous energy, good-natured, alert, quick to scheme and to act — yet holding something of the power of the sphinx in his narrowed eyes; carrying his hands in his pockets and his shoulders high; as good a listener as he was a talker, — he seemed to carry corner lots in the hollow of his hand, and to sell them without really desiring to sell.

When Kulshan was eighteen months old it boasted of ten thousand inhabitants. Charred stumps stood thickly on vacant lots between buildings on the business streets. Fortunes were made, and lost, daily. Many an old pioneer found himself the owner of a ranch adjoining a "booming" town; he laid it out in town lots and became wealthy.

One evening in February Mrs. Palmer came into the sitting-room, where her husband sat smoking. "Mis' Martin was just here," she announced. "They've made a clean twenty thousand out o' their ranch. It wa'n't half as good as our'n was. You're just as easy. You don't know any more about tradin' than them no-account Pollards. Five thousand dollars! We could of got fifty thousand without sneezin'. Five thousand fiddlesticks! You ain't worth shucks. It's just as I say. You go a jacketty-pinchin' around, a-tryin' to make a bargain, but the other fellow always gets the bargain! It makes my soul ache."

"It makes mine ache, too," said Mr. Palmer, wearily. "I do the best I can, but I always get the worst of everything. Didn't I come in from the field and ask you what you thought about it? Didn't you just *jump* at five thousand dollars, an' talk about changin' the old organ off for one with a high back an' three knee-swells an' twenty-seven stops, an' *figgers* on it? Aigh? Didn't you? Didn't you think it was a Jerusha-snap itself? Now because it's turned out hind part before, I get all the blame. Didn't you go to ponderin' who'd take a notion to Mariella an' cut Mahlon out? An' now, all is. We've got five thousand dollars in the bank."

"We might just as well have fifty thousand! You snap everything up just like a snappin'-turtle! Good grieve!"

—"An' we've got our home an' the orchard an' out-buildin's, an' cows, an' hens—"

"An' Mariella to dress! My soul! Don't we have to have clo's for a girl that's got all the young fellows 'n the neighborhood a-danglin' after her, an' her only twenty-one? It does my soul good." Mrs. Palmer's anger cooled off suddenly. Her voice took on a confidential tone, unconsciously. "It does my soul good to see Mis' Mall'ry act up about Isaphene. She thinks the sun raises an' sets in her, especially when she gets her dressed up in buff! 'I admire to see buff,' she says, a-squintin' her eyes. 'I do admire to see it. Not a rill yellow, but just a buff, like the under feathers on a young chicken. Isaphene looks terrible well in buff,' she says. 'I ketch all the young men a-castin' sheep's-eyes at her in church.' Sheep's-eyes at Isaphene Mall'ry! I don't wonder. Nothin' but a sheep would cast any kind of eyes at her. She coughs an' says, 'Yes, ma'am,' to everything you say to her. She holds her elbows in as if they was glued to her sides."

'I bet she can't spell tic-douloureux!" piped out Mr. Palmer, suddenly.

"I bet she can't, either. Her mother makes her walk as if she had a pail of water on her head. She turns one toe out this way, an' one toe out that way, like this—" Mrs. Palmer held up her dress and illustrated; her audience was all attention now. "An' she carries her hands like this, down below her waist. 'She learned how to conduct herself at boardin'-school,' says

Mis' Mall'ry; 'I was bound an' determined Isaphene should get the best there is to be got.' That was a dab at me. My-O, she gives me more dabs. I dab back. Isaphene never could hold a candle to Mariella — an' Mariella never saw the inside of a boardin'-school. She didn't have to. She never took a dancin' lesson, an' look at her dance! It's just in her. I never see her set still a dance. They all want her. She ain't so terrible pretty, but there's somethin' about her eyes. She just looks at a man, an' he never sees another girl after that. He just goes to danglin' an' danglin' after her. Leaming's a-danglin' now."

"I want to know!" Mr. Palmer stopped rubbing his thumb and his forefinger together. His face flushed weakly with pleasure. "Not in earnest?"

"In earnest? I guess. He's only been here two months. She's dodged him ever since he come."

"She was sick the first week, wa'n't she?"

"Yes, she was; but she wa'n't sick the second week, was she? Nor the third, nor the fourth, was she? You do pin a body down, as if you was made o' pins. He come three or four times while she was sick. Of course she couldn't see him then; but he come two or three times since, an' she went out the back door an' off in the woods, like a killdeer."

"What ails her?"

"Why, she never got over his up an' goin' off to England the way he did — all of a sudden so! She never got over it."

"Hunh!"

"That's what I say — hunh! Now, here he's come back rich, they say. That Englishman died, an' his son died, an' all their money went to Leaming. An' now she won't look at him, little goose-head! Well, all is. I told him to come in the evenin'."

"She needn't to look at him if she don't want to."

"She needn't to, aigh! You'd just as lieve she'd go an' take up with Mahlon Proudfoot, after all! She never will take a notion to anybody else if she mopes around after him forever. Leaming's the chance of a lifetime, if she'll make up with him. He ain't only cashier. He's a director, too, an' one o' the big stockholders. He just about owns the hull bank. That Sunday Mariella an' me dropped in to Mis' Mall'ry's — you may shoot me if they hadn't got him there to dinner. He was a-settin' a-lookin' as wretched. Isaphene was primped all up on the organ-stool, *in buff*, with her elbows in an' her shoulders up, a-playin' for all. He give one look at Mariella — an' he never took his eyes off o' her. When we said we must be goin', he jumps up an' says — 'I'll walk home with you.' If you could of see their faces! I thought they'd both have duck-fits. 'It ain't dark,' says Mis' Mall'ry. 'It aint *near* dark,' says Isaphene. 'Isaphene ain't sung for you yet.' 'I'll come again, if you'll let me,' he says, as polite as a basket o' chips. I says, 'Oh, pshaw, now, Mr. Leaming, it ain't necessary' — but he cut me short. 'But a great pleasure,' he says, lookin' at Mariella. An' her! — well, all is. The little mischief, she laughs right in his face. 'You'd better stay an' hear the music,' she says. 'Isaphene sings beautifully.' 'I'll be glad to hear her next time I come,' he says. 'We asked you to dinner an' spend the evenin',' says Mis' Mall'ry, kind of feeble. 'It was good of you to take pity on my loneliness,' says he, smiling and showing his teeth — I swan! I never see such white teeth. 'I'll beg you to ask me again sometime' — an' with that up he picks his hat. Isaphene looked as if she'd been drawed through a knot-hole; an' 's for Mis' Mallory's chin — well, you could of stepped on it! Their hands was just like bird claws when we shook hands. An' Mariella — she just walked along as cool as a cucumber. She wa'n't dashed. I didn't know what to do when we got to the gate. I was afraid to ask him in, for fear you'd be a-settin' by the fire with your shoes off, a-toastin' your chilblains — "

She stopped suddenly as the door opened. "That you, Mariella? Where you been till after dark this way?"

"Down on the beach," said Mariella. She took off her hat and drew her arms out of her jacket. She had grown into a tall, slender girl, and was possessed of a powerful attraction, which seemed to lie first in one charm and then in another. The great braids of bronze hair coiled loosely around her head gave her a queenly, distinguished look. The poise of her throat was beautiful. Her eyes were those deep, rich, brown ones which take the velvety red of old wine when the sun strikes into them. The coloring of her face and throat was exquisite. Her figure was delicately rounded, with no suggestion of her childish thinness.

"Down on the beach?" said Mrs. Palmer. "Hunh! A pretty time o' night for you to be down on the beach. It's a-gettin' so's it ain't safe for a girl to go a-traipsin' around alone the way you do."

"I'm not afraid," said Mariella, smiling.

"Oh, I know you ain't afraid o' anything. But it's gettin' terrible rough with all these strange men a-prowlin'. Anybody on the beach with you?" she asked, suddenly.

"No one."

"Well, you'd better light a fire in the parlor."

"In the parlor!" Mariella's face dimpled into interrogation-marks. She was not allowed to waste wood on fires in the parlor unless company was expected.

"Yes; somebody might come."

"Who?" asked the girl, briefly.

"Oh, I do' know; anybody. Oscar Nelson might; or Henry Bonning might; or" — Mrs. Palmer hesitated visibly — "Mr. Leaming might."

Mariella laughed.

"The sitting-room is good enough," she said, drawing a low rocking-chair to the fire and sinking lazily into it.

"You do beat all! It's good enough for Oscar Nelson or Henry Bonning, I'll allow; but it ain't good enough to set the cashier of a bank down into!"

"What's good enough for us," said the girl, calmly, but with a sudden flash in her eyes, "is good enough for the cashier in any bank. What do I care about cashiers in banks?"

"What do you care about cashiers in banks, aigh?" mimicked her mother, furiously. "Let me tell you, they don't grow on every tree — single, an' nice-lookin', an' danglin' after you. You hold your head a little too high, missy. I suppose if the governor come up here from Olympia, you'd think the settin'-room was good enough for him."

"It is — if he is the kind of man a governor ought to be," said Mariella, quietly. "It is much better than the parlor; it doesn't pretend to be nice. The parlor is horrid."

"You — ungrateful — mink!" Mrs. Palmer breathed deep and hard. "After the awful time I had to get it furnished! I peddled strawberries myself to buy that Brussels-carpet lounge an' them lace curtains. I milked cows, an' churned butter, an' sold it, to buy chairs an' a carpet. I fed hens, an' raised chickens, an' gethered eggs, to buy that org'n an' that org'n-stool; an' now you set there an' tell me to my face that the parlor is horrid. You're an ungrateful mink!"

A note in her mother's voice touched Mariella's heart. It was as if the woman's soul had been suddenly hurt and had spoken the hurt aloud. The girl felt herself shrink and turn pale. She was shaken with the helplessness of one who has selfishly wounded another, and has at hand no balm for the wound. But not a word of repentance could she speak. Her lips seemed frozen shut. The touch of sympathy for her mother was new; and it had come upon her unexpectedly. She could not remember a time when she had not seen through, and scorned, her mother's dual nature. She had always had the feeling that her mother was sincere only when she was in a rage. The characters of hostess, polite to effusiveness; affectionate wife; indulgent mother; faithful church member; obliging neighbor; catechism teacher—Mariella had come to consider these all assumed. There had seemed to her no grace in belonging to a church and continuing to do nearly all of the things which that church taught should not be done—in making fun of the creed of others and not living up to one's own; or in sitting up all night with a sick neighbor, only to come home in the morning and criticise the neighbor's household conveniences and mode of living.

But now, as her mother spoke in this new tone, she suddenly felt her blood singing in her ears. With a blur before her eyes she made her way hurriedly to the door.

"I'm going to bed," she said, speaking low and running her words together. "Good night."

CHAPTER XX

When Mariella reached her room in the attic she went straight to the window in the gable that overlooked the orchard. It was quite dark now. She stood there, silently looking out, and in a moment her eyes, which had seemed to go searching uncertainly here and there through the night, steadied their vision upon the object they sought.

A smile of tenderness came upon her lips; her eyes and her heart were tender, too. It was as if all her maidenly tenderness came out into sudden fragrant flower, as a lily might open its petals in the dark where no eye could behold it.

She stood for a long time watching the light. It neither moved nor wavered, but shone out across that dark mile to her, as brightly and unchangeably as constancy itself. After a while she turned back into the room, and groped around with her hands upon a little table for matches. She groped with her eyes closed tightly.

"Don't you ever sly around in the dark with your eyes open," her mother had once sternly admonished her, when she was a little girl. "Don't you ever let me ketch you. That's how come Helen Henderson got her blindedness. She went slyin' around in the dark, an' stooped down sudden an' struck both her eyes on the knobs in the footboard of the bed. It put 'em clean out. I hear —" her voice sank to tragic depths — "it mashed 'em both to a jell. I guess it's so; she wears

them blue goggles all over 'em, so's nobody can see 'em."

This awful tale had made such an impression upon the sensitive child that she had been unable to sleep for several nights because of the conviction that sometime, sooner or later, she would forget her mother's warning and stoop in the dark with her eyes open. The habit clung to her all through her girlhood, so that now she closed her eyes unconsciously as she bent over the table.

Her little lamp was well filled and trimmed, and the chimney was polished carefully. "There's just one thing Mariella never forgets," Mrs. Palmer often declared, half in praise and half in blame, "an that's her lamp. She most forgets her own name; but she fills and cleans that lamp like clockwork. She brings it down in the mornin' just as sure as she brings herself." Once she had mentioned it by chance to Mahlon's mother.

"Why, I declare!" exclaimed Mrs. Proudfoot, and her kind face fairly beamed. "If that isn't just like Mahlon! If I am not well, I can let any of his room work go but the lamp. It's the only thing ever makes him a bit impatient with me. He brings it down, too, every mornin', an' if I do happen to forget it till he's ready to light it he cries out—'Oh, mother! You went an' forgot my lamp again!' Then he goes an' takes it clear out behind the woodshed in the dark to fill it, so 'he won't tamper with the insurance.' I often tell him it would burn three nights, an' then's when he speaks up impatient. 'I want it *bright*,' he says, kind o' fierce, 'just as bright as I can get it.'"

The two women smiled together sociably over the common idiosyncrasy of their children, not suspecting that there was a reason for it.

When Mariella had lighted the lamp she drew back her white Swiss curtain, that the light might have a free path; then she sat down in her low cane rocker, close to the window, but a little to one side. She leaned her head back against her chair, with her hands lying loosely together in her lap. Her eyelids fell halfway over her eyes, like the curved petals of a lily, as her gaze went across the night; her slender white neck came out of her dark dress with the bending grace of a lily's stem. Her mother frequently lamented that she had not named her Lily. "If ever a mortal looked like one!" she would declare proudly to Mrs. Mallory. "She even turns herself around like one." And that lady would sniff and lift her eyebrows, and say, "Why, do you think so?"

In the year that followed the birth of the new town Mariella had changed rapidly in mind and character. She bloomed out like a rare rose that has been grafted on a common stem. She had not gone out into the world, but the world had come to her and woven its mesh about her.

At first she was confused by the strangeness of the society in which she found herself; but she was possessed of a certain dauntless something which carried her through.

Mrs. Palmer dwelt in wretchedness and wore anxiety for a daily garment. When Mrs. Laramier gave her historic reception, she sent cards to every one she had met. She had met Mariella, so cards were sent to her and her mother. Mariella, coming in one day, found her mother helplessly studying hers through her spectacles.

"What in the land does this thing mean?" she asked, relinquishing it with a long sigh. "'Mrs. P. D. Laramier, *at home*, Thursday, three to six!' That's too much for me. It might just as well be in Chinese."

"It's an invitation to a reception," said Mariella.

"Invitation!" Mrs. Palmer reached out stiffly. "Give it here. I'd like to know where the invitation comes in. It don't say 'will you come' or 'won't you come,' or 'can you come' anywheres on it."

"That's the way they send invitations," said Mariella, smiling. "We were taught that the last year at school."

"All is, it's a fool way," said Mrs. Palmer.

She dressed soon afterward, and went out without explanation as to her errand. When she returned, an hour afterward, she was breathing hard; her face was flushed with triumph.

"There!" she said, laying a large book on the table beside Mariella. "The next time any fool thing comes, I guess I'll know what it means. That's the best book on etyquette in town, an' it cost three dollars an' a ha'f! If it ain't good, it ought to be."

"Oh, mother!"

"That'll do now. I don't want one word. Mis' Mall'ry 'll be a-comin' in before night with a made-up errand, just to find out if we got a bid. I'll study that book till I go blind but what I won't let her out me. I bet I'll forget more in it than she ever knew."

Mariella smiled at that; but her face was red.

"Oh, mother, I don't like to read a book about how to behave. I should rather go and do just as others do."

"That's all very well to talk," replied Mrs. Palmer, firmly, turning the leaves in search of a chapter headed "Receptions"; "but I won't even know how to get there if I don't read about it first. I won't know whether to walk or pace or run! I won't know whether to hold my dress up in front, or behind, or on both sides at once! That's just what I paid three dollars an' a ha'f for this book for. I don't propose to have Mis' Mall'ry a-teeheein' behind my back."

Mrs. Palmer studied the book faithfully, making

Mariella read and explain all that she could not understand. She got through the reception without disaster, although Mariella trembled more than once. In the very door of the reception room she paused and stood as still as if rooted there. Her gaze was moving sternly over the room, full of gayly dressed women.

"I won't go in a step!" she announced fiercely, to Mariella. "Not a step. I'll balk right here. They ain't a one of 'em got on a Paisley shawl."

"It doesn't make any difference," replied Mariella, in an agonized whisper; her heart was beating in her throat. "You can't go back now. They are looking at us."

"Let 'em look! I won't go in a step. The book didn't say a word about a Paisley shawl. Pretty kind of a book, I must say! I'll take it back to-morrow. Three dollars an' a ha'f! An' not a word—"

"Oh, mother, do go on. They are looking—"

"I tell you, let 'em look. I won't go in a—"

The hall behind them had filled with ladies while she was talking and she was now pressed on in spite of her remonstrances, to Mariella's relief.

They were graciously welcomed by Mrs. Laramier and the ladies who stood with her, and presently made their way into the small, crowded room where the refreshments were served.

"You may shoot me," said Mrs. Palmer, in a hissing whisper, after a long look around the room, "if there's a chair in the whole room. Not a one! Do we have to stand up here like dumb loons?"

"Please, please, mother—"

"You can stop your 'please, pleasin'' me—now! The book didn't say a word about standin' up. My land, look at this!" she added helplessly, with a sound of near tears in her voice. "If they ain't holdin' their plates in one hand an' eatin' with the other! An' me with this Paisley shawl over both arms, an' the fringe a-danglin'! I know *now* why they didn't a one of 'em wear a Paisley shawl!"

An hour later Mrs. Palmer emerged from the crowded rooms, purple and perspiring.

"Pfew!" she said, making futile dashes at her neck with her kerchief. "That's the awfullest hour I ever went through. I'm wringin' wet. Of all tom-fool doin's! You ever drag me to another! You see Mis' Mall'ry? I see her — stiff an' ugly in a new alpaco. An' Isaphene a-pigeon-toein' along with her in buff, a-holdin' her head just so, an' her hands just so, like she learned at boardin'-school. Hunh! I'd rather go to a quiltin'-bee, or a church social, where they sew all the afternoon an' the men come in in the evenin' — any time! You ketch me at another!"

But in less than a week she had recovered so completely that she was watching the post for another card.

It was about this time that Mariella went one evening to the Pollards' on an errand. Returning at dusk, she suddenly found herself, upon turning a bend in the forest road, face to face with Mahlon Proudfoot. When he recognized her he uttered a cry of joy, and went stumbling forward to meet her. He was in his working-clothes, and she was dainty and sweet in a ruffled dimity dress. She was dismayed to find herself recoiling from him when he gathered her with eager, but trembling, arms to his breast.

"Oh, Mariella, Mariella!" he whispered passionately. "Kiss me! Kiss me! It has seemed like a thousand years since you kissed me!"

The girl trembled, too, in his arms, moved strongly by his ill-controlled emotion. She kissed him lightly, and put her arm up around his neck in the way he had been dreaming about for months. Then she drew away from him gently, all unconscious that her feeling as she did so was one of relief, and that the caress itself had been one of duty rather than inclination. The indefinable rapture of the kisses she had once shyly given Mahlon Proudfoot was not in this one.

"Let me look at you before it gets so dark I can't see you, Mariella," said Mahlon, holding her hands tightly, as if afraid of losing her. "Look at me" — his voice shook. "I want to see your eyes."

Mariella looked up at him and smiled kindly.

"Well, then," she said.

"Good God!" he cried out, with a kind of rough passion. "If you could look at me that way every day — every night! Every night — every night — for nearly two year I've dreamed that you come and stood alongside my bed and looked at me like that! I've seen your eyes just as kind and tender, and I've felt your breath on my face; and I've heard you say *Mahlon*, just as plain. But when I fling out my arms to you — you're always gone! Sometimes" — he hesitated and gripped her hands harder — "your eyes look sad, as if you pitied me about something — "

"Oh, Mahlon!"

"Yes. I never know what; but I wake up with something as heavy as a stun on my breast, and can't sleep any more that night."

The girl was deeply touched; yet at the same time she was conscious of shrinking away from the word "stun."

"You mustn't dream such foolish things," she said embarrassedly, not knowing what to say.

"They're not foolish, Mariella. I don't have hardly a thought but you all day, and I don't want a dream but you all night. I can't dream nice about you all the time, and I'd rather dream bad about you than not to dream about you at all."

Mahlon pronounced the last two words "a-tall." Mariella noticed it, and loathed herself at once for noticing it. "How could he be expected to pronounce words correctly?" she thought, with fierce self-reproach. "His parents talk that way, and he had to leave school and work. He doesn't talk half so badly as his parents or my parents."

For the first time she realized that, beside his love for her, her love for him was a small and mean feeling. A wave of guilt and shame swept over her.

"I don't deserve such love, Mahlon," she said remorsefully.

"I'll love you that way as long as I live," said Mahlon, simply. "I couldn't love you any different if I tried."

He hesitated a moment and then went on, as if talking to himself: "I don't expect you to love me the way I love you, Mariella. I've been alone so much the last year and a half that I've had a chance to think it all out. We love just according to our own hearts. There's no two ways about it. Some men — most men — if they're disappointed in love, get over caring after a while; I never would. It isn't in me to. I've built every thought for seven year, and every hope, on you; you've been in my heart all this time, and I never had a thought of any other girl. I couldn't get you out of my heart without tearing my heart out — "

"Oh, hush — hush! I don't want you to put me out of your heart, Mahlon."

She released one hand and drew the soft inner fulness of her fingers over his wrist soothingly.

"I know you don't. I'm just telling you; I'm just explaining how I feel about you. God knows I don't get much chance to tell you about it, and it'll make me happy when I'm sitting alone thinking about you to feel that you know it."

"Don't talk about sad things, Mahlon. I'll have to go in a minute."

"Are you going to leave me already?" he asked, almost roughly. "When I haven't even touched your hand for a year!"

"I must."

"Must!" He drew her toward him with powerful arms. "Don't you know I'm starving for your kisses, your breath? Don't you know that I suffer daily, hourly, without you? Don't you know that I fight myself, my passions, to keep myself away from you and do my duty to my parents? Oh, Mariella!"

He broke down suddenly and bowed his head upon hers, with sobs thick in his throat.

"Oh, Mariella! Before you go away again and leave me alone, and in such loneliness — tell me that I am doing right in denying myself happiness for my mother! Tell me! Sometimes I doubt it — and then I suffer the torments of hell."

"Hush, hush!" whispered the girl. "Of course it is right. I should hate you if you deserted your mother. She has only you to depend upon. We can wait; we are young."

"Thank God, Mariella!" He lifted up his head. "You do not fail me. You are my hope and strength. I can go on again now. But there is one thing more —"

"Let us walk on; it is getting late."

"No, I want to hold you here in my arms while I say

it." He drew her closer. "Mariella, you are young and enjoy company. I want you to have a good time. I can't go with you and take you to places, and a girl can't go alone. I want to prove to you how much I trust you. I want you to feel free to go with other young men —"

"Oh," said Mariella, quickly, drawing from him, "you want to go with other girls!"

"I'll never go with any girl but you," he replied gravely. "But you are young and enjoy parties and company. I want you to have a good time. You will have cares and to spare when you are my wife. I want to love you unselfishly — I'm bound to love you unselfishly. You can go with other men in a friendly way — they all want to go with you; I've had to face that for years, — and I'll always trust you and believe in you."

He hesitated, and then added, "Just as long as I see your light in the window; I'll know that means you are true to me."

It had cost Mahlon Proudfoot many a bitter night of torment to bring himself to say this. At first the mere thought of Mariella's walking through the soft spring darkness, late at night, with her hand on another's arm, had kindled fires of fiercest jealousy in his veins. His body and spirit had grappled together and fought it out.

It had been a long struggle. He remembered the torture of his school-days, when some other boy had walked up boldly and given Mariella a red apple, and she had thanked him with a smile and blush which Mahlon felt were stolen from him. Now that she was a woman and any man might desire her for his wife, the thought of standing aside and leaving her free had been a thousand times harder to face.

But he had faced it. He had been vanquished an hundred times; but Mahlon Proudfoot never gave up in a struggle with his lower self. "If I can't have a fine education," he kept saying, over and over in his heart, "I can be a man. I can conquer myself, and I will. That's an education of itself. Lots of college men never learned that." In the end he conquered.

"It's a poor love that can't trust, Mariella," he said. "I don't want to love you that way. I don't say I won't go through fire on account of it; but I do say that I know it's right, and I'm going to stand it, just as I stand paying off mortgages. Anybody can do pleasant things."

Then Mahlon Proudfoot had his reward. Mariella suddenly threw both arms around his neck, and leaned her slender body upon his breast in a rapturous abandon of love as sweet and spontaneous as it had been on that April night, years before, when Mahlon had first confessed his love for her. Her soft, cool cheek, pressed upon his, was wet with tears.

"Oh, Mahlon, Mahlon," she said, "I do love you, but I do not deserve you. I could not be so generous. I want all of you, and I would not share you with any one."

Mahlon strained her closer.

"That's the way I want you to love me. I don't want you to be willing to share me with any one. You couldn't make me happier than to say that, Mariella."

"But that isn't the way you love me."

"It's exactly the way I love you. My first thought is to get my hands on the throat of any man that pays you notice. That's the way I love you. But I had to overcome that feeling for your sake. I want you to have a good time while you are young and like to go out in company. You can't go alone. You can't go," —he dropped his face to hers again, shuddering,— "without men paying you attention and trying to make you love 'em—"

"No, no, Mahlon — "

"Don't deceive yourself, Mariella. Don't I know? A man can't look at you without going mad with love."

"You mustn't think because you love me — "

"Don't contradict me, dear. We have such a few minutes to talk. I know more about men than you do. The hell of my life till I can marry you 'll be knowing that men want you and try to get you, while I — God help me! — can't go near you. The heaven of it — "

"Yes, Mahlon?" Her hands caressed him softly.

"The heaven of it 'll be feeling sure they can't get you."

She lifted her head and looked at him steadily through the dusk. Her eyes burned like dark stars. The silence of the night was broken by the jarring musical note of a nighthawk. The rich perfume of wild musk was loose on the air about them. Mahlon never smelled it afterward without a swift thrill of ecstasy and a wild beat of his pulses.

"Mahlon," said Mariella, almost solemnly, for she was deeply moved by his devotion; "as long as you love me this way and want my love, I promise to be true to you. So do not doubt me."

Mahlon put his face down to hers, and held her a little while without speaking.

"I'll have to let you go now," he said, at last, and his voice trembled. "God knows when I'll see you again; but at least I've got something to live on again for a while. Good-by, dear; I mustn't go any farther, but I'll wait here till you're safe home."

He loosened his arms, and Mariella sped two or three steps from him; then she stood still. "Mahlon," she called softly.

"What-a-say?"

He reached her side with a bound; but for a moment

Mariella was speechless. His voice had such vibrations of tenderness in it that her very soul was shaken by it — but through it all she was conscious that he had said "What-a-say."

"I — I — only wanted to tell you good-by again," she faltered out at last, and then fled away through the shadows and left him standing there alone.

Mariella watched that night until she saw Mahlon's light; then she undressed, and, worn with the emotion of the unexpected meeting, crept into bed.

"Oh, God," she cried, passionately, burying her face in her pillow, "I know you'll hate me, and I hate myself — but, oh, I *wish* he wouldn't say 'What-a-say'!"

CHAPTER XXI

Two or three evenings after Mariella had met Leaming at the Mallorys', she was sitting by the big fireplace with her parents, when a low rap came upon the rattling door.

She arose, with a deep color flaming over her face and neck. Her parents had both made little wild leaps out of their chairs. Both started for the door at the same time with great strides.

"*Set down!*" exclaimed Mrs. Palmer, in a hissing whisper, seizing her husband's arm and trying to force him back into his chair. "*It's him!* Nobody ever knocked that way on that door. You don't look fit to be seen! My land! Hadn't you best go to bed? Them old suspenders!"

"Bed!" faltered back Mr. Palmer. "What for? Am I to be druv out of my own house?"

"Mule! He'll never come again after seein' you look that way. It's Leaming."

"What if it is! Let him in."

Mrs. Palmer smoothed the thunder out of her face, and opened the door.

"W'y, it's Mr. Leaming," she declared, in a tone of cordial surprise. "Step right in. Mariella."

Mariella smiled faintly. Mr. Leaming went across the room and took her hand, with a look of grave pleasure.

"I have found you at home at last!" he exclaimed. "Have you been hiding from me all these weeks?"

Mariella colored. "You have not seen my father, either," she said. "You would not accuse him of running away from you. Father," she added simply, "this is Mr. Leaming."

Mr. Palmer fairly jumped out of his chair and shook hands with Mr. Leaming.

"Well, how are you, Mr. Leaming. You're a cure for sore eyes. I reckon you never would of come back if it hadn't been for the boom. I tell you," he bragged, with twinkling eyes, "the boom brings 'em."

"It did not bring me, Mr. Palmer," said Leaming, smiling; "but I am glad to find it here, nevertheless."

"Set down," said Mrs. Palmer. "I'll build a fire 'n the parlor. It must of gone out."

She took some lamp-lighters made out of twisted paper from a cup on the mantel, and went, heavily and consciously, into the parlor.

"I saw you down on the beach," said Mr. Leaming, looking across Mr. Palmer at Mariella. "I tried to overtake you, but you walked too fast."

Mariella smiled. The firelight brought out the red velvet of her eyes. "It was getting dark."

"She's a regular sandpiper," spoke up her father. "Run? She can run like a killdeer! How's things down town? Corner lots gone up any?"

Mr. Leaming looked bored. He had not come to talk shop. One could talk shop when Mariella was not looking at one with those marvellous eyes.

"Yes," he said, "Hill was here to-day. That stirred things up."

"I want to know! Hunh!" Mr. Palmer's blue eyes beamed upon his visitor. He rubbed his thumb and his

forefinger together with a little irritating noise, which was broken at regular intervals by a snap.

"Hill's a reg'lar hummer, ain't he? He don't let grass grow under his feet, I can tell you. Wilson Benner ain't very fur behind him for makin' things hum. W'y, tic-douloureux! I was a-talkin' to a poor relation o' Benner's that was here when the town first started, an' if I'd of followed her advice! I swan! I'd be ownin' banks myself now. She was reel clever to me. She says, 'Don't you tell a soul I said so, but you buy lots. Buy lots — an' keep a-buyin'. I asked Cousin Benner how much of a town 'u'd be built here; an' he stood around, an' says, "You keep a still tongue in your head an' buy lots, buy lots"' — but I was too much of a durn ijjit to believe her. She went ahead an' bought lots at a couple o' hundred apiece, and pretty soon she was a-sellin' 'em at two-three, three-four thousand apiece. She makes more money 'n any man in town. She just buys an' sells. She'll walk right up to a passel o' men all talkin' reel estate, an' the first thing they know she's chipped right in like a chipperdale bird, a-offerin' em a bargain in corner lots. I never see her beat. You know her?"

Mr. Leaming stiffly admitted that he did.

"I expect she banks with you?"

Mr. Leaming failed to recognize the interrogation-point.

"It's worth a farm to see a New York dandy's face the first time she buttonholes him on the street an' begins to talk reel estate an' corner lot at him! These here tenderfeet, they give me seventeen tickles! A woman boomer just gets away with 'em —"

He paused in the middle of a sentence and stared in open-eyed, questioning amazement at his wife. She had returned to the room, and was making furious signs at him behind the visitor's back to keep still and not monopolize the conversation.

"So — that — a — So — that — a —" he kept saying over and over, struggling to continue his discourse and at the same time make out the meaning of the dumb show.

"The fire's all lit," announced Mrs. Palmer, coming around to the front. "The parlor 'll be all het up d'rec'ly."

"What was you wantin', mamma?" queried her husband, in his company tone, still looking mystified.

Mrs. Palmer felt that she must shout "Dry up!" at him. As it was, she looked it at him.

Before she could reply, however, there was another rap upon the door. This was a welcome interruption to the momentary embarrassment. She opened the door.

"How are you, Mis' Parmer?" spoke up a woman's voice outside.

"W'y, — I — declare!" said Mrs. Palmer, with feeble hospitality. "If it ain't Mis' Worstel. I — declare! At this hour?"

The visitor stepped right in. She was thin, of medium height, and of middle age. She wore a full, blue dress-skirt, reaching just to her shoe tops, a black cloth cape, and a queer black bonnet, with a blue ribbon rosette set on the very front of it. Her thin face was all glow and animation. She moved with short, quick movements. She seemed to be enveloped in fresh particles of outdoors, which shook loose from her as she went about the room, shaking hands.

"How are you, Mr. Parmer? He'll be here in an hour or so. He had business down town, so I come along by, to set awhile. Well, Mariella? You well? You ain't got married yet? I ain't see you for a coon's age. . . . Mr. — aigh, what's the name? I didn't ketch the name. Leaming? I'm honored. You in the bank? I've see you through the window. He's met you. He 'tends to all the business we have at the bank. We do most of our trading in that way at the post-office. Well, Mis' Parmer?"

"Have a seat?" said Mrs. Palmer, in a cold way. "It must be chillish outdoors."

"It is so." She sat down, and taking a black cloth bag on her lap, commenced pulling out the drawing-string.

"He come home to-day an' said he'd heard you had a touch o' rheumatiz. I said, 'Oh, I'll hasten right over there to-night, swift, an' let her try my Oxydonor Victory.' It'll cure anything on earth. It ain't a medicine. It's a kind of an egg-shaped instrument. You put it in a pitcher of cold water, and then you see this long wire. This elastic is buckled around the ankle" — she stopped talking suddenly and looked at Mr. Leaming. "Ever see one?"

Mr. Leaming had never had that pleasure.

"It's terrible fine. Cures everything. I couldn't live without it. You wear it five hours a day, or a night — it don't make any difference which."

"No, I guess not," said Mrs. Palmer, with a sniff of contempt.

"I declare, you must try it. I'd be condemned if I didn't lend it to you to try. As sure's you try it, you'll buy one."

"How much is it?" asked Mr. Palmer, in a discouraging tone.

Mrs. Worstel turned to him. Her eager eyes beamed upon him.

"Only twenty-five dollars. You'll save it in doctor bills in no time. I cured the salt-rheum on myself; an' the stun cancer on him — yes, he had a stun cancer;

every doctor that see him give him up; he'd got so he weighed terrible — an' this cured him; an' the children all had mumps an' scarlet fever — this Oxydonor Victory cured 'em — "

"I ain't much faith in a thing that cures all outdoors an' in, too," said Mrs. Palmer. "I ain't one o' the faithful kind myself."

"You will be. You just try this. I feel ten years younger. It'll cure anything down from a case o' consumption or pneumony. It — "

Mrs. Palmer was seized with a violent spell of coughing. Mrs. Worstel fidgeted in her chair, but finally settled down with a resigned air until the attack should subside. Suddenly she leaned forward with a start. Her eyes glowed.

"You're coughin' terrible," she said eagerly, almost triumphantly. "This 'll cure you. This 'll — "

"Mariella," spoke up her mother, from the depths of her assumed strangulation, "I guess the parlor is all het up. I guess Mr. Leaming don't care much about stun cancers an' Oxydonor Victorys. I guess you might as well take him in the parlor an' entertain him."

Mr. Leaming arose at once with an air of relief, Mariella with a frown of embarrassment.

The parlor was a big square room with the indescribable odor of the unused parlor pervading it. Mariella disliked the room, and entered it only when compelled to do so. Her mother had completed its furnishing before Mariella was old enough to assist.

The floor was covered with a carpet largely figured in brilliant scarlets and greens. The walls wore a paper out of whose dark background started flame-colored roses. "It don't look just right with the carpet," Mrs. Palmer had said, with a perplexed air, studying the effect with half-closed eyes when the paste was dry

— she had papered the room herself. "The figgers are both red, but they don't seem to go just right together. I can't see what ails 'em!"

There were several rugs. Some were made out of braided rags sewed together, round and round, until large enough. Others, and these predominated, were made of men's clothing cut into points and worked, like buttonholes, around the edges with colored yarns. These points were sewed on a heavy foundation of gunnysacking in such wise that each point fell between, and a little behind, two other points. These rugs were lying before the organ, the bookcase, the centre table, and wherever unusual use might befall the carpet. The polished walnut of the table was concealed by a gorgeous "crazy" cover of silk and velvet pieces, embroidered with letters and unimaginable designs.

The organ stood in one corner. It was a high organ. Little shelves started out unexpectedly here and there over it. It had nineteen stops, two knee-swells, and four pedals, two wide ones and two narrow ones. A vase on one end of the organ held a tall bouquet of money-plant; one on the opposite end held a tall bouquet of "pearly everlasting" flowers. There was a hair wreath in a deep frame on the wall. There was a landscape made of feathers. There was a white wax cross, twined about with a green vine, under a glass case. There were several "enlarged" family portraits — one of Mrs. Palmer, in all her finery, with her Paisley shawl falling coquettishly away from one shoulder, and her hair curled, and a self-conscious look across her eyes; and one of Mr. Palmer, stiff and wretched, with one prong of the head-rest sticking out over his ear and maledictions in his eyes, with a frown of bashful pain on his brow, his chin held high above the prick of the starched collar, and his tie askew. There were crocheted tidies everywhere: on the organ, on the organ-stool, on the chair backs, and on the Brussels-carpet lounge. There were green Holland shades and coarse lace curtains over the windows. A big brass lamp hung from the ceiling; a china shade, painted with crimson poppies, was suspended above it.

Mariella was fifteen years old when this lamp made its advent. She laughed when she first saw it. "The red in the poppies doesn't match the carpet, nor the paper, nor *anything*," she said.

"You little heifer!" her mother had responded promptly. "You'll talk about reds a-matchin', will you? The awful time I've had a-gettin' a parlor together that'll be fit for you to take young men beaux into!"

And Mariella had scornfully retorted, "Young men fiddlesticks!"

Accidents were always happening to things in the Palmer household. The narrow strip of walnut that folded over the edges of the organ keys had been broken off, revealing the ends of the keys. These ends were not covered with ivory, and the wood had turned yellow. This gave the organ the appearance of having drawn back its lips in a snarl and showing its teeth.

To Mrs. Palmer's unspeakable dismay, Mrs. Worstel at once arose and walked into the parlor after Mariella. She slipped the drawing-string of her bag over her arm, and fairly beamed upon everything in the room.

"Well, I declare!" she said. "This is reel nice. I never get an invite in here myself," she added, with a confidential nod and wink at Mr. Leaming. "It's kept shut up in a bandbox. It's sacred for Mariella's beaux — oh, yes, an' the minister. I guess he sees the inside of it. I come a laugh on Mis' Parmer about her parlor every time I come here. She's so secluded with it. My, oh, me! She secludes all her best friends from her parlor — she's so afraid somethin' 'll get hurt."

She turned to beam pleasantly upon her hostess; but the beam was not warm enough to penetrate the inch of frost coating that lady's face. She stood in a stiff, temporary attitude, just inside the door.

"Shall we go back an' keep him company?" she asked, with bitter politeness.

"I want to see your parlor first. W'y, me-O! Can't Mariella an' her beau find time enough to spark after I'm gone?" she asked, with an injured air.

Mariella, herself, having overcome her embarrassment, was trembling with laughter. "Won't you sit down, Mrs. Worstel?" she asked sweetly, ignoring her mother's frowns. "You might persuade Mr. Leaming to try an Oxydonor Victory. Do you ever have any aches or pains?" she asked, turning to him with eyes full of enchanting fun.

"Never," he replied, smiling, and beginning to see the humor of the situation, now that she was pointing it out to him.

"Never have *anything?*" queried Mrs. Worstel, fumbling with the drawing-strings of the bag. "Consumption, pneumony of the lungs, ja'ndice, ague, colds — don't you ever ketch cold? It'll cure a cold in twenty-four hours! — sore throat, chilblains — say, he cured every chilblain he had! Oh, it's just wonderful! The doctors hate it like poison. . . . I'm going to leave it for you to try, Mis' Parmer, whether or no. Just put it in a pitcher of cold water an' buckle this elastic around your ankle, an' go to bed. You'll wake up *well.* I expect you'll have to let out this elastic some," she added, with a reflective air, as if mentally comparing Mrs. Palmer's charms with her own.

There was a stamping and a scraping of feet out on the porch.

"W'y, blessed land!" cried Mrs. Worstel, gathering

herself out of her chair. "If he ain't come for me! A'ready! I ain't got ha'f through a-telling you what an Oxydonor Victory will do for you. . . . Well, I'll step into the bank some day, Mr. — Mr. Randall. — Sir? Oh, Leaming; much obliged — an' see if you don't want one o' these to try. If you never have anything, maybe somebody else in the bank does. . . . Yes, father, I'm a-coming. Why don't you let me be? I never see a man that didn't get in a stew an' holler out, 'Come on, now!' to his women-folks, just the minute *he's* ready to go. Men are awful dumb about such things, Mariella. They're so dumb that sometimes I think they want to be dumb. Well, good-evening, Mariella; come an' see me. . . . Good-evening, Mr. Randall. . . . Well, Mis' Parmer?" — she began laughing in a good-natured, infuriating way. "I'm glad I got to see the inside o' your bandbox. I declare, it's reel nice. How much a yard was your carpet?"

"I don't remember."

"Well, there! You had it long as that? An' I never even saw it. Your things don't match terrible well; but it's reel nice. Your table is walnut, ain't it? What did you have to pay to get a table like that, may I ask?"

"Fifteen dollars," replied Mrs. Palmer, with bitter reluctance.

Mrs. Worstel lifted her eyebrows and kept them up. "Fifteen? Well, me-*O!*"

She hesitated, and lingered. Once she made a movement toward the door. Then she turned and gave a long, deprecatory look at the table. "Yes, father," she called out, "I'm a-coming. Keep still, can't you? Fifteen? . . . You paid a plenty for it, didn't you? I got to go, or he'll have a tew. He nearly tews his head off, if I keep him waiting. I'd give anything to cure him of tewing — "

"Buckle the Oxydonor around his ankle, and put him to bed," called Mariella, saucily. But her mother fairly pushed Mrs. Worstel out of the room before she could retort, and closed the door.

CHAPTER XXII

When Mariella found herself alone with Mr. Leaming, she felt her embarrassment returning. She had loved him dearly when she was a little girl; yet now he seemed so strange that she did not know what to say to him.

Leaming, also, found the situation difficult. He had expected a warm welcome from her; but at first he had felt that she avoided meeting him, and her air of reserve and diffidence when he met her at the Mallorys' had increased his disappointment. He had always remembered her, and had hoped that, when he returned, he would find the promise of her childhood fulfilled. He had even hoped that she would develop into a woman whom he might love and marry. It was this hope that had brought him back.

His eagerness to meet her after his return was increased by her avoidance of him. He had fleeting glimpses of her that revealed her unusual beauty and grace. His impatience to meet her increased daily. He had not expected to be put at a distance and kept there.

The meeting had been easy enough while others were present; but now that they were for the first time alone together, he was conscious that he was most absurdly embarrassed.

He hesitated to break the silence, for it suddenly seemed to him one of the great moments of his life. He was on the verge of discovering whether the girl had developed into the unusual, or whether her hard life had narrowed her into the groove of the commonplace.

But break the silence he must.

"I find everything very different, Mariella," he said, looking about the room. "I remember one or two pictures, but everything else seems changed."

The sound of his voice gave her courage. She turned toward him, and gave him a long, asking look. She tried to smile, but her nerves were so tense that her lips only trembled.

"You are changed, too," she said.

"And you, Mariella," he said kindly. Her eyes fell; her hands were clasped closely together in her lap.

"Of course I am changed," she said, still with her eyes cast down, "but not so much as you — not in the way you are changed. You have been away in a different world."

She lifted her eyes unexpectedly, and gave him a look that was at once wistful and appealing.

A feeling of quick sympathy and understanding possessed him. "Oh, Mariella!" he exclaimed. Involuntarily he arose, and, going to her, took one of her clasped hands out of her lap, and holding it in one hand, stroked it tenderly with the other, as he had done so often to soothe her when she was a child.

The color came up into her face. It seemed to spring up in beating waves, each deeper than the ones before it. As a child, she had been able to bear his anger without tears, but not his tenderness. Now, at his first touch of sympathy, she felt the tears coming. She tried to hold them back, but they filled her eyes full and fell upon her hand and Leaming's.

She dropped her burning face upon his arm, and let them fall without restraint.

"I was mistaken," said Leaming, presently, in a low

voice. "I thought you were changed, but you are not. You are the same little sensitive girl."

He said no more then, until the color had burned itself out of her face and the tears had ceased to fall.

When she had drawn away from him, he said, still holding her hand: "Why did you never write to me? Do you think it did not hurt to have the little girl of my heart treat me with such indifference?"

His reproachful tone made her heart ache dully.

"I suppose it is useless to try to make you understand how your going made me suffer," she said. "I was a lonely, sensitive child, and you were the only one who helped me; who understood my lawless nature, my violent temper; the only one who could interest me; the only one who seemed — I say seemed — to love me." She hesitated, remembering Mahlon; then she went on: "You were all the world to me. I worshipped you. I was bitterly jealous of every little girl you spoke to or noticed. When you went I suffered so passionately I could not forgive you. I could not write to you. I used to try, — at first, — but something always came up into my throat and set me to trembling so I could not hold my pen. It must have been unforgiveness."

"Did you know how hard it was for me, too?" he asked presently.

Her lip curled with her old scorn. "For you? A man! Hard to go out and face the world, and learn? If it was hard for you to leave me, think what it must have been for me — a poor lonely child in what they call the backwoods — to have you go!"

There was a silence. Her voice had broken in a sob.

"Forgive me, little girl," he pleaded then, very gently. "I am only now beginning to realize what you suffered. I was selfish — all men are; yet there has not been a day that I have not thought of you, and wondered what

kind of a woman you were growing to be. What I did seemed the only thing I could do. . . . I found my benefactor dying, slowly; he lingered for months. When he died, he made me promise to remain as long as his son, who had an incurable malady, lived; it might be weeks, months, or years, the doctor said; but he had left me all his fortune at his son's death; he had been a father — more — everything to me. I could not refuse to stay. The son grew more and more like a brother to me. I took care of him, travelled with him, managed his estates. He died a few months ago. . . . Now you know all, or nearly all — all that can be told here and now. Can you forgive me for what I have made you suffer?"

She looked up at him with a grave movement of her lips that was hardly a smile, yet tried to be one.

"You expect five minutes' repentance to make up for seven years' forgetfulness!" she said, with a flash of her old scorn. "Well" — she smiled now — "I've not forgiven you yet. Maybe I will sometime. I'll tell you when I do."

Leaming put her hand down in her lap again, and seating himself, regarded her intently.

"I wonder how I could have thought you changed. You are the same. Your moods always did change as rapidly as the fire in an opal, but you yourself do not change. You are the only Mariella."

Her mouth curved into saucy lines.

"Oh, but I have changed. My temper is not half so bad. Even mother gives me a little grudging praise now and then." She laughed in sudden remembrance. "If Gus were here now, and called you my sweetheart, and teased me about you, I should hesitate about throwing potatoes at him and calling him a fool — really, I should."

Leaming felt his face slowly redden. As Mariella regained her ease, he grew more embarrassed.

"How furious he used to make me!" she went on, still with laughing, reminiscent eyes, from which all traces of tears had vanished. "But I forgave him long ago."

"Oh! One must be an hired man to win your forgiveness!"

She laughed outright. At the thought of her mother's pride in "the cashier," beautiful mirth dimples flashed out in her cheeks.

"Yes," she said, "a cashier —"

"I beg your pardon, but I am filling the cashier's place only until we can find one that is satisfactory."

"Oh!" The scornful curve came back to her mouth. "Then there's no hope for you. I might in time forgive a cashier — but never a president."

He felt himself coloring again.

"You used to forgive your teacher in the old log schoolhouse, Mariella," he said, smiling gravely. "But let us stop talking nonsense. I am glad to see that you have an organ. I remember it was the wish of your heart when you were a child."

"I have had it several years."

"Do you play?"

"Not well."

Her eyelids fell over her eyes to hide the sudden mischief in them. "I couldn't think of playing for you after Isaphene Mallory had played for you."

Her eyelids flickered and lifted; he saw a thousand little laughter devils in her eyes. "I might show you the album," she said. She drew it between them on the table, and went through it with him as she had seen Semia and Isaphene do when young men came to see them.

"That's my grandmother. Do you think she looks like my mother?"

"Very much," he assented wretchedly.

Mariella did not offer the information that it was her father's mother. "And this is my grandfather. Aren't his whiskers dear? And this is my father's sister's sister-in-law's baby." She glanced at him obliquely; he was perfectly serious. "Isn't it cunning? Why do they have babies taken with their mouths open? And this" — she held the leaf at a little scared girl — "is — yes, it is" — she turned now and gave him one of her deep, long looks — "it is *I*. Don't you think I was sweet — then?"

Mr. Leaming admitted with warmth that he did.

"See what dear shoulders I had" — she placed the faintest emphasis on the had, but uttered it in such a way that it seemed as if a question-mark belonged after it. "And dimples in them, too?" She turned the leaf, hiding the pretty bare shoulders and arms. "This is the minister. He's dreadful. He's a Presbyterian. He thinks awful things are going to happen to me. There's a new Episcopal minister, isn't there?" she asked, innocent of the distinction between minister and clergyman.

"Yes," said Leaming, "but I attend the Unitarian church — that is, when I attend any, which is seldom. They have a good choir. Do you know Mrs. Flush?"

Mariella did not know Mrs. Flush — "the gay Mrs. Flush," she was called. There had scarcely been a day since Kulshan was founded that she had not heard Mrs. Flush's name mentioned.

The Flushes had come from somewhere in the East. Mr. Flush was a banker. Mrs. Flush was about thirty, but she did not look more than twenty. She had golden hair and dark eyes, and the most innocent, appealing look imaginable. She dressed stylishly and carried herself with such an air that no man ever passed her without taking a second look at her.

The Flushes had hastily built a home. They entertained lavishly. They seemed to have a great deal of money. Mrs. Flush's innocent and appealing look was reserved for men. With women she assumed the haughty and snobbish manner which always indicates that a woman has known what it is to be snubbed, and has come to consider it more comfortable to take the initiative in this practice. Such women are always to be met in the society of a new mining, or a new railroad, town.

"Mrs. Flush takes a great interest in the church," said Mr. Leaming. "I'll introduce you to her, if you'll come to church."

"What an inducement!" said Mariella, laughing with the quick scorn she never could control just at the first second. "I have seen her several times. We were introduced once, but she has never recognized me since."

"One who is strange in a place meets so many," he said apologetically. "You'll like her when you know her."

Mariella returned mischievously to the album.

"Here's Isaphene — Isaphene dressed for a dance! Isn't she dear and precise? Every lock of her hair lies in the right place. How can some girls keep their hair so smooth? I can't."

"I hope you will not try," said Mr. Leaming, with an involuntary glance at her loose, heavy braids and rebellious curls.

Mariella glanced sidewise at him. She was beginning to forgive him. There was a kind of dignified strength in him that compelled her respect. She had never until that year known any society save that of the neighborhood — the Sunday visit, the church sociable, the school entertainment, the summer picnic, the occasional dance.

But the people who came to the new town of Kulshan were from all parts of the world. They were all sorts and conditions of people. Mariella had attended dances and receptions from the first; and she soon realized the difference between her old provincial life and this gay cosmopolitan society.

She looked now at Mr. Leaming with interest. She liked the grave lines about his mouth, and the steadiness with which he returned her searching look.

She turned another leaf and came full upon Leaming's picture — Leaming as he had looked seven years before — young, even boyish. She turned the leaf quickly. But for the first time he showed interest in the album. He put out his hand and turned back the leaf.

"Ah, who is this?"

"He was a teacher — when I was a child. He was very dear to me, but he went away and left me."

"Oh," said Mr. Leaming, with a start, flushing; "is it I?"

They sat in silence, then, looking at the picture. It was one which he had entirely forgotten. The sight of it gave him keener memories of his youth than he had had for many years. As for Mariella, her thought went across the darkness of the night to the little lonely girl who had sobbed herself to sleep on the night Leaming left for England.

He had written faithfully at first; but she had been too hurt by his going to reply. He had finally written to her father, and had asked him about Mariella. How was she doing at school, and at home? Why did she never write to him?

Mr. Palmer had laboriously indited the following reply:

"Dear Sir and Friend:—I have received your letter. We are all well and glad to here you are the same Mariella is a doing well at school She is as smart as a steal-trap she gives them all dust The little Mallory gal she can't hold a candel to Mariella no sir Ely or any other She is a little clever to Semy since you went away Semys ma is a having elecktrick belt spells these days she will go and have more spells to git the belt then the belt cud kure her of if it went intoo the kuring bisness for the rest of its life

"I'm willing to bet my best harro the one with the spring sete that them their spells will kill that poor antie before they kill the speller You remember that blak heffer we had not a white hare on her well sir shes had a caff as white as any duv not a blak hare on it

"Hopping that you are enjoying good helth when you git this with best respex from Mariella and her ma I remane your truely sir and friend

"Jerry Palmer"

After that no word reached her from Learning. Then came Mahlon Proudfoot's love to fill her life. Gradually the thought of Learning had faded with the years. When she did think of him, it was with a dull sense of injury.

Now he was sitting beside her; but he seemed like a stranger to her. After a while she went on turning the pages slowly. When the last one had been reached, she closed the album and looked at him. His face was perfectly serious.

He was, in fact, both bored and disappointed. He had expected to find the girl provincial in many ways. With her parents and environments, he told himself that he must be prepared for it, that it was inevitable. But he had not expected anything so bad as the family album. She had acted the part so well that his spirits sank low.

He stood up. "It is late," he said, formally. "I must apologize for staying so long."

Mariella arose, too, and stood before him. Her eyes were cast down. She had long brown lashes, and they rested now upon her cheeks. Once in a while, when she was shaken with repressed mirth, the most enchanting dimples flashed across her face and were gone as if they had never been. Leaming looked down just in time to see a flight of them disappear. He knew them of old.

"Mariella," he said at once, "look at me."

She lifted her eyes.

"You are laughing at me!"

"How can I help it? You took it so seriously."

"What?"

"The album. You looked so wretched. I was only doing a little character sketch. I have studied Isaphene dozens of times when she has been showing her album. It is considered an accomplishment; and through it all you were so polite—and so wretched!"

He stood looking at her a full minute without speaking, so amazed and so relieved was he. At last he smiled reluctantly.

"I am coming again," he said quietly, "and please bear in mind that I am not the only one in need of forgiveness."

"W'y, are you going *so soon?*" exclaimed Mrs. Palmer, getting to her feet, stiffly. "W'y, it's only ten o'clock. Father's gone to bed, but he always goes early. Sir? Oh—yes, indeed; come just as often as you can. Mariella, I guess she'll ruin her eyes, a-settin' around so a-readin' evenin's. She just reads and reads. Well.

Look out for the step at the end of the porch — w'y, it's terrible dark! Have the lantern?"

"Oh, no, indeed; thank you."

"Now do. It'll only take a minute. I'd feel condemned to let you go away in the dark so."

But Mr. Leaming was firm. If his life depended upon its cheering rays, he would not go home with a lantern making a myriapod of him in his shadow.

It seemed as if Mrs. Palmer could not let him go. "Well, be sure you come again soon," she said, filling up the doorway with her dark bulk. When he had disappeared, finally, she came in and closed the door.

She sat down, breathing hard. "That's a terrible triumph," she said, and there was a crow of that triumph down in her throat. "I'd like you to see Mis' Mall'ry's eyes, when I tell her how long he stayed. I know just how to bring it in. I'll tell her as easy an' ca'm as if cashiers 'n banks grew on trees."

"Oh, mother!" said Mariella, shrinking.

"Well, if it ain't a triumph, I'd like to know what it is. Here he's come a dozen times; an' the first time he found you at home, he's stayed till nearly midnight."

"What if he has, mother? It is provincial to suppose that the first time a gentleman goes to see a young lady, he — he — "

"Oh, you hush! The only man of any style that's ever looked at you! You keep your chin up in the air, an' you'll drive your pigs to a pretty market, or die an old maid."

"I'd rather be an old maid fifty times over, than to have all this talk about marrying."

Her eyes fell, and she hesitated; then she went on. "Get married and slave, and raise children!"

"Yes, an' then have 'em turn around an' sass you an' abuse you," said her mother, bitterly. "That's the way.

That's all the thanks a body ever gets for slavin' for their children."

Mariella looked at her mother under level brows.

"My conscience is surely as clear as yours, mother," she said. "I have surely treated you as well as you have treated me."

"Oh, you talk so! Here you turn up your nose at a cashier 'n a bank — an' then talk about your conscience! That's a pretty way to treat your parents, when they want to see you make the best match 'n town. Ain't I just slaved my soul out to get that parlor fixed up, so's you'd have some place to take young men beaux into when they come?"

"You know I wouldn't care if no young man ever looked at me," said Mariella, furiously. Then a smile came reluctantly to her lips. "Unless Semia wanted him."

"Oh, *talk!*" cried her mother, helplessly. "What are you goin' to do when you're left all alone in the world? Your pa is a-gettin' along in years, an' he can't last always; an' I'm a-gettin' no-account; an' you're a little delicate thing — you ain't worth shucks. You could no more do the housework 'n you could *fly*. Your pa ain't worth so terrible much property but what you'll have to do somethin', when him an' me can't work any longer. What you goin' to do?"

The girl turned her head from side to side.

"I don't know," she said. "Don't worry about me. I'll get along somehow."

"That's a pretty way to talk. You'll let this cashier slip through your fingers. You act the *dumb*-head so! They don't grow on trees. Here he only met you once an' went to danglin' right away. You wouldn't act the loon so, if he hadn't went an' put fool-notions in your head, while you was little; goin' out 'n the woods to study birds an' flowers two-three, three-four days out of a week. Lots o' good it ever done you! You don't make much money by it. He'd better learned you something so's you could make a little money. You ain't worth your salt. But he was the only one ever could keep you out of mischief."

"I might have done something — been something — if he had not gone away," said Mariella, with emotion. "His is the only refining influence I ever had."

"Oh, that's right. Ta'nt your mother — ta'nt your mother! I ain't got any feelin's. Ta'nt away. I'm coarse an' uneducated. I never had any refinement or education to teach to you, or I'd of worked the flesh off my finger-bones a-teachin' it to you. But I *have* got feelin's —"

Her face worked convulsively; tears filled her eyes and rolled down her cheeks.

"Mother — *mother!*" cried the girl. She ran to her mother, and, throwing her arms around her, kissed her tenderly. Then she went quickly out of the room.

CHAPTER XXIII

Mrs. Pollard was sitting, propped up with pillows, on the lounge one pleasant afternoon. Semia was washing dishes in the kitchen; the door between the two rooms was open. Mrs. Pollard was in a hard "fishing spell," and auntie was sitting upright beside her, fanning patiently.

"Oh, my Lord," moaned Mrs. Pollard, "will I ever live through this spell! Did any poor mortal ever suffer the way I suffer? Oh, what a welcome relief death 'u'd be."

"Oh, sister," quavered auntie, "don't you take on so. You work yourself up so. What would the rest of us do if you was to be taken?"

Mrs. Pollard opened her eyes suddenly. "Aigh?" she said.

"W'y, I say what would the rest of us do if you was to be taken? Think of that."

Mrs. Pollard looked bewildered. She was stricken with a thought that had never presented itself, nor been presented, before.

"I do' know," she replied, in the tone of one who weighs a mighty question. "Fan hard."

Auntie fanned hard.

Semia appeared at the open door. She was drying a plate with a tea-towel. She had grown into a tall. pretty girl. She wore a blue gingham dress and a white apron, with jaunty straps that were tied in pretty bows on her shoulders.

"Mrs. Worstel's coming."

"Oh — my — goodness!" Mrs. Pollard cast a rapid glance around the room. "The room looks so. It looks like all. How near is she?"

"Oh, right in the yard. The room's all right. Don't worry about the room."

"Well, there!" announced Mrs. Worstel, putting her head in at the open door. "It's only me. Well. You sick again? Poor sufferin' soul! I know all about it. I've been a sufferer all my life."

There is always in the tone of one making this announcement a note of triumph that is indescribable. It is not like any other triumph on earth. It holds itself haughty and aloof from other cases of triumph.

"Ain't I glad I come! I didn't know it was one of your spellin' days, so I thinks, says I, well, I'll go over an' set with Mis' Pollard."

Mrs. Pollard received her visitor without enthusiasm. "Well," she said, between hard breathings, "you, is it? Have a chair?"

Mrs. Worstel sat down and began pulling off her black woollen gloves.

"I can't stop fannin' long enough to take your things," said auntie, apologetically. "Semy!" She lifted her thin voice so high it quavered and broke, making her cough. "Come an' take Mis' Worstel's things. I can't leave off fannin'."

"I can't stay so terrible long," said Mrs. Worstel, cheerfully. "How is your lung to-day? I thought I'd come in an' set a spell."

Without waiting for a reply she arose to give Semia her cape and hat. She rolled her gloves carefully together. Then she sat down again.

"I've been to the revival meetin' this morning," she said. "I wish you could of been there."

"It's a-feeling worse to-day," said Mrs. Pollard, coldly. "It's a-aching me."

"There wa'n't a man out — not a one! The church was full of women. They go three times a day, I bet, seven days a week; an' the revival runs two or three weeks at a time. They go the whole during time."

"I coughed terrible last night," said Mrs. Pollard. "I coughed till I couldn't sleep for coughing. Every five minutes. If ever a mortal suffered!"

"I want to know," said Mrs. Worstel, absently, but with perfect politeness. She beamed pleasantly upon the invalid and the pale, fanning auntie.

"You must get tired," she said to the latter. "It must make your arm ache you." Then she turned back to Mrs. Pollard. "How did you say your lung was a-feeling?"

"It's in an awful condition." Mrs. Pollard's face had an injured expression, as if she had suffered in vain. "I'm a-going by inches!" she declared, with a kind of triumphant fierceness. "Oh, my Lord! if ever a poor mortal suffered from the cradle to the grave, it's me! Fan hard."

Mrs. Worstel's face brightened. She leaned forward suddenly and said, "If you won't tell a soul, I'll throw off my profit and sell you one for twenty dollars."

"One what?"

"W'y, Oxydonor Victory, of course."

Mrs. Pollard opened her eyes and smiled feebly. "Do you sell 'em for your health?" she asked, with irony, between gasps.

"No," said Mrs. Worstel, with prompt humor, "for *your* health."

"Well, I don't want none of your humbug things. You don't go a-bucklin' your humbug things around *my* ankle. They may cure the kind of ails you have — but they don't cure Lord-sent mortal ails. My ail is mortal. I've got the worst case on record. Every doctor that ever saw my case, give it up — "

"An Oxydonor wouldn't give it up," said Mrs. Worstel, firmly. "It ain't like a doctor. It 'u'd just buckle itself around your ankle an' go to work."

"Well, excuse *me*."

"Oh, I'll excuse you." Mrs. Worstel sighed. "I didn't suppose you'd take one. You drether have spells. You like spells. If you got cured of 'em, you'd have a regretful spell, I expect. Well, Semy?"

Semia smiled faintly.

"Shall I fan, auntie?"

"No, I'll fan. You set down an' rest a spell."

"Rest a spell?" echoed Mrs. Worstel. "I declare, I wouldn't think anything could rest a spell."

Mrs. Pollard opened her eyes and looked at her; then she closed them again.

"Mrs. Palmer's coming," announced Semia.

"It never rains but it pours," remarked Mrs. Pollard, grimly, from her pillows.

Mrs. Palmer was ushered in by Semia. Her cheerful countenance fell when she saw Mrs. Pollard propped up on the couch.

"You sick again, aigh?" she said, in an indescribable tone. "Well, it does seem — "

"Take off your hat," said Mrs. Pollard, in an expiring tone.

"No, I can't set long. I told Mariella I wouldn't stay long. She wanted to come over an' see Semia a little while, an' we couldn't both leave at once — with salt-risin' set. She stayed to home to watch it till I get back. Mariella loves salt-risin' bread. I've been over to the Mallorys', but I stepped out my way to come in an' see you a minute."

"You're real clever," said Mrs. Pollard, feebly, with her eyes closed. "I wish it was so's you could stay long enough to take off your things."

"Mrs. Mallory well?" asked Mrs. Worstel.

"About as usual. She always looks as if a gust 'u'd blow her away."

Mrs. Worstel nodded her head with a significant look.

"I don't wonder," she declared mysteriously. "Poor woman! There's a reason for her looking as if a gust 'u'd blow her away."

Mrs. Pollard moved her head on the prop and opened one eye. A startled look flashed across Mrs. Palmer's face. She moved nervously in her chair.

"How?" said Mrs. Pollard.

"Why, I say there's a plenty reason for her looking as if a gust 'u'd blow her away. With a husband a-carryin' on the way her husband does!"

Mrs. Pollard opened the other eye. She forgot to breathe hard. A faint pink, like that of a sea-shell, went in one flash across auntie's face.

Mrs. Palmer felt hot waves of scarlet pushing one another up into her face. A wild singing sprang into her ears. She sat motionless. It seemed to her as if a great weight were upon her, and she could not move. She tried to hitch her chair into the shadow, so the light would not strike upon her face, but she could not. She sat still, feeling the scarlet deepen to purple.

Mrs. Worstel dropped her voice. "If you lived where I live! That fly-away Mis' Caruthers lives within a stone's throw. Mr. Mallory, he goes there two-three, three-four times a week."

"Semia," Mrs. Pollard fairly hissed out, "you go out in the kitchen an' finish up your work."

Semia blushed, and went out of the room reluctantly.

"She's a regular fly-away, that Mis' Caruthers. She's pretty, too. She's got a complexion like milk an' roses, an' light hair that curls all over her temples natural, like a baby's. She ain't more 'n thirty, an' gay — well, good grieve! The men's all crazy about her. Them's the kind to take the men!"

The three married women sighed unconsciously. Auntie made no sign, but fanned as if she had not heard.

"She don't turn her hand over." Mrs. Worstel illustrated. "She lays abed mornin's an' her husband gets his own breakfast an' hers. He thinks the sun fairly raises an' sets in her."

"Hunh," said Mrs. Pollard.

"If she worked herself all stiff, an' her hands all sore, to make him comf'terble, he wouldn't throw her a two-penny smile once a day. He'd come in an' growl, an' eat, an' growl, an' pick up his hat an' go down to set in the back room of the cigar-store an' play cards an' drink beer. But just take one of the gay *helpless* kind — an' me-O! The men all fall over themselves to wait on her an' carry her around on two chips!"

"How long has Mr. Mallory been a-goin' there?" asked Mrs. Pollard, her curiosity getting the better of the spell. The color was ebbing out of Mrs. Palmer's face.

"Nigh onto six months."

"I wouldn't think Mrs. Mallory was one to stand her husband's paying attention to other women."

"Stand it?" Mrs. Worstel looked surprised. "Why, what's she been doin' for the last ten years? Ain't she been a-standing it?"

Mrs. Palmer's face had grown as gray as ashes. There was a drawn look about her mouth.

"This is all I've see with my own eyes, but I've hear

time an' again that he was always a-making some fool woman or other think he was a-dying for her."

"Hunh."

"Some women are such fools for believing! They can't help it; they're born foolish. It's my idee that it's the woman's fault. Whenever you hear talk, you just study the woman, an' you'll find she's a little wrong in the upper story. She looks 'n the glass a good deal."

"She — what?"

"Looks 'n the glass. Oh, pats her hair, an' puts her hand up to her face when she laughs; an' she takes to flattery like a duck to water."

"You must have been around that kind of women a good deal."

"Well, there's a plenty of 'em, wherever you go. I've about made up my mind it's a disease."

"Oh, now," said Mrs. Pollard, sarcastically, "you're workin' around to an Oxydonor!"

"No, I'm not," declared Mrs. Worstel, vigorously; but at once her countenance changed and she fell to faltering — "No, I'm not — I'm not — that is, I wa'n't, but now I come to think of it, I believe on my soul an' all that an Oxydonor 'u'd help it as well as anything. I don't see why not."

"I knew you'd get around to it in time."

"Well, why not? You take any married woman that's foolish after men, an' it's a disease, as sure as you're born! So, instead o' remonstrating with her, or trying to keep her away from him, if you'd just buckle an Oxydonor around her ankle, it 'u'd cure her in no time."

"Then every time she fell in love 'twould cost her twenty-five dollars," said Mrs. Pollard; "for I'm sure she'd use an Oxydonor all to pieces a-curin' each spell."

"Well, what if she did?" returned Mrs. Worstel,

undaunted. "An Oxydonor 's cheaper 'n a divorce, ain't it?"

"Well, I'll dare you to go an' try to sell Mis' Caruthers one!"

"I'll go to-morrow; but I won't try to sell it to her. I ain't a dumby. I'll sell it to her husband, an' tell him to lock it on her ankle an' lose the key."

"You'd ought to sell Mis' Mallory one — to buckle around his ankle — "

"I'll have to be a-goin'," said Mrs. Palmer, gathering herself together as she felt a little strength returning to her. "Mariella 'll be a-tewin' if I don't get back on time. She wants to step over an' see Semy a few minutes."

"You well to-day?" inquired Mrs. Worstel, with a sudden solicitous look. "Why, I declare! I hadn't noticed how bad you look. You look as gray! Be you sick?"

"No; I got all het up a-walkin' so fast, I expect. I felt all flushed up when I come in. After I set, I paled off. I felt myself a-paling off. I look sick, I expect, whenever I'm tired an' pale off so all of a sudden."

"I bet. I never see you look so. Why, your lips are just as pale as your cheeks! An' they're both the color of ashes."

"It looks as if you got paler every minute," said Mrs. Pollard, with a faint show of interest, turning her head on the prop.

Mrs. Palmer faltered out some commonplaces and finally got out of the house. Then her face grew still grayer and her expression more haggard. She walked rapidly until she got out of sight in the woods.

She was shaken with powerful emotion which she could not control. Her thumbs were locked in the palms of her hands by the fingers; there were tiny scarlet splashes blurring her vision — spots like new blood started out here and there on the dull atmosphere; her lips jerked convulsively.

Presently she turned with a moan of stifled anguish into a narrow path that crossed the road. It was seldom used, and the ferns, devil's-clubs, and thimbleberry bushes had grown on each side. The thimbleberry's broad leaves and the graceful boughs of young alders met above her head.

It was such a relief to be alone that she commenced sobbing. Wild and terrible sobs they were, deep in her breast, sobs of vital distress.

She went far into the wood, talking to herself. There was no other person in all the world to whom she might speak the guilty secret that had been burning her heart out for years.

Poor, ignorant, passionate woman that she was, she had loved her husband when she married him with all the intensity that such natures are capable of. And he had loved her. But the ceaseless drudgery of a hard frontier life had worn their early passion to indifference, and this, as they grew older, had led to daily complainings and reproaches; and finally to bitter taunts and quarrels.

Then Mr. Mallory came upon the scene, handsome, flattering, loving himself and his own pleasure better than anything on earth.

Mrs. Palmer was the comeliest and the most spirited woman in the neighborhood. She had a keen sense of humor, and she was constantly doing the unexpected. She kept him entertained.

He flattered her with words when they chanced to be alone together; at other times, with his eyes, being one of those men who can express whole volumes of passion in this silent and effective way.

Mrs. Palmer had a strong, coarse nature; in many ways she was a powerful woman; but she had the weakness that may be found in many women — the desire for love, the kind of love that bears ceaseless homage with it.

This kind of love does not last long after marriage. Mrs. Palmer, with her head high in the air and her mouth scornful, declined the milder and more comfortable attachment which is known as affection.

She would have devotion from her husband, or she would have nothing. So for many years she had nothing. Then another man offered her devotion, and she accepted it.

She struggled long against herself, for she was not a bad woman, but in the end she yielded; for her desire for this one thing was as great as a miser's lust for gold.

As many a finer lady has done, this poor woman went stark blind to everything save the thing she wanted and thought she had. She went blind to honor, truth, and virtue, most of all.

And it had lasted two years. Two years of deception and falsehood and shameless intrigue—those three deathless thorns hidden under the rose of guilty love!

Then the man had tired of it and had released himself. He had the one manliness to lie to her, to make her believe that only a sense of honor and a fine loathing of the wrong he was doing her in yielding to a selfish passion for her could force him out of her life.

The wretched humor of that and the ease with which he had made her believe it appealed to her now powerfully. She laughed aloud; but it was a terrible laugh, and the sobs came up her throat thick after it. They were not like human sobs, but more like the sounds that come from the throat of an animal in torture.

For several years she had not seen him alone; but

through the amazing readiness of such women to be deceived, he had been able to make her believe, by an occasional deep look or sigh, that he worshipped her in silence, and suffered because of his noble renunciation.

The most dangerous of all libertines is the one with a gift for acting and a strong touch of poetry in his nature. He must really believe that he feels, for the time at least, the emotion he puts into words. The born actor must act — even if in the backwoods and solely for his own unconscious but intense love of acting. A deep look in the eyes, a broad breast swelling with repressed passion, a poetic description of her fairness, and a murmur — a mere hint — of a life-long sorrow because of a lofty renunciation that is for her sake alone, — no woman can be counted on to see the humor of such fine acting as that. She may see the evil of it, and she may be able to resist it; but her inborn vanity will dull her senses to the healthful and saving humor of it.

Poor Mrs. Palmer had been able to endure the separation because she was so firmly convinced that she was not the chief sufferer.

The gossip of a couple of women had now dispelled the delusion of ten years.

Now, for the first time, she knew everything; the blindness fell from her eyes. She saw herself for what she really was. She imagined herself the gossip of the neighborhood, like that Mrs. Caruthers. She shuddered hard at that thought. Then she remembered the reference to the Oxydonor. Did they laugh behind her back and say that she ought to wear one buckled around her ankle? . . . Would Mariella — would Mariella's father — ever stand in her presence unable to lift their eyes to hers for very shame of her?

She did not laugh now. She uttered a loud but sobbing cry and pressed on into the forest, not knowing that she walked.

For this one time she yielded to an abandonment of grief, shame, remorse. Not many hours could she steal out of her crowded life for the luxury of woe. She must let it all out in one wild, passionate hour.

"O God, God!" she cried out, fiercely, beating the dull air with her hands. "If I could only be alone! I deserved it, an' I never see the time yet I couldn't bear what I deserved. I'll bear this. I swear I'll bear it somehow — but oh! for a little time alone! To get used to it where nobody could see me. . . . Fool, fool, fool! . . . Lord God — if there is a Lord God! — listen here. If you'd of hunted high an' low — in earth an' heaven an' hell — you couldn't of found an awfuller punishment for me than this. . . . To know that it was all for nothin'! That he never cared! That he fooled me, lied to me day an' night, laughed at me for believin' him! That he was *just that kind of a man!* . . . To learn it after all these years! Did any fool woman ever get punishment like that — an' not have some place to go an' hide in till she'd learn to bear it?"

Through all her suffering she was now, with her powerful sense of humor, alive to the ridiculous side of the situation. She saw herself, portly, middle-aged, uneducated, going through torment because of betrayed love for a man other than her husband — and he a handsome country libertine!

Her vision had of a sudden grown wondrously clear. It seemed to her that she could draw her inner self away from her outer, or physical self, and stand and look at the Mrs. Palmer her neighbors knew. She saw herself going up the aisle in church in her best black dress, with the Paisley shawl falling in even folds from her shoulders, and her girlish hat covered with blue corn-

flowers. She saw her eyes set anxiously but stealthily upon a far corner of the church, and she cried out angrily: "Fool, fool! She's a-lookin' to see if *he's* there!" — for the vision had for the instant cheated her into the belief that it was reality.

Then she saw herself seated in a pew, with her head bowed in prayer, the blue corn-flowers falling over her abundant hair. She could not endure that vision.

"O my God!" she cried wildly. "What a hypocrite I was! To bow my head as if I prayed, an' then go around laughin' in my sleeve at religion! Me with a daughter to bring up! I never prayed in my life in earnest. I would now, only I expect it's too late to be sorry, too late to be good, too late for everything but to have Mariella ashamed of me, an' to have Mis' Worstel come, a-grinnin', to try to sell me an Oxydonor Victory!"

She burst into a kind of ferocious laughter, but it ended in sobs.

"Hear me laugh," she cried, pressing on farther into the forest. "Fool, fool! It's a good thing I can laugh, or I'd go mad this night!"

But suddenly she stood still. "If there is a Lord God," she said, in a low and solemn tone, "look at here! It ain't for *him* I'm a-takin' on so. All that foolishness dropped right off o' me when I heard them women talk. I'd hugged it to my heart for ten year — but it's gone. It ain't for that. It's because it's done, an' can't be undone. Listen here. If you can do everything, why didn't you make sin so's it 'u'd look as ugly before it's done as it looks afterward?"

But no reply ever comes to this question when it is wrung from a tortured heart. After a moment she walked on again.

It was long past dark when Mrs. Palmer entered the kitchen. Mr. Palmer was doing the barn chores, and Mariella was washing dishes.

She looked around at her mother inquiringly.

"Why, mother! We were growing anxious about you. You said you would be home early. Did you stay to supper, — are you ill?" she broke off suddenly, for her mother had advanced into the light, and Mariella saw the haggardness of her appearance.

"I took a queer spell on the road home," said Mrs. Palmer, turning to the stove, to get her back to Mariella. "I stayed longer 'n I expected, an' then I took this queer spell an' wandered off a path an' set down; an' I wa'n't able to get home till night."

"Oh, mother!" cried Mariella, with quick tenderness and remorse. "We ought to have looked for you. You might have died out there all alone! We thought you had stayed to supper."

As usual, Mrs. Palmer saw the humor of that. A faint smile unclosed her gray lips.

"At them Mizzourians'! I never heard of them askin' anybody to supper. I feel better now, but I guess I'll go right to bed."

"You must have some tea first. Sit here while I pour it for you."

Mrs. Palmer fell in a kind of helpless huddle into the chair Mariella pushed close to the stove for her.

"Oh, mother," said Mariella again, and stooping, she put her arms around her mother's neck. "You might have died out there alone. Do you feel quite well now?"

The girl's tenderness and solicitude shook the guilty woman through.

"Don't go to actin' up, now," she cried harshly. "You know I ain't never sick, an' this don't amount to a hill o' beans. You act as if you was possessed."

Mariella shrank back, but a quick, hurt glance discovered tears running silently down her mother's face.

She stooped and kissed her cold cheek without a word. Then she brought the tea and stood silently by her mother while she drank it.

CHAPTER XXIV

One afternoon, a few days later, Mariella from her window saw a storm coming up the bay. There was a grove far down the shore, where, safely sheltered, she had enjoyed many a storm. Putting on her hat and a warm wrap, she set out for a race with the rain.

As she went down the path that led to a lonely part of the beach, it was like descending into a world of lavender, violet, and white-edged black. The water, as far as the eye could reach, was black, but every wave, as it came flinging and curving toward the shore, was edged with glittering pearls. The wind came in strong, recurrent pushes, that made her struggle against it.

She reached the beach and made her way along the water's edge for half a mile. The sea-birds were beaten in by the storm, and circled above her in silvery rings, uttering their plaintive screams.

Mariella's love for the outdoors was so genuine that she could in a moment fit her mood to nature's. The coming storm awakened her pulses and sent the blood racing, sweet and warm, along her veins. It brought a rich color to her cheeks and a brilliancy to her eyes.

Finding herself after a while unable to struggle longer against the wind, she turned from it to regain her breath, and almost at once saw Learning making his way along the beach toward her.

She was conscious that a thrill of pleasure went through her when she recognized him. She realized, as she had not before, that he was of really noble pres-

ence. He was tall and of splendid figure; and even as he battled with the storm, his bearing was distinguished.

As for her, Leaming thought he had never seen a woman of such indescribable loveliness, as she stood, swaying, wind-beaten, against the sea, the red of roses in her cheeks, her eyes brilliant with dark red lights, and her lips parted, scarlet, in a smile of happy welcome to him. A man, he thought, could forget everything looking into those eyes, so deep and marvellously beautiful.

"Your father calls you a sandpiper," he said, breathlessly, as he reached her. "The name is appropriate. I have been trying to overtake you for fifteen minutes at least."

"You are too dignified to run," said Mariella, saucily, as she put her hand, cold and drenched with the salt spray, into his warm palm. "You are too — "

She was interrupted by the long roll of the thunder, so near and terrific that he involuntarily drew her closer to him, and held her there until it had passed, and died away in faint fragments of sound that seemed to break themselves into particles on distant mountain peaks.

"Now we must make for shelter!" he cried, putting her from him. But he kept her hand, and they went running, like two children, across the beach, and climbed the steep bank, to stop finally, laughing and breathless, under some heavy-foliaged firs whose branches drooped to the ground. The first large drops of rain were falling; but under the trees the moisture was faint and sifting so finely that it was more of a mist than a rain. Leaming took off his heavy ulster, and folding it about her, bade her sit down on the dead ferns. Her first impulse was to decline it, but one glance at his face caused her to change her mind.

"Now," he said, sinking beside her, "let me look at you. I could not see you the other night."

His eyes dwelt upon her. In the last year she had grown beautiful. At the least embarrassment or emotion the blood came beating up into her cheeks and bloomed there into deep roses. Her hair, either for its abundance or its rare reddish bronze, would have distinguished any woman. Her eyes, in the half dusk of the trees, made him think of stars shining in dark water; her lips were scarlet and trembling, and her chin delicate and sensitive. Her figure grew more beautiful constantly — rounder and fuller, without losing its slenderness. Her shoulders, the tapering, firm beauty of her arms, the poise of her head and body, would have filled an artist's soul with delight.

"Well," said Learning, at last, "it is my little Mariella, isn't it? After all these years the eyes, the soul, are the same. How does her old teacher look to her eyes?"

"Beautiful," she answered, smiling.

The color came up his face.

"Not beautiful!"

She nodded her head, her eyes still upon him. "Yes; there is no other word for a man except handsome, and I dislike that word too much even to think it, as describing you."

"Why?"

"Oh, you know the look and air a man has when he is considered handsome — that sleek, smooth, self-satisfied look! His eyes go out from woman to woman, smiling, insinuating." She shivered and then laughed. "A handsome man thinks every woman looks at him with admiration and would accept any attention from him. They believe themselves to be irresistible. They twist the ends of their mustaches and their eyes rove."

He looked surprised.

"Mariella, who has been teaching you?"

"Kulshan," she replied, laughing, with a touch of scorn. "A new 'boom' town is an education of itself."

The informality of their unexpected meeting had put them both at ease. Mariella wondered how she could have been so embarrassed in his presence before.

But presently Leaming's face grew grave.

"I find your parents greatly changed, Mariella."

A shadow fell upon her happy face. "I know," she said gently.

"They seem so much older than their years; care-worn and" — he hesitated, then added — "hopeless."

"It is this hard pioneer life!" cried the girl, bitterly. "They have had nothing but work and hardship. They bend their backs to toil, like horses or cattle. They do not know the meaning of comfort, nor of ease, nor of pleasure."

Tears trembled in her eyes.

"I am only beginning now to understand it," she went on, after a moment's silence. "I have been so thoughtless, so impatient, with my mother. I could not see that it was all because she never had a chance to be different. Have you seen her to-day?" she asked abruptly.

"Yes, I reached the house before you were out of sight. She asked me to come home with you to dinner."

"Supper," corrected Mariella, coloring.

"Supper — yes," he said easily.

"I am glad she asked you. Father is away, and the evenings are lonely."

"I shall be happy to serve in relieving your loneliness," said Leaming, stiffly.

Mariella looked full into his eyes and laughed.

"Oh, I should be glad to have you, even if it were not lonely."

He smiled reluctantly.

"You have not forgiven me yet," he said, "or you would be more kind. That scornful sudden curve of your lips — how well I remember it! Child though you were, it used to make me afraid of you."

A ribbon of lightning uncoiled across the west; the heavy thunder bellowed after it. Mariella closed her eyes. Then came the rain in great drops, driving and pelting everything before it. Some of the drops, striking the trees, shattered themselves into a fine spray that sifted down through the needles. Leaming drew the ulster more closely about Mariella's neck.

"Talk to me," he said, then. "I want to hear all that you have done, read, learned, since I went away."

The girl's first thought was of Mahlon. But she shrank from telling Leaming about him. She laughed uneasily and moved her head from side to side.

"Oh, I have been rising at six o'clock, and eating three meals a day, and going to bed at ten. At first, of course, there was school — such as it was; and after my graduation I learned to sew a little and to darn and mend and crochet. I learned cooking and housework, too, but I detest it all and do it in a half-hearted way that distracts poor mother."

"But what did you do for pleasure?" asked Leaming, gravely.

"Oh, I walked and rode, and explored the forest for miles around. I know every road and trail!" she boasted, with kindling eyes. "And I rowed and sailed. Then, of course," — she laughed suddenly, — "I went to picnics and apple bees and cherry parties. Sometimes there was a quilting party, but I made such long stitches that they soon let me off."

"And who was your escort to the evening parties?" asked Leaming, with a fine indifference.

Mariella colored faintly, and flecked some raindrops from her hair with her kerchief, to gain time.

"Mahlon Proudfoot used to be when I was quite young," she said easily; "but of late he has not been going out, so I have gone with any one."

"Any one — or some particular one?" asked Leaming, smiling, but intensely in earnest, nevertheless.

"Any one," replied Mariella, smiling too; "no particular one."

"But these are not pleasures," said Leaming, presently.

"Apple bees, sewing parties, cherry parties?" Mariella laughed. "No, they are not pleasures; but walking, riding, sailing, rowing — these are more than pleasures; and there are others."

"And these others? I want to know everything."

"You will laugh at me; and yet" — she looked at him soberly and rather wistfully — "you taught me how to enjoy nature; so I will tell you. The most intense pleasures I have ever known have been those of nature: the forest, the sea, the snow-mountains, the rich coloring of the sunsets; finding the first flower, or the last; listening to the wind and rain, especially late at night. I could lie awake all night listening to the frogs, the nightjar, the mourning-dove, the owl; I could sit all day listening to the meadow-lark. I have spent every day for a week at a time searching for the *Calypso borealis*."

"Continue," said Leaming, when she paused; "I want to know everything."

"I am telling you all these things," said the girl, somewhat proudly, "because, ever since you came, I have been afraid — I have felt sure — that you would pity me. I want you to know that I am not for pity. I confess that in certain rebellious moods I pity myself for having missed many things which — well, let us say *you* consider necessary to happiness, satisfaction, even life. But I really am not to be pitied — "

" No — no," said Leaming.

" Every one must miss something in life. Those who have all that I have missed, that I am daily missing, have themselves missed what I have; therefore their education is as one-sided and narrow in its way as mine. I shall never feel uneducated, nor the need of pity, while I can take such passionate pleasure in simple things. And for this " — she added, looking gravely and sweetly at Leaming — " I have to thank you."

" Why ? " asked Leaming.

She smiled, half sadly. " Have you forgotten the red flash of the woodpecker's wing ? I might never have known the beauty of that if you had not pointed it out to me when I was a child."

Leaming was silent for a little while.

" Mariella," he said at last, very thoughtfully, " you make me ashamed — as if I had wasted my opportunities ! I thought I was getting everything out of life that one can get. I have travelled all over the world, and I have come back to the place where I was born in ignorance and obscurity, to find a little girl, whom I once taught, holding fast to joys which I have been missing — joys of which I had forgotten all that I ever knew."

" It is because you have lived too much with people," said Mariella, carefully plucking a broad blade of grass on which glistened a chain of raindrops. " You have not had to depend upon yourself for pleasure. But when one does have to depend upon one's self, it is a great comfort to be able to feel equal to it. It is the [illegible]t perfect independence I can imagine — not to have [illegible]epend upon any one for pleasure or enjoyment !

When I read of some great painting or statue which I shall never see, or of some great singer whom I shall never hear, after the first keen sense of loss has been dulled, I can always take heart, remembering all that I have. I know—*I know*," she said, with convincing earnestness, "that there is no painting on earth to match this stretch of sea, if only I have it in me to feel its beauty and significance; and if I haven't, why, then, I should not be able to read the message of the painting. Tell me"—she leaned suddenly toward him and looked wistfully into his eyes,—"am I right or wrong? I have reasoned it all out for myself after much reading and thinking. I believe that I am right; and yet"—her straight, dark brows drew together—"of course, I have hours of doubt. . . . Am I right or wrong?"

Leaming stood up slowly, and took her hand to assist her to rise.

"The rain has ceased," he said, "and the sun shines across the sea. We must run home between showers; I promised your mother not to let you get wet."

Then, as they walked homeward together, he said, in a lower, different tone, "I think you are right, Mariella."

He walked beside her with his eyes bent thoughtfully upon the ground for several minutes; then he lifted his head with a long breath, as if dismissing a serious subject, and said, lightly: "But since the 'boom' came, Mariella? How has it been since then?"

The girl's most mischievous smile flashed across her face.

"Oh," she said, "since then I have been entertained by people instead of nature. It has been an education of itself, entirely different from that of nature, or even that of books. So, you see, so far from being an object of pity, I have really had very unusual blessings. There is the old woman who two years ago lived in a one-room shack down on the beach and sold oysters and clams; her daughter, Jane, opened the shells all day long with a little sharp knife — by evening she stood knee-deep in shells. I used to go down there to buy the oysters, and I always stood and watched her. They 'jumped' some tide-lands and sold them for ten thousand dollars. Then they invested in real estate and made a fortune in six months. Now they live in a big green house, trimmed with shingled bands in lavender, rose, and paler green. It has two towers — two — and a great plate window across every corner. It is as much as any one's life is worth to mention oysters or clams in their presence. They have had their name changed from Harrow to De Haro. Mrs. De Haro wears purple velvet, and there are no words to describe her haughtiness; her chin and neck fairly swell out with it, like a pouter-pigeon. She" — Mariella burst out laughing and looked up at Leaming, who was smiling with grave reluctance — "she gave a valuable painting to the Catholic church, and she had the Madonna's head painted out and her own substituted!"

Leaming was laughing now without restraint, but with a kind of amused reproach in his eyes.

"Let me assure you," he said, "that you may tell that kind of story to real Englishmen, but not to an American who has only lived for a time in England."

"It is the truth," she assured him at once, so seriously that he could no longer doubt. "She also had John the Baptist's head painted out and her young son's substituted. I have been expecting," she commenced laughing again, "to see Jane's face on a Magdalen! She has a tall glass case, framed with gold, in the drawing-room, and in it is the white brocaded satin gown she wore when she dined with the President."

"Really," said Leaming, "do you expect me to believe your western stories? I have heard — since my return; I never heard it when I lived here — that one can walk across your greatest rivers on live salmon when they are 'running'; but your Madonna story is new to me, also your satin gown one."

"They are true," said the girl, simply. "You have only to call on the De Haro's to verify the one, and to attend service at the Catholic church to verify the other. Please understand that, with all this and more, I should not laugh at them if they were kind-hearted; but they draw their velvet draperies around them, and will not recognize any one worth less than a million. Poor Mrs. Worstel knew them very well when they sold oysters; she was kind to them and gave them clothing. After they made their fortune they went to Europe for three months, and when they returned Mrs. Worstel called on them, hoping to sell them an Oxydonor. They were entertaining visitors on the piazza. Mrs. Worstel approached them with the fearlessness of a kind and honest heart. 'How do you do, Mrs. Harrow,' she said, stretching out her hand with the ribbon of the Oxydonor bag around her wrist. 'I'm glad to see you back.' But Mrs. De Haro did not move. She looked Mrs. Worstel straight in the eyes, with a face of stone. 'Did you want the housekeeper?' she asked. 'No,' said poor Mrs. Worstel, 'I came to see you and Janie' — her name is Jeannette now," added Mariella. "'I am your old neighbor, Mis' Worstel — ' Here Mrs. De Haro turned to a servant. 'Mary,' said she, haughtily, 'take this person to the housekeeper and find out what she wants.' Mrs. Worstel came home crying. So," concluded Mariella, looking saucily up at Leaming, "you must stop scolding me with your eyes for laughing at them. I never, never, laugh at kind-hearted people. I should not be telling you these things now, only you would know everything. Studying such people has been one of my pleasures since the 'boom.' Mrs. De Haro says Jeannette has a recherché nose."

"Was I scolding you with my eyes?" said Leaming. "I did not know it. I had no intention of scolding you. I have never been more charmingly entertained."

They had reached her home. As they went up the narrow path Mariella turned once more to look at him. Her eyes were soft and deep with a satisfaction that was almost happiness.

"I cannot tell you how glad I am that you are here," she said simply.

Leaming took her hand.

"Then you have forgiven me," he said, "and all is peace between us."

CHAPTER XXV

Mrs. Palmer met them on the porch. She stood poised backward on her heels, her curved hand roofing the light from her eyes. She was dressed in black; she looked ten years older than her age. Her face brightened as they came around the house.

"He ketch up with you?" she asked Mariella, briefly.

The girl nodded. She was looking at her mother with asking eyes. Had she told him about Mahlon? She was dully conscious that she did not wish him to know. Oh, to be alone with her mother for one second.

"Where'd he ketch up with you?"

"Oh, nearly a mile down the beach. The storm caught us, and we climbed the cliff to the trees. Then we came home by the hill path. My boots and skirts are wet; but the sunset after the storm was glorious — all violet, rose, and green."

"Hunh! You'll violet, rose, an' green yourself yet! You'll get pneumony o' the lungs yet, a-traipsin' so!" She turned to Leaming, kindly. "Why can't you stay right here? We've got a spare room, an' you'd be so much comp'ny. You an' Mariella could read an' study. Since Mahlon don't —"

Mariella laughed nervously. There was a splash of scarlet in each cheek.

"Oh, mother! Think what Mrs. Mallory would say!"

"I don't care a picayune what sixteen Mrs. Mallorys 'd say. She said enough about Mah —"

"Well, do let us have supper, and talk about it afterward, mother. We are both starved."

Leaming, left alone in the sitting-room, looked about wonderingly. During the last year Mariella had given a soft touch of her own to the room here and there. Dotted Swiss curtains fell in straight full folds over the windows; the walls were freshly and daintily papered; there was a rag carpet on the floor, and portières woven beautifully of rags hung over the doors. A fire burned redly on the hearth; a bowl on the mantel held creamy clusters of shad-bush blooms. Everything else was familiar to him — the old-fashioned horsehair lounge, upon which, he recalled with a smile, one could not sit without sliding gently forward; the big cane rocker which belonged to Mrs. Palmer; the little green chair with the rawhide seat, in which Mr. Palmer had always sat smoking, tipped back against the wall and staring into the fire with half-closed eyes; the andirons, the uneven hearth, the swinging crane — these were as if he had left them but yesterday.

Mariella, arranging the table with light movements, said with a fine carelessness at last, "Oh, mother, I wish you would not mention my engagement to Mr. Leaming."

Mrs. Palmer was mashing potatoes in a big pan. She dropped in a generous piece of butter, and dusted salt and pepper over the creamy mixture. Then she said slowly, "Aigh?"

Mariella's tone lost some of its carelessness in repeating her words.

"Oh," said Mrs. Palmer. She held her head on one side and beat the potatoes long and hard, until they looked like beaten cream. "Why?" she asked then.

"There is no special reason," replied the girl, with some petulance; "only, we told no one; and I do not care to have it known. I think — when he is told, I'd like to tell him myself."

"I ain't likely to tell it," said Mrs. Palmer, scornfully.

Nothing more was said. The potatoes were heaped lightly in a dish, with bits of butter pressed in here and there to melt deliciously. Mariella broiled the steak herself. Over it she poured some fresh mushrooms which she had gathered, peeled, and fried.

Learning felt Mariella's softening touch in the dining-room also. The floor had been painted, and rugs were scattered over it; there were white Swiss curtains at the windows; the dishes and linen were good. The table was arranged daintily and correctly; in the centre was a small bowl of wake-robins which she had found in the forest.

"Wake-robins!" exclaimed Learning, with kindling eyes. "How they take me back to my boyhood on the island."

"Do you remember where we used to find them?" asked Mariella, with happy eyes.

"In the hollow on the other side of the hill —"

"For pity's sake!" interrupted Mrs. Palmer, "what are you gassin' about? Set down. You must be hungry enough, a-traipsin' so far in the rain."

"I confess I am hungry," said Learning. He stood, unconsciously waiting for Mrs. Palmer to be seated. But she was moving about with high heel-steps, adding touches here and there to the supper. Suddenly she observed him with amazed eyes.

"Is anything the matter of your chair?"

"My chair?"

"Yes. Is anything the matter of it?"

"No; nothing."

"Then, why in the land don't you set down? You

must be pushed! A-standin' up so! I'd smile to see myself a-standin' up so! Set down."

Leaming sat down, but not until Mariella had slipped into her chair, two vivid red spots burning in her cheeks.

"I expect," continued Mrs. Palmer, when she had finally settled into her chair with as many flutterings as a hen brooding her chickens, "you're ust to pretty tony things an' ways by this time, Mr. Leaming? Sir? Oh, yes, sir, Mariella gethered 'em. She knows 'em from toadstools, an' I guess you learned her. She goes crazy over getherin' em. . . . Well, we're not very tony here. We don't feel to afford it. Mariella tries it. These here three forks strung around the plates like a silver shop!" Mrs. Palmer laughed with good-humored sarcasm. "Them's her doin's. I don't put on any airs myself. But she can if it does her any good. . . . Did you see any lords in England?"

"Yes, several," replied Leaming, not looking at Mariella, but feeling that her face was scarlet with humiliation.

"Not to speak to, I expect?"

"Yes, I was acquainted with them. Do you remember, Mariella, when you used to cook mushrooms in the woods?"

Mariella gave him a grateful smile. "I never see a mushroom without remembering that."

"Do you mean to say you was *intimate* with *lords?*" persisted Mrs. Palmer, returning bravely to the attack, there being no bravery like that of curiosity.

"I was very well acquainted with several," returned Leaming, politely. "They visited frequently at our home, and we returned their visits."

Mrs. Palmer threw a large hand out toward him playfully. "Oh, *you!* You expect us to believe the moon is made out of green cheese! You'll be telling us next you eat with the queen, an' she asked you for your mother's buckwheat cake receipt! *You!*"

Leaming laughed without restraint; and after a little hesitation Mariella joined him.

"You think you're so smart!" grumbled Mrs. Palmer, good-naturedly; "but you can't fool this chicken. Now, come, own up. How clos'd you git to a lord?"

"Really, I told you the truth." He was still laughing. "Mr. Hampton was a younger son of an earl himself."

"He was, aigh?" Mrs. Palmer gave a sniff of contempt. "How comes he didn't have any title?"

"His elder brother is living."

"Did you ever know him?"

"Very well."

"Hunh," pondered Mrs. Palmer, slowly. "He look down on you?"

"I really do not know."

"Well, if he was the son of an earl, what on my soul did he come out here for an' live in the woods on an island?"

Leaming remembered the portrait that had hung on the wall at the foot of his benefactor's bed, — the portrait of a beautiful, wistful-eyed girl, — but he answered, slowly — "I do not know."

"Well, it looks terrible queer. He must of done somethin' disgraceful. Was he well off?"

"Yes."

"An' left it all to you! You feathered your nest."

She pondered silently a few seconds with drawn brows; then her face cleared. "Well, I declare I'm rill glad for you, Mr. Leaming. You deserve your good luck. You was terrible good to Mariella. I didn't sense it then, but I do now. You goin' back?"

"I have not decided."

"Well. You'll see. You'll have to go as soon as the girls here find out you've got a fortune an' been runnin' around with lords. They'll set their caps at you."

She looked at her daughter thoughtfully. "Let me see," she said then. "How old are you, Mr. Learning? I ust to know, but I forget."

"I am thirty-one, Mrs. Palmer. I suppose," he added, smiling, to Mariella, "that must seem very old to twenty."

"Oh, but I am twenty-one!" she retorted, with an air.

"Mahlon's twenty-eight," said Mrs. Palmer, absently. Her face grew purple. "I just happened to think o' him," she exclaimed hastily, replying to Leaming's inquiring look. "He used to come here a good deal. He's awful busy now. He — "

She drew a long breath, coughed deeply, and then finished weakly, "He used to come a good deal to gass with pa."

But the humor of this caused her features to relax in a grim smile.

"These delicious mushrooms," said Leaming, not interested in Mahlon, "remind me of the Sunday we all waited breathlessly for Mrs. Pollard to die. Do you remember?"

Mariella smiled; Mrs. Palmer sniffed. "Oh, her an' her spells! She has 'em yet, just the same, one after another. Set there an' fan! That poor down-trod auntie! She looks like a breeze 'u'd blow her over. If anybody'd fan her as hard as she has to fan, she'd keel right over. I never see the beat o' that woman an' her spells!"

"Did Semia grow into a nice girl? She seemed a shy, modest child."

Mrs. Palmer set her lips together. "She ain't nice,

as I see. She might of been if her ma hadn't been too busy a-havin' spells to look after her. She's got to gaddin' around nights on the streets; an' now that Mis' Flush has took her up, an' I guess she's done for."

"Oh, mother! Semia is only — lively and — thoughtless. She is very kind-hearted."

"Oh, fudge! If she's kind-hearted, she'd best take some work an' fannin' off that poor fagged-out auntie. Well, in my mind she ain't worth talkin' about. . . . Now, Mr. Leaming, what do you say? Will you stay right here with us? You know all about us. You know I'm a good cook. I never spare butter an' eggs an' cream — an' them's the things in cookin'! An' Mariella — she's a-gettin' so's the things she does cook she cooks fine."

"I will give you my decision after supper," said Leaming, gently. "Believe me, I appreciate your kindness; and I hesitate only — "

"Well, take your time. Only, you'd best decide to come. You can have your own way about everything. I guess — well, I do' know, either — yes, I guess," she repeated deliberately, making the most important concession she could think of, — "you might set in the parlor whenever you wanted. I don't feel to want cigar-smoke in there, though; that's all."

When the dishes were washed and the kitchen was swept that evening, Mrs. Palmer put a black shawl over her head and held it together beneath her chin. "I'm just a-goin' to step over to Mis' Winter's a minute, Mariella. I'm out o' Kansas-starter, an' I have to set bread yet to-night. You go in an' entertain Mr. Leaming. An' say," — she lowered her voice, — "do all you can to get him to stay here. Just think of him associatin' with *lords!* W'y, everybody in town 'u'd fairly be *green!* You get him."

"Oh, mother! You promised you wouldn't care any more for what people think. I wouldn't say a word — not one word — to influence him to stay. Let him do as he wishes."

"Well, have your own way," said Mrs. Palmer, turning to the door, huffily. "You're so contrary. I never see!"

A moment after she had closed the door she opened it, and put her head inside. "You make hay now," she said, in a loud whisper. "I shan't stay long. Mercy! don't forget to take off your apron. If he's a-tellin' the truth about *lords*, he must of been intimate with *ladies*, too; an' I bet Lady This, That an' the Other Things don't wear aprons into the settin'-room, when they go in to set down after supper, anyhow. You make hay!"

When her mother was finally gone, Mariella went out on the porch and stood alone in the darkness. In the south Orion and the Great Triangle shone resplendent; above them were Aldebaran and the misty Hyades; and fluttering on toward the north, the pale doves, and all the other splendid, sleepless ones of the night. Her eyes dwelt upon them through bitter tears. Never had she suffered so acutely, so hopelessly, because of her mother's vulgarity. It was a hurt that sank much deeper than formerly because, of late, she had been conscious of a change in her mother — a softening, a kind of gentleness, an evident desire to please Mariella, even an occasional display of affection. The change had touched Mariella, awakened and strengthened the best in her. She was learning patience and endurance; she was cultivating consideration for her mother. Yet this very fact of their growing nearer together caused her to shrink in keener agony of soul over each vulgar act or speech, which once would have aroused in her only contempt.

Never, never before had her mother seemed so coarse, so impossible, as now. Leaming's natural refinement had impressed her deeply, even when a child; but now she recognized the added polish which he had acquired unconsciously through contact with the world and polite society. To the bitter, hungry-souled girl the red, scintillating lamp of Sirius seemed no farther, higher, above her than Leaming. A kind of awe of him grew upon her. She had no desire to go in where he was — rather, where she supposed he was; for presently there was a movement beside her in the darkness, and then she felt his hand upon her shoulder.

"Oh," he said musingly, "Orion is more interesting than an old teacher? I am honored. Where is your mother, that you stand here alone with the stars?"

"She is gone for 'Kansas-starter,'" replied she, with an unwilling laugh, in which he joined. "But I think I hear her coming."

"Oh, she is coming?" There was a note of disappointment in his tone. "Why did you not come in? Did you not know I wanted you? — wanted to ask you something?"

"No. How should I know? You are a stranger."

"Mariella! Am I?"

"What was it you wished to ask me?"

"About remaining here. Shall I?"

"As you wish."

"What do *you* wish? That is the question. I wish to do what will please you."

"And I," she said, very softly and sweetly, "wish you to please yourself."

"Obstinate girl! Would my constant presence here be a pleasure or an annoyance?"

"A pleasure."

"Would it cause you more work, or take your attention from your favorite pastimes?"

"No; or, if it did, I should not mind."

"Mariella, you used to obey me, — you shall obey me now. You shall answer me when I ask you again; so be prepared."

He waited a moment; the darkness throbbed around them; her mother's step sounded nearer.

"I will not stay unless you say you want me. Mariella, do you want me?"

She turned her head and laid her cheek in a swift, impulsive caress for three heart-beats against his hand, as it rested on her shoulder. Then she slipped away and was gone before he could speak.

CHAPTER XXVI

It was about this time that auntie began to fail in health. Her sister refused to believe that it was anything serious. "Take some sarsaf'rilly," she said fretfully. "It's your blood that's the matter. Where you feel bad?"

"Oh, I don't know," said auntie, deathly pale; "it feels like it was my heart."

"Your heart!" Here was an affront, indeed, to Mrs. Pollard. For any one else, particularly her own sister, to walk right in and claim one of her pet and patented ailments! And anything as serious as the heart! What right, even, had she to a heart at all? "Your heart, aigh?" she sniffed. "Well, you must be gettin' foolish. You never had any heart trouble. I'm the poor sufferin' mortal with my heart. I expect you'll go to wantin' heart-trouble, just because I've got it."

"Oh, sister," said auntie, faintly. "It's the first time I've ever been sick in my life. And I do feel terrible gone. I feel most as if I'd have to let all holts go. I'd be condemned, if I just had to give up an' couldn't wait on you any longer."

"The idy," cried Mrs. Pollard, indignantly, "of you a-thinkin' such a thing! You know I couldn't *live* without bein' fanned. What makes you talk the tom-fool so? Take some sarsaf'rilly, I tell you, and don't think so much about it, an' you won't be sick."

"I don't think it's my blood, sister. It — it — scares me sometimes."

"You must be gettin' foolish. It scares you sometimes! Fiddlesticks you! You think it's your heart, just because here I'm a poor lifelong, unfortunate sufferer with my heart; next thing you'll think it's creepin' paralysis, because ma died with that. You'll get to thinkin' you've got everything you ever heard of, if you ain't careful." She began crying suddenly. "I suppose you're tired of taking care of me. I know I'm an' awful burden. The Lord Almighty has laid sufferin' an' helplessness on me; an' now, as I'm gettin' old, an Semy's wild, an' her pa no earthly account, except to go a fishin', you're a-goin' to turn agen me and say you can't wait on me." She sobbed childishly and heart-brokenly. "May the good Lord have mercy on a poor, wretched, forsaken mortal!"

"Oh, *sister!*" cried poor auntie, stung to the soul. "I'll wait on you just as long as I can; an' I'll want to wait on you as long 's I have a drop of blood in me. I only thought — maybe — that is — why, sometimes I feel so terrible gone, I thought the time might come when I couldn't. I'm sorry I said a single word. Don't cry; it'll make you worse. I'll take sarsaf'rilly, faithful."

But at one o'clock that night the fan fell from auntie's hand; the hand itself fell limply at her side. When Mrs. Pollard awoke from a refreshing slumber, she uttered a great cry that brought Mr. Pollard and Semia from their beds, for all had been resting pleasantly but auntie.

They carried her to her bed. It was the poorest in the house, and had been the least occupied. But there, at last, she lay now, helpless, suffering, but giving as little trouble as possible. She lay on her back, with her hands crossed over her flat waist, and her sharp features turned upward.

Mariella came as soon as she learned that auntie was ill, and stayed at her bedside, day after day, waiting upon her tenderly and faithfully.

"Oh, it's awful — to be so much trouble," auntie kept whispering over and over. "I never thought I'd be a trouble to anybody — never."

It was in vain that Mariella assured her it was no trouble, but a pleasure to serve her. She kept turning her head from side to side, and moaning, "Oh, I never thought I'd be such a trouble."

Sometimes she was delirious; then she would lift her poor tired hand and make a fanning movement, ceaselessly, for hours. "Don't stop me," she would plead, pathetically, when Mariella tried to hold her hand. "Poor sister! She can't get along without fanning. She can't get her breath. I've fanned her most all my life. . . . An' I fanned my mother just so. If it hadn't of been for havin' to fan my mother so, I'd be his wife now; an' have children of my own, mebbe, to take care of me, so's I wouldn't have to be beholdin' to strangers. But the Lord knows I don't regret takin' care of my mother. Mothers come first in this world. That ain't what hurts me. . . . What's been hurtin' me all these years is that he never meant it; he never 'd of said it if he hadn't been mad an' out of patience so — an' yet he's had to suffer for it all his life, same as I have. It don't seem right. . . . Night after night, night after night, year in an' year out, I've set an' fanned an' looked out the window — an' thought. I was always thankful when spring come. Then I could have the window open an' smell things a-growin', an' hear the frogs down in the pond; I could hear the ducks an' geese swimmin', too. Then my thoughts 'u'd be pleasanter an' almost peaceful. But when winter come, an' the rain was on the roof, an' the wind cried down the chimbly mournful, then I just set an' thought bitter thoughts; an' kept a-goin' over 'em. . . . Well, all is. Havin' so much to think about, bitter an' sweet together, made fannin' easy. Some couldn't fan for fallin' asleep. But I had so much to think about I never got sleepy."

Mariella, moved by a great pity, stooped and kissed the wrinkled brow, upon which few kisses, indeed, had fallen. This poor lonely creature had lived solely for others. She had gone through life shackled to Duty, that most unrelenting of mates when once one has looked into her eyes and bowed before her will. She had given up all her own hopes and desires without a murmur, with no conscious rebellion; and now that she had come to her death-bed, her thought was still for others.

"Tell Semy to remember her pa's corn-bread," she would open her eyes to say faintly, when supper time drew near. "He always likes it hot for supper. An' don't let her forget the apple-sauce; he likes that, too. Her ma needs some beef tea or some chicken broth; she has to have one or the other when she's in a spell — an' Semy's so afraid of a little work. She'd rather gad around with the boys than to work. She's gettin' terrible wild — a-stayin' out late nights the way she does. Mariella, you look after her if — anything, howbe, happens me."

"I will, auntie," whispered Mariella, with a choke in her throat, pressing the bony hand. "I promise."

"She's too pretty to be let run wild, an' nobody ever took any care of her 'ceptin' me. Her ma never. She's been sick so, she never had no time to look after poor Semy."

She awoke one midnight from a troubled sleep. Mariella was sitting, wakeful and patient, beside her. All the best in the girl's nature was stirred and strengthened by the tragedy of this humble passing. Mrs. Pollard was having "neglect" spells, one after another. Semia was impatient and fanned too hard; Mr. Pollard was sleepy and fanned too little; nobody had ever

fanned just right but auntie — and now she was so inconsiderate as to be dying. So into neglect spells went Mrs. Pollard.

Neighbor women came in during the day to assist; but at night Mariella sat alone beside auntie, facing death for the first time, yet unafraid. Sometimes, when the breathing was unusually labored and a grayness overspread the face, making the eyebrows stand out dark and startling, a feeling of sudden terror would overcome the girl. But in a moment her strong will would conquer. "If she is not afraid, why should I be?" she would ask herself, sternly.

Therefore, when auntie awoke that midnight, she was not alone, but she did not know the girl sitting beside her. She stretched out a trembling hand and struggled up in bed.

"Oh, Perry," she whispered, "you'll have to wait."

She looked earnestly at Mariella, searching her face; then she burst into piteous weeping. "Oh, don't say that," she wailed, as if pleading for her life. "If you love me — if you love me — you can wait. You will wait. Don't say that! I can't leave my mother, an' I can't put her on you. . . . But we're both young! We can wait. I can do my duty by both. . . ."

There was a long silence. Suddenly she burst into childish and convulsive sobbing, and fell upon her pillow in a stiff, helpless huddle. "Oh, don't say that!" she wailed. "Don't say that."

Thoroughly frightened now, Mariella aroused the family. The end was near. Even Mrs. Pollard got into the room, somehow, and forgot all about her spell in the presence of Death.

"Whatever 'll I do now?" she kept saying. "It ain't like her to be so selfish an' go an' leave me. Who'll fan me, an' make me beef broth without too much pepper, I'd like to know. What 'll become of me now, the Lord knows!"

Mariella gave her one look of bitter scorn; then she sank upon her knees beside the bed, obeying an uncontrollable impulse, and lifting her eyes, prayed aloud solemnly — as solemnly as she had once before, when a little child, in that same house, shaken Leaming's soul with her prayer which had seemed to the young man to be lifted and laid at the very feet of God: "O Lord God, it is auntie. Be kind to her and take care of her. She has taken care of other people all her life. She is worn out with work and thinking and sorrow — O God, be good to her —" She stopped, shaken with sobs.

In that moment the dying woman struggled up again. There was a far-seeing look in her eyes and a smile — the first Mariella had ever seen there — on her gray and trembling lips. "I hear the bells," she uttered, in that death-stricken voice which, once heard, can never be forgotten — that thick and shaken and failing voice.

"I hear — them plain; an' they — are — sweet. It's the first — time since that — Sunday — that they have — sounded sweet. They sound like — they used to — summer evenin's when he — took me to church. . . . I smell the — locusts along — the lane. . . . Oh, the — sweet bells! Thank Thee, God — the bells sound sweet — once more. . . . But he'll soon be here — an' I'm not ready. Oh, sister — I hate to trouble you so — but I want my lawn — dress . . . the one with — violets scattered — over it; he always wanted — I should wear — it to church. . . . Not the weddin'-dress — it ain't lucky. . . . I'm keepin' it to be — buried in. Buried?" A long shudder passed over her. "Did I say — buried? What makes me think of bein' buried — now — the first time the bells — sound sweet? Every so often I seem to see — a — pile of fresh earth dug up. . . . Is any-

body a-dyin'? It looks like a grave. But the bells wouldn't — sound — so sweet. Would they? Oh, sister! I hope no poor soul is — a-dyin' to-day, when he's comin' an' I'm — so happy. It 'u'd seem wicked to be so — happy if anybody — was a-dyin'. Lord God, have mercy," she prayed, fervently but brokenly, "on all poor souls that be a-goin' out to-night — in the dark."

Mariella, still kneeling, laid her cheek on auntie's stiffening hand.

"It's all right, auntie," she whispered, through sobs. "God will take care of them. *I know.*"

"Poor souls! Poor souls! My heart aches for 'em — a-goin' out in the cold an' dark so — an' me so rested — an' happy; an' the bells — so sweet. I ain't felt so rested for years — an' years — an' it's mighty sweet, I tell you. . . . Sister! You'll fan ma till I get home from church, won't you? Then I'll set up with her all the rest — o' the night. . . . Where's my dress with the violets in? I want it."

She ceased talking and lay motionless. The gray of ashes came over her face. Her body stretched out and struggled; then she lay still. Her eyebrows became darkly outlined against the gray of her face. There is no sign of approaching death so sure or so dread as that sudden coming out of the eyebrows. The lids fell, and the lashes made a dark shadow on the cheek. She breathed slowly, but easily.

Mr. and Mrs. Pollard and Semia were weeping now. "I'll have an awful spell after this," sobbed Mrs. Pollard to Mariella; but the girl did not hear her. She was still kneeling by the bedside, and praying with lifted eyes.

For the last time, without stirring or opening her eyes, auntie spoke. "I never — rested so — in all my life. I never knew — what rest was. It seems as if I —

couldn't — ever get enough of it. It seems wicked to be so lazy —" She lifted her hand feebly and tried to make a fanning movement that ought to have broken her sister's heart; but her hand fell limply. "It's no use. I can't. I'll just rest. . . . Hear the bells! . . . They make me smell the — locusts along the — lane —"

CHAPTER XXVII

One afternoon Mariella and Semia were returning from a visit to Isaphene Mallory. They dallied and loitered as girls do, under the trees, pausing now and then to gather flowers or sit for a few moments in a shady place.

They did not care for each other. Mariella had always felt a tolerant scorn for Semia, and Semia had never forgiven Mariella for taking Mahlon Proudfoot away from her.

But they visited and kept up a cheerful pretence of friendliness.

"Let's sit here on this bank a few moments," said Mariella, taking off her hat. "It is cool and sweet under this locust tree."

As they sat down a man came around a bend in the path near them.

"Here's Mahlon Proudfoot!" whispered Semia. "You saw him coming and sat down on purpose!"

"I did not," declared Mariella, indignantly; but her cheeks grew red.

"Oh, but you're sharp. You took off your hat on purpose — to show your hair!"

"I look better with my hat on," said Mariella, laughing. Then she stood up, still laughing and blushing, and put her cool hand in Mahlon's warm, eager one.

"How do you do, Mahlon? I want you to tell Semia that you do not know whether I have a hat on or not. She is accusing me of taking mine off to let you see my hair."

"I've known just how your hair looks for ten years," said Mahlon, simply; but there was no mistaking his eyes. They were gravely tender.

He scarcely saw Semia as he shook hands with her. His look dwelt on Mariella.

"She snatched her hat off the minute she saw you!" said Semia, reddening.

"She didn't do it a-purpose," said Mahlon, stubbornly. She isn't that kind of a girl."

Mariella sat down again and drew her dainty skirts aside to make a place for him. He sat down, trembling with happiness. His movements were awkward.

Mariella was unconsciously comparing him to Mr. Leaming. She had noticed that he said "a-purpose." Her ears seemed strained to catch his faintest mispronunciation.

"Have you seen Mr. Leaming?" he asked suddenly.

A deeper color rose in her cheeks. "Yes, several times," she replied. "He is coming to stay at our house soon."

"He came to see me," said Mahlon, simply, "but I was working in the up meadow, and didn't see him. Mother said I'd never know him."

"He has changed a great deal."

"He's grand, *I* think," said Semia. "He's a great swell. He went with the swellest people in England, I heard."

"He's cashier in the bank here, ain't he?"

"Just till they get a regular one," said Semia, loftily. "He's president and one of the largest owners. I heard he owned nearly the whole bank. Oh, he's rich, all right enough."

She put up her hand to adjust a lock of hair with a lofty air, as much as to say: "You needn't think I'm dying for you, Mahlon Proudfoot. There are others."

But Mahlon did not notice. He was looking at Mariella with adoring eyes.

"I wish you could see the house, dear," he said rapidly, in a low tone. "It is beginning to make a show."

"I can see from the road," she replied, with a sudden beat in her throat. She blushed, then she lifted her eyes to his resolutely.

"You know I love it just as much as if I saw it every day," she said loyally.

"I know, dear," said Mahlon Proudfoot, sighing; "but you don't know how hard it is for me to not have you see it."

Semia, who had strolled a few steps from them, now came back with her arms full of dogwood blooms.

"Who's this coming?" she asked, narrowing her eyes a little to look down the path.

Mariella turned and looked, and the color came up her face and neck again.

"It's Mr. Leaming," she said, and gave him a smile of welcome as he approached.

"This is a pleasure, but not an unexpected one," he said, shaking hands with her and Semia. "Your mother said you were out this way, so I followed in the hope of meeting you."

"This is Mahlon, Mr. Leaming," said Mariella, shyly. "I know you have not forgotten him."

Leaming gave a start of surprise. He had observed, as he approached, that their companion wore working clothes and had an uncouth appearance generally, and it had passed through his mind that it must be a farm hand, who was serving them in some way during their afternoon walk. The thought that it might be a friend of Mariella's, enjoying her companionship, had not presented itself.

"Why — Mahlon!" he faltered out, extending a ready hand. "I hope you will pardon me for not recognizing you. You have changed more than I, being so much younger."

"And poorer," said Mahlon, with a quick, uncontrollable bitterness that was new to him. "That makes more difference than the age."

His face had reddened with mortification. He was conscious of the vast difference between them, in looks, manner, speech, bearing. He, for the first time, felt his own awkwardness. He had an impulse to plunge out into the forest and hide himself and his misery.

"I'm very glad to see you again, Mahlon, after all these years," said Leaming, kindly, ignoring Mahlon's rude speech. "I have been to see you, but you were not at home."

"I'm always working," said Mahlon, feeling ashamed, yet still speaking bitterly. "I'm only at home when I'm in bed."

"Don't work so hard, Mahlon," said Leaming. "It doesn't pay."

"Oh, doesn't it?" cried Mahlon with a kind of fierceness. "Well, I thought it was the only thing that *does* pay" — he drew a long shivering breath, and added — "mortgages."

Just then Mariella flashed one swift, hurt look full into his eyes. He softened instantly.

"I hope you'll forgive me, Mr. Leaming," he said, in the old manly way in which, as a lad, he had confessed many a fault to his teacher. "I guess I do work too hard. That's what makes me feel bitter sometimes. It isn't often. I'm sorry I was in this mood to-day."

"Don't think of it again, Mahlon," said Leaming. He put his arm across the young man's shoulders with simple and genuine feeling. Then he turned and walked on with Semia, who was leading the way homeward. Mahlon fell behind with Mariella.

"I know you're angry," he said wretchedly. "And I'm ashamed to speak that way to him — the first time I've seen him! But I can't explain how I felt. It seemed as if ten years' shut-up bitterness spilt out when he didn't know me — and then told me I'm changed! My God!" he said passionately. "Don't I know I'm changed? Couldn't I see the difference between him and me without his telling me? After I'd looked at him once I didn't know what to do with my hands or my feet; I didn't even know what to do with *myself!* And you — oh, Mariella! You standing there to see the difference, too! Is it any wonder I went mad?"

"Hush," said Mariella. A bend in the alder-lined path had shut the others from view. She paused and put both hands on his arm in a shy, quick caress. Mahlon threw his arms around her and dropped his hot face down to hers.

"Lord God, forgive me once more!" he exclaimed fervently. "I don't know what ailed me. I don't envy him, nor any man on earth — not while you love me."

His powerful passion thrilled the girl through; yet in the same moment she was conscious of a strong physical repulsion at the touch of his coarse and not over-clean clothing. She shrank from his kiss even while returning it.

"We must go on," she said hurriedly, withdrawing from his arms; "they will wonder why we are so far behind."

"I don't care much," said Mahlon, keeping her hand as they walked on.

"But I care, Mahlon."

"All right, dear," he said gently, "if you care."

They walked fast and soon overtook the others. Semia looked around, laughing significantly.

"You ought to thank us, Mahlon Proudfoot," she said. "We walked real fast."

Mahlon and Mariella both flushed, but neither replied.

"We didn't look back once, either! Did we, Mr. Leaming?"

"I really do not know," replied Mr. Leaming, coldly; a look of extreme annoyance passed over his face.

"Oh, thank you!" cried Semia, flashing a coquettish glance at him. "That is a compliment, indeed!"

Leaming looked at her, not understanding. A slow color came up his face. "I meant," he said simply, "that the thought of looking or not looking would certainly never occur to me; so I could not remember."

"I'll have to turn off here," said Mahlon, pausing reluctantly. Leaming turned back and grasped his hand.

"I'm coming to see you again, Mahlon," he said heartily; "and I wish you would come to see me. Drop into the bank any time. You'll be sure of a welcome."

"Thank you," said Mahlon, and his embarrassment was painful as he stood awkwardly for a moment before turning away.

The parting scene arose before him as he walked along his lonely way home. He saw Leaming, grave, kind, at perfect ease; Semia, gay, fluffy, smiling scornfully at his embarrassment; and Mariella, sweet and tall in her delicate dress, with a deep blush across her face which he knew was for him.

His face burned hotly.

"I'm a country clown beside him!" he cried aloud, wretchedly. "And she sees it. She can't help seeing it. I wish he hadn't come back! Yes — kind as he

always was, I wish he'd stayed in England! He was her teacher and he always took such an interest in her, of course he'll be with her a great deal, and she'll see the difference! She can't help it. Look at me to-day alongside of him! Me, all stiffened up and clumsy with hard work and not knowing what to do with my hands and feet, sunburnt and smelling of perspiration, and him, clean and cool and easy — Oh, God!" he cried out passionately. "It's too much — it's too much! It was torture to her! I could see it in her face!"

His mood was one of his bitterest and most rebellious; but at the sight of his home the old choke came to his throat and his heart softened.

"Poor mother!" he said, in his throat. "I'm not sorry things are just as they are. I *can't* be sorry when I think that having them this way is all that saves her home for her. She ain't got a comfort on earth but her home and me. She don't care how coarse my clothes and manners are — and Mariella don't, either, God bless her!" he added resolutely. "It was for my sake the difference between him and me hurt her, it wa'n't for hers. Didn't she tell me" — his voice took on the tone of one making a plea for his life — "that she wouldn't love me if I went away to the university and deserted my mother? Didn't she say she'd rather have me do my duty than get an education? I'll never forget how her eyes flashed when she said that. . . . Oh, Mahlon Proudfoot!" he added, slowly and firmly. "You're a coward to complain at anything while she loves you."

The three walked on together after Mahlon left them until they came to Semia's gate.

"You're coming in, aren't you?" she said to both, but looking at Leaming with soulful eyes.

"Not to-day, thank you," said Mariella; "it is late now, and I expected to be home earlier."

"That's Mahlon Proudfoot's fault," said Semia, significantly. "You sat down on the bank the minute you saw him coming. You took off your hat, too, to show your hair! She did that very thing!" she added gayly, to Mr. Leaming.

"Mahlon has seen her hair many times," said Leaming, coldly.

"Well, you're surely coming in, aren't you, Mr. Leaming?"

"Why, no — not now, thank you," faltered that gentleman, taken unawares. "I — er — it is so late now. I should only have a moment to stay. I'll come some other time. I'll walk back with Mariella if she'll let me."

"That wasn't nice of you," said Mariella, calmly, as they walked on. "You should have gone in a little while."

"Oh, should I? And missed you altogether! I only came to walk home with you. Your mother said you were out here, and that it was about time for you to return. I walked slowly, hoping to meet you. . . . You make me feel that I was rude," he added, after a hesitation. "I suppose I ought to have gone in — after it turned out so awkwardly. I'll go soon; I will really," he promised, smiling into Mariella's doubtful eyes.

They walked a little way in silence. Then he said diffidently, "I came to ask you to go with me to a dance at Mrs. Flush's, Friday night."

"I do not know her — thank you," replied Mariella, after a moment's surprise.

"I know," he said quickly. "We discussed that. She said your mother had never called on her, so she couldn't call on you."

"Mother seldom makes calls." The girl spoke evenly, but a tinge of color came beating up into her cheeks.

"That is what I said — explained — supposed," stammered Leaming, aware suddenly that he was on delicate ground. "And so, as this was to be a very informal dance, I thought — I hoped — you would take my word that Mrs. Flush desires very much to have you, and — that you might respond to her cordial advance in a way to make us all happy."

"You are very kind," said Mariella, gently, "but — "

"Now, you are thinking of a chaperon!" exclaimed Mr. Leaming, in a tone of dismay. "But as the town is so small, and the dance so informal, I thought — "

Mariella interrupted him by laughing out merrily.

"I haven't thought of a chaperon," she said, unable to get the mirth out of her face.

"If you were not thinking of a chaperon," said Leaming, rather stiffly, "perhaps I can persuade you — "

"Thank you," said Mariella, composedly, as he hesitated, "I will go. I was only wondering if my one party-gown would be gay enough," she added frankly, laughing and letting him look into her eyes, as he had been vainly trying for some time to do.

"Oh, if that's all," he returned, with a relieved air; and then he suddenly forgot what he was saying, and looked at her so long that the color came into her cheeks again, and her eyelids fell, like the curved petals of a cherry bloom, over her deep eyes.

"Oh, but it is not a small matter, I assure you," she said quickly, to conceal her embarrassment.

"I am sure it could never matter what you wear," said he, with a delicate emphasis on the pronoun.

"Oh, but it does! I'm perfectly beautiful in pale green." She said this, laughing, in a kind of childishness that had clung to her through all the years, and made her adorable. "But my one party-gown is white, and I'm not at my best in white. So it was really a question to ponder over seriously."

He smiled indulgently, as men do over matters of dress. When they reached her home he said, "I'm afraid you're not going to ask me to come in."

"No, indeed," she answered, promptly and saucily. "You declined Semia's invitation because it was late. I shouldn't like to have one of my invitations declined; so I'll make them so rare that there will be no danger."

"Try me," he pleaded.

She shook her head. "Not to-night."

"Mariella!" called her mother, loudly, from within. "That you? I thought you'd stay till doomsday. Leaming's been here a-lookin' high an' low for you. Serves you right! Why don't you —"

Here she appeared in the open door. The words froze on her lips.

"W'y, Mr. Leaming!" she faltered out. "I was just a-sayin' — just a-goin' to say —" her voice had fallen swiftly to company modulations — "for you to step in an' have supper with us."

"I've just been forbidden, thank you," he said, smiling kindly, and deeply pitying Mariella, who covered her humiliation by a powerful effort.

"Never mind her," said Mrs. Palmer, with hearty familiarity. He was so stiff, she decided he needed encouragement. "She ain't got the whole say yet a while. You step right in an' eat with us, I tell you."

But, tempting though the invitation was in that it promised another hour, even two, with Mariella, one look at the girl's wretched face caused him firmly to decline, softening the declination with, "Another time, it may be."

"May-bees don't fly in April, nor in March either!"

retorted Mrs. Palmer, with that provincial smartness which always cut Mariella into speechlessness.

"Good night, Mrs. Palmer," said Leaming, lifting his hat; and then he took the girl's hand, as it hung tense at her side. There was no mistaking the pressure he gave it, a pressure that expressed tenderness and sympathy. Understanding what he meant delicately to express by it, her heart warmed to him gratefully; he felt her hand relax and respond to his; a pulse in her palm beat full and strong upon a pulse in his own palm.

"Good night," he said, very low; and when Mariella had gently replied, he released her hand and went away through the early violet dusk. "Poor girl, dear girl!" he said, under his breath.

Mariella went in and found her mother in a state of mind.

"Oh, jaw!" she exclaimed bitterly. "I know you want to, and I deserve it this time. I'll take my medicine. That's one thing I can say for myself — an' it ain't everybody that can say it, either; I take my medicine. When I deserve nasty, I take nasty, an' I don't make any complaints, either. *Pay*, I say. . . . So jaw away. I know he heard what I said; an' I know I oughtn't to of hollered out that way."

"There's no use talking about it now," said Mariella, heavily. "But I do wish you would not think about such things; then you would never say them."

"Well, thank mercy!" said Mrs. Palmer, who was great on self-consolation, "it ain't half as bad as it would of been if I hadn't of see him just as I did. I was just a-goin' to say if you didn't set your cap a little harder you'd let him slip through your fingers."

And at this even Mariella, finding the humor of it more powerful than the humiliation, was forced to laugh, although it was with reluctance.

CHAPTER XXVIII

The one-streeted new town had gone on a gallop two miles around the bay to meet the old town; but half-way between the two was one strip of uncleared forest through which ran an old corduroy wagon road, which had been impassable, both for pedestrians and teams, all winter, on account of mud and chuck-holes. Travel between the two towns was therefore confined to the beach—when the tide was out—and to small steam launches which made round trips hourly.

Mrs. Flush lived in the old town, although her husband's office was in Kulshan, because desirable property was so much more "reasonable" there, and besides, it was only a question of a few months when the two towns would be one town. The launches landed just below her home, and she was a daily passenger, in her jaunty hats and gay gowns.

The house had been planned by herself—and it was like herself, showy. It was be-shingled and be-towered and be-porticoed; and it was adorned with five shades of paint. Its gingerwork was the awe of the town, as was also its cheap and tawdry interior decoration.

But Mrs. Flush was gay; she gave parties, and had made herself the leader of the light set; she knew how to snub undesirable people and keep them out of that set. She was "talked about"; but she knew it, and calmly repeated the talk and laughed about it. Her hair was bleached, it is true; but then it was such a successful bleach! There was nothing dull or indescribable about it; it was a pure, deep gold.

The society of the whole bay had been shaken upon the advent of Mrs. Flush. How about her cheeks, and her lips? How about her gayety and her dash? How about her showy gowns and the recklessness with which she spent money? How about — this in a whisper — her bleached hair? Should society receive her?

And lo! while society was deep in the throes of the discussion, it grew into a question of, not who would receive Mrs. Flush, but whom Mrs. Flush would receive. New people were coming in so constantly that it soon became her privilege to make the first visit and offer the first hospitality.

She soon drew a small set about her, and made it as exclusive as such society can be. When she was visited by any of those people who had hesitated too long in receiving her, she snubbed them, and declined both to receive them and to be received by them. If she met them in society, after having been introduced to them, she never quite saw them; she looked sweetly and fixedly at their chins, their ears, their noses, but never, by any chance, into their eyes; she never permitted them to bow to her. Yet on all such occasions her expression was positively angelic. The eyes that fixed their gaze upon an unfortunate chin never seemed to see the chin itself, but to look clear through it, lost in a vision of seraphs.

For the gossip about her, Mrs. Flush welcomed it; Kulshan would have been unendurable without it. It kept her before the public and gave her a notoriety which she mistook for fame. She knew that she was called "the gay Mrs. Flush," and she considered it a compliment. She strove to deserve the title.

For Mr. Flush, little need be said. He was a grave,

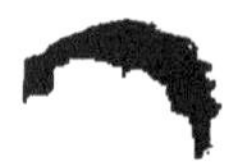

on the wind, as if it were a voice that smelled sweet, and all you need do is to follow it."

"Oh, now," said Leaming, "you are laughing at me! Yet," he added, more thoughtfully, "I suppose what you really mean is that some have a sense made up of all the others which enables them to respond to the finer calls of nature in an indefinable way."

"I don't know what it is," said Mariella, simply. "I only know that something tells me to go to a certain spot or along a certain path; and if I go, I find flowers."

"And I know," said Leaming, "that some can find flowers and that others cannot; but I never knew before that there was such a thing as a flower-call. And 'wake-robin' wind! Who but you would have named it that? I remember that when you were quite a little girl, you named Puget Sound the 'Sea of Opal'; you said the sunsets looked like Mrs. Mallory's fire-opal," he added, smiling.

They now reached the launch. The tide was low, and they were compelled to descend eight feet by a narrow ladder. The launch was rolling, and the ladder constantly lifted and swung from side to side, although two men were trying to hold it.

"This is dangerous," said Leaming. "I can't let you try to go down that ladder."

Mariella laughed, and set her foot firmly on the topmost rung.

"One doesn't live all his life in the West," she said, "without learning to love danger and adventure. This is nothing to a trip to Victoria in an Indian canoe. I did that once. And I crossed the Frazer River alone in a basket twenty feet above the water; pulled myself across with a rope and pulley, you know, with the water tearing and thundering beneath me. You'll have to hold my hand firmly, though, and come down after me."

She wrapped her skirts tightly about her, and with Leaming holding her hand, descended dauntlessly. When she was three rungs from the bottom, one of the men reached up and lifted her down.

"It is more trouble to get to a party in this fashion," said Leaming, in a tone of annoyance, reaching her side, "than the party is worth. I am humiliated to have exposed you to such hardships by my thoughtless invitation."

"Oh, please, please understand once for all," said she, looking at him with sweetly honest eyes, "that what seem hardships to you are pleasures to us of the West. We are not accustomed to ease and luxuries, and we rather scorn them — as yet. I suppose," she added, sighing, "we'll lose that with civilization coming upon us in the guise of a boom and Mrs. Flush. Now, here you are bored with the difficulties of getting across the bay in this chinook to a party; and I consider the trip across the bay — yes, even one sweep of this warm wind — worth a dozen parties."

Leaming did not at once reply. The launch was rolling heavily, and he assisted her to a seat behind the tiny cabin, where they were sheltered from the wind.

"I strongly object to your making an outsider of me," he said, then. "'Us of the West,' indeed! I am of the West."

"I should have said the Out-West," said Mariella, laughing.

"Then I am of your Out-West."

"Yes, I know. But" — there was a vague wistfulness in her tone — "you have been living for many years in so fine a civilization that you have forgotten the old hardships and difficulties of this life out here. I can see that it all seems new and crude to you. You love the mountains and the forests, the lakes and rivers and seas, but" — she laughed out suddenly in a kind of bitter mirth — "your very soul shrinks within you at the thought of asking a lady to scramble eight feet down a perpendicular ladder into a rolling launch to get to a party. That proves that you are not of the Out-West; for to us the perpendicular ladder and the rolling launch are half the party." She laughed again, more softly. "*You* would never —

"'breast high water,
And swim the North Fork, and all that,
Just to dance with old Folinsbee's daughter,
The lily of Poverty Flat.'"

Mariella was charming, indeed, when she talked. What she said mattered little; but her manner of saying it, much. Her voice was sweet, her language simple and unaffected. Leaming himself had taught her, when she was a child, never to use a long word if several short ones would express her meaning, and always to choose the simplest words possible. Her smile was brief and beautiful; but the chief charm of her talking — it was never conversation — lay in her eyes, in the deep look that held her listener's eyes when she was earnest, or in swift, flashing glances, trembling with mirth. She had lost completely the awkwardness and self-consciousness of her youth.

Precocious and of unusual intellect and discernment, she had easily familiarized herself with the small customs and conventions of the society in which she found herself. Good reading had developed her understanding and refined her taste; so that, as the town grew about her, she was soon able to perceive the real inferiority of the people who concealed the emptiness of their minds by gayety and show. She could not help feeling a quiet scorn for their shallow pretensions; and grad-

ually but surely she grew above them, and acquired serenity and ease of manner while they had only smartness and flippancy.

From the intellectual and cultured people who had been borne to Kulshan on the compelling tide of the boom, she learned much, and was quick to acknowledge her obligation to them; but they were not many.

There were a few moments of silence on the way across the bay, and then Mariella's thought went straight, with a pang of self-reproach, to Mahlon. Her whole self seemed to have been taken up by the roots and set out afresh — so changed did she feel by the new experiences and associations of the past year. For a long time a conflict, of which she was but dimly conscious, had been going on within her. It was only, as yet, the result of the growing pain of her soul; and it penetrated her consciousness only in such a way as to give her many moments of grave disquiet and doubt when the thought of Mahlon presented itself. The picture of his tired face, bent above the little table in his lonely attic, was one that flashed often before her, swiftly and clearly, in scenes of gayety and brightness; and it never failed to cloud her face with deep thought after the first sharp stab of self-reproachful pain.

When the picture swung itself before her that night, half-way across the bay, she put it from her as quickly as possible, and commenced talking again. Leaming was surprised when the launch swung in to the pier and made fast. The rocking ladder was climbed. Before them stood Mrs. Flush's home. There was a sound of music from within; lights shone softly through deep red curtains from every window.

CHAPTER XXIX

Mrs. Flush stood near the door of the reception-room to receive her guests. Mr. Flush stood beside her in faultless evening dress. She wore a rich red silk gown, cut very low and sleeveless. Her face was enamelled and her hair was "bleached," and every one knew it; but she looked very pretty and childish, nevertheless. Her eyes were innocence itself, and the touch of her small hand was so velvety and clinging that it was like a caress. There was just a hint of delicate and pensive sadness in her smile — as if a rose-leaf sorrow might lie somewhere out of sight, covered by a gayety that had been assumed for that purpose.

She received Mariella and Leaming with cordiality, holding the former's hand in both her own while she told her, with a gracious but languid manner, how glad she was to know her, and how good it was of Miss Palmer to come. "I'm *really* glad," she said, letting her teeth flash white and glistening through the languor of her smile.

For Mrs. Flush was always languid with women, even when cordial; her gayety and her vivacity were reserved for men — and she was not always gay with them; sometimes a sweet pensiveness was more effective. There were only two women with whom she was really lively, and they were her intimate friends.

"Was it very bad coming across?" she asked, with ready tact, observing that Mariella had no society small talk.

"I suppose it was bad," replied the girl, smiling, "but I enjoyed every minute of it."

"Ah?" cried Mrs. Flush, with an arch glance at Mr. Leaming. "I always declared you were an interesting talker."

"It was the wind I enjoyed," said Mariella, impulsively, coloring, "and the rolling of the boat, and — the darkness, the night. Mr. Leaming did not talk at all, I am afraid. I talked chinook wind to him all the way over."

"It is a charming subject," said Mrs. Flush.

"She was laughing at me," said Mariella, as they passed on to make room for some new arrivals. "But I don't care. I know, since I've had one good look at her, that I am not afraid of her. I suppose," she added, coloring more deeply and frowning, "it was rude of me to say what it was I enjoyed. But she should not have forced me to say it." She looked at him perplexedly as they paused by a table. "Tell me, what reply would she have made if I had asked the question?"

Leaming smiled kindly, and wondered how he could keep her looking at him in that entreating way. "Oh, if she had heard, she would probably have made the first laughing response that came to her lips. But the chances are she would have been so full of her own chatter she would not have heard it. Anyhow, she would never have thought of it again."

He walked with her, talking, through the drawing-rooms, which were over-furnished, as all American rooms are.

The floors were polished and covered partly with rich rugs. There were elegant tables and couches and chairs; tea-tables and ottomans, and cushions piled two or three deep on the floor; heavy red velvet curtains fell over the windows; bits of china were scattered throughout the rooms, costly and beautiful, but quite modern; there was a guitar here, and a mandolin there; there were innumerable things to be in one's way and to be stumbled over or upset, if one breathed near them. There was an effect of crowding, of massing color on color, of getting as many costly and dazzling things into the rooms as possible.

Mariella was interested and amused. Her eyes went again and again, in a kind of scornful admiration, to Mrs. Flush. She was surrounded by men. They held her flowers, they fanned her, they looked into her eyes, they did her bidding in a dozen ways. She kept them away from younger women unblushingly; she returned and encouraged their glances; when she was fatigued and sat, a young man was at her feet on a low stool instantly, fanning her, or toying with her fan while she held it, and looking up into her eyes. This was her favorite attitude, for then her drooping lids concealed whatever she might put into her eyes from all save the poor fool at her feet.

A few of the men present were faultlessly attired. Others wore dress coats with light trousers; others wore Prince Alberts; and there were a few frock coats and cutaways; several went wrong on their ties only, and more on their shoes. The women were dressed in all colors and all styles — from gowns that were cut too low, like that of the hostess, to ones whose collars harassed the ears and held the chins high and stiff. When it came to a large party, Mrs. Flush was obliged to go outside of her small set; later on she and her few nearest and dearest would entertain one another with witty and merciless descriptions of those present who did not belong to the charmed circle. But that would be in the early morning hours, when the hostess and the favored ones would gather around the fireplace in the library,

after Mr. Flush had laid aside his devotion and retired. Then would the light trousers and the four-in-hand ties come in for a good share of attention; and few of the unsuspecting guests would escape criticism. This was the postscript to the dance; and, like the proverbial woman's postscript, it was more entertaining than the dance itself.

When they reached the ballroom at the top of the house, Leaming learned what dancing with Mariella was like. She was the very poetry of motion. She seemed as light as the blown silk of a thistle. The music always got into her blood, and mixed with her pulses until drops of delicious fire went bubbling along her veins, wrapping her in a kind of intoxication — a rhythmic exaltation. We are told in the Bible to worship God in the dance. If any one ever obeyed that command faithfully, yet unconsciously, it was Mariella.

After his first waltz with her, Leaming led her to a seat in a quiet corner. Almost at once three or four ladies and gentlemen approached with great assurance, and seated themselves in front of Leaming and Mariella in such a way that their view of the ballroom was completely shut off.

Leaming's face flushed, and he made a movement to rise, but Mariella laid her fan across his arm to detain him.

"Do not go for the world," she breathed, with an arch glance, "it is Mrs. De Haro and Jeannette. They are with some people who have just come from Boston to buy all the mines on Mount Kulshan; their conversation will be better than all the dancing. It will convince you of the truth of my Madonna and satin gown stories."

Mrs. De Haro's massive bare shoulders, rising out of their violet velvet and point lace, had been settled squarely in front of Mariella, whose slender and modest person had received from that lady's eyes one sweeping and haughty glance, — a glance which had said more plainly than words, — "Oh, I may sit in front of you; you do not count."

She did not recognize Leaming as the "wealthy Englishman" whom she had been manœuvring to meet ever since rumors of his great wealth had been whispered through the town. Her eyes were now narrowed into a close investigation of the lace on her companion's gown. When she had convinced herself that it was genuine — for the ease with which such a woman will educate herself in these matters, while the simplest rules of grammar remain as Greek to her to the end of life, is marvellous — she turned her attention to the ballroom. Then she leaned her large head, be-feathered and bejewelled, over toward her companion.

"I expect you don't know many o' these people, Mis' Harrington," she said loudly.

"I think not," replied Mrs. Harrington, with a languid air which implied that she did not consider this a misfortune.

"I expected not. Well, you see the lady in green silk dancin' with the tall man with side-whiskers? Over there," she pointed with her fan. "She's Mis' Abernethy an' he's Mr. Fountain. They're both awful swell. Rich is no name for it. She's cannery people an' he's a cedar shingle man."

Leaming looked at Mariella. "That is our aristocracy," she whispered. "The most wonderful fortunes are to be made here now in cedar shingles, coal-mines, real estate, gold-mines, fish-traps, canneries, railroads, and a few more things — oh, I must not forget jumping timber claims and tide-lands. Unless one is engaged in some of these enterprises, one is not of the inner circle. I am afraid a bank would never do," she added, turning her head on one side and studying him with questioning and mocking eyes.

Leaming laughed.

"You must go into something else," she insisted, with assumed languor. "Fish-traps are the most desirable. You have only to go off around the sound on a pile-driver and drive piles in a good location; then sell it next day for fifty thousand dollars — oh, we are missing things."

"It seems so very new and crude here," Mrs. Harrington was saying in a bored tone. "I am sure I cannot be contented here, even for a short time. Only think of that tiny library with two or three thousand books in it! I don't know how to live without access to a good library, after having been accustomed to those of *Boston* all my life."

"I'm sure you're quite welcome to mine," said Mrs. De Haro; her chin doubled a little more than usual. "I'm getting quite a good one; I'm havin' the costliest bindin's I can get on all of 'em," she boasted. "I can't begin to name over all I've got a'ready. I buy every book that every agent brings along. I don't care a picayune what it costs. Mr. De Haro, he says let *me* alone to get the costliest that's goin'. Well, I'm sure! I don't see what great wealth is for, if it ain't to get the costliest that's goin'. I do it every time." Her voice grew louder; she was warming to her own praise. "Look at my stained-glass front door with a full-length nude on it! That's a fair sample of the way I buy. I could 'a' got a half-length for half the money, but Mr. De Haro, he says not *me*, I'd have full length or nothin'. I guess that's so. That front door, it cost enough for a family to live on the rest of their life, if it was put out on interest. But that didn't faze *me!*"

"No, indeed," said Mrs. Harrington, purringly. She

and her husband had been regarding each other intently, during the recital of the front door story. "I should think not, indeed."

"So you're quite welcome to use my liberry. I ain't cause to be ashamed of a thing in my house. I bought the costliest of everything right straight through — oh, look-ee, look-ee there! That lady in pink silk an' Valenceens, she's Mis' Dalton. They're fish-trap people. She's dancin' with Mr. Minewell, he's only an author. And so it is. My carpets are the best Axminster an' Wilton clear through; an' when it comes to the liberry, I've got the best bindin's an' the best books. What's great wealth for? You can have your pick. I bought all Julius Verne's an' Mary J. Holmes's an' Albert Ross's an' E. P. Roe's —" Here Jane turned from her conversation with Mr. Harrington. "And the 'Duchess,' mamma; and Rhoda Broughton and Laura Jean Libby —"

"Oh, yes, an' Mary Corelia; an' — oh, just set after set, set after set. It's a great big room, an' it's fairly alive with books. It's all furnished up in leather."

"You are very kind," said Mrs. Harrington, with lowered lids. "I find it very dull here already. I miss the fine lectures and, of course, most of all, the Symphony Concerts."

Mrs. De Haro stared.

"The — aigh?"

"The Symphony Concerts."

"Oh," said Mrs. De Haro, coloring, and fanning herself hard. "Oh — yes; I dare say."

Jane turned her glance again, smiling sweetly. She nodded her head to give the impression that she understood.

"I expect you miss the op'ries, too," Mrs. De Haro said, still fanning hard. "I've always been crazy to hear Florence Nightingale sing. I've often thought, well, dear me! Why not charter a special car an' bring a troupe of big op'ry singers out here to Kulshan, an' let 'em just sing us up full for once. If the turn-out didn't pay expenses," — her chin swelled again — "I guess I could stand it. Mr. De Haro, he says, let *me* alone. I'm sure I don't know what great wealth is for if it ain't to bring an op'ry company out here, if a body wants to."

"Yes, indeed," murmured Mrs. Harrington. "It would be lovely of you."

"I don't think it would take, like a minstrel show or jubilee singers, but it's worth tryin'. I could entertain the whole troupe at dinner, and give the swellest ball you ever heard of afterwards. I could have guests come down from Seattle an' Tacoma on a private Pullman. When I was back East everybody was so outed to see me travellin' around in a private Pullman! I told 'em," she bragged, laughing, "that wasn't anything for out here."

"No, indeed," said Mrs. Harrington. "This West is really a very great country. It is a pity that it is so new and — er — crude."

Jeannette gave her the sympathetic smile of a kindred spirit. "Yes, isn't it?" she sighed.

"There seems to be so little refinement, so little real culture."

Mrs. De Haro was silent for a full minute.

"Yes, that's so," she said, beginning to fan. "But times have been hard so many years, an' people poor. It'll get better now, with everybody makin' money, hand over fist. Why, everything we touch just fairly turns to gold." She lowered her voice. "The worst thing about it is that a body meets all kinds of people now at a party."

"Yes?" said Mrs. Harrington, looking at her husband.

"Yes. You'd be astonished at the people that push theirselves in. Some of 'em without a silk dress to their backs. The velvet that Mis' Anson has got on to-night, for instance — well, my bedroom porteers are enough sight finer! She holds her chin as high as anybody's, though. She actually ast Mr. Leaming to dinner. He's the greatest swell here. He's English, an' he fairly lived with lords — "

Leaming turned pale and arose at once, as did Mariella. Mr. Harrington, observing them for the first time, stood aside for them to pass.

"Great Heavens!" said Jeannette, in a horrified whisper. "It's Mr. Leaming himself! And that Palmer girl! He couldn't help hearing — you do talk so loud."

Mrs. De Haro purpled and fanned hard.

"Well, I'm sure," she said, at last, "it ain't as bad as it might be. I didn't say any harm of him. What on earth" — her eyes narrowed on Mariella — "does he want to go around with that Palmer girl for? They're nobody on earth. I saw her mother at a reception in a *Paisley shawl!* — an' look at the way this girl is dressed to-night. They live just like farmers; an' she never has a chaperoon to her name."

"She's mighty fine-looking," said Mr. Harrington, following Mariella's beautiful figure with admiring eyes.

"She is certainly the prettiest girl I have seen here; her eyes are like claret-colored velvet," said Mrs. Harrington, who had a poetic vein in her nature.

"Pretty?" said Mr. Harrington, contemptuously. "She's not pretty at all. Pretty! With such eyes and hair and such a figure and bearing. She walks as if she owned Kulshan. She would be distinguished anywhere."

"It's a pity she's so common," said Mrs. De Haro, hurriedly while Jeannette followed Mariella with envious eyes. "They are just as common! The parents are awful. I assure you we do not know them at all. They are not in our set. Yet this girl is actually tryin' to be; she is very pushin'. The men all take a notion to her," she added, with a significant glance at Mrs. Harrington. "That's the way she manages it; she's that kind of a girl."

"Ah," said Mrs. Harrington, more coldly, lifting her eyebrows faintly. "We never meet such young women in Boston."

"Oh, come, my dear!" said her husband, impatiently.

CHAPTER XXX

THROUGH some misunderstanding Leaming and Mariella missed the midnight trip of the boat, by which all the guests departed save the few invited to remain.

"Oh, this is lovely," cried Mrs. Flush, holding Mariella's hand. "Now you'll both remain for the orgy. Don't be shocked, Miss Palmer — it isn't half as bad as it sounds. We'll be a shade more proper than usual, too, in your honor. Have they all gone? 'All,'" she explained to Mariella, "means the Philistines, because they've been upon us. You're not a Philistine, because you have remained with us. That makes you one of us. Come, then, to the library. Is every one here — Oh, my love!" she suddenly became aware that her husband was beside her. "Are you still here? I thought — fancied — are you going now? Good night, then." She put a fond look into her eyes as readily as she would have eaten a chocolate cream. "I wish you didn't scorn our orgies — we'd love to have you join us. Well, if you will go, bad boy" — she stood on tiptoe and lifted her lips entreatingly. He smiled, and, bending his head with a charming manner, kissed her cheek. Mariella had hardly noticed him before, considering him insignificant; but now she suddenly felt sorry for him; she was sorry for every man who was compelled to kiss his wife in company — no real man, she thought, ever doing it willingly. In another moment she was following her hostess to the library; but the remembrance of that enforced kiss had left a half-reluctant, half-scornful smile

on her lips. Leaming saw it and drew nearer to her, involuntarily.

"If you are amused already," he said, in a low tone, "there is a brilliant hour before you."

"That kiss!" said Mariella, in the same tone. "Poor man! Will I ever forget the conscious look that went across his eyes? Does he have to do it often?"

"Rather."

"And does he always look so — well, reluctant, about it?"

"I think he does."

The library was inviting. There was a low fire in the room, but no lights — only shadows. There were low couches and lounging chairs.

"Now," said Mrs. Flush, sinking languidly into her chair, "we will be comfortable. We must have some wine. Ralph, will you ring?"

One of the young men whom she had made her slaves, who danced attendance upon her faintest whim, like puppets, sprang to do her bidding.

"You may as well give the wine-ring," she advised. "Three long and a short. Rose knows it. In fact, she knows it rather better than any of the other rings. I know it sounds like a hotel; but when one gets notice once a week that one's best maid will leave unless her work is 'eased up,' why, one will do anything. I'm reduced to the verge of nervous exhaustion. I'm even thinking of getting silver knives — and I never thought I would sink to that! — so she'll not have so much cleaning to do."

Mariella felt her face grow warm, remembering how her mother had worked and skimped and saved to buy a half-dozen silver-plated knives.

"One can't go into a cheap restaurant," continued Mrs. Flush, settling herself and making room for young

Warfle to stretch himself at her feet after giving the wine-ring, "without finding silver-plated knives with blue streaks running through them — clammy things!"

"You must say *clk*-ammy things, like the Siwashes," said Weston, who was studying the country and writing a book.

The door was opened noisily and the maid entered. She stumbled over a rug. She had a conscious, awkward air. Her eyes went nervously and curiously from one guest to another.

"Put the tray here on the tabourette, Rose," said Mrs. Flush, encouragingly.

The girl set the tray down; her hands were shaking; the glasses jingled musically together; she turned quickly and stumbled over the rug again. She wore a black dress and a long white apron with a deep hem and wide strings; there was a white cap on her dark hair. She went out of the room hastily; the door closed with a bang. It was opened immediately, and the girl's pale, large-eyed face appeared.

Mrs. Flush turned her head and looked at her. "Was you speaking?" asked the girl, faintly.

Mrs. Flush shook her head, gently. The door closed once more. There was a silence. "That," said Mrs. Flush, at last, deliberately, "is my best maid. She has been with me two months, and the mere sight of a man sets her into agonies of nervousness. The first week she was with me Mr. Flush brought Mr. Ashley home one evening unexpectedly to dinner. Rose positively refused to wait on the table. Her 'hair wasn't curled,' she said. She balked in the china closet, and there she stayed. Nothing would budge her. I did have wild ideas of lighting a fire under her, as we are told to do with a horse that doesn't go the right way. Fancy me!"

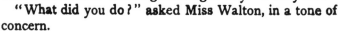

"What did you do?" asked Miss Walton, in a tone of concern.

"I'll never tell. But I fear" — she cast down her eyes, modestly — "you do not see what a big compliment her continued flutter at the sight of a man pays to my wifely qualities. It means that she sees few men here."

There was a laugh at this. The wine had been passed. Mrs. Flush held her glass daintily by the stem, and looked at it dreamily.

"I had worse luck than that once," she said deliberately. "I thoughtlessly invited three guests, one being Mr. Ashley, to dinner, and Rose played sick three whole days. At the last minute I found a woman who was willing to *try* to wait on the table. I drilled her faithfully; but she passed things at the right side, and removed them at the left unfailingly. Once she upset a salt-cup, and threw her hand up to her face, and giggled, and exclaimed, 'Oh, look at me!' But that wasn't the worst!" Mrs. Flush sipped her wine, reflectively. "While I was expecting the finger-bowls to be brought on, I observed Mr. Ashley gazing in a fascinated way at the sideboard. I glanced there, and found my waitress going placidly along, cleansing her fingers in first one finger-bowl and then another, until she had used the five; then she looked at me in a puzzled way, and said, 'What next, mum?' I learned afterward that she believed me to be a Catholic, and thought she was performing some holy rites for me."

While they were laughing — for that was one of the duties of her guests — Mrs. Flush sipped her wine.

"Did any one notice," she asked, with half-closed, meditative eyes, "how charming Mrs. Pump-handle Anson was in a low and sleeveless gown?"

"She was perfectly stunning," said Miss Peabody. "She made me positively dizzy. I couldn't take my eyes off her."

"I couldn't, either," said Dr. Jetts. "Her clavicle and her olecranon processes were things to dream about."

One's natural delicacy may be determined by the kind of humor he enjoys. Mariella had considered it bad enough for Mrs. Flush to discuss her servants; but how much worse was it to ridicule her guests — and so coarsely?

She knew Mrs. Anson to be a very good and amiable woman, although certainly tiresome.

"Why do they call her 'pump-handle'?" she asked Miss Peabody, gravely.

"Because she is tall and thin; and when she shakes hands she works her elbow up and down — this way." She illustrated, smiling.

"I don't think it is amusing," said the girl, coldly.

"You mustn't mind our calling people names," said Miss Walton, who had overheard. "We call one another dreadful names. And really, 'pump-handle' is a nice name for Mrs. Anson. We might give her a worse one, if we wished to be mean, for the very tone of her eye, as Dr. Jetts says, when she looks at us, is so disapproving. She doesn't like the style of us. We are too gay, too flippant; we go in for too good a time; we don't fit into her ideas of theology. She's a Presbyterian because she loves to walk on thorns and curry her soul; we are mostly Episcopalians because we love to dance and play the fiddle, and be bad and comfortable. An Episcopalian," added this gay young Episcopalian, nodding her head, "may do anything she wants to do and be as larky and frivolous as she chooses, if only she goes to church regularly, and has the proper prayer-books — and carries them properly; that's important. And she mustn't dance during Lent, and she mustn't play cards — except in 'back rooms,' as the gamblers say — and she must cast down her eyes, and learn to bend from the waist when she says, 'We beseech thee' — but all the rest is easy. Oh, we are hypocrites," confessed this frank young woman. "And now, what is your church, Miss Palmer?"

Mariella smiled. "I am not a member of any church. I think one can be just as good without belonging to a church."

Miss Walton spread both hands over her face and peeped through her fingers at Mariella in a shocked way.

"Sh-h-h!" she whispered. "You're a heathen. You mustn't confess that you think it. That's where the fine point of respectability comes in. You *may* be respectable and not belong to church, but there's always a doubt about it; but if you belong to church, everybody *knows* you're all right. Look at me, for instance!"

She crossed her hands on her breast and cast her eyes upward in a rapt Mater Dolorosa pose that made every one laugh heartily.

"I was doing the Episcopal Lenten pose for Miss Palmer," explained Miss Walton. "She's a Unitarian," she added, gravely. "A Unitarian," she drawled in a monotone, "is one who calmly, and without any sense of humor, preaches that his belief is the only progressive and enlightened one; he also points his moral and adorns his tale (did I get that right?) by asserting with vigorous originality that if you put your hand in the fire, you'll be burned. I have heard dozens of Unitarians talk, and the only one who didn't say that said that all other beliefs were narrow."

"I am not a Unitarian," said Mariella, laughing, "but Mr. Leaming is."

"Oh, no, he isn't. He — "

"My dear," said Miss Peabody, languidly, "don't you

see that you are shocking Miss Palmer? I am surprised at you. Besides"—there was a wicked flicker of her eyelids—"you should not make fun of things that people can't help."

She had read this thought in Mariella's eyes.

"Mrs. De Haro can't help being stout—laugh at her full-length front door if you must laugh; and Mrs. Anson can't help being thin—"

"She could if she'd drink a pint of milk every day," drawled Mrs. Flush, who found the conversation getting away from her, which was intolerable. "I've been drinking milk a month, and I've gained five pounds. I'll send my milkman around to Mrs. Pump—"

"He'll go! he'll go!" cried out Miss Peabody, brilliantly. "He'd give anybody with 'pump' to her name milk for nothing!"

"There's our launch!" said Mariella, suddenly, to Leaming, as a shrill whistle smote the night. "We must go at once."

"I'm awfully sorry you can't stay," said Mrs. Flush, sweetly, rising. She held her glass in one hand, and gave Mariella the other. "Really, the orgy hasn't begun. We've been afraid of you."

"You needn't be," said the girl, simply. "I have enjoyed it very much. Thank you for asking me to come."

CHAPTER XXXI

One evening, about a month after Mrs. Flush's party, Mariella saw Leaming coming up the path. She was dressed for a walk, and she ran down to the gate to meet him; her face was aglow with excitement.

"Oh, Mr. Leaming! The Lummis and the Nooksacks are camped down on the beach; they are going to have a big sing-gamble game. It begins at nine o'clock and lasts all night. I've always wished to see one, but there has never been one near enough for me to go. And I can't go now unless you will take me, for I am sure mother would say no. Please, please, take me," she pleaded.

"With great pleasure," said Leaming, smiling. "Is it time to go?"

"Yes, this minute. There will be such a crowd, we cannot get to the front, and I want to see all of it."

She passed through the gate which he was holding open for her, and went swinging along beside him with her free, graceful stride.

"How is it you never saw an Indian gambling-game?" asked Leaming, greatly amused at her excitement.

"Oh, the town has been too small to raise enough money. They'll be having canoe races now. The Alaskas may come down. Their canoes are beautifully carven and the Indians are splendid."

The game was to be held on a partly cleared block between the two towns. When they came in sight of it, Mariella gave a little cry and quickened her pace. "Oh, let us walk faster! See the crowd! We'll never get close enough to see."

They were soon pressing through the excited crowd. Mariella's face was flushed to a rose-color; her eyes were brilliant, and sent eager flashing glances on all sides in search of avenues by which they might make their way to the front. Leaming, smiling and amused at her pleasure, scarcely took his eyes from her face. He pressed with her through the crowd, and protected her from contact with rough people. She kept a little in advance of him, and whenever he paused, looked back with such entreating eyes that he could only smile and press on again.

Finally they arrived, laughing and breathless, at the open space wherein the Indians sat. A great fire was burning redly, and on each side of it a long board was laid. Behind the board the opposing players half knelt, half squatted, seven on each side. Sharpened cedar sticks, to serve as counters, were set in the ground between the boards and the fire.

The game was played with alder-wood sticks, three inches long and an inch in diameter. Some of these were peeled entirely; around the middle of others remained rings of the silvery bark.

"They haven't begun!" cried Mariella, her eyes shining red in the firelight. "Oh, I'm so glad. How good you were to bring me!"

"Good!" said Leaming. "I would take you to the other side of the world — if I might go with you."

The players were making their bets. This consumed much time, and was arranged satisfactorily to all the Indians only after long and tiresome parley and bitter dispute.

"Down in front! *Sit down!*" yelled the crowd, hoarsely and furiously.

Mariella laughed, and sank down upon the trampled grass, drawing Leaming, to whose arm she had been clinging for protection, down beside her.

It was a weird scene. The Indians were still betting. Canoes, ponies, watches, clothing, and all kinds of trinkets were put up on both sides. One man offered his klootchman, but she was declined with roars of derision, evidently not being a belle.

At last the game was commenced, and Mariella settled down with a long breath of relief.

Two players on one side picked up the alder sticks. Each took two sticks, one smooth, the other belted with bark. Holding these in his hands, each man passed them rapidly from one hand to the other under a coat lying across his knees; then, above the coat, in full view of the guessers.

The other Indians on that side began a loud beating on the boards with sticks, and a guttural, monotonous chant — in which "hi-ah, hi-ah," seemed to be uttered incessantly, the voice rising on the first syllable and falling on the last.

The two leading players swung their closed hands to and fro in front of them. They held their arms bent rigidly at the elbow. Frequently, without losing time to the melodious din of the beating and chanting, they tossed the sticks into the air, caught them, and fumbled them under their coats, still keeping perfect time by regular movements of their arms and bodies. Sometimes they threw their heads back and laughed a wild, triumphant accompaniment; other times they bent forward almost to the ground; but never was there a break in rhythm.

All the while the Indians on the opposing side were trying to guess which hand held the peeled stick, and which the belted one. When a correct guess was made, the winners set a cedar stick in the ground before them, and the two short alder sticks were tossed through the fire to them.

The weird music with its fierce, perfect rhythm got into Mariella's blood and beat through her pulses. The scene was barbaric. The Indians were naked to the waist. The scarlet-blanketed squaws sat behind them, stolidly watching the game, their faces revealing neither triumph nor disappointment.

Leaming cared little for the game. His eyes never left Mariella for more than a glance. Not an expression of that exquisitely sensitive face escaped him.

Suddenly she turned to him, flushed and glowing with excitement. She struck her bare palms together with an exclamation of delight.

"Oh, isn't it worth coming to see?"

He smiled. Something in his eyes made her look away.

"Your pleasure is; yes."

"You know I meant the game," she said, after a hesitation, in a tone of gentle reproof. "Why can't you enjoy it?"

"Because I am enjoying your pleasure so much that I can enjoy nothing else."

The firelight cast a richer red on Mariella's cheek.

"Isn't the big Indian with the slahals splendid?" she said hurriedly. "His muscles are like ropes. His neck and chest are like brown marble. How his eyes flash! And how perfectly his movements keep time to the beating and the chanting! I am fascinated!"

"Ah? So am I," said Leaming, so heartily that Mariella could not help laughing and looking at him again; but she looked away at once.

"Do be serious," she said. "I meant it. There *is* a fascination in it all — although," she added, after a slight

hesitation, "I cannot tell in what particular feature it lies. Is it in the music? Or the weird light? Or the rhythm —"

"In none of those," replied Leaming, smiling gravely as she looked up at him for an answer; "in the eyes, I should say; or the tremble of the lips; or the bronze hair — it is almost red in this light, Mariella; most of all, in the pulse beating so sweetly in the throat."

Mariella, with a tremulous laugh, put her hand up quickly to her throat. Her brows drew together in a swift frown of embarrassment. "It *is* beating," she confessed, "but I am excited. One doesn't see a sing-gamble game every night. But do be serious. You are only laughing at me, and I am enjoying it, oh" — she laughed out clearly — "so much more than Mrs. Flush's dance."

"I don't know about that," said Leaming, remembering the waltzes.

They were as completely alone in that crowd as they could have been in a forest. The girl was trembling with intense excitement and happiness; and she did not know that half her pleasure was due to Leaming's presence. As she looked up at him reproachfully their eyes met in a deep look that increased her pleasure to a kind of exquisite pain.

The thought of Mahlon Proudfoot went like a swift knife through her heart, carrying a brief shudder of accusation with it. Accusation of what? She found no answer to the still question. The crowd, the leaping fire, the rigidly swaying Indians, the chanting, all blended into one blur that seemed to swim round her and Leaming, closing them in alone and away from all the world.

A deafening roar of yells arose. An Indian had made his guess, accompanying it by the usual picturesque movement of throwing out one bronze arm straight and pointing, at the same time bringing the other arm around with a sweep and resting the hand over the pointing arm at the elbow. His guess had proved correct. The noise had ceased for a second while the players opened their hands; then the yells of victory arose; the alder slahals were tossed across the fire to the winners; a cedar stick was set in the ground.

There was a moment's silence before the winning side would begin the game; and straight through this silence Mrs. Palmer's surprised and unwelcome voice spoke: —

"Well, good grieve! You two here? Well, if this ain't a great note! Been a-lookin' high an' low for you! Why didn't you tell me you was a-comin'? You needn't to be so sequestered, I'm sure! It's a great note if you can't take your mother somewheres once in a coon's age!"

Leaming and Mariella turned, startled, to find Mrs. Palmer settling herself almost between them. Leaming forced a smile to his face as he made space for her. Mariella, too, greeted her mother with a smile; but hers was not forced. The humor of the situation appealed to her. Her smile deepened; then suddenly her whole face trembled with laughter, and, looking at her, Leaming, notwithstanding his chagrin, was compelled to laugh, too.

"Oh, it's funny, ain't it?" exclaimed Mrs. Palmer, huffily. "You think I didn't know you run away from me! Smart Ellics! I ain't as green as you think I am. Not by a jugful!"

With a roar the successful guessers now began their beating, chanting, and wild gesticulations. Mrs. Palmer turned to them with eyes wide with wonder.

"What in the land are they a-doin'?" she cried. "They drunk? I believe on my soul they are!" She turned stern eyes on Leaming. "Well, this is a sweet place to bring Mariella to, I must say. A lot of old drunk Indians a-gamblin'! I don't admire your gum'tion."

"They're not drunken," Leaming assured her, patiently. "Their actions are a part of the game. Else, it would not be 'sing-gamble.'"

Then he explained the game to her, simply and clearly. She listened, but her face was eloquent with disgust.

"Dumb-heads! Loons!" she kept saying, over and over. "What of it? Who cares whether the peeled stick is in that fellow's right hand or his left? Such a to-do! Well, I must say, I'm not surprised at Mariella a-settin' here in the damp, a-ketchin' her death o' cold, but I did think you'd know better, Mr. Leaming. I did think you'd make her walk the chalk better than this. W'y, I bet even Mahlon —"

She coughed suddenly. "Well, there! Just look at there! See that loon-head throw them things up 'n the air an' ketch 'em — an' his body a-goin' here an' yon for all that's out the whole durin' time. I've got enough of it a'ready. How long they keep it up?"

"Until morning." Leaming sighed as he answered. The joy of the evening was gone. He glanced at Mariella, and observed with satisfaction that the glow was dying out of her face too.

"Until morning! That tom-foolery?"

"Yes; they continue until they are too hoarse to chant and too exhausted to beat longer on the boards and swing their arms."

"Well, all is, this is a plenty for me. I've see idiots before now. We'll just mosey out of here; this is a good place to vamoose from."

"Oh, mother," pleaded Mariella, "do not go yet. Why did you come?"

"I come because I thought it 'u'd be one of your tricks to sly off down here. When I got here people kep' a-sayin', 'You'll find Mariella way up in front.' You can just come on now. This is a sweet place for a young lady, I must say."

"Please, mother, let me stay an hour. It can't be wrong when I'm with Mr. Leaming," urged Mariella.

"You'll come right on now, I tell you," said Mrs. Palmer, firmly. "I'd be ashamed. Mr. Leaming, you go ahead an' be the thin edge o' the wedge through this crowd. Mariella, you come. I feel just like pinchin' you. Go an' sly off to a place like this! It's a pretty note."

Leaming went unwillingly. But his reluctant obedience was rewarded.

"Mariella," commanded her mother, "you follow close behind him. Mr. Leaming, you take holt o' her hand, or pretty soon she'll be anywheres on Puget Sound but where she ought to be."

So for twenty blessed moments Leaming held Mariella's soft palm pressed against his own.

CHAPTER XXXII

Mahlon Proudfoot was hoeing down through the long, green rows of young corn. He had been up since yellow dawn, and it was now late afternoon. He knew by the width of the shadow the cottonwoods cast along the creek that it must be nearly five o'clock. He was hot and soil-stained and tired. His back ached and his soul ached.

He worked on fiercely, with his teeth set together. It was one of his bitter days. He hated the thought of going home almost as much as he hated the work he was doing. He thought of the cows to milk, the horses to feed and water, the slops to be carried to the troughs for the hogs to squeal and fight over.

He thought of his mother, with the little, pathetic stoop that had come of late to her frail figure and the weariness on her face; of his father shuffling about, fierce and scowling, m-m-ming in his throat and thumping the floor with his cane.

Then, at last, like a benediction, came the thought of his attic and the small lamp, cheap and plain, but oh, so exquisitely clear and steady of flame! to be set on the table by the window for Mariella.

This attic was the barest and most cheerless place that could be imagined; but happily Mahlon Proudfoot did not know it. To him the room was so walled and furnitured and hallowed with thoughts of Mariella that it seemed beautiful.

His love for the girl, through long patience, repressed

passion, and almost sublime unselfishness, had grown into a feeling that approached holiness. The spirit in which he nightly went to set a light burning across the dark to her was, although he knew it not, somewhat like that in which a devout Catholic lights the candles about the Virgin in a shrine.

He never analyzed his love nor his way of loving; he simply loved her—with all his heart, and all his strength, and all his life.

In the last year hope had grown stronger within him. He was beginning to see his way clear to paying the mortgage; part of it had already been paid, and by winter he was counting on having his mother's home free of debt.

When the home was free, he would be a free man. He could go forth boldly to claim Mariella before their small world. But until that time death itself could not break his stubborn pride, and force him to seek admission to the house that had been forbidden him.

"Don't you ever set foot under my roof again!" Mariella's father had thundered at him on that black day that had separated him from her.

"So help me God, I never will, till I can take Mariella from under it!" Mahlon had answered, not aloud, for Mariella's agonized eyes were upon his, but deep in his throat.

The words had stuck there, repeating themselves daily and nightly ever since. Whenever a moment of weakness or yielding seized upon him, the words took voice suddenly, and spoke themselves in his throat as clearly and fiercely as on that day.

Mahlon Proudfoot could not take back words uttered as those had been. He could endure the torments of hell in his passionate longing to see Mariella, to be near her, to touch her hand, to hear the soft rustle of her garments, to look into her deep eyes; but he could not go to her, and not for the love of God would he have had her come to him.

One night he had dreamed that she came, sweet and delicate in her dainty gown, to the closed door, and beat upon it with fragile hands; and, when he ran to open it, she threw herself upon his breast, with his father glowering at her and mumbling, "Huzzy!" and cried out wildly: "Oh, Mahlon, Mahlon! You wouldn't come to me, and so I have come to you! I know you want me — and so I have come!"

Mahlon awoke with a sweat of agony cold upon him; he was trembling as in a chill. "What if I do want you?" he was crying aloud in a terrible voice. "What if you want me? Haven't you got any pride?"

And then he fell down on his pillows, from which he had started, and groaned out: "My God, don't ever let her come! Help her to bear anything — only don't let her break her pride. Don't ever let her come!"

Once his mother, coming upon him as he sat alone with his head bowed upon his breast, looking into the fire, had put her arms around him, and leaned her face down to him.

"Oh, my son," she said tenderly, "don't feel so about it. We all say things we don't mean, when we're worked up. What's the use of you and Mariella both making yourselves wretched? All for a little stubborn pride about knuckling down! Be the first to knuckle down, my son. Put on your best clothes to-night, and step right over there, and up to the door, and say, 'I've come to see Mariella,' just as if there wa'n't anything wrong. You'll see, they'll never mention it or hint to it."

"*They* wouldn't; but *she* would if she's got any pride. A girl 'u'd hate a man that 'u'd swallow an insult like that."

"Oh, no, Mahlon; she ain't your disposition. She's forgiving. You're"—she hesitated, and then said timidly—"terrible stubborn, Mahlon. You're as set as putty. You're just like your father in that one thing. A body can't turn you round, once you're faced a certain way."

Then Mahlon Proudfoot turned a tortured face upon his mother.

"*Mother*—Lord God! I can't help the way I'm made. I can't help what's in me, and I can't get it out. *I don't want to get it out!* Can't you understand that wild beasts themselves couldn't drag me over there alive till I can bring her away with me? They could gnaw the flesh off my bones—*slow*—but I tell you they couldn't drag me over there alive."

"Don't talk so, son; it's wicked. I know Mariella don't feel that way. I know she'd humble her pride and come to you in a minute."

Mahlon threw out his hands with a hoarse cry.

"For the love of God, mother! You'll drive me mad! I'd hate her—loathe the very thought of her—if she did! Oh, mother, if you love me, pray, pray on your knees, pray to God, pray to Christ, pray, like the Catholics, to the Virgin Mary—pray to anybody or anything you believe in—only pray that she'll never come!"

He had arisen and stood, trembling, convulsed with the desperate abandon of his passion. His face was pale, but great cords stood out in his temples, beating full and strong.

"I wish you wouldn't work yourself up so," said his mother, drawing back gently, but with a frightened, appealing look. "When you look that way you remind me so much of your father that it almost scares me."

"Lord knows I don't want to remind anybody of

him," said Mahlon. He dropped his arms to his sides, and went slowly and heavily out of the room, leaving his mother standing still in gentle wonder at his fierce mood.

Mahlon's face was drawn with thought as he hoed down through the straight rows of corn. He hoed steadily with strong muscles swelling out in his arms. The bright blade of the hoe, glittering as it lifted and sank through the late sunlight, made his eyes burn.

When he reached the end of the row nearest the road he suddenly felt, without looking, that some one stood there waiting for him. In another moment he caught the flutter of light skirts, and his heart stood still.

But it was Semia's voice, not Mariella's, that saluted him. She stood before him, close to him, holding up her dress coquettishly, and looking at him with a mocking smile. Her eyes were narrowed like a serpent's. Semia had never forgotten that she had offered herself to Mahlon Proudfoot, and that he had scorned her.

"Hello, Mahlon Proudfoot," she cried gayly.

He gave her a long, cold look. "How d'you do," he responded, without changing countenance.

"You needn't be so cool." Her face had flushed slightly beneath his steady, asking look. "I came around this way on purpose to do you a favor."

"Thank you."

"Oh, wait till you hear what it is. Maybe you won't thank me. It's" — she broke off the head of a velvet-hearted field daisy with a nervous snap, and began pulling off the petals one by one — "it's something I thought you might want to know about Mariella."

Mahlon paled through all his sunburn; his eyes glanced away from her coldly.

"I guess I know as much about her as you do."

"I guess you do," admitted Semia, casting the petals

down in an endless white chain, "but maybe not just the same things that I know."

She waited, but he did not speak. He stood motionless — graceful, because he was too indifferent to her to be self-conscious.

"Did you know that Mr. Leaming was cutting you out?" she asked, then, in a voice that was like velvet.

Mahlon felt himself start. His face flamed red, and his hands clutched convulsively around the hoe handle.

"Did you?" said the soft voice. "Did you know that, Mahlon Proudfoot?"

"No, I didn't know it," he answered briefly.

"Well, everybody else knows it. Everybody is laughing about her taking up with him so of a sudden. They say she must be pushed for a sweetheart to throw off on you so quick and take up with him."

"She hasn't done it," said Mahlon, quietly, but he felt his throat trembling strongly.

"Oh, hasn't she, though?" Semia snapped off the head of another daisy, and commenced casting another white chain down her dress. "Well — you don't have to take my word. Ask anybody, everybody. You don't have to take anybody's word, for that matter. Find out for yourself. He's at her house every day. Her mother goes around bragging high and low about cashiers in banks and lords in England."

Semia laughed out shrilly, and suddenly flung down the daisies, and, folding her hands in front of her, began strutting around with high heel-steps in perfect imitation of Mrs. Palmer's most pompous manner.

"I tell you, Mariella's got the best there is to be got," she bragged out, imitating Mrs. Palmer's tone of lofty indifference. "I tell you, she holds her head high. It ain't every girl that has cashiers 'n banks a-danglin' after 'em high an' low. No ordinary cashier 'd do for her, either. She had to have one that owns the whole bank itself, an' that skuroped around with lords an' all in England. He's here half his time, an' he's comin' here to stay as soon as he finds another cashier. I tell you!" bragged out Semia, bursting into laughter at her own successful imitation.

Mahlon had turned cold all over. The girl's acting was so faithful that he knew, with something like terror, that she must have heard those very words from Mrs. Palmer's lips. But at once he was able to reflect that Mariella's lips were very different from her mother's. What more natural than that Mrs. Palmer should see an admirer in every eligible man that looked at Mariella?

He turned a pale face toward Semia, and looked steadily into her laughing eyes.

"I don't care what her mother says. It's all tommy-rot."

Semia tossed her head and laughed tantalizingly.

"Oh, you don't have to take her mother's say-so. Find out. It's easy enough."

"Mr. Leaming was her teacher when she was a little girl," said Mahlon, doggedly, controlling his temper. "He thought a great deal of her then."

"He thinks a great deal of her now." Semia's teeth flashed white between her curled lips. "He took her to Mrs. Flush's party—it was a dance, and he danced half the dances with her; and he took her down to the Indian gambling game — " She threw her hand over her face and laughed outright. Mahlon's face went white to his hair. "They stayed half the night. They'd be there yet if her mother hadn't gone after them."

"I don't want to hear any more." Mahlon clutched the handle of the hoe spasmodically, and stooped as if to go on with his work.

"Just as you like," said Semia, gathering up her skirts

with a rustling sweep. "It's nothing to me. You stay squatted on this ranch till, pretty soon, you'll take root, if you don't look out. I thought I'd tell you — that's all. Nobody but an idiot would think a man would follow a girl like her shadow unless he was in love with her, nor" — she lifted her head and looked calmly and coldly into his fierce eyes — "nor unless the girl encouraged his attentions."

"I want her to go around and have a good time," said Mahlon, his hands closing and unclosing on the hoe. "I can't go with her, and she can't go alone. I'd rather she'd go with Mr. Leaming than any one else."

"She *could* go walking alone, I suppose, though," said Semia, purringly. "He goes walking with her every night."

Mahlon's fingers trembled helplessly upon the hoe.

"It's all right, whatever she does," he said, beginning to hoe irresolutely. "I feel ashamed to even take her part."

Semia drew a long breath. "Well," she said finally, "it's all right if you're satisfied. I wouldn't have come if I hadn't known it was the truth. I'll put it in plain words, and then you can find out easy enough if it's so. Mariella's in love with Leaming, and he's in love with her."

Two or three minutes afterward Mahlon seemed to see himself emerging from a dense fog. He became conscious that Semia was flitting lightly down through the tall brakes; and that he, swaying upon the support of the hoe, with dull red flecks blurring his vision, was uttering over and over, hoarsely, in his throat: "It's a lie! It's a lie! Lord Almighty, if she was only a man!"

"Are you sick, Mahlon?" said his mother that night, after supper.

"No, mother."

"Why, you look sick. I never see you look so. Does anything ail you?"

"Nothing that I care to talk about, mother."

She smoothed his hair with her coarse but gentle hand. "I thought everything was going well about the mortgage."

"So it is, mother." He leaned his cheek against her hand for a moment; then he stood up. "Don't worry about me, mother; I'm not worth it. I'll be all right by morning. Good night. I'm going upstairs now."

Once in his room, Mahlon stumbled through the darkness to his window, and strained his eyes through the night in the search for Mariella's light. It was not burning.

"It's early yet," he thought; but he remembered that for several weeks it had been growing later and later before the light appeared. Twice he had sat waiting until midnight before its slender flame thrilled and warmed his heart, and let him go to his needed rest.

Now its absence intensified his feeling of dread.

After a while he stood up, trembling. Semia had said that it would be easy to discover the truth or falsity of her charge for himself. He knew what she meant. With his hands clenched almost painfully, he took two or three steps toward the stairway. Then he stood still, his arms fell at his sides, the veins swelled out in his throat and temples.

"No, by God!" said Mahlon Proudfoot. "I won't watch her! I love her, and I told her I trusted her. I do trust her. Watching is a poor way to show love or trust, or to keep them. If I ever do watch her — if I ever do stoop so low! — I pray God" — he said it through set teeth — "I pray God that He'll let me see and hear things that'll break the heart inside of me!"

But when he had looked again in vain for her light, he threw himself roughly upon the floor, and, burying his face in his arms, moaned out, like an animal in torture, "Oh, Mariella, Mariella, Mariella!"

CHAPTER XXXIII

One day in late summer, Leaming invited a party for a sail across the bay to Smuggler's Cove. Mariella arose early, and stood for a few moments at her window, looking down over the town and sea. The morning was in tones of lavender and purple, as if some mighty amethyst had been pounded fine, and its dust blown loose upon the air. She felt, rather than saw, the beauty of the morning. Her eyes had gone far, to the yellow glimmer of Mahlon Proudfoot's new house among the firs and alders. She never looked down in that direction without feeling a strange tremble of her heart.

She saw the faint line of smoke curling from the kitchen chimney of his home, and knew that in a few minutes he would be going to his day's monotonous work, while she would be sailing away over the blue sea with gay and careless people.

"Oh, Mahlon, poor Mahlon!" she murmured. "You are too good, too unselfish, for me. But I'll make it up to you some day. I'll make you so happy that you will forget all these bitter days of separation."

She did not know that the feeling in her heart was passionate pity instead of love. She did not know why her heart trembled when she looked down toward the house he was building for her. Nor did she know why she had kept her engagement from Mr. Leaming. "I'll tell him myself," she had said to her mother; but the time never came when she could put the announcement into words. The mere thought of it made her shrink and turn pale.

She finally turned from the window with a sigh. Breakfast was on the table and her parents were seating themselves when she entered the dining-room. Leaming was living with them now, but he had arisen early, and expected to breakfast on the launch. They kept no servant, and only one man, and he, being married, lived in a small house in one corner of the orchard.

Mrs. Palmer gave her a dark look as she entered. "It takes you a pretty spell to dress! This is a nice caper! It wouldn't of hurt you to help me get breakfast, an' dress afterwards. I ain't as young as I was."

Mrs. Palmer had changed much and living with her was far more comfortable than it had ever been before; but she still had many dark moods when her violent temper mastered her, and Mariella and her father could secure peace only by fleeing from the reach of her tongue.

Mariella colored.

"You have forgotten that I offered to cook breakfast, but you were afraid I might be late, and insisted upon doing it yourself."

"Mebbe I did an' mebbe I didn't. I never thought it 'u'd take you all day to dress. Take off your jacket an' let me see how your waist sets. . . . Hunh. It sets all right. That green is terrible becomin'. There ain't one girl in a thousand complected like you. Most skins like your'n freckle all up. I bet you'll either freckle or tan to-day."

After a moment's silence she added: "You're as straight as a fir. It makes me laugh to see women try to hold themselves that new-fangled way. That Mis' Flush! She must hurt herself! She'll get a tumor yet, a-holdin' in her stomach so an' a-protrudin' in the back.

But if anything was new-fangled, she'd do it if it give her five tumors all at once."

"Oh, mother!" Mariella laughed reluctantly. Mrs. Palmer laughed, too.

"Well, she would. I declare I don't like your goin' around with her. I wish she wa'n't goin' to-day. Next thing you'll come out with red paint on your cheeks and yellow hair."

"No, she won't," said Mr. Palmer, stirring his coffee round and round until it sank into a little smooth whirlpool. He looked at Mariella with kind, faded eyes that touched her heart. His illness had changed him strangely. The look of one who has toiled and waited and hoped, only to fail utterly in the end, was upon him. It was in his listless glance, his dragging step, his sunken chest, and stooping shoulders; it was in the frequent quiver of his chin and the tremble of his great brown hands; it was in the helpless bend of his thin knees. He would often stand for hours leaning on the gate, and looking out over the water with far, level gaze that seemed as if it must reach to the very end of life.

At such times, Mariella thought, a great artist would have painted him upon a piece of canvas and named the picture "Failure."

His whole nature seemed changed. He had grown gentle and patient and uncomplaining. He never lost his temper, and he never quarrelled with his wife. When she scolded, reproached, or upbraided, he turned his eyes away from her, and listened in a silent patience that was pathetic.

Mariella had been greatly affected by the change in her father. It had dignified him, even as death dignifies the weakest and the most insignificant. He had always defended her so far as he dared from her mother's violent outbursts of temper and rage, but he now showed her affection and even tenderness. What touched her most was a kind of humility — an embarrassed shame of himself — which caused him to absent himself when she had company. If a knock came upon the door in the evening, he would rise in feeble haste, dropping the ashes out of his pipe.

"Don't go, father," Mariella would entreat in distress.

"I'll go to bed," was always his reply, with a flickering smile. "I ain't fit to see comp'ny. I smell of tobacco smoke, your ma says. Never mind, Petty; I'd just as live. Bed's the place for us when we get old an' no account. I'd just as live."

Mariella looked across the breakfast table now and smiled at her father. "No," she said, "I'll not paint my cheeks, father; and I like my hair as it is. You must promise me you'll not work any to-day. You always work too hard when I am not here to watch you."

"For the land's sake!" exclaimed her mother; a splash of red came into each cheek. "What does he work so hard at? He don't do a thing but the chores. He can't gether fruit, because his back aches him so. He can't pare vegetables for me, because his hands trimble him so. He can't make out the accounts, because his eyes hurt him so. The hired man can't do everything, an' it all comes on me when you're a-gaddin' around. You don't ever tell me not to work so hard, I notice."

"I'll stay at home hereafter," said Mariella, quietly, but with white lips.

"No, you won't!" Mrs. Palmer lifted her voice loudly; her face was almost purple. "You'll go every time Leaming asks you. I don't mind doin' the work, but I do mind your whinin' about your father's workin'."

"He is not able to work. He shall not work." Her [illegible]s flamed into her mother's.

"Oh, that's big talk. You're a pretty one to talk. You'd set the well a-fire a-workin'. You couldn't earn a dollar if we all starved; an' you wouldn't have Leaming if you could get him. You make a big fuss about your father, but you wouldn't turn your hand over to help him."

Mariella arose. Her father had already left the room. She followed him. He was standing on the porch, looking out over the water with wistful eyes, and rubbing his thumb and forefinger together softly.

All her life Mariella had starved for tenderness and close, warm affection, and now that her father seemed to be turning to her with childish fondness and dependence, her rich heart went out to him in passionate, forgiving response. She was so hungry for love that even the poorest crumbs were sweet.

She went to him now, and put her arms around his neck, and kissed him. He looked at her with tears in his eyes; then he looked away.

"Never mind, Petty," he said, patting her clumsily on the back. "I know I'm awful tryin'—not a durn bit o' use to her; an' she does have to work hard." His eyes fell. "I wish you *could* take a notion to Leaming. It 'u'd make things easy for her; an' there's no use in denyin' it, she's had an awful hard life, an' there don't seem to be much ahead for her."

He patted her on the back again, as if to take away the sting of his words, and went shuffling feebly away in the direction of the barns.

Mariella stood where he left her, pale and shaken with emotion.

At nine o'clock the yachts were drifting with blown sails into the purple distance that led to the islands. Mrs. Flush, gayly and showily dressed, as usual, sat in the stern, with her delicately gloved hand on the tiller. To secure this seat she always pretended to steer the boat; it was the most comfortable seat.

Mariella preferred the bow. She liked to lie prone on a soft rug, with her cheek on her arm, and listen to the music of the waves that met and kissed, and parted as the sharp cutwater pierced them, only to fling them into long liquid banks of glistening pearls.

When they were well away from the wharf, Leaming, knowing her preference, bestowed her carefully on soft rugs in the bow. There was a stiff breeze. He wrapped her in a warm shawl before seating himself.

"It is a violet day," she said, smiling in sheer sensuous enjoyment of the water, "when the sky is pale blue, the sea deep blue, and the distance purple. The three tints blend into violet. And a violet day on Puget Sound is perfect for sailing. That low island to the south —" she looked into the distance with dreamily narrowed eyes — "is Columbine. See how the firs are bent by the wind. Do you remember how in June its rocky shores are so covered with columbines that it seems to be wrapped in a red mist?"

"I remember," said Leaming. "But as I think of it, it does not seem so beautiful to me as Fireweed Island — that little mound, scarcely larger than a room, that slopes up and seems to float like a rosy cloud upon the water. A single tree would have spoiled its beauty."

"There were trees upon it once and they were burned, or there would be no fireweed," said Mariella, with her little air of knowledge of all things western which always amused Leaming.

"What a picture!" cried a gay voice, and Semia came climbing up behind them. Leaming had invited her to please Mrs. Flush, who had taken her up, and was rapidly converting her into a young lady of fashion after her own heart — one of the gayest of the gay. "Upon my soul! I've always wondered what fascination the bowsprit held for Mariella! Now, it is clear. There are possibilities in the bowsprit. Will some one come and enjoy this original picture with me? Mrs. Flush — oh!" Her tone changed suddenly. "Are you coming up here, Mrs. Hamlin?"

Mrs. Hamlin grasped Semia's reluctant hand and pulled herself up delicately. She was large, middle-aged, and dignified. She was from Boston, and she was the compound extract of the literature and culture of Kulshan. She could not talk fifteen minutes without mentioning the Symphony Concerts. She had belonged to a Woman's Culture Club in Boston; and as there was then not a club in Kulshan, she was distinguished indeed.

Mariella was desperately in awe of her. So much culture, higher education, and perfect propriety filled her with dismay whenever she was brought in contact with them. To add to her discomfiture, Mrs. Hamlin always showed marked and cold disapproval of her. Usually Mariella managed to escape with an embarrassed greeting; but now escape was impossible.

Leaming at once arose and assisted Mrs. Hamlin to his place on the rugs. "How do you do?" she said, narrowing her eyes and coldly studying the girl, as she settled herself in stiff and dignified state. There was a deliberation in her every movement that was exasperating to Mariella.

Mariella returned the greeting civilly, but with secret wretchedness. Leaming, reading her glance of entreaty aright, remained. So did Semia; but her eyes were full of delighted anticipation.

Mrs. Hamlin held her kerchief in one hand, and smoothed it with the other, as she talked. She had made up her mind that this girl was not a proper person to be in polite society. She was too original, for one thing, and too bold in expressing her opinions —and such opinions! They always differed from the opinions of every one else. She was too independent and scornful of manner; and there was something like a challenge in her very carriage and in her flashing glance that never wavered. Then her family was, of course, worse than no family at all. She was determined to discover what there was in an ignorant country girl to attract and hold a man like Mr. Leaming, and to force a recognized position for herself in society, in spite of the fact that her parents had no position and the girl herself no chaperon.

She had been given to understand that Mariella held her own by cleverness.

"It requires a very clever girl to go about alone with men and be received," she had replied. "An unusually clever girl. They do that kind of thing in villages, of course, and nothing is thought of it; but there is no excuse for it here. We are trying to be civilized."

"But who would chaperon her?" some one, of a kind heart, protested. "You see what her parents are."

"That is precisely what I mean," returned Mrs. Hamlin, calmly and cruelly. "In Boston young women of that class — without presentable parents, without chaperons — are not in society."

Now she smoothed her kerchief and kept her searching eyes on Mariella.

"The breeze is very cold up here," she said deliberately. "Would you not be more comfortable down in the cockpit with the others?"

"Oh, no!" said Mariella. "I love to be up here."

"Few young ladies care to separate themselves from the others for so long a time."

"Yes, I know." Mariella let her white teeth flash for

an instant in one of her dazzling smiles. "That is why I monopolize this particular place. No one else seems to want it. I *always* sit here," — she looked Mrs. Hamlin unwaveringly in the eyes,—"*the whole way!* It is delicious. The wind beats you like whips. . . . Do you have neuralgia?"

Mrs. Hamlin did have neuralgia; but she would not admit it.

"It will give one neuralgia, if he ever has it . . . and rheumatism. Do you ever have rheumatism? . . . You are fortunate. This is only a fair breeze. I like it when the yacht heels over and runs with her rail a-wash. *That's* sailing. Are you ever ill?"

"Sometimes — naturally," replied Mrs. Hamlin, with an inflection calculated to suppress the girl. "I suppose every one is ill when it is very rough."

"I'm *never*," cried Mariella, joyfully. "The rougher it is the better I feel. But then," she added innocently, "I go sailing because I love it. Some go because it is the thing to do; then they turn pale and large-eyed, and they cry 'Oh!' and scramble to the high side of the cockpit when the rail goes under; they are very ill when it is rough; but they go home, and declare they had a lovely time."

"You have lived in the West some time, Miss Palmer, have you not?" asked Mrs. Hamlin, with a cold ignorement of Mariella's little speech, meant to crush that young person.

"Always," replied Mariella, nodding her head merrily.

"Not — always, surely?"

"Why not?" demanded Mariella, nettled by the tone.

"Why — er — it seems impossible. It is — er — inconceivable to a New Englander, or even an Easterner, that any one should have lived out in this country *always*."

"Why?"

"Well, I don't know exactly why. One's mind doesn't seem able to grasp it, somehow. It seems too awful. To have been born here in this crude place, and to have lived here always! With no advantages of society, education, refinement, culture, association! To have sat here in this wilderness of stumps always. To have associated only with backwoodsmen; to have heard no lectures, no music, none of the world's famous singers; to have seen no great plays, no famed paintings; in a word, to have had nothing that tends to refine and broaden, and elevate; to make fit for polite and gentle society! It is inconceivable, I say, to us."

Something in the girl's face — something dauntless, challenging — had made Mrs. Hamlin say more than she had intended to say, had, in fact, made her utterly merciless. As she began speaking Mrs. Flush and two or three others had come up from the cockpit, so that Mariella was forced to the further humiliation of a larger audience to Mrs. Hamlin's words, — every one of which cut the girl's heart cruelly.

At first, as the even, well-modulated voice went on with slow, deliberate cruelty, a kind of despair seized her; she turned pale and cold. But when the voice ceased and there was silence of human sounds, she heard of a sudden the long washing ripple of the waves about the prow, the whistling music of the wind in the bellying sails, the thrilling cry of the gull; she turned her eyes away from Mrs. Hamlin's cold face and saw the distance stretching away, purple and beautiful and full of possibilities like a future, — and something strong and unconquerable swelled within her. The rose-flush came slowly back to her face, the deep red lights to her marvellous eyes, the outward curl to her lips. Her throat commenced beating, as it always did when she was angry or moved by any strong emotion; a full, ner-

vous beating that seemed to her to shake her slender body, although outwardly she was the picture of control. The islands arose, dark and strong, out of the mist, and far away the great soft roses of the snow-mountains bloomed pink upon the pale green of the morning skies.

She turned back to Mrs. Hamlin with a deliberation that equalled that lady's own. Her eyes went full into hers.

"These advantages," she said slowly, "according to your own showing, should certainly refine and polish the manners. They should also ennoble the nature, broaden the character, and give a wide and generous outlook on life. It seems to me that education should first of all make it impossible for those possessing it to criticise others who have not been so fortunate. Whatever else it may do, if it doesn't do that, it fails. And it does fail sometimes. It all depends, I suppose, upon the material it has to work upon. I should say, for instance," she added, more slowly, "that America could get along better without all her college graduates than without her one great backwoodsman, Abraham Lincoln. When it is given to one to be noble or great, it doesn't matter where he lives, nor what his advantages have been. He can get education from mountains and forests, and from the people about him, while others are getting it from colleges and paintings and music. If he cannot, he is not one of those who count in the world. And when one has had all the advantages of higher education, and yet has not received from it that which makes it impossible for him to criticise another less fortunate, nor that which gives him a kind and generous heart, he is also one of those who do not count."

When Mariella had ceased speaking, she was as much astonished as the others at what she had done. Her eyes fell at last beneath the cold gaze of Mrs. Hamlin, the exponent of education and culture. She felt herself trembling. What had possessed her? A moment before she began speaking she had had no consciousness of her intention to do so. It seemed to her now that the words had suddenly, but quietly, come against her will.

Then she remembered that Mrs. Hamlin had never missed an opportunity to slight her and hurt her. With a pang of dismay she thought of Isaphene and the currant stains on the white chip hat. "It is the same thing," she thought bitterly. "They both hurt me, and stung me into doing wrong; and after it is done, I can only cry, 'What *made* me do it?'"

The color was gone out of her face. She sat pale and aghast at the effect of her words. Mrs. Hamlin was speechless, with red spots of fury burning in her cheeks.

She arose haughtily, and prepared to descend into the cockpit. Her curiosity was satisfied. She had learned how Mariella held her own without a chaperon in Kulshan society. The others, including Semia, followed her. They were bored by Mrs. Hamlin's culture-pose, and were really pleased to see her chagrin, yet they carefully concealed their satisfaction. Mrs. Hamlin's social position could not be ignored.

CHAPTER XXXIV

MARIELLA found herself alone again with Leaming. She had not looked at him. She was afraid of seeing disapproval in his eyes; and in the present tumult of her emotions she felt that she could not bear that. She was even having all she could do to keep tears out of her eyes, although she seldom allowed them to come to the relief of her sufferings. No one understood her, she did not even understand herself; yet, somehow, she had always expected Leaming to understand her and excuse her, to himself, if not to others. It was one of her childish faiths which she had not let go.

But after a while she felt that she could bear anything better than the silence which held such uncertainty in it. She lifted her eyes shrinkingly, and looked at him. Then her heart leaped. He had returned her look with grave and sympathetic tenderness.

"You're not angry?" she exclaimed, with almost childish relief; and it seemed as if her heart opened out to him sudden petals of gratitude.

"How could I be angry with you?" he replied, moving nearer.

She shook her head slowly. Her eyes filled with tears now, but she looked at him steadily through them.

"I deserve your anger. I was rude and unkind. You were my teacher — and you would be more proud of me if I had ignored her rudeness. It must have displeased you; only — please do not scold me, even with your eyes, as you used to do, for I am sorry enough without that."

"Dear girl," said Leaming, and he put out his hand and laid it, trembling, upon hers, "don't be afraid of me. I'll never scold you again — and I don't believe I ever did! But if you had flung your calm but stinging truths at me, I should not have been angry — should not even have disapproved of you. For it *is* the truth. It is hard to see it as truth, harder to admit that it is the truth; but we'll get to it in time. For myself, I am free to say that I am so sunken in my narrow college groove that only the enlightenment of being with you could have made me see it. Only think," he said, smiling, "of coming out here, to a new 'boom' town, cut out of a forest, and having the cherished opinions and the culture of ages laughed at by a slip of a girl who has lived Out-West all her life — who never saw a college or a school of higher education of any kind; a girl who looks us in the eyes and tells us that there are things we do not know, and other ways of getting an education than the ones we know; who tells us even" — his voice sank lower — "that there are better ways of getting close to God, and to an appreciation of God's largeness, than the ones we have been following for centuries. We don't like to be laughed at, and after we 'leave school' we don't like to be taught — unless we love the teacher! I confess that this ruthless hand of yours has been tearing up culture by the root in me for some months; at first it hurt; and although I have grown to like it now, I can appreciate Mrs. Hamlin's emotions."

The girl laughed. "I couldn't help it. Even if you had scolded me, I should do it all over again at the first provocation. You don't know, of course, how exasperating it is. As soon as a woman comes here from the East and shakes the dust off her clothes, she narrows up her eyes and goes poking around in the woods, holding up her skirts, looking for culture — as if it were something that grows wild! When I am introduced to a tenderfoot, I count the number of times my heart beats before she asks me if there are many 'cultured people' here. We have to laugh at them, or teach them better, or go mad! The last would be easiest, really. . . . Tell me," she wheedled, changing her tone, "what is the most amusing thing a Westerner does when he goes East?"

Leaming considered a moment; then he laughed, as in reluctant remembrance. "Oh, I think it is the stern look he puts on his face."

"Why does he look stern?"

"Well, you can hardly expect me to know."

"But why do you think it is?"

"Well, I *fancy* it is because he is awed by the strangeness, the unusualness, of it all, and not wishing any one to suspect that he is overpowered, he puts on that almost fierce look, as much as to say: 'I'm not curious; I'm used to all this sort of thing. Is *that* your Statue of Liberty and your *World's* Tower? Hunh!'"

Mariella struck her hands together and laughed gayly.

"Oh, that's delicious! Do we really do that when we go East the first time? Are we ashamed of our curiosity and our awe?"

Then her face grew serious. "But you taught me all these things," she said, "years ago. These truths, as you call them, which I have been putting to Mrs. Hamlin — you taught them to me. Had you forgotten?"

"Yes," said Leaming, with a sigh, "I had forgotten. The world has got hold of me, somehow, and I have let many of my old sweet beliefs go. After all, Mariella, solitude is the thing to keep the soul sweet and simple.

I want to come back to my early teaching; will you help me?"

Mariella shook her head. "No," she said; "you helped me, but I cannot help you. It is too late." She looked at him with a kind of sadness. "This town is only two years old, but it has already eaten something out of me. I don't know what. I find myself shrinking from the fear of being considered different from other women. I surprise myself studying Mrs. Flush's style or Miss Walton's manner, solely because I dread being peculiar. I have even found myself wondering how far I may imitate them without losing my own individuality."

"You could never lose that," said Leaming, hurriedly. "You never could be at all like them."

"I *could* be just like them," she replied bitterly. "Or I could have been; I do hope it is too late now. I have missed many good things, but I have at least missed — "

She paused, and Leaming finished the sentence for her.

"Thank heaven," he said, "you have missed the half-education and the half-culture that produces such women — so self-satisfied that they never realize how little they know, and how little they have that is worth having."

They were silent for a moment, then the color went across Mariella's face in a leap. She looked him resolutely in the eyes.

"Those were beautiful things I said to Mrs. Hamlin, were they not?"

"Yes, Mariella."

"There was no reply she could make, was there?"

"I can think of none."

"I want to make a confession. I believe what I said to be the truth, and yet — "

"And yet?" questioned Leaming, smiling as she hesitated.

"And yet," — she spoke very low, — "I, too, shrink from certain results of living in the backwoods. I shrink from them in myself, and I shrink more from them in others."

The color was faded from her face, leaving her pale. She was thinking now, unconscious of the thought, of Mahlon Proudfoot, awkward and toil-stooped and poorly dressed. How different he might have been with education and the advantages of a city — the thought went no further; she remembered suddenly what she had said to Mrs. Hamlin. Poor Mahlon! Was he only of those, then, who do not count? She was filled with quick self-reproach.

Before Leaming could reply, there was a scramble in the cockpit.

"*Hey!*" came a bellow behind them. "What's the matter? We've been shouting ourselves hoarse at you. Here's Smuggler's Cove. Look out! The jib's coming!"

Leaming got to his feet in amazement, and lifting Mariella, steadied her with his arm, for the yacht was heeling far over on one side. It was true. They had sailed ten miles across the bay, rounded the Cape of the Windbent Trees, and were just entering the small but beautiful Smuggler's Cove. The entrance was narrow; on either side masses of long olive kelp coiled and twisted, and floated over dangerous rocks. Inside, the bay widened to the curve of a horseshoe; the heavily timbered shores sloped up steeply to a height of a thousand feet; there was a small beach of sand, pebbles, and agates. The shores were rocky, but the shallow-rooted firs had managed to get a footing to the water's edge, to grow straight and tall, and blend into the dark green background of forest. A kind of purple twilight, sown with flecks of sunlight as the night is sown with stars, dwelt always in that sequestered cove. On the warmest day it held the poetic, alluring cool of evening. The rocks were covered with mosses and lichen, lighting up the shadows with rich tones of green, rose, lavender and yellow. In the deepest shadow a waterfall let loose its pale green liquid thunder; and from high on the mountainside sank the u-lu-lu of an owl.

Mariella went through that long summer day in a dream. She was conscious that Leaming was almost constantly at her side, anticipating her slightest need or wish, and serving her with unobtrusive delicacy. Semia tried in vain to lure him to her, and Mrs. Flush set herself boldly to the pleasant effort to secure his attention. He was unfailingly courteous to all his guests; but he gravely permitted them to see that his chief desire was to please Mariella.

Quite unconsciously she put the thought of Mahlon from her. The day was full of soft, compelling dreaminess, and she yielded to its spell. As the day wore on the people about her grew more unreal to her. She talked, moved from one place to another, and rested with her lap full of blue harebells which Leaming had gathered on the cliff above the waterfall; but faces and voices and laughter came to her but dimly through it all. She had a sense of desire, a passionate longing to enjoy the day to the utmost; to get something rich and full and deep out of it and out of all her life afterward. She wanted the day to lead on to something nobly sweet in her future — something that would ease her unrest and give her a clearer understanding of life.

The dream grew sweeter as night came on, and the beach fires sent up their scarlet flames through the dark. "For this one day," her heart kept saying, "I will be perfectly happy."

"For this one day," the waves repeated, as they came pushing and curling up the sand to break into musical speech, ere they drew away to be lost in the ocean.

At midnight they sailed out of the little cove. As the yacht swept between the masses of kelp, Mariella, curled up in the bow with Leaming beside her, turned and gave a long, regretful look backward. The cove was weirdly lighted by the smouldering fires, whose embers, falling now and then one upon another, sent up columns of scarlet sparks that finally parted company, and swam hither and thither through the violet dusk among the firs like beautiful wandering fireflies. She thought of the hundreds of years the cove had been hidden there, with the tall dark trees rising above like sentinels. She thought how many times the sun had turned them to glittering shattered lances; how many times the moon had silvered them and flooded that lonely place with poetic radiance.

A few moments later they were rounding the Cape of the Wind-bent Trees. Low in the east Orion's beautiful three were slowly rising. The splendid Aldebaran, the peerless Capella, and all the other glittering ones of the heavens burned in the violet spaces above; and of a sudden the east whitened to a chaste glow that seemed to cast a great thistle-down of light upon the sea; presently the moon came pushing, dark and strong, into the light — so slowly that at first it was but a slender curving sickle that gradually filled and rounded out into the full moon.

The charm of the night possessed Mariella more powerfully than that of the day. She was conscious now of a rich, satisfying happiness, which she did not connect in her thought with Leaming, although she was aware of an intense and throbbing appreciation of his nearness, and of their complete isolation from the others.

It seemed to her that a small world of joy swam around them, closing them in alone; but just outside its circling rim lay a great world of sorrow, through whose dark, blurred spaces she occasionally caught a glimpse of Mahlon Proudfoot's face, white and haggard, but always fading away and eluding her like a face in a dream, as she strained her eyes for a second glimpse.

At first they talked, in low and broken sentences, the girl sitting upright against the mast, Leaming lying beside her, leaning upon his elbow. Then their voices fell lower; their sentences grew fewer and more broken, their pauses longer; at last they fell under the thrall of the night's noble beauty, and the silence was broken only by the push of the wind in the sails and the long, singing wash of the waves.

Through it all Mariella was only dimly conscious that her hand, its pulses large and full with delight, was folded close in Leaming's.

CHAPTER XXXV

DAWN was drawing long beryl and pink ribbons across the east when Mariella entered her home after that day and night on the water. A door opened noiselessly, and her mother came tottering toward her. She was uncombed and only half clad. One look at her face told the girl that she was facing some great trouble; it was gray, and furrowed deep with continuous and bitter weeping. Mariella stood still; she could not speak. Pulses of terror were beating in her throat. Her mother fell upon her, sobbing.

"Oh, Mariella, your pa, your pa! He's a-dyin'. He was took with an awful spell this mornin', not long after you left. Out in the barn, an' we didn't find him till noon. The doctor says he can't live."

"Is he suffering?" came struggling from the girl's lips.

"No; he just lays an' moans — *an' talks!* Oh, my God! it breaks my heart to hear him — to hear the things he says to *me!*" She staggered back against the wall, and stood tearing her finger-nails with her teeth and staring down at the floor. She was talking to herself now, and seemed to have forgotten the girl's presence. "He called me Polly, just as he ust to do when we were first married — before we'd ever quarrelled any, or got cold an' bitter an' stubborn to each other, or struggled so for money. Much good it ever done us to work an' pinch an' scrimp! Much good it does *him* a-layin' there a-dyin'! If he had scrimped up a million, he wouldn't be a-thinkin' of it now. It couldn't keep his mind from goin' back to the time we was young an' first married, an' never quarrelled or hated each other, an' I was Polly. *Polly!*" She burst out into convulsive sobbing that seemed to tear her breast. "I ain't hear that name for twenty years. And to hear it now, an' him a-dyin'! If I had thought he would ever speak tender to me again, I never'd of — never'd of — been so wicked. May the Lord have mercy on me and forgive me! My God, my God!" She walked up and down the room, wringing her hands; those great hands knotted and red with coarse labor appealed to Mariella now with a terrible pathos. "Do people know everything — *everything* — after they die? Will *he* know everything? Oh, my God, my God, spare me that! Never let him know! Punish me any other way! Give me suffering, torture, hell — but never let him know!"

Mariella had stood speechless in that fear which the young have of grief and death. But now at last she summoned courage to go to her mother, and put her arms around her.

"*Oh, mother!*" It was all she could say; but tenderness and pity for her mother beat through her voice. Her mother looked at her a moment with dazed eyes, not understanding; then her head sank forward upon her breast, and such dumb anguish shook her as set the girl to sobbing passionately upon her neck. After a while these words struggled from her mother, sounding as if torn from deep in her breast: "Oh, Mariella! *You kind, too!* Why wasn't you kind before? Long ago? When you was little? I never'd of done wrong if somebody'd been kind an' tender to me."

"Why weren't you kind to me?" cried the girl, in a voice of pain.

"Oh, God knows why! I don't. At least, I suppose

He knows why He makes people an' puts *devils* in 'em, an' then binds 'em out when they're children in the backwoods to slave year in an' year out, without a chance to git any learnin' except to follow their own wills, right or wrong. I've had devils in me all my life, an' nobody ever teached me how to git 'em out. Am I to blame? Who *is* to blame? Nobody ever said, 'Don't do that; it's wicked,' or, 'Don't swear; it's wrong,' to me. I never had a chance. It was born in me an' it stayed in me. But you, — you've had some chance. You might of been kinder to your mother."

A moan came from the bedroom. She started heavily and tried to compose her features. "He's awake. Come right in, Mariella. No knowin' how soon it'll come, the doctor says."

Mariella followed her tremblingly. The bedroom was gray and cheerless. Not a picture hung on the walls, painted drab, like the dining-room. A dull calico curtain was drawn across one corner to make a clothes-closet; another across another corner, to conceal shelves of medicines in bottles and boxes. There was a little home-made table, with combs and brushes upon it and a wavy mirror hanging above it; a drab window-shade, worn to lace on the edges, had been rolled up and tied with a string to let in the daylight.

In one corner stood the bed. Mr. Palmer lay supine and still upon this hard bed, his head well back upon the pillow. His hair and his long straggling beard had grown quite gray during the illness of the summer, and they had an unkempt look that filled Mariella with self-reproach. Why had she not taken better care of him? Why had she not shown him more tenderness? What had he gotten of love, or joy, or satisfaction, out of life? And now it was too late to do anything for him. He was dying. It would soon all be over. She went to him silently, and took his rough brown hand in both her own.

"Father," she murmured; and all the love, all the pity, all the fondness she had kept from him, kept locked in her heart, throbbed through the word. He moved his head and looked at her. A sudden moisture went across those blue eyes of his, now more strangely, intensely blue than she had ever seen them.

"Oh, Mariella, you've come back in time. I'm so glad, so thankful. I didn't want to leave Polly all alone. Poor Polly!" Then he called her, in quite a young, cheerful voice; yet oh, so feebly! "Polly! Polly! What you doin', Polly? You gettin' supper?"

Mariella raised her head. She had knelt down beside him.

"It is morning, father."

"Well, there, look at me!" he exclaimed weakly. "Polly'll think I'm gettin' silly. She gettin' breakfast?"

Mrs. Palmer came to the bed. Mariella moved to make room for her. Mr. Palmer took his wife's great hand and patted it tenderly.

"Polly," he said, "you must forgive me everything. I'd give all my life if I could live one year more an' see things as they look to me now. I see how mean an' stingy an' naggin' an' stubborn I've been to you always. I'd like to just be good an' kind to you one year, an' make you happy — so you'd run an' set on my lap an' kiss me the way you did that first year we was married. I'd put on white shirts for church an' comp'ny; an' buy you a black silk dress an' a new bunnit with hollyhocks in it; an' I wouldn't eat apple-sass with my knife if the cashier was here. I wouldn't do a thing to pester you an' make you mad, like I've done all my life." He sighed heavily. "But it's all too late, Polly. We always want to do bad things too soon, an' good ones too late. But, Polly — listen here! I can say one thing as many men can't say. *There's never been any other woman but you.* No matter how mad I'd get at you, or how mean I'd treat you, I never looked at any other woman without feelin' proud all over an' thinkin', says you, she can't hold a candle to Polly! That Mallory. He ust to make me so mad! Always a-slyin' around that no-account Lize Appleby, an' then a-braggin' about it, an' a-sayin' she was the finest lookin' woman in the county. Heifer! she couldn't hold a candle to you for looks."

Mrs. Palmer lifted a face like stone. She knew his mind was wandering, or he would not talk of such things now; and yet —

"Is he, Mr. Mallory — that kind of a man?" she asked, and God only knew how her heart trembled.

"What kind?" He looked at her vacantly, and began picking the bedclothes. "Oh, after women? Yes; always a-boastin' about some woman or other. He wa'n't fit for a woman to wipe her feet on! But some women are such fools!"

Mrs. Palmer leaned her head on her hand. Her eyes were set on her husband's face.

"Why didn't you ever tell me this before?"

"I do' know, Polly."

"How long has he been — been actin' that way?"

"What way, Polly? W'y, years an' years. He knowed just how to make every woman think she was the only one. Them's the men! It's so easy for 'em to fool women that they fool their wives. They're so nice to their wives that they think the sun rises an' sets in 'em; they don't know all the other women thinks so, too."

"Oh, mother," said Mariella, very low, and with a strange new gentleness, "don't let him talk about such things now."

She stopped, struck by the haggardness of her mother's face.

"I'll make some coffee for you, mother," she said, and went hastily out to the kitchen. She was afraid to be left alone in that room with her father. It seemed to her that something pale and shadowy sat there waiting.

The day wore on. Neighbor women came and looked in with stern, but eager, eyes, and went away disappointed, to stand and talk in low tones out in the yard, casting frequent but surreptitious glances at the bedroom window. Once Mariella raised it two or three inches. They left off talking immediately, and came in with long, stealthy strides and beckoning looks.

"— ain't got a thing but white clumatis, but it'll work up well with green sparrowgrass," one was saying.

"Sparrowgrass is terrible common," said another, frigidly.

Late in the afternoon Mariella looked up from the side of the bed to see Mrs. Worstel standing outside, signalling with a bent finger. She went out and was drawn aside.

"I *couldn't* help coming. I know an Oxydonor has been known to work miracles; an' it *couldn't* hurt him just to try."

Mariella declined; they were following the doctor's instructions, and in spite of Mrs. Worstel's "fiddling" the doctors high and low, she was firm; but her eyes were full of tears, and at last Mrs. Worstel yielded, and kissed her without offence. "It's worked wonders, though," she said, sighing. "I wish you wa'n't so set. You are just as set as gelatine!"

All day and all night, worn with grief and loss of sleep, Mariella watched with her mother at the bedside. The neighbors cooked dinner for them, disputing firmly

to the end. Should the potatoes be boiled or baked? Should the croquettes be fried in butter or lard?

Leaming sat in the parlor all night, smoking cigar after cigar, to keep awake. The neighbors whispered in the kitchen, and drank many cups of strong coffee. At midnight Mrs. Worstel carried one in to Leaming. He accepted it gratefully. She waited while he drank it. To apologize for the rings of smoke circling around the room, he remarked that he smoked because he found it so difficult to remain awake. She made no reply; but when she had taken away the cup she returned and placed a big pitcher of water on the floor. Then she held something out to him; yards of yellow cord fell, coiling beneath her hands. "Try this," she pleaded. "Just put it in the pitcher, an' buckle this elastic around your ankle, agen the flesh, an' set down an' read. It'll keep you awake; or, when you want to go to sleep, it'll put you to sleep. It'll do anything."

It was dawn — a dawn as yellow as a primrose — when the tired spirit ceased struggling with death. He had slept; and awaking at that hour which takes so many souls out to a new day, he looked wistfully at Mariella and her mother; then his sunken eyes turned to the light.

"I see it all, Polly." The words were painfully broken by struggles for breath. "I can see my whole life stretched out behind me, an' it seems a terrible failure. What worries me is that I wa'n't kinder to you."

Mrs. Palmer had been sitting, holding his hand, with her head bowed down upon it. Now she raised a face in which grief and remorse had eaten great wrinkles over night. "Oh, my God!" she uttered, chokingly. "Don't talk about not being kind — unless you want to drive me mad!"

"It's a lonesome thing, this dyin'," he continued, still staring, as if for help, at the light. "It seems as if the whole world ort to stop an' help, or be sorry, or somethin'." He lay a long time with closed eyes; then he looked again at the light. "I never had a chance here, Miss Rachel," he said earnestly. "Do you s'pose I'll have a chance hereafter?"

Mrs. Palmer looked at Mariella through drowned eyes. "She was his Sunday-school teacher," she whispered. "He thought the world of her. He always called her just Miss Rachel; but I ain't hear him speak her name for twenty years."

"You was my only chance, Miss Rachel, but I was such a little fellow I couldn't quite understand. You ust to say a prayer with me. Would you mind sayin' it now?"

He paused and waited. There was intense silence in the room. A shaft of sunlight fell across the bed. The clock ticked off the moments ceaselessly. Outside the window a bird burst into full and joyous song. It ceased. Another sound struck on Mariella's tense hearing, the shrill monotonous beating of a woodpecker's beak upon a dead tree.

With one awful sob, she fell upon her knees beside her father. "O Lord God," she prayed, in a voice shaken powerfully with heart-beats, "be with my father, who is going away. He is old and lonely, and afraid to go alone. Be with him. Dear God, you have given me strength so many times when I have asked you. Now I ask you for my father. Give him strength and courage — and oh, my God, my God —"

She broke down, sobbing. Her brow sank to her hands, folded on the bed.

"Thank you, Miss Rachel," said the dying man, with a pathetic politeness. "But there was another prayer we ust to say together. I hadn't thought of it for years an' years; but it seems as if I could say it clear through. You learned it to me . . . I was such a little fellow, and I didn't have any mother . . . I'll see if I can say it over. Seems as if God 'u'd hear a prayer an old dying man had learned, when he was such a little fellow, at his Sund'y-school teacher's knee. I couldn't of said it a month ago, but I can say it now. Miss Rachel, hear?"

He set the tips of his trembling fingers together, and lifted his eyes, as little children do, and repeated, slowly and in a tone of childish solemnity, the Lord's beautiful Prayer — that sublime plea that no man or woman of mature years can hear without a full heart and full eyes.

"Our Father, Who art in heaven, hallowed be Thy name! Thy kingdom come; Thy will be done on earth, as it is in heaven. Give us this day our daily bread; and forgive us our tres-passes as we forgive them that tres-pass agen us. Lead us not —" he paused. "Forgive us our tres-passes as we forgive them that tres-pass agen us," he repeated faintly. "I never sensed that before. Everything seems so clear now. *As we forgive them* —"

He was silent a long time. "I do," he spoke out at last, in a stronger tone. "Polly, I do forgive every one that ever trespassed agen me."

Mrs. Palmer lifted her head. "Every one?" she whispered.

"Every one, Polly."

"If they trespassed agen you an' you never knowed it?"

"Every one."

"If they sinned terrible agen you? Could you say you forgive 'em without knowin' *what* you are forgivin'?"

"Every one. The Lord'll have to forgive some ter-

rible sins if He forgives me. Didn't I ask him to forgive me as I forgive them?" Then he went on slowly: "Lead us not into tem'tation; but deliver us from evil; for Thine is — the kingdom — and the power — and the glory — forever. Polly?"

He ceased. There was silence in the room. The sound of the woodpecker's hammering struck on Mariella's quivering and drawn heart-strings.

"Oh, my God, my God!" she cried, in passionate entreaty.

The dawn drew a long bright ribbon across the room, and left it on the girl's head. Then Leaming's strong arms lifted her, and she heard his kind, gentle voice say, "Come."

CHAPTER XXXVI

THE funeral was a large one. Every one had liked Mr. Palmer, and now that his kind blue eyes were closed in death they came from far and near to pay him the last respect in their power.

Conveyances of all kinds were ranged along the fence. The women all crowded, pale and breathing hard, into the house, where they stood or sat, large-eyed, with their heads tipped forward, alert for a word of gossip; the men stood around the yard in groups, talking low.

"He liked his joke," one said, with a sepulchral smile. "I never see a man so ready for his joke."

"He was the straightest man on a horse-trade in the county," said another, chewing a fine stick which he had whittled white. "I God, I bet nobody ever fooled around him on a horse-trade. He dealt square, an' you had to deal square with him."

"If you didn't, you got your eye-teeth cut in a hurry," said another, forgetting the occasion and grinning broadly.

"Yes, I God, an' your wisdom-ones, too!"

"It's a good thing he'd git fired up about somethin'. He"—the speaker lowered his voice—"let his wife walk all over him. He hardly dast say his soul was his own. My wife, she come over here one day an' walked right into the kitchen, an' there was Mr. Palmer over by the sink a-drinkin' somethin' out of a teacup. 'You takin' medicine?' says she. 'No,' says he, right out, with his face all red, 'I'm a-takin' whiskey. I'm all of a trimble, an' just feel like lettin' all holts go, an' I've wanted whiskey for a week, but she just hooted at the idy, an' kept pourin' root-beer down me. She's just stepped out to a neighbor's, an' I took this chance to git some whiskey down me.' Then he looks my wife in the eye an' hisses out: '*Root-beer!* Damn it all! When a man is all of a trimble!' My wife come home a-titterin'."

"Darn'dest man for a joke!" repeated the first speaker, as if he had a mortgage on the bit of information. "He'd set up half the night to come a joke on somebody."

"This is what we all have to come to," said one woman, sitting on the edge of her chair, as if poised for flight.

"Did you hear that dog howl the night before he died?" asked another, sinking her voice to a mysterious whisper.

"What dog?"

"Oh, I don't know *what* dog. It howled an' howled, just as mournful. I said at the time there was goin' to be a death," added the woman, triumphantly.

"I wonder if she'll wear black," whispered another. "Somebody offered to lend 'em mournin' veils for the funeral, but Mariella refused 'em."

"She needn't to hold her head so high. They ain't left any too well off, I guess."

"Well, they say Leaming can't see anybody but her, an' he's as rich as they make 'em."

"Well, listen. She ain't got him yet. I hear she's engaged to Mahlon Proudfoot — "

"Sh-sh! There's his mother over there; she'll hear you."

Both glanced over at Mrs. Proudfoot, who sat alone in one corner of the room, looking sweet and gentle in her old-fashioned black dress and hat.

"I wouldn't of thought she'd come; she hardly ever gets out."

"Mahlon, he come with her. He's stayed out in the yard with the men. I'd think he'd come in an' walk with Mariella. Mr. Pollard, he's a-goin' to walk with Mis' Parmer."

"I see. Well, anyhow, Semy Pollard is after Mr. Leaming, might an' main; so maybe Mariella won't hold her head so high after all. I'd think" — the woman laughed in a stifled way — "Mr. Mallory would walk with Mis' Parmer."

The other woman smiled with her hand over her mouth.

"I'd think so too, but I guess his wife might raise objections. Don't it beat all, the way some men can draw the wool over their wives' eyes all their lives! It's that Mis' Caruthers now, an' his wife don't suspect a thing."

"Who's Mis' Caruthers?"

"Oh, I don't know who she is. They come here from Cincinnata, Ohio — that's all I know about them. She's pretty lookin', an' Mr. Mallory, he commenced slyin' around her right away. I know just how he manages it," added the woman, with a shrewd look; "he says poetry to 'em! He sighs an' looks sad an' says mournful poetry about stiflin' his feelin's — an' the fool woman feels sorry for him, an' thinks he's a-sufferin', soul an' body, for her. She always wants him to stifle his feelin's till she sees he's a-doin' it an' a-sufferin', an' then she gits in an' does her best to keep him from stiflin' 'em. I tell you," bragged the woman, drawing up her chin, "I have seen a lot in my time, an' you can't fool me."

"Tap wood," said the other woman, admiringly; and her companion tapped the door, beside which they were sitting, with hard, crooked fingers.

Then their faces straightened out and grew slowly red; they drew apart and moved their chairs back with little squeaks on the bare floor of the dining-room; they looked significantly at each other, and then fixed their gaze solemnly on the floor. Mr. and Mrs. Mallory had just entered the room. Isaphene accompanied them. She had an air of importance. She whispered with her mother for a moment, and then made her way, holding her head high, into the parlor; she was to play the organ. Her mother looked after her with eyes narrowed to conceal the pride in them; her face fairly glowed. Mr. Mallory looked around the room at the ladies, caressing his cheek with his full fingers.

Out in the yard Mahlon Proudfoot stood with, and yet apart from, the other men. He hated them for talking. How could they talk and laugh down in their throats when Mariella was suffering?

His heart was sore for her and yearned over her. He wanted to hold her in his arms, close, close to his breast, and soothe her and kiss her soft hair, and promise to take care of her and be good to her. It seemed to him that a thousand devils were trying to drag him into the house to find her; but he stood as motionless and stiff as if his feet had been great stones. He had been forbidden that roof, and he would not go under it until he could lead Mariella out from under it with him.

Once he heard her sobbing at an open window. His face went white to his lips. The veins swelled out like cords in his temples, and great drops grew upon his brow and hung there.

"Ain't you goin' in?" questioned Mr. Worstel, in a whisper.

"I guess I won't," said Mahlon, shortly.

"I'd think you would. I'd think Mariella 'd expect you."

"I guess I won't."

"W'y, her ma, she's goin' to walk with Mr. Pollard. Who'll Mariella walk with?"

"I don't know."

Mahlon's thumbs sank into his palms.

"You'd ought to go in an' walk with her, Mahlon."

"I guess I won't."

"I'd think she'd expect you —"

"For God's sake," interrupted Mahlon, hoarsely, "let me alone!"

After a while the solemn tones of the organ pealed out, followed soon by the familiar words of "Nearer, my God, to Thee."

Mahlon's throat ached. He could not bear it, and he walked a few steps away and stood alone, with his hat drawn over his eyes. He knew what Mariella was suffering, and his very soul trembled for her.

"I wish they'd keep their music still," he thought savagely. "It pulls anybody's heart out — and then, to think what it is for her to bear, poor, little, delicate thing!"

It seemed a long time to Mahlon Proudfoot before the silent procession came from the house. His heart went out with a sickening leap to the slender figure in black drooping upon Mr. Leaming's arm. Then, in an anguish of whose selfishness he was ashamed even in that moment, he turned aside and did not look at her again.

"Mahlon," said his mother, that evening, following him out upon the back porch after supper, "are you goin' over to see Mariella to-night?"

"No, mother," he said, without looking at her.

"Don't you think you'd ought to, son?"

"I don't know," he replied, wearily.

"I think you'd ought," she advised, encouraged by his brevity.

He was silent.

"Shall I help you get ready?"

"No, mother, I'm not going."

"I wish you wouldn't act so. What will Mariella think? You haven't been a-near her in her trouble."

Mahlon winced.

"She'll understand," he said, after a faint hesitation.

"I don't see anything to understand. There ain't a thing to understand, so far as I see."

She seized hold of a broom, not angrily but tremblingly, and commenced sweeping the porch, which was already clean; her thin hands, in whose backs the veins stood out large and blue, shook upon the handle.

"There ain't a thing to see but your disposition. There ain't a thing the matter but that. If it wa'n't for your disposition, you'd have overlooked everything an' gone over there months ago, instead of leavin' the way open for other men. Semy says — "

She stopped, frightened by the look on his face.

"What does she say, mother?"

"Why, that — that — Leaming is a-cutting you out. Of course — it ain't so. He walked with her to-day, though. It was your place. By rights, you'd ought to walked with her, but you never went a-near. If it hadn't been for your disposition — "

Mahlon turned upon his mother with a white face. His chest lifted and fell powerfully as he breathed.

"See here, mother," he said; his voice was kind, but thick with repressed passion. "You are torturing me; and it isn't a bit of use. I know the reason I don't go there, an' the reason I couldn't walk with Mariella to-day. I've known it all these years that I've been separated from her. I know it's my disposition — just that and nothing else — that keeps me away from her when all the time my heart is eating and burning itself up with wanting to be with her, to have her, to take her and keep her away from everybody else. It's all my disposition. But Lord Almighty!" he burst out ferociously, and his throat purpled and swelled; "what is it that makes a person but his disposition? If it was my disposition to let a man order me from under his roof, when I didn't deserve it, and then go back, cringing, under it again, just to be easy and happy, I wouldn't be Mahlon Proudfoot, would I? I'd be somebody else! If it wasn't your disposition to bear everything, sweet and patient; if you flew mad at father and went into a spell once a week to let off your rage, — you wouldn't be you, would you? You'd be Mrs. Pollard. This thing you call disposition — as if it was a *straw* a body could knock off! — is the thing that a person's life depends on, as I see it. It makes all his happiness and it makes his trouble; if it ain't his own disposition that gives him the trouble, it's the disposition of somebody he loves. There isn't a man alive that hasn't got some one thing in him he can't conquer. In one it's drink, and in another it's gambling, and in another it's women, and in another it's an ugly temper, and in another it's cheating in little mean ways or stinginess about money. In me, it's stubbornness. I'm so stubborn that at times I seem to fairly go mad with it. *I can't give in* — not to save my life, and not to save Mariella's. I know it's my disposition, and I know it's stronger than life itself. If it separated me from her forever, — if it — if it — turned her away from me and" — the words seemed to shake in his throat — "and gave her to another man, I couldn't change it. Mother, can't you understand it and let me alone? You can't reproach me any more than I reproach myself." Then his voice trembled and broke.

He went to his mother, who had put her face down into her hands, and laid his arm around her shoulders. "Don't cry, mother," he whispered tenderly; "you know how I love you, and how hard it is for me to hurt you; but don't you see how it hurts me, too? Come, come, mother; try to forgive me. I'll have the mortgage paid off soon now, and then all the waiting and unhappiness will be at an end."

"That's fine talk," said Mrs. Proudfoot, between her sobs, being wholly unable to see that the unconquerable thing in her own disposition was a gentle, persistent nagging, "but in the meantime Mr. Leaming 'll walk off with Mariella. You could see it in his eyes to-day plain every time he looked at her. I heard two-three, three-four nudge each other and whisper at the way he looked at her, just as if he worshipped her."

"I don't doubt he does!" cried Mahlon, with a groan. "He couldn't help it. But that's no saying she'd be untrue to me —"

"Maybe it's no saying, but —"

"Don't you dar' to say she's a light woman that thinks nothing of her word."

"I won't say that, and I don't mean that," replied his mother, in a tone of gentle perplexity and worry. "I only think, with him following her around all the time, and you with your disposition, actin' so —"

Here Mahlon groaned aloud in utter anguish of soul, and, turning away from his mother, went up to his lonely attic. As usual, he went groping straight to his window to look for Mariella's light. It was not yet shining. He drew a chair to his window, and sitting down in the darkness, rested his elbows upon the little table and his face in his hands. His eyes went burning and aching through the night. An odd strained look had been growing of late about his eyes.

"You'd ought to wear a wider-brimmed hat, son," his mother frequently said; "the hot sun is makin' your eyes weak. The lids are gettin' a wrinkled-up look, as if you strained 'em lookin' too far through the sun."

It was not straining his eyes too far through the sun, but through the darkness, that had brought the wrinkled-up look to his eyelids.

CHAPTER XXXVII

In the days that followed her father's death Mariella was all tenderness to her mother. Her own nature seemed to have been enriched and ennobled by this great sorrow. Life took on new and deep meanings for her. It seemed to her that she had always been a child, and was suddenly become a woman, assuming all a woman's earnestness and responsibilities.

One night she and Leaming returned from their customary walk later than usual. They had not talked much, nor lightly, since her father's death; but that night they had scarcely talked at all. Leaming was so completely possessed by his deep feeling for the girl that silence seemed fuller and richer than any speech; and Mariella was no longer able to misunderstand his chivalrous and unobtrusive attentions. Every look he gave her, every cadence of his voice, told her that he loved her.

And at last she knew her own heart. She knew, with a guilty, passionate joy that would not be crushed, that she loved him, and that she had never loved Mahlon Proudfoot. She thought of Mahlon, stiff and awkward, saying "what-a-say," and not knowing what to do with his hands in company; she always compared unconsciously his embarrassment with Leaming's grave ease, and the comparison made her shudder.

Each day she told herself that she could never marry Mahlon Proudfoot; but one glimpse of the new house,

growing slowly and patiently among the trees, or one look at his light, shining steadily and constantly to her, and she would bow her head, pale to the lips with the certainty that her nobler self would not allow her to break a heart that had no one but her.

She realized that she had outgrown him in everything save constancy; yet she remembered, with torturing clearness, that she had urged him to do his duty at the sacrifice of his desire for a higher education. She remembered the night when the odor of wild musk was about them, and she had told him that she would hate him if he deserted his mother, and had promised him solemnly to be true to him and wait. She remembered the day and the hour when he had taken her out to the headland to select a site for their house — she remembered the new green firs and the wake-robins at their feet that day, and how his emotion had shaken her with an answering one that seemed almost holy. She remembered sometimes, with her pale face deep in her arms, how she had thrilled and trembled with joy when he had first kissed her under the white drift of the shadbush.

She had been only a young girl then, starving for love. Now she had outgrown it all. She was a woman, and she loved Leaming in a way that she had never dreamed of. It seemed to her now that she always had loved him, even as a child, and that it was as a lover he had come back to her.

That night they had walked along the cliffs in silence. The splendor of the sunset burned itself out about them. The sun was sinking through a deep purplish haze; each wave flung out a fleck of scarlet that flashed once and was gone. It was as if thousands of fireflies were floating above the sea.

When the last one had flashed and disappeared and

the evening had faded into gray, they turned homeward. It was already dusk, and the stars were out when they reached the porch. Mrs. Palmer had retired, and the house was in darkness.

"Good night," said Leaming; "I am going to stay out here awhile."

His voice had deep vibrations of tenderness in it.

"Good night," said Mariella, and her own voice trembled. He found her hand in the darkness and pressed it; then suddenly he stooped and laid his lips upon her arm, soft and warm through its thin sleeve.

She drew away from him tremblingly and opened the door; but his voice, low and firm, arrested her flight.

"*Mariella!*"

She stood still.

"Come back a moment. I have something to say to you."

She returned a step or two toward him, without speaking. He put his arm around her and drew her to him.

"Mariella," he said, very low and in a shaken voice, "forgive me if it seems too soon after your father's death to tell you that I love you — that I want to comfort you and take care of you. It is your very sorrow and loneliness that make it impossible for me to keep back the words any longer. Mariella — "

The girl had for a moment rested, trembling, in his arms, he had felt the intoxicating rapture of her yielding to his embrace; then she had started away from him, like a frightened bird taking flight. He held her hand firmly.

"Mariella, — dearest, — do not be afraid of me. I ask nothing of you to-night but your forgiveness and your tenderest thought. I do not ask an answer — nor a [illegible] I only ask you to believe that I love you, that

I came back from England hoping to love you, having had you always in my heart; and that it is my earnest desire to save you from all worry for the future, concerning which your mother has consulted me."

Fearful of frightening her into an immediate and embarrassed answer, Leaming had spoken with a repression of which he had not considered himself capable. Comparing his speech, when he was alone, with his real passion, he was struck with the humor of it. "It sounded like the proposal of a scientist," he told himself, in chagrin.

But his object was gained; Mariella slipped away from him in the darkness, when he lingeringly released her hand, without making reply.

Mariella went straight to her attic. Trembling with guilty happiness, she knelt down by her window, and laid her face in her hands. "Oh, Mahlon, Mahlon, Mahlon!" she cried; but even as she cried to him, pitying him, her heart shrank from him and yearned to Leaming. She did not go to bed that night. For hours she heard Leaming's step as he slowly paced the porch beneath her window. At last, however, she heard only the mournful cry of the night-owl on the hill. At one moment her pulses surged with joy; at the next she was bowed down in almost unbearable anguish at the thought that now her happiness could only mean sorrow for Mahlon Proudfoot; and his peace of mind, her own hourly torture.

Once, late at night, she tried to imagine the future as his wife. She saw herself rising in the gray dawns, year after year, to cook his breakfasts; toiling all day at housework, cooking his dinner and his supper; sitting for an hour or two in the evening, with an aching body and a tortured mind, to listen to his dull talk about the crops, the cattle, the hop-yield; and then giving herself to the tired, dreamless sleep of the brute that chews its cud in the barnyard.

She saw herself stepping soberly along in the narrow path Mahlon Proudfoot had worn hard with his ceaseless walking to and fro, never turning aside. She realized the powerful growth her mind had made since she parted from him. She laid herself upon the cold floor, and buried her face in her arms, with dry, passionate sobs.

"Oh, my God!" she cried. "Why must this have been? Is anything on earth sadder, or more terrible, than this — for one to outgrow another? Why could not he have grown, too, and filled and satisfied my mind and heart? Or if, to work out Thy plans, it was necessary to bind him down to the bitter treadmill, why was not I crushed down, too, with my face to the earth? Why was I allowed to spread my wings and fly out into wider fields, and find my strength, my power — *Oh, God!* my power to win the love of a man like — "

The name died in her heart, unspoken. She sank lower still, shivering.

"Why did he ever come back to me? Why was I permitted to feel the torment of the difference? What am I to do now? Marry another, loving him as I love him and knowing that he loves me — or break a heart that had only me?"

So she lay in the fierce grip of her heart's anguish, while hour after hour wore away. She had sown the seed of her happiness with a light hand, but it had fallen in rich soil and taken swift and deep root.

Gradually her sobs ceased as the thought of Learning obtruded itself into her mind, bringing with it a warmth that diffused through her body.

As she went back in thought over their acquaintance, the silence of her room seemed to burn with Leaming's presence; it was as if she could put out her hand and touch him.

She asked herself why she cared so much for him, but could find no lucid answer. All she knew was that he met and satisfied every thought she sent out to him. She realized now that it had from the first been a delight merely to be with him and speak of the simple things that had filled her life, — things in which no one else had ever seemed interested, — or to walk silently beside him while he told her of the different life in England.

The feeling of understanding and happiness had remained with her from the moment of their meeting. It had been enough for their eyes to meet, to make any day rich; for their fingers to touch, to make the silence loud with voiceless speech.

She began to see, now that her consciousness was cleared of the passionate joy that had been obscuring it for months, her grave error in not having told him the truth about Mahlon Proudfoot. She had frequently formed the resolve to do so; but always, when the moment came, her strength failed her. There was something in Leaming's attitude toward Mahlon, — a certain pitying kindness, a consideration, such, almost, as a man physically strong might unconsciously show for a cripple, — which had always closed her lips helplessly when she would have spoken.

She knew instinctively that in Leaming's broad vision Mahlon really appeared as a mental cripple. His mind had become dwarfed by the low roof of his outlook on life. His back had become bent with toil, and his mind with the bitter burden of ceaseless and unchanging thought. Perhaps the fact that had, more than any other, made it impossible for her to tell Leaming, was that, although he must have frequently heard intimations of Mahlon's attachment to her from Semia and others, it seemed to have never once presented itself to him that she could feel anything more than a sympathetic and friendly interest in Mahlon.

She went over and over the months she had spent with Leaming. To youth there is a grayness about sorrow that is like the first chill light of dawn; it makes the heart shudder with terror of the unknown and the unbearable it may bring with it. "How shall I bear it?" was the girl's wild cry. "What shall I do? How shall I decide?"

Later, she pressed her tear-stained face into the hollow of her arms, folded upon the floor, and moaned out —"Oh, I love him, — I love him! How could I have thought that other was love? I can never marry another — it would be sacrilege — sin — "

But her thought never went farther than that; it stopped short of perfect happiness. Between her and her heart's desire arose constantly the white, drawn face of Mahlon Proudfoot, — like the face of a drowning man it seemed to float, helpless and pleading, on the black waves of despair that surged around her. And with it came memories that were like blows upon an exposed nerve in their exquisite torture: memories of that house among the firs and alders, growing slowly, an hour at a time, every stroke a stroke of love — a house in which she knew no woman but herself would ever live while Mahlon Proudfoot lived; of that tone which made the utterance of her name an impassioned endearment; of the look of grave and absolute devotion in his eyes.

But she had heard the same tone in Leaming's voice, and had seen the same look in his eyes, and every fibre of her being had thrilled in response.

The night wore away at last, and in the chill dawn Mariella lifted herself from the floor and, worn with her long vigil, pushed back her curtains, and saw the sun's first ray of misty red trembling from the crest of the hill above her and widening across the town and sea.

But no help came to her with the day. Her eyes

were drawn, against her will, to the new house shining out in the red light. She bowed her head, remembering that for the first time she had forgotten to light her lamp, and that Mahlon must have spent a night of anxiety in consequence.

"Oh, what shall I do?" she moaned, looking across the distance with her eyes full of tears. "Poor Mahlon! Must I break your heart or my own?"

When Mariella finally went downstairs she was calm, but pale. There seemed to be a new darkness about her eyes and in them.

Leaming stood at the window, waiting for her. He turned quickly at her entrance, and was at once touched by the look of suffering on her face. He went to her quickly and took both her hands.

"Dearest," he said, in a tone that thrilled her heart through and brought the color to her face in one leap, "I have caused you more trouble. I have spoken too soon. I wished most of all—"

The door opened, and Mrs. Palmer came in with her customary rush, bearing a dish in her hand. She took three steps and stood still, staring at them, large-eyed.

After his first flush of annoyance, Leaming went straight to her, with his usual grave ease.

"I want to marry Mariella," he said simply.

Mrs. Palmer stood back on her heels and looked at him. Her face flushed and quivered with exultation.

"Aigh?"

"I want to marry Mariella."

"Oh!" Little mirthful quivers ran away from her mouth, nose, and eyes. "You do, aigh?" She lifted her chin. Mariella felt, with a sinking heart, that her mother had never seemed so coarse. "Well, there's a plenty been in the same boat. Ha'f the county's wanted her, sometime or other."

"*Mother!*"

"What ails you? You know it's so. Can't I tell Mr. Leaming? I'm sure I never boasted ha'f as much as I might of. But now that he wants you, too, I'd think he'd want to know about the others."

"I don't care anything about it," said Leaming, rather quickly. "Mariella is not well this morning, and after breakfast she must lie down and rest. But first I wanted to tell you."

"Wanted to tell me what?" Mrs. Palmer looked perplexed. Then she smiled again. "Oh! about wantin' to marry her. Well, I'm sure I'd like you to first-rate. I would, really. You know how to manage her. For the land's sake, why didn't you come sooner?"

"What has that to do with it?" asked Leaming, gravely. "I want her now; I always have wanted her — at least, I have always hoped that she would grow into the woman she promised to be, and that I might find favor in her eyes."

Mrs. Palmer stood staring at him in unabashed perplexity. There were interrogation-points all over her face. "Yes," she said ponderously, "I see. But —"

"But what?" Leaming's face reflected the perplexity of her own. He had feared hesitation from Mariella, but not from her mother. "You know," he said now, with some embarrassment, "that I am wealthy, that I can give her a beautiful home and every luxury — here or in England, as she may choose."

"Hunh," said Mrs. Palmer, reflectively, "I knew you was rich, but I didn't know you was so terrible rich."

She burst into sudden, nervous laughter. "I guess she wouldn't have to fry potatoes the rest of her life if she married you. I guess she wouldn't. But that's what Mahlon Proudfoot's wife 'll have to do."

She turned for the first time to look at the girl, and received a look in return that made her stare.

"Aigh?" she faltered out, as if Mariella had spoken.

"I did not speak," said Mariella.

"You might as well of," said Mrs. Palmer, helplessly. "I can't make out what ails you. You look so."

Then she turned back to Leaming.

"Well, as I live an' breathe! To think you really want to marry her. I'd like to see Mis' Mallory's nose. Wouldn't it go up? My-*O!* Her pa always said she was as smart as a steel trap; but I didn't think she'd catch you. An' now, I bet my soul an' all, she goes to actin' up in her fool notions an' thinks she's bound not to marry you! Would dukes an' lords take notice of her, too, if you took her to England?"

"Without a doubt; they couldn't help it if they would."

He turned to smile at the girl. She was deathly pale, and stood leaning against the dark door like a white lily. He thought her mother's vulgarity had worn out her strength.

"We will talk about it another time," he said hastily. "Mariella is tired."

"Not much good to talk about it, as I see. She's such a mule when she takes a notion! I'm willin', but it all depends on whether she thinks she's bound to ruin a chance like this. If she does, the Old Harry hisself couldn't move her."

"May I ask," said Leaming, who had turned pale and rather stern, "if you are — that is, if I am to understand — "

Mariella came forward suddenly. She was still pale, save for two red spots of resolution that burned in her cheeks.

"Don't let us talk any more about it now," she said calmly. "Let us have breakfast."

Mrs. Palmer got herself heavily down into a chair at

the head of the table, and poured coffee with a shaking hand. Her face was eloquent. She talked to herself in a low tone. For the most part they could not distinguish one word from another; but twice they heard her say emphatically, "You may knock me over with a feather!"

After breakfast Mrs. Palmer went out into the kitchen. She closed the door securely behind her, smiling grimly as she did so.

But Mariella did not wish to be alone with Leaming. She arose and followed her mother into the kitchen.

"Now look at here!" said Mrs. Palmer, facing her and breathing heavily. "Just look at here, Mariella Parmer! If you go an' ruin a chance like this, I'll feel just like pinchin' you. You hear? I say I'll feel just like pinchin' you! I feel like it now. You've got your lips set together, an' you're as pale as putty—just the way you always look when you're countin' on makin' a tom-fool of yourself."

"Mother," said the girl, still pale, but resolute, "I love Mr. Leaming, and I wish to marry him more than you can possibly desire it. I know now—I seem to have known ever since he came—that I never did love Mahlon. I was so young, I did not know what love was. But, oh, mother!"—her lips trembled, and her eyes filled with tears, but she went on,—"I have promised to marry Mahlon. He has counted on it all these years; his house is almost finished—it would break his heart! I do not know what to do, and I have not told Mr. Leaming about Mahlon—"

"Well, why on earth didn't you post me? I might of put my foot in it."

"Please, mother, do not say any more. Mr. Leaming has given me time to decide—don't mention it again. I will do the best I can, but I must have time,

and — please, please do not mention it again either to Mr. Leaming or me."

"Hunh," said Mrs. Palmer, with a reluctant smile, "I ain't very likely to mention it to him. I'd be sure to put my foot in it, if I did."

She pondered a moment; then she said solemnly: "Well, in all my born days! If you don't beat all! For a girl raised in the Out-West! A body 'd think a storekeeper 'd be the top-notch, but nothin' but the next thing to a lord 'u'd satisfy you. You go a-steppin' up. I bet if you take him you won't be satisfied no time, but 'll go a-settin' your cap at a lord hisself." Mariella winced. She turned to leave the kitchen, and her mother called after her, lifting her voice to a penetrating whisper: "I know now what you'll decide. I know it by that pale putty-look on your face. You'll decide to *fry potatoes* the rest of your natural life! You wouldn't take a lord, if you got a chance! Not you! You'd rather fry potatoes, an' try out the drippin's to fry 'em in!"

CHAPTER XXXVIII

When Mahlon Proudfoot came down that same morning to breakfast, his mother, who was frying hot-cakes on a long griddle, looked up at him anxiously.

"Why, what was the matter last night, son?" she asked at once. "I heard you a-prowlin' around your room several times. There's a board that screaks when you step on it. The last time you woke me up steppin' on it, I lit a match an' it was three o'clock. If the curtain had been up, it would 'a' been daylight."

"I couldn't sleep," said Mahlon, briefly. He went out on the porch and pumped the basin full of water. The strained look of one that watches had settled upon his face during the last year. To this was now added the haggardness of anxiety.

"You wasn't sick, was you?" questioned his mother, coming to the door, with the shining cake-turner in her hand.

"No, mother, I wasn't sick." Mahlon scooped up great handfuls of water and plunged his face down into it. He had a natural and unconscious grace of movement when he was not in company.

"Then you're still worryin' about that mortgage," said his mother, with a sigh.

Mahlon did not reply. He was more anxious than he would confess, even to himself, concerning the absence of Mariella's light. He recognized the feeling that had at last grown up in his heart from the careless seed sown by Semia. It was fear. Not, as yet, real

doubt of Mariella's constancy, but an indefinable fear — strong enough and terrible enough to make him turn suddenly cold in the noonday heat, and lean, shuddering, upon his hoe.

When he seated himself at the table his mother placed a plate of hot-cakes before him; then she drew her hand across his hair. Mahlon shrank a little; he knew what was coming, and he dreaded it.

"Has something gone wrong about the mortgage?"

"No, mother; I'll pay the last cent inside of a month. Don't worry, mother; it's all right."

"Then it's about Mariella."

Mahlon was silent.

"I've been hearin' things about her an' Leaming. I expect you've heard 'em too. Now, all I've got to say is just this, son: if she's that kind of a girl, I mean a light one that takes up with first one an' then another, you're lucky to find it out in time. Suppose you'd marry her an' she'd turn out" — Mrs. Proudfoot dropped her voice suddenly, and glanced about her in a scared way — "like her mother!"

Mahlon went white to his hair. "You mustn't say a thing like that, mother," he said, looking steadily at his plate.

"Well, I won't say it if you don't want I should, Mahlon, but I can't help it if the thought comes to me. A mother with a young man son can't help thinkin'."

"Well, don't think such things aloud, mother." His voice was steady.

"Well, I won't, then. But it does seem to me that where there's so much smoke there must be a little fire. An' it seems to me you ain't the kind to stand even a little fire?"

She said this with a rising inflection.

"No," said Mahlon, after a slight hesitation.

"An' what with the mortgage paid off, an' your house that you've worked on so faithful almost finished, an' you all ready to go to savin' up for yourself," boasted his mother, her imagination surging ahead in leaps, "I don't want to see you left in the lurch by Mariella Parmer or any other girl alive. What's more, you don't have to be. There's a plenty girls would be *glad* to live in that house."

At that Mahlon's lips drew apart in a kind of wretched humor; at the thought of any other girl after Mariella, he was unconsciously eased of the fierce pain in his heart. He looked up at his mother, smiling, yet serious.

"Dear mother," he said, "you are too ridiculous."

"I don't see why," she replied, with a perplexed look. "Mariella ain't the only girl in the world, is she?"

"She's the only one in the world for me," said Mahlon, with a deep sigh. "Oh, mother! why don't you know me and understand me better? There will never be any girl but Mariella. I'll never know what any other girl looks like."

"Mis' Worstel was here yesterday, Mahlon. She ain't much of a hand to gossip; but she said everybody's a-talkin' high an' low that Mr. Leaming an' Mariella are in love with each other. She says it's as plain as the nose on a man's face. You know he stays there, an' has for a long time. He takes her every place, an' they go walkin' every night it don't rain."

Mahlon leaned his head in his hands and looked at his mother. In his eyes was that which in a woman's eyes would have been tears.

"How is it," he said, in a voice of deepest feeling, "that you can be my mother and yet torture me so needlessly. In the name of God, mother, let me bear my troubles alone!"

"Well, I will," said his mother, giving up her one luxury with a sigh; "still, I'll always have my thoughts. A mother with a young man son can't help havin' her thoughts."

"Then have them all to yourself, please, mother," said Mahlon, turning at last to his breakfast.

But when he was working, out in the field alone, he found work harder than usual. At times he was amazed to find himself trembling strongly.

It was near noon that a shadow fell before him, and he heard a rustle of draperies as once before. Semia stood between the tall rows of pale green peas. When he looked up, with a great dread in his heart, she was standing still, holding up her ruffled skirts high on one side and smiling down at him mockingly. He thought of a pretty snake coiled to spring.

"Well, Mahlon Proudfoot," she cried saucily, "how are you? You look as if you'd seen a ghost! And no wonder! I'm not surprised that you look like a death's-head at a feast."

"Now look at here," said Mahlon, straightening up and putting back his shoulders, "if you've come here to talk to me about the girl I love and trust — why — you can go back again without sayin' one word. You're no friend of hers, nor mine either."

Semia put her hands on her pretty hips.

"That's where you are mistaken," she said, giving him a long look. "I am a friend of yours, Mahlon. I always have been. Because I'm a friend of yours, I don't want to see all the county laughing at the way you're being fooled. I've known you such a long time; you might say we've grown up together; and I'm tired of hearing folks laugh about your new house that you've worked so hard over — "

"I don't want to talk about it," said Mahlon; his

face was as white as death, and his eyes burned out of it.

"You don't have to; let me do the talking. I only want to tell you —"

"I don't want to hear!"

"I'm going to tell you, anyhow —"

"I don't want to hear."

"He has asked her to marry him, and her mother is fairly bursting with it."

Semia swelled out her chin, and commenced walking between the peas, stepping high and stiffly, and looking from side to side, like a hen. "Nothin' but a lord for Mariella!" she bragged haughtily, imitating Mrs. Palmer. "I tell you! She goes a-steppin' up. A lord hisself is none too high for a girl like her. She fairly beats all. I'll feel like pinchin' her if she don't take him — as rich as he is. Why, in England he lives with lords an' dukes!"

Semia burst out laughing, but at sight of Mahlon's white face she grew serious.

"See here, Mahlon. I told you a long time ago you'd never marry Mariella. I told you she wouldn't be true to you. Now, I know she isn't, and I want to prove it to you. She and Leaming are going out in the forest some evening soon to find that dell where the twin-flowers grow. You needn't take my word for anything. Be out there some place, and see and hear for yourself. It's the only way you can find out the exact truth."

She stood looking at him; the cords had swelled out in his temples and neck, and he was breathing hard.

"Are you through?" he asked hoarsely, without taking his eyes from her face. It seemed to him that her eyes had taken on the pale green of the peas.

"Yes, I'm through. You needn't to ask how I know they're going, but I do know. I'll let you know the

exact time, and then you can do just as you please. If you go on in this uncertainty, you'll die. You look like death now."

"I'm not in any uncertainty!" he almost hissed at her. "You're the one that's uncertain."

"Mahlon Proudfoot," said Semia, in a tone of such conviction that it made his very heart tremble, "if you don't believe what I tell you, you're not only a fool, but you must *want* to be one. If I didn't know what I say is true, you suppose I'd tell you how to prove it? Why, any man alive would find out if it's true or not. If it isn't true, it's your business to stop all this talk."

"If you're through," said Mahlon, "I wish you'd go. I wish you'd go right away."

Semia stood motionless before him, and quite close to him. She was thinking rapidly. She would not have married him, now that she knew Mariella did not want him, for a fortune; she was, in truth, in love with a married man, a friend of Mrs. Flush's. But Mariella had taken two men away from her. Would it not be a fine revenge on both her and Mahlon Proudfoot —

She was compelled to cast down her eyes to hide the smile in them. Would it not be delicious to let the whole neighborhood see that Mariella's lover of a lifetime could be so easily consoled? Judging Mariella by her own narrow and mean nature, she was convinced that it would pique her deeply.

She lifted her eyes, with the pale green lights playing in them, and looked at him. It was a strong, pleading look, and for a few seconds it held him with the fascination of a serpent. She moved quickly to him, and folded her smooth, long fingers around his wrist.

"Mahlon," she sighed, in a voice like honey, "give her up. She doesn't care for you; she never did care for you. Let Leaming have her, and let me help you to forget her."

Mahlon flung her hands from him and plunged backward a step or two. His face in the shadow of the tall peas was ghastly. His look was an unintentional insult.

"You snake!" he burst out furiously, in a rage too fierce to let him choose his words. "You creeping, deceitful thing! You pretend to be her friend — and mine — good God! If friends are made of such stuff, I'll take enemies!"

Semia's face flushed scarlet at his first words. If her feeling had been sincere, she could not have spoken again; but the play was only a comedy to her. Still, she would play a comedy well, or not at all. The greatest actress of all is the one who, in real life, can assume emotion at will. She cast down her eyes, as if hurt to the soul. A real tear shone on her lashes.

"You are mistaken, Mahlon," she said, almost inaudibly. "I am the truest friend you ever had; I would save you from ridicule, shame, betrayal. See how I come to you again and again, sacrificing my modesty —"

"Do not sacrifice it, then," burst out Mahlon again. "It is no use on earth. I have only contempt for a girl who would throw herself at a man. If you want my respect, — even my respect! — stay away from me! When a man wants some particular girl he's never too bashful to let her know it. That's where women fool themselves. A man is only bashful with the women he doesn't want. If women could only understand that, they'd stop throwing themselves at men who don't want them."

When he had hurled these words at her, like stones, he was almost frightened, angry as he was. But Semia stood her ground.

"I'm not throwing myself at you, Mahlon," she said, in a soft, pleading way. "Have I not stayed away from you since you told me you loved Mariella? Have I not let you alone, and eaten my heart out in silence? But that is like a man," she added, bitterly, with a sudden leaping stroke of diplomacy. "You think only of your own suffering. You are very sorry for yourself. You never think that what you suffer for her, I suffer for you. One would think suffering would make you kind, Mahlon Proudfoot, but it only makes you cruel."

For the first time she had touched the right chord. He swept her with the first look of interest he had ever given her. For almost a moment she gathered, from his silence and hesitation, that she was making her way with him.

But suddenly his old repulsion for her seized him. His eyes flamed at her in unspeakable rage.

"The idea of any other girl — after *her!*" he burst out, flinging his sarcasm at her in words that were like blows. "It would make me laugh, if it did not make me — ill! You say I am like a man. Well, you are like a woman! — like the average woman! When another woman is so far above you — so entirely apart from you — that you are not worthy to tie her shoes, you never know it, you never guess it. You have to be told. For God's sake, go away and leave me! After what you've said to me to-day, I — I — feel — unclean — "

He hissed the words out at her in the most terrible and unrestrained rage of his life. There was no mercy in him. Was she not trying to take Mariella's place?

At last the girl realized that it was all useless. She could never triumph over Mariella. She was at once filled with fury and shaken with laughter over her failure. For almost a moment she stood silently looking down; then she lifted her eyes slowly and gave him a long, broken-hearted look that haunted him and thrilled him with a vague remorse for his cruel words as long as he lived.

If she had spoken, her voice would have betrayed her; but she did not speak. She drew one long breath that broke on a sob in her throat, and then the tears rushed to her eyes, filling them. She turned blindly, reaching out her hands against the peas, as if she could not see, and vanished slowly through the misty green. But the moment she was out of sight, she flung her arms above her head. The undeveloped wanton in her leaped in a laugh to her lips and in a flame of triumph to her eyes, low-lidded and long.

"If it were worth while," she said, "I could do it yet! But he is such a fool — and the world is before me! It was good practice, and — there are other men!"

She gathered her skirts in her hand, and, bending her lithe body forward at the waist, fled, laughing, down between the tall green walls.

CHAPTER XXXIX

One day, in late summer, Mariella started to walk around by the cliff path to see Mrs. Flush. She had learned of Semia's entanglement with a married man who was a guest of the Flushes. Remembering her promise to auntie, she had resolved to make an appeal to Mrs. Flush, rather than Semia.

It was near sunset. A mile away, across the dark tide-lands, there was a line of silver rising, and falling and rising again, each time a little higher, breaking here and there into clouds of beaded spray.

She walked rapidly; and as she walked, with her eyes turned to the water, that silver line crept ever nearer the shore. The sea-birds wheeled above it, uttering shrill cries of triumph, and dipping into the bubbling foam only to rise again and fling opalescent drops from wings and breast. There was a faint shivering murmur that swelled softly and harmoniously louder and louder as that white line rippled nearer. The coloring was all in steel-blues and purples.

At last one tiny wave, driven harder than its companions, gave a wild leap and reached the shore. In a moment more all the countless millions of little wild water-people were leaping and laughing and struggling against the cliffs. With a sigh, Mariella, who had paused to watch them, walked on.

Mrs. Flush was alone. She received Mariella in her "study," as she called a pretty den at the top of the house. With all her other accomplishments Mrs. Flush was literary. She wrote what she lightly mentioned as "little things" for magazines that do not pay. She was a dilettante in everything, — even love, — and frankly confessed it. "But I have no children, you know," she always added, with a sigh, casting down her eyes in her Madonna look.

"Oh, my dear," she said to Mariella, without rising from her exquisitely dainty writing-table; "I'm so glad to see you. Come here and shake hands with me. I'm too dead tired to get up. I've been at work all day on a little thing for the *Clever Folks' Magazine*. Sit here by the table. Did you walk?"

She leaned back, threw her body slightly forward, crossed one knee over the other, and put her hands — covered with rings — on her hips.

Mariella sat down gravely. The full glory of the sunset blazed in through the window. It set a halo above Mrs. Flush's blond head.

"I've been so bored too," she said, with a rose-leaf sigh. "Mrs. Culbert has been here. Mrs. Culbert is an 'impossible.'"

"What is an 'impossible'?"

"Don't you know?" Mrs. Flush shivered slightly. "Why, an 'impossible' just puts your teeth on edge. She sits on the side of her chair, and slides her foot around on the carpet or works it up and down while she talks; her veil is too long or too short, too loose or too tight; if it is too long she keeps trying to pull it up over the brim of her hat and make it stay there; if too short, she pulls it down persistently over her chin, and it as persistently springs back, curving in as she breathes; she plays with her rings nervously, or makes little regular movements with her fingers; she clears her throat too often" — Mrs. Flush imitated; "she stays too long, says nothing she should say and everything

she should not say; asks one how much one pays one's 'girl,' and if she, the 'girl,' is 'wasteful' and breaks 'dishes'; she will probably offer the information that her 'girl' uses four pounds of butter a week, which she thinks just 'sinful'; she asks for receipts and calls them rules; she asks one if one had an 'invite' to a party — when she is *very* impossible she calls it a 'bid'; the party itself she calls an 'at home.' Mrs. Culbert is an 'impossible' who will never be a 'tolerable'; she remained an hour and a half, although one might have skated on the ice surrounding me. It is delightful to see you; you'll be nice and restful, I know."

"I fear I shall be anything but that to you," said Mariella, smiling.

"What do you mean by that?"

"Mrs. Flush," said Mariella, plunging straight into the disagreeable subject, "I came on an unpleasant errand, not my own."

"Ah?"

"I have heard —"

"Wait a minute," interrupted Mrs. Flush. She began rolling a cigarette. "You said it was not your errand; is it your business?"

"No, it is not; only, I promised —"

"Don't make promises; if you make them, don't keep them. It sounds like a hard-shell Baptist. Let me give you some advice right here: If it isn't your business, don't attend to it; if it isn't your errand, don't tell it."

"I came to tell it," said Mariella, coldly. "Naturally, I thought it over carefully before deciding to come."

Speaking rather quickly, she added, "There are disagreeable stories about Semia and Mr. Charlton, stories to the effect that they are in love with each other, and that it is serious."

There was the faintest lift of Mrs. Flush's lovely brows; after that her features were under perfect control.

"It isn't love," she said coolly, finishing the cigarette and lighting it gracefully. "Pardon me for not asking you to have one; I know you never smoke. It isn't love; it's only affection — mild, at that."

"Oh!" said Mariella, scornfully. "What is the difference?"

Mrs. Flush opened her eyes in languid surprise.

"Don't you know? But of course you do. Really? Well, I don't say that it always holds good; but as a general thing —"

She paused, smiling reflectively, and summoned her small dog to her side.

"As a general thing," she repeated languidly, balancing a chocolate cream on her dog's nose and watching her flip it up and catch it, "affection is comfortable, and love is the reverse; affection gives mild and serene pleasure, love gives ecstasy; affection can wait years without seeing the one upon whom it is set, love cannot wait a day; affection looks at the weather before going to see its sweetheart, love just goes and doesn't know there is any weather; Miss Ollie, *will* you flip that chocolate properly, or must I punish you? Affection never loses its appetite, and love never had one to lose; affection spends its evenings at the club, love with the one it loves — for love is wise; affection never suffers, being a philosopher, but love dies of a broken heart; affection thinks a real sealskin jacket makes up for all neglect, love knows better — my dear, why do you look at me so? What are you thinking?"

"I am thinking you are perfectly disagreeable," said Mariella, with an unwilling smile. "You are so disagreeable that I do not believe any one ever loved you!"

"Perhaps not," said Mrs. Flush, smiling sweetly and dreamily, "but, at least, one or two, my dear, have been affectionate. Affection is considered more enduring than love — but sometimes endurance can hardly be called a virtue."

"All this," said Mariella, becoming grave again, "wanders too far from the subject."

"May I ask," said Mrs. Flush, after a brief hesitation, "why you come to me with gossip? I detest gossip — save when I have a fresh, witty morsel to tell about myself."

"Because Semia and I have grown up together, and I thought she might receive it more kindly from you."

"Might receive what?"

"Why — remonstrance, advice — "

Mrs. Flush threw back her head and laughed long and heartily, laughed until Mariella's face grew red.

"Fancy *me!* Giving advice! Remonstrating! Oh, you are delicious!"

"Also because," continued Mariella, her cheeks burning hotly with anger, "according to the stories, they meet constantly at your house, and you have been encouraging the intimacy."

Yellow lights played now under Mrs. Flush's drooping eyelids.

"Be careful," she said, in a purring tone.

"You forced me to say it, Mrs. Flush. I promised Semia's dying aunt that I would do all I could for her. I came here in all seriousness, all earnestness, to ask you to do what any good woman would gladly do for a young girl. You have ridiculed me for coming — simply treated my errand with scorn."

Mrs. Flush smiled again.

"I don't believe in errands, I don't believe in promising dying folks things, either. If you do, don't keep your promise. The next worst thing to making a promise is keeping it."

"You do not mean what you say, Mrs. Flush. This old auntie was a mother to Semia, was devoted to her; and dying, asked me to be a friend to her. I now make the same request of you."

"Thank you." Mrs. Flush turned in her chair, and smiled coldly into Mariella's eyes. "I am a friend to her. I give her a good time. If she enjoys flirting,— even falling in love,— let her!"

"Mrs. Flush! With a married man?"

"Why not?" Mrs. Flush laughed deliberately; the yellow lights still played in her eyes. Mariella looked at her, and without intending it, or even being conscious of it, her look was an insult. She was pale with anger.

"Mrs. Flush, you ask me why not, but you must be jesting."

"I assure you I am not jesting. On the contrary, you must have come here on such an errand in jest— to *me!*"

"Mrs. Flush— I was convinced the stories were true before I came."

Mrs. Flush leaned her elbow on the back of her chair, and pushed her beautiful hand through the loose waves of her hair; the sunset sent brilliant flashes out from her rings. Her eyes narrowed and fastened upon Mariella's like a serpent's.

"My dear girl," she said sweetly, "don't waste your breath further. Go home and play with your dolls."

Mariella arose and got herself somehow, without a word, out of the room. She went blindly down the stairs and through the hall; but at the door she paused. She had only done Semia harm. Surely Mrs. Flush must have some good in her nature, if it could be found. If she, Mariella, had been more patient, more humble—

With a swift resolution she turned back. She was so absorbed in her own deep thought that she forgot to knock. She turned the knob mechanically; the door swung open noiselessly. One of the young men who were devoted to Mrs. Flush was coming from behind a tall screen in one corner.

"Is the coast clear?" he was saying. "Is the little blue lightning gone?"

Mrs. Flush sprang up gayly and laughed — a laugh of triumph — as she ran to him; the mask of demureness had fallen from her face.

A moment later a sound at the door caused the man and the woman to turn. Mariella, unable to escape, had shuddered back against the wall and stood there with wide, fascinated eyes.

Mrs. Flush uttered a violent word in her throat, and involuntarily took three steps forward. Then she stood still, pale and breathing hard. The girl had the look of one who has received an unexpected blow full in the face; there was a scarlet stain of shame across each cheek — as if the back of a hand had left it there.

"I beg your pardon — for not knocking," she faltered out, at last.

"I wish I could kill you!" said Mrs. Flush, in a low, hissing tone. "And I will if you ever tell! You eavesdropper!"

"*Tell!*" repeated Mariella; and all her repulsion, all her loathing, all her horror, struggled out in her tone.

The woman before her flew at her like a beast, and seized her by the arms, and shook her, with a face distorted by fearful emotions.

"Tell!" she hissed, "if you dare! Tell! And *I'll* tell — about your mother!"

"About — my — mother!" The words hurt the girl's throat.

"About your mother! Oh, you thought nobody knew that old, that ten-year-old, scandal — about your mother and that Mallory! That *common* Mallory!"

She released the girl, and stood back and looked at her, with the unbridled rage of a beast in her face. Her lips drew away from her teeth in spasmodic jerks; her breath escaped in sounds that were like sobs; she was like a female panther couched to spring. The violence of her passion could no longer be controlled; fragments of it burst from her swollen throat in words. "You eavesdropper! You spy! You cursed pretender and upholder of virtue! You'll look at me with such horror — such loathing — will you? You! With *such* a mother! What is she? Get out of my house! And if you ever tell — "

Mariella stood still, crushed, quivering, against the door, grasping it, as if to save herself from falling. The words had struck her like real blows until she was stunned; even after they ceased, she continued to shrink and shudder as if they still rained upon her. Her first impulse had been to cry out that it was false; but cruel, pitiless, as were the blows of the violent words, they were not so stupefying as those dealt her in quick succession by memory. Before her dazed eyes flashed two scenes. In one she saw herself kneeling, a child, by her open window in the darkness; the sound of a sliding bolt quivered through her; and then, a shaft of light struck across a man's face, — a man's face with a smile on it that she had remembered all these years. In the other she saw herself and Semia sitting on the cliff, eating their lunch together; she heard again the words: "I'd rather have my ma than your'n! Any day! *Mr. Mallory don't come to see my ma!*"

The words hurt her now like a knife struck into an old wound. She had forgotten the two episodes long

before she was old enough to understand either; but now they were clear and distinct before her, and with their return ached through her again the old dull wonder and dread as to their meaning. So do words, scenes, scents, faces — even peculiar expressions on faces,— impress themselves upon a child's memory, and lie hidden there until, many years after, they may suddenly be called out and understood in the flashlight turned on them by a mature knowledge. She knew now what they had meant. They had meant this shameful thing which this shameless woman was flinging in her face — was lashing her with; this shameless, desperate woman, trying to save herself.

CHAPTER XL

MARIELLA never remembered how she got out of the house. After a while she found herself running along the cliff path toward home. She was like a wild thing. She breathed hard, her breast struggled and ached, her eyes felt large and strained; the trees, the water, the path before her, were studded with scarlet blurs. She seemed to be full of awful pulses, beating; they were in her hands, her temples, her ears, her throat; they were beating the same words over and over: *"You — with such a mother! What is she?"*

The summer evenings are long on Puget Sound. It never grows really dark on a clear night. The last glow of the sunset lingers until ten o'clock, and after that the twilight, scented of sea and forest, hovers silently for two or three hours and then pales softly into dawn.

The sunset still burnished the hill as Mariella climbed the last steep. She approached the house resolutely, but as she put out her hand to open the gate she shrank suddenly away from it, and turned into a narrow path that led over the hill to the right. She climbed it with a sidewise movement, and kept looking back at the house, with eyes full of dread and horror, — as one looks at a house where murder has been committed, — trembling, asking eyes. How could she ever look into her mother's eyes again?

It was dusk when Leaming, searching for her, came upon her in the little mossy glen which they had made their own. She was lying prone upon the ground. Her face was buried in her arms. She was suffering intensely, but dumbly. Her mind was quite clear now. The blots of deception and easy falsehood in her own nature were no longer things to marvel at; they were born in her, they would stay in her forever.

And this other vile thing that was in her mother. Was it in *her*, too? She thought of the feeling she had for Mahlon and which she had mistaken for love; she remembered the momentary thrill of pleasure that had gone through her at his touch, his kiss. . . . She shuddered lower. "My God, my God," she whispered. "It wasn't love. What was it? Was it the thing that is in *her?*"

Here Leaming found her in a wordless anguish that terrified him. He lifted her and held her against his breast. When she felt him, warm and trembling, against her, the first tears came to relieve her. She wept long, passionately, speechlessly, with those awful sobs that seem to tear the breast from which they come. She wept herself at last into a dull calm that was numb to further suffering for the time. Then she drew from him, and told him rapidly, in a monotone, what Mrs. Flush had said to her about her mother. "And it is true," she concluded dully. "I remember things now that make me know it to be true, make me marvel that I never knew it before. It is true. You will not want to marry me now."

Leaming sat silent awhile, considering. He was still holding her hand and stroking it. He drew it up now and kissed it, lingeringly; then he pressed it against his cheek and held it there. "My own," he said, at last, and his voice had deep vibrations of tenderness in it, "my very own — I knew all this years ago. It did not keep me from wanting to marry you. Why should it now?"

"You knew it too? Every one has known it! And

I—I have been holding my head up! You knew it too! And to think what I have suffered here alone making my resolve to tell you. I never—never—could have done it, had I not loved you so; had I not held you as close and dear as my very self. . . . And you knew it all the time! . . . And loved me in spite of it . . . trusted me . . . wanted to marry me!"

"Yes, oh, yes."

"How could you? I do not understand."

"How could I not?"

"Oh, say something to help me!" she cried out, more passionately than before. "Is there nothing you can say to help me bear it? She is my mother! I am her daughter—her flesh and blood!—and I cannot look at her!"

Leaming had never felt such distress for another as now. His heart was throbbing wildly with the joy of her confession of love, but he was scarcely conscious of it, so deep was his anxiety to relieve her suffering. He had risen above his human love in his earnest desire to say the words that might be a comfort and a help to her in the extremity of her pain. His early years spent on an island, completely under the influence of a spiritual and lofty nature, had left their impress upon his whole character. Notwithstanding his years of travel, —years full of broad education and rich with experience,—there remained in him something of the austerity of the priest. Men respected him and women adored him; but neither men nor women were quite easy in his company. He might be with them, but never of them. He was always apart from them. He was deeply conscious of his isolation. He had never been able to escape a feeling of loneliness until he had loved Mariella.

She had filled his heart. In his brief separations from her, his mind had dwelt continually upon her in a pure and most beautiful feeling which had gradually grown to adoration — an adoration made human by deep passion. She satisfied all sides — all heights and depths — of his nature.

Although intolerant of creeds and dogmas, he was of a deeply religious nature. Realizing this, he had from his youth been so fearful of growing into a cold and unapproachable asceticism, — which he deemed as undesirable and as useless as an over-development of the flesh, — that he had always held his spiritual inclinations under as stern control as his fleshly ones.

But now, — although the girl's slightest touch, after her involuntary confession of love, set his blood thrilling along his veins like drops of liquid fire, — the priest in him arose above the man. In this deep hour her suffering and helplessness called all his spiritual strength to her aid; he was conscious of an almost painful desire to put his own feeling out of sight for the present and to be of assistance to her.

He put his arm around her, and drew her gently to him again. His look was rapt and exalted.

"Mariella," he said slowly, "does not the rose bloom in the swamp, the lily in the mire? Does not the new and beautiful tree spring from the decaying log, from the charred and broken stump? Will God not give us the chance He has given these? No character is so beautiful as the one that has struggled up; that has climbed upon its own faults, its own deceptions, yea, its own sins. Mariella, do not judge your mother too harshly —"

She lifted her head suddenly; her eyes shone at him through the dusk.

"Judge her!" she said, with subdued emotion. "My poor, poor mother! My heart is one awful ache for her. I have judged her and criticised her all my life.

And all the time she has been needing my tenderness and my love. How can I make it up to her and be a comfort to her? How can I get close to her and make her feel that I love her? It is only" — she faltered — "in this last year that I have been thinking her changed, kinder, more human; that I have been drawing nearer to her, pitying her, loving her! And now —"

"Your mother is changed, Mariella. She was never a bad woman, only a coarse, uneducated woman, to whose nature deception and sin came easily. Only think; she can barely read and write! How about her parents? What opportunities had *she*, Mariella, when she was a child?"

"You and I have both been holding to the opinion that there is an education of nature as well as of books."

"We have. But did she receive this education? Was she taught the beauty, the poetry, the religious significance, of nature? That is what I mean by education. The sublime lesson of nature is that the beautiful and the pure may spring, erect and strong, from the old and the decayed. Did any one teach this to your poor mother? No. What she has learned of life has been through her own bitter experiences, her own mistakes and sins and repentances, her own deep and silent sufferings away from the eyes of the world. The fire of her sin burned itself to ashes years ago; the fire of her remorse burns to-day in her heart with a quenchless flame. Mariella, one day, a month ago, entering the house unexpectedly, I found your mother upon her knees, bowed down in such prayer as only a soul in the extremity of anguish can know. She did not hear me, and I came away softly. But since that day I have had a new feeling for your mother."

Mariella was silent, remembering her father's death, and understanding now what had been a mystery to her at

the time in the questions her mother had asked him; but suddenly she leaned upon Leaming with a moan of pain.

"Oh, what shall *I* do?" she cried piteously. "Tell me. Help me. It is in the blood. It is in me, too. There is no need to struggle against it; I should only be a little wave struggling against the awful rock of heredity. Oh, the wrong of it! The sin of it! For such a nature to bring a child into the world!"

Leaming put both arms about her with an utterance of deep and passionate tenderness, and held her close.

"Mariella, everything depends upon character, and character is not born; it is made. The making of a noble character is the highest object one can have in life, for it must be founded upon truth — and truth is another name for God. It is the God in us that impels us to speak the truth when a lie would be so much easier, and would perhaps save us trouble or suffering —"

"Oh, hush, hush!"

They were facing each other in a stress of passion and emotion that lifted them out of themselves, and set them upon a spiritual plane so remote that the flesh could not follow. Mariella had no longer a sense of physical distress. She had the feeling which comes to every person of fine sensibilities in an hour of great emotion, that her soul had somehow escaped her body, and was at once appealing to and opposing the stronger, calmer soul of Leaming. She had no realization of the fact that she was in his arms; he seemed at a great distance.

"Nay, let me continue. We can make character only by successfully overcoming many impulses, many temptations, to wrong action. We may fail to overcome many times; but each failure will help us rise to an ultimate and sure success. It cannot be otherwise if we are resolved that we will have it so — that we will eventually succeed. Each failure must be counted one step toward victory. Defeat may be used to broaden and deepen and chasten character. The fire of defeat burns slowly, but it chastens as it burns. Oh, my own! Look at those who have always trodden rose leaves, those who have had no obstacles to overcome, no burdens to bear, no curses of heredity to embitter, no mistakes and failures, yea, and sins, to set their feet upon and rise above! Are they great? Are they noble? Are they purified by fire? Are they made simple and human through suffering, and bearing, and giving up? And giving up! Mariella, what we give up enters more deeply into the making of character than what we have, what we hold fast to; what we — "

"Oh, hush!" Her voice was harsh with pain. "You are torturing me. What we give up! Oh, it is so easy to say it; but could you do it? Bring it home to yourself. Could you give up the — the — let us say the dearest thing on earth to you, if your having it meant wrong to another; if your having it cheapened you in your own eyes; if your having it made you live a lie; if your having it became a canker in your heart that ate day and night? If it were the dearest thing you had, and if you never had any other dear ones, could you give it up? Could you?"

"The dearest thing on earth to me," said Leaming, slowly, "is yourself. To give up you would be giving up the dearest part of myself. But what joy would there be in keeping you if therein lay a wrong to another; if therein lay anything that could stain or cheapen the character, the honor, the truth, of either of us? Oh, Mariella! God could ask of me no sacrifice so terrible as that — to give up you, after all these years that have been sweet with the hope of one day having you; after these months — these months — that have been too sweet, too perfect, to be described in words — that must be lived to be understood! But if my keeping you meant wrong to another; if my keeping you cheapened myself in my own eyes, or made me live a lie — " He paused; the long wash of the waves came up to them; above them, high and lone, glowed the beautiful stars; through the still air was blown the weird note of a night-hawk; the lights of the town far down below came out, one by one, like glowworms. At last Leaming drew a deep breath. "Yes," he said, softly, "I could give you up. It would break my heart; but I could do it. I would rather keep you as a beautiful pure memory than as my very own, stained by your dishonor or mine. Think what a little while, what a few brief years, we have to love one another here. Shall we, then, lift ecstasy's cup and drink it, at the cost of honor, to the dregs? Mariella, Mariella, we lie, we cheat and deceive ourselves, when we call a love great that has not greatness of character behind it. Passion says — 'Let me have; let me have, at any cost!' But Great Love bows and says with trembling lips, 'If need be, let me give up.' The love that is not founded on truth and honor is an insult to the one to whom it is offered."

Mariella had sat listening with bowed head. Her hands were strained together. Every nerve was tense. The pulses in her ears beat like the swift, regular blows of a thousand tiny hammers, but she heard every word. The beauty of the night ached in through her senses. It seemed to her that Leaming's voice was the voice of God speaking the truths she had already known, but which she had been silencing in her heart. It was the supreme moment of her life. All the good and all the evil in her nature were struggling together.

Worn out at last, she sank down in the soft moss and

buried her face in her arms with a moan of pain. With the act came a sudden consciousness of her body's suffering and her body's desires. "Oh, I do love you, I do love you!" she cried. "Whatever I do, believe that."

In an instant he was kneeling beside her and had lifted her again upon his breast. The night was sweet and still about them. For a few moments she yielded to his embrace, and her lips trembled upon his with answering passion. Then, with a great effort, she freed herself a little, and knelt backward from him. She spoke rapidly and almost harshly. "I have been deceiving you," she said. "Deception is in me. I have not been honest with you. I love you and have allowed you to love me and all the time I have been deceiving you. I have promised to marry another man."

There was silence for a full minute. They could not see each other's face; but when he finally spoke his voice hurt her. He uttered the one word "*Whom?*"

She answered so low that he could scarcely hear, "Mahlon Proudfoot."

"*Mahlon Proudfoot!*" he repeated, in amazed unbelief. "Not Mahlon — surely! Mariella, is this a jest?"

"It is not a jest," said the girl.

"But — not Mahlon!" Astonishment had taken all feeling for the present out of him. "Surely, Mariella, not Mahlon."

The girl was wincing keenly. "Why?" she asked, just audibly.

"Why?" he repeated stupidly. He had released her hands, and now stood up, looking down at her, although he could only see the outlines of her figure in the dusk. "Why? I hardly know; it seems, somehow, preposterous."

Leaming was only human, and in those first moments he was not generous. The unexpected announcement

had struck a blow to his self-love as well as to his faith in Mariella. He had come to consider Mahlon so entirely outside of his own world that it was not possible at first to connect him with Mariella in his imagination. His affection for Mahlon had always had pity in the heart of it, pity for the failure of his life, and a helpless rebellion at the circumstances that had caused it.

He had secretly entertained the belief — as successful men usually do — that if Mahlon had been more ambitious and energetic, the sacrifice of himself need not have been. The education might have been acquired and the mortgage paid — somehow.

At this moment his keenest remembrance of Mahlon was that he had said "Sir?" when he had not understood a remark of Leaming's, although Leaming was heartily ashamed, later on, of having remembered it; at the time of its occurrence he had not even been conscious of making mental note of it.

Then Mariella, still kneeling, spoke in a low voice, flute-like in its clearness.

"Do not say one word against him," she said, "whatever you say against me. When you went away and left me, I had only him. He always loved me, and — till you came — I thought I loved him. I thought I loved him," — she repeated slowly and convincingly, — "and I made him believe it; made him believe in me. For a long time now I have known that I never did love him, have known that I love you. But oh!" — she threw herself down again upon the moss in an abandon of despair, — "I can never tell him. I must break my own heart instead of his!"

It was quite dusk now. The lights of the town glimmered below through the purple mist of evening; scarlet, blue, and green serpents of flame wavered out across the water from the wharves; the forest climbed, dark and still, above them.

Leaming stood in silence for some moments. It seemed a long time to the wretched girl lying at his feet.

At last he stooped and lifted her, and held her close to him; but he was trembling now.

"You are cold," he said, very low and gravely. "Stay here in my arms a moment, Mariella, and let my love make you warm. If you love me, you belong here and I must have you. I will not give you up! The very thought of — of — *him* is maddening, preposterous! It must not be; cannot be."

His lips found hers in the darkness and trembled upon them. "Tell me you love me," he whispered.

"I do, I do," said the girl, so low he could scarcely hear her; her tones were as sweet as the notes of a love-bird alone with its mate.

"Then I will never give you up," said Leaming, exultingly. "Never. If you did not love me — But you do!" he broke off, still trembling with the first exultation of the assurance of love. "My own, just for a little while forget everything but that we love each other. Presently we must face trouble and sorrow and heartbreak, — if not our own, then his, — but let us forget it all for a little while to-night."

When they reached home Mrs. Palmer had gone to bed. When Mariella had said good-night to Mr. Leaming, she went to the door of her mother's room, and stood there, trembling.

The rapture of her love had died out of her. Her face was pale, and the look of suffering had come back to it. After a few moments had passed she opened the door resolutely, and entered the room. Her mother was

on her knees by the bed. Her face was in her hands and she was praying aloud. Mariella could not move. She stood still, with her hand on the door, and heard.

"O Lord God, have mercy! I don't deserve any, but oh, have mercy! I ain't any excuse, O Lord, except that I never had much chance. The people I was bound out to lied an' swore an' stole, an' I don't know anything about my parents. It ain't much excuse, but it's some. An', O Lord, you know that I've been a-tryin' to be a better woman for a long time. I can't change my whole natur' at my age — but oh, my God!" she cried, bursting out into wild sobbing, "give me some credit for wantin' to an' tryin'. An' help me! Oh, for Mariella's sake, help me! I don't know how to go 'bout it. It ain't in me to get religion an' confess my sins, an' have folks a-watchin' to see if I backslide — it ain't in me an' I don't believe in it, an' I can't do it. There must be some way besides that for people with their sins a-eatin' their hearts out. I want it just between you an' me. Oh, help me, help me! I'll go mad yet for thinkin' o' the way Mariella's pa talked when he was dyin' — "

But Mariella could bear no more. She stole out of the room, and closed the door noiselessly. She groped up to the attic in the dark, and threw herself upon her bed.

"Oh, what is life for?" she cried passionately, "if we are only to get started right after we have broken our own hearts or somebody else's!"

CHAPTER XLI

One night, when Mahlon Proudfoot came home, his mother met him on the back porch. There was an air of important mystery about her. She was full of repressed excitement.

"What do you think, son?" she said. "There's a letter come for you. Mr. Grandy brought it when he was comin' by home. It's been all scented up. Who'd you expect it's from?"

"I don't know, mother," Mahlon replied quietly, but his face was going from pale to red and back again. He was sure it must be from Mariella; and at once he wondered why he had never written to her.

"To make her write first!" he groaned to himself, as he stooped over the wash-bench to hide his face from his mother's gentle curiosity. "Oh, I'm a country clown—and she so dainty and sweet! Think of me alongside of *him!*"

"It's in a blue envelope, Mahlon, an' it's got a white splotch of wax on the back of it, with some kind of a figger in it. It looks like a windmill."

Mariella and a windmill! Mahlon smiled reluctantly.

"I guess it's not a windmill, mother."

"Well, I don't say as it is one; but it looks like one. Shall I open it while you're a-washin'?"

"No, never mind, mother."

"Why, I'd just as lieve mind. It wouldn't be a bit of trouble. I'd be glad to."

She moved away eagerly.

"No, no, mother," said Mahlon, authoritatively, lifting his voice. "I'd rather open my own letters, please."

Her face fell.

"It's the first you ever got from a lady, as I've see. D' you expect it's from Mariella?"

"I don't know, mother. Is supper ready?"

"Yes, it's all ready to put on the table. It's a queer kind of handwrite. It kind of sprawls all over the envelope. Do you know anybody that writes that way?"

Mahlon went in as if he had not heard, and sat down at the table. The square lavender envelope lay on his plate. He reflected that he did not even know Mariella's writing, but it must be from her. He laid it to one side. A thrill of joy went through him as he touched it, mixed with self-reproach for the awful fear of her constancy that had been taking the flesh off him of late. How could he have doubted her?

"W'y, ain't you goin' to open it?" said his mother, in a tone of sharp disappointment.

"Not now, mother."

"W'y, why not?"

"I'd rather open it in my room." Then he looked up at his mother and said, with the gentle but unmistakable firmness which she knew so well: "You must let me manage such things myself, mother. It's my letter. If there's anything in it that concerns you, I'll tell you in good time."

Mrs. Proudfoot's face flushed, and she said no more for some time. Mahlon ate rapidly. He breathed loudly as he ate, and swallowed distinctly; sometimes it was more of a gulp than a swallow. Even when she was young, Mariella had shrunk from his manners at the table. She had not been taught better herself, but she was possessed of a natural delicacy and refinement which

it is. Sometimes, for hours, I feel just as sure of her as I do of God; and then, all at once, something black and awful comes into my heart, and I feel a thousand miles away from her and afraid of her — afraid of what I'd find in her eyes if I looked at her! Whatever this is, it's in my heart now. I've always been able to conquer it, but to-night I feel as if it had me. See!" He stared into his eyes in the mirror. "It's as strong as seven devils. I feel weak alongside of it. It tells me to go — to go! — and ease this pain that's been in me so long. It tells me" — he burst out suddenly into terrible laughter — "to go and spy on the girl I love and honor, the girl I've loved and trusted all my life! It tells me to do that, and I feel too weak to resist it. . . . I am going. . . . I feel that I am going! I don't want to go — I want to be honorable to the very last, and every breath I draw is a cry to God to not let me go — and yet, I know that I am going! I know that I am going to dishonor myself. Oh, it's awful for a man to grip a thing like this and find that it's stronger than he is — to find himself going down before it! I'd rather die — God, I'd rather die! — than go out there and spy on her; and yet I am going! I prayed to God once that, if I ever did fall so low as to doubt her and spy on her, He would make me see and hear things that would break the heart inside of me. I prayed that to God" — cried out Mahlon Proudfoot, in a terrible voice — "and yet — I am going to do it! I have fallen so low — and I am going to do it!"

CHAPTER XLII

In the middle of the warm August night Mariella and Leaming stood alone in the forest. They had set out early in the evening to find the glen of twin-flowers. They had not found it.

"Never mind," said Mariella, giving it up, with a little sigh, "the blooms would be all gone, anyhow; but it must be beautiful with the vines banked over everything, as it is said they are."

When they first set out they had walked in silence. The road ran, a narrow gray ribbon, through the forest. It was an old, forgotten road, overgrown with clover and wild geranium. The firs — the beautiful, wonderful firs of the West — grew close together, and lifted their tapering crests three hundred feet through the purple spaces of the night. Looking upward, each seemed to have stars shining upon its quivering tip. The ferns grew tall in the shade of the firs, grew to twice a man's height, and cast their slender-fingered palms to meet and interlace across the path.

The large, flat leaves of the devil's-club floated on the air, motionless. Out in the sun their edges drooped, but in the depth of the forest they were spread out flat — as were the leaves of the vine-maple, which also droop in the sun. The wild pea climbed high and drew a line of blue wherever it went; the meadow-sweet and the steeple bush waved their soft plumes in every open space where the flames had been, beside the spires of the fireweed and the goldenrod.

But as they went on, there were no more open spaces. The ferns parted at their coming, and closed together behind them. They found themselves in a fragrant lavender twilight. Their feet sank noiselessly in deep layers of moss. Long fragments of gray moss hung from the branches of the trees.

There is something in the beautiful, dim silence of the Western forests that is like holiness. One steps softly, and bends his head, as if expecting to hear a benediction sink earthward. For silent centuries on silent centuries the needles of the pine and of the fir have sifted down by day and by night, to carpet the shadowy aisles with stillness; the dark greens of the foliage, the paler greens of new growth and mosses, the purple and the silver of barks, the warm browns wrought by decay, and all the dull reds and yellows of dying woods blend into one hovering mist of Persian splendor. And over it all, like an invisible dove with outstretched, quivering wings, seems to brood holiness.

"Mariella," said Leaming, at last, "we are lost. I have tried for an hour to find the path. Are you afraid?"

"Not with you," she answered sweetly. "I have always dreamed of spending a night with you in the forest."

"But your mother?"

"She will be asleep and will never know; for as soon as daylight comes I shall know the way out."

"But you will be cold. I shall never forgive myself."

"I am dressed warmly." She came closer to him, and he reached out in the dusk, and finding her hand, clasped it. "Oh," she said, "do not reproach yourself. Only think! How beautiful to spend a whole night together alone in the forest. Let us sit down and rest — and talk."

She spoke calmly; but Leaming's voice shook when he replied.

"Let me push in through these ferns first, and see what is there. It seems to be an open space. Do not move from this place."

He left her. In a few moments he cried to her: — "Oh, Mariella! I have found the glen! I have found it!"

It was still faintly light as he helped her over an old log, out of whose moss-covered decay ferns and young trees were growing luxuriantly.

When they sprang down on the other side they sank deep in the drifted needles and mosses of centuries.

They were in the glen they had been seeking. It was a small space, not larger than a room. It was round, and was walled in by firs and logs, out of which grew tall ferns and thimbleberry bushes. Leaming had by chance found its only entrance.

The long branches of the firs drooped gracefully until their tips touched the ground. The twin-flower vine grew luxuriantly on all sides; it was twined thickly over the logs and banked deep around the trees.

"This is the place," said Mariella, low, as a mother speaks who has a sleeping child. "How beautiful it is — and how sweet. But I am tired. Let us sit down and rest."

"Are you not afraid?" asked Leaming, uncertainly.

"With you?" she said, only.

He still hesitated. "I am tired," she repeated gently.

He sank down then in the deep softness, and drew her down beside him and held her there. He was trembling.

Mariella lifted her face and looked upward. Far above them was the sky between the trees. Stars were burning there; and a gradual silvering told that the moon would soon be moving patiently above them.

They sat in silence. Somewhere a bird called drowsily, but in a kind of delirious ecstasy, to its mate.

"Oh, how beautiful it is!" murmured Mariella. "I never dreamed it could be so beautiful in the forest at night. It is so still one might hear the needles falling, if one listened. It seems" — her voice sank lower and took on vibrations of sweetness — "as if one might reach out in the darkness and touch God. . . . Do you understand?"

"I understand," said Leaming, in a tone of deep emotion. He leaned his face down upon her hair as she sat beside him. She stretched out her hand, as a child might have done, — so natural and innocent it seemed to him, — and laid it upon his hand.

"You are cold," she said quickly.

"I am not cold," said Leaming.

"You are trembling."

"Am I trembling?"

"Your hand is." . . . Then, after a moment, she asked, very low, "Have you forgiven me?"

"I have forgiven you."

"I knew you would. I would forgive you anything."

"It was the thought of giving you up —"

"I know; I know."

They sat silent then. Loneliness lay heavy and still upon the forest. The only sounds were the drowsy notes of the birds, the ceaseless sifting of the needles, the faint sighing murmur of the wind — perhaps a mere vibration of air — in the far tree-tops, the musical stir of ferns and broad-bladed grasses, the distant, hesitating

speech of a brook; and these sounds, noted together, made a lullaby.

At last Leaming lifted himself from the deep silence of his thought.

"Mariella," he said, in the deep tone of one who has passed through a bitter struggle and has at last arrived at a decision which he knows will bring another struggle with it, "I cannot give you up. I cannot let you marry Mahlon Proudfoot. However you may look at it, you must see that it cannot be. If you had not confessed that you love me — but you have, you have! That makes you mine; it gives me a right above all others. You must marry me."

"I will never marry you," said Mariella, in a voice that was firm, although it trembled. "I will never break Mahlon's heart. I should loathe myself forever, if I did. I have been going through a terrible struggle for months; but I am at last resolved."

"I am resolved, too, Mariella — dearest," replied Leaming, in a tone of dangerous determination. "Neither of us is to blame. Love cannot be set down at the door of any heart one chooses. You were only a child when you promised to marry him."

"I must marry him, if I ever marry any one."

"Would that be fair to him, dearest? Would it be honest? Would he wish you to marry him when you do not love him — when you love me?"

He had nerved himself for the ordeal through which he saw he must go.

Mariella felt the blood rush to her face; she, too, had nerved herself for what she felt must come.

"He must never know it," she said, in a tone of decision. "Never."

"You would deceive him?" questioned Leaming, in bitter sarcasm.

"I would do anything that God would give me the strength to do rather than let him know the truth," said Mariella, firmly but despairingly.

Leaming was silent for a little while. She heard his deep breathing. When he spoke again his tone was of such vibrating and pleading passion that she was terrified at the sudden yearning leap her heart gave toward him.

"Why do you consider only him, dearest? Is my suffering nothing, then, to you?"

"I do not seem to think of it," she replied, steadily enough, although her heart was beating wildly. "I am selfish; and when I am not thinking of his suffering, I am thinking of my own."

Leaming uttered an exclamation of passionate love, and pressed her hands in his.

"God bless you for saying that, dearest! And I am selfish too. Since I am suffering, I want you to suffer — so much that you cannot give me up. Give me up!" he burst forth, vehemently. "What foolishness! You can't give me up! Can such love as ours give up? You little wild thing! Do you think I needed your confession of love? Do you think I did not know that you loved me? Has not your hand trembled if I touched it, and the color rushed to your face if I looked at you? Feel your hand tremble now in mine, like a frightened bird — it sets every pulse in me beating to madness! For six months, Mariella, I have not been able to approach you without this tumult of my pulses; and yet" — his voice sank low, but pierced the dark, pointed sharp with reproach — "because the world has taught me to keep perfect control of myself, you think only of his suffering and your own, not once of mine."

"Since you have such perfect self-control," said Mariella, clearly and calmly, "continue to use it."

Then, with an edge of irony in her voice, she added, "We can make character only by overcoming many impulses, many temptations, to wrong-doing — "

"My own!"

"Look at those who have not had to overcome themselves — are they great, are they purified by fire? Does not what we give up count more in the making of character than what we hold fast to?"

There was silence for a moment. She felt a slight loosening of his hand, and her heart reproached her sharply, even before he spoke. When he did speak, she knew by his tone that he was hurt.

"I do not deserve your irony, dearest. I had thought of all that before I came to this decision. I went over it all again and again during this last week. I remembered all the fine things I said to you the other night about duty, about the making of character, about — oh, all of it. I talked finely, did I not? Well, this is the human nature of it, my own. I could apply my fine reasonings to that situation, but not to this. I could use them to help another, but when it comes to myself, they sheer off and leave me stranded. But I had already felt the humor of that — and its tragedy; I did not deserve your irony."

"Oh, forgive me, forgive me!" exclaimed Mariella, in her warm, impulsive way; her fingers closed around his with entreating tenderness. When he was all fire she could be all ice; but now that his clasp had loosened, she was all yielding and melting warmth. "It was unkind, ungenerous, of me to remind you! I was not really serious. It was half in bitterness and half in jest. It seemed such irony: that all you said the other evening had worked back against yourself; had helped me to resist you."

His hands closed firmly about hers again.

"What I said shall *not* help you to resist me, Mariella. The situations are different. There is only one right in this, and you must follow it."

"I know," she said, very low. "There is only one right, and I intend to follow it."

"Dearest, the right is love. Love is always right — such love as ours. It can't be wrong. What I said the other day fitted another situation. We were facing a sin, and I was trying to make you feel that one can rise above a sin, and that if one is born without a noble character, he may make one for himself."

"I know," said the girl, distinctly. "I was born without one. I am trying to make up for it. It may be late — but you started me right."

"This is nonsense," exclaimed Leaming, in a kind of terrified impatience. "It is not to the point. It is not the same thing." She uttered a low cry of distress, and laid her brow down upon their clasped hands.

"Why will you cheat and deceive yourself?" she asked him, desperately, for she perceived that she was making no progress with him. "What you want me to do would be a sin. Can't you understand it? He has given up everything to pay off that mortgage. He gave up an education — the university — even the grammar-school, —" Mariella faltered and broke down, remembering how Mahlon had gone out into the forest and prayed to God to make a way for him to go to the university; she could not tell that to his rival, although she knew it would appeal to Leaming more powerfully than any plea. "He gave up parties and all amusements. His only happiness was in building the house —"

"*The house!*" said Leaming, in a tone of poignant pain and surprise. "Mariella, what house?"

"What house?" faltered Mariella, taken unawares; "why, the — the — our house. Did you not know?"

"Oh, Mariella!" exclaimed Leaming, in a tone of deepest, gravest emotion. "This is terrible. Your house! *Yours and Mahlon Proudfoot's!* You said it as calmly — Good God!" he burst out passionately. "Don't you know how that hurts me? Can't you guess? Can you imagine the thoughts, the dreams, a man must have while he sees going up the house that is to hold him alone with the woman he loves?"

The girl shuddered. She need not imagine; she knew. "Can *you* imagine," she said, meaning the cruelty to herself rather than to him, "what his thoughts and dreams are when, to have the house, he must build it himself, hour by hour, and nail by nail, before and after his hard day's work? Don't you think it must mean more to him then?"

"This is terrible!" repeated Leaming; his voice was shaking. "To think that another man has built a house for you; has had such thoughts — such dreams — such hopes —"

"It is the only happiness he has had for three years," said Mariella, gently. "Do not begrudge it to him; but consider it. Consider how hard and narrow his life has been, and how into such a life the few joys grow so deep that taking the dearest one away is like tearing the heart out."

"Oh, this is terrible!" said Leaming once more, in a tone of despairing wretchedness. He released her hands, and drew away from her, sitting alone with his head bowed on his breast. "Oh, Mariella, this is torture! I do not know how to bear this! Why didn't you tell me at first — when I first came?"

"Why?" said she, in tones of profound sorrow and remorse. "Because, whenever I would have spoken, I felt a strange shrinking which would not let me. I did not understand it; I was only conscious that I did not want you to know it. I know now that it was because from the first moment of your return my heart yearned to you — and I was so weak, so selfish — and deception was in my nature, and helped me out so easily! That first afternoon, when you went home to supper with me, when I saw my mother standing in the door, it went through me that I did not want you to know; and when we were alone I asked her not to tell you."

She moved an inch nearer to him, and, reaching out in the darkness, laid her trembling, asking hand on his.

"Do not be angry with me," she said, with a pleading tenderness that set every fibre of his being throbbing with answering tenderness and passion. "I was weak and I did wrong; but" — and she made her most powerful plea so low that it was just audible — "I did it because I loved you. Try to forgive me that."

"Forgive you!" exclaimed Leaming, throwing his arms around her, and drawing her swiftly to him in a kind of rough, wretched, but uncontrollable passion of tenderness, "who could do anything *but* forgive you, whether you ask or do not ask? You sweet, tormenting, torturing, irresistible girl!"

He was suddenly wrought to the highest, fiercest emotion. She felt the compelling warmth of his body and of his breath, as he gripped her so fiercely in his arms that she could neither resist nor move; his very voice seemed to carry fire with it as it issued from his lips. "What is it in you, Mariella, that takes hold of a man like this? There is nothing I would not do to possess you — to hold you — to make you mine utterly — utterly — so that no man dared claim you! — so that no man dared even think of you! I can't give you up — Good God!" The cry trembled from him, hoarse with jealous love and rage. "The thought of another man holding you as I am holding you drives me mad! What is it in you, you little wild, sweet, maddening thing? It isn't beauty of face or form. *That* gives birth to a different love—although you have physical fascination to spare. It is the wild, lawless spirit in you that always seems to be mocking me and eluding me. It is slipping away from me now when I would force you against your will to my wish—I *could* force you!" he cried fiercely, between set teeth, pressing his hot face to her cool, soft one.

For the first time, for one or two heart-beats, Mariella felt fear. But at once a self-reproachful shame filled her. Fear of Mr. Leaming and love! That would be fear of heaven itself. That would be to sweep the solid ground out from beneath her. That would be to make more utter shipwreck of her heart than to give him up and never see him again. That would be to shake her very belief in God.

She had been holding her face away from his passionate caresses; but now, swiftly and impulsively, she turned upon his breast and kissed him for the first time full upon the mouth, sweetly and trustingly; she put her arm up around his shoulder, and pressed the inner softness of her hand gently against his neck; and as she kissed him, she breathed one word upon his lips, with breath which Leaming thought held all the pure sweetness of heaven—the one word "*Dearest*"—and once again her tone was as sweet and pleading as the love-note of a bird when it is alone with its mate.

The madness went out of Leaming. After a little while,—a few moments of despairing rapture,—he put her gently from him.

"It is as I said, Mariella; when I would have you at any cost, with your consent or without it, your spirit eludes me and flies away from me, mocks me, defies me, and finally looks down at me calmly from a nobler height. But when, in grief and despair, I turn from you, desperate in my loneliness, mad in my misery, then back it flies to your eyes like an undaunted, innocent bird — calls me, lures me, enchants me, until my strength is beaten down, and I am like a broken reed in your hands. Here I am, Mariella, broken to your wish. What are you going to do with me?"

The vibrations of love and pain in his voice thrilled her to the soul. Her pulses were beating full and heavily — she felt big with pulses; the soft-cushioned ends of her fingers felt twice their usual size; her heart leaped and fluttered with every beat. Again she felt fear, but this time it was of herself. Her whole being was yearning to him — with such power, with such aching agony of desire, that she was terrified. If he discovered that there was one yielding impulse in her heart, she could never hold out against him. All her being seemed to be flowing out to him in waves of unconquerable desire.

The sweetness of the night, too, and the stillness of the forest had taken powerful hold upon her senses, numbing them to a kind of passive, delicious drowsiness. She felt, creeping sweetly and insidiously upon her, an exquisite weakness and indifference to duty, right, honor — everything save love; she felt ebbing away from her — slowly and languidly, with a kind of lulling music, as the waves ebb away from the shore — every strength save the one strength to love and to be happy. She felt all this, and it terrified her, but even her terror seemed passive and remote; it pierced her yielding ecstasy only as the touch of the surgeon's knife makes itself felt through the delicious drowsiness of the chloroform trance, too dully to awaken to a consciousness of pain. The very calls of the birds sounded faint and far away, as if heard in a dream.

Leaming broke the spell. He leaned toward her and took her hands again. "Oh, Mariella — dearest — come to me! Be my wife. I would not force you if I could. I kneel to you and entreat you. Do not break my heart and send me wandering, God knows where. I am all yours; do not throw me away for a distorted sense of duty. We trust each other; our love is stronger than everything else, and it is right."

"It is not right," said Mariella, now thoroughly awakened to a sense of the danger that threatened her from her own weakness. "Try to put yourself in my place; or in his place. Try to see how wrong it would be for me to marry you. It would break his heart — "

"And how about mine, Mariella?" he asked her, in that deep, submissive tone which she found harder to resist than his anger. She pressed her hands to her temples.

"I can't think of you," she cried, passionately. "I must think of him. I can't forget the years he has worked and waited, loving me and trusting me. Every night for five years he has set a light in his window and watched for mine. This last year — since you came" — the words came so fast and so vehemently now that they seemed to push one another from her lips — "my lamp has been lighted later and later — yet not once has his window been dark. Night after night I have seen his light with the guiltiest pang a woman could know. I was deceiving you, but how much more was I deceiving him! I have seen" — her voice fell suddenly — "the house growing day by day, and my heart has been sick with despair and misery. . . . Oh, don't you understand how much harder it would be for him to give me up than for you? His life has been so hard and narrow. It has had only this one thing; but he has had it all these years, and you would take it from him in one little year. You do not know how he loves me —"

"Oh, do I not?" said Leaming, in an irony so bitter that it was almost a grim humor.

"But *I* know," she went on, not heeding. "It would kill him. He has nothing else to turn to. If I were so selfish, so wicked, as to do what you wish, I should never have more than a few moments' happiness at a time. I could never forget him — his love — the promises I have made him! I should hear the hammer and see the house grow in my dreams . . . his eyes would haunt me and follow me in the dark with the look of love deep in them. . . . I should hear him say 'Mariella' in that tone — that tone — oh, it would drive me mad in time!"

She broke off, sobbing. Leaming pressed her hands, speechless with misery; her sobs cut him to the heart. When she grew calmer, she continued, but more brokenly — "Don't you see that it can never be? If he knew the truth he would release me; but no happiness that I might know as your wife could make me ever forget the look that would be in his eyes when he first knew — if it ever left them at all! It would be the look of death."

She leaned her face down upon their clasped hands, her tears falling upon them.

"Oh, dearest," she cried, beseechingly. "You are pleading against your own nature, against your own ideals of right and honor. You spoke the other night from your nobler self, your real self. You said if keeping me meant wrong to another and cheapened you in your own eyes, you could give me up —"

"I was a fool!" said Leaming, hoarsely, between his teeth; she felt the cords swell out in his wrists again, and she pressed her quivering lips almost convulsively upon them. "Men talk that way — before they are tempted!"

"You said that we cheated ourselves when we called a love great that did not have greatness of character behind it. . . . Oh, my dearest, my dearest," she pleaded, kneeling up to his breast, "all your life you have lived up to your ideals, and I have fallen below mine! The words you spoke the other night seemed to open life out before me and show me the way to live — the peace of self-denial — the heights a soul may climb to — in the making of a beautiful character. Your few words revealed my whole life, my whole nature, to me, like a searchlight, and helped me to rise above myself for the first time — gave me the exaltation of a first self-victory. And now" — the words came in a passionate cry — "you would dash from my lips the cup you put there! At the first temptation, you would let me drag myself down again, and you with me!"

Learning was trembling like a wind-swept reed under the tumultuous passion of her entreaty. He pushed her almost roughly away from him, loosening his hands from her clinging fingers, whose touch he felt dearer than heaven to him.

"In God's name," he said brokenly, "say no more. You have conquered me. You have won. It shall be as you desire. . . . *Only* — if you love me — do not touch me! Do not let me hear your voice again! And let us go — anywhere to be moving. . . . Go before me — so I cannot turn back. I will follow. And as you go" — the words were almost inaudible — "pray, pray to God, Mariella, as you never prayed before, to show you the way out of this forest."

CHAPTER XLIII

Coming into the kitchen later than usual, Mrs. Proudfoot was surprised to find no fire in the stove.

"W'y, my land," she said, standing still, "what does this mean? Mahlon must o' gone out to fodder before buildin' the fire." She tried the outside door and found it unlocked. "Yes, that's it," she said, and her face cleared with relief. "It give me a turn at first. He ain't been actin' natural lately; he's been actin' up, an' I didn't know —"

She did not finish the sentence, but took the lids off the stove, and crushed a newspaper down into the fire-box. Then she slanted some sticks of kindling-wood and two or three larger sticks over the paper, and held the blue flame of a match under it all. As the flames roared up the stove-pipe, she heard Mahlon coming slowly across the porch.

"W'y, how come you didn't start the fire, son, before goin' out to fodder?" she said, in her gently complaining way, without looking round; she was dusting off the stove-hearth with a turkey's wing. "It'll make breakfast late, an' you wanted to get an early start gatherin' truck for the store, didn't you? You'd ought to be more particular. It's the greatest accident on earth I woke up as early as I did. If I hadn't, it 'u'd be all hours before you got to gatherin' truck — eight-nine, nine-ten o'clock, just like as not."

Receiving no reply, she turned to look at him. He was walking to the stair-door, and his face was toward her. It was like the face of the dead. It was a gray-white to the hair — as if the blood had been dashed out of it at a blow; his lips were colorless and a little apart; his eyes were like those of a tortured animal — they were big with a terrible anguish, as if it had been distilled there slowly, drop by drop, until they could hold no more.

"*Mahlon!*" cried out Mrs. Proudfoot, in a loud voice, her knees trembling under her, — "what ails you? You look like a corpse. Be you sick?"

Mahlon put up his hand, with the palm toward her. "Hush, mother," he said, "don't speak to me; and don't get any breakfast for me. Just let me alone."

He passed into the stairway, and closed the door behind him. But curiosity, leaping within her, propelled Mrs. Proudfoot after him. She pulled the door open.

"Son," she called, in a tone of plaintive entreaty. "Oh, son! Just answer me one thing. Is it about the mortgage?"

"No," said Mahlon, without turning his head.

She closed the door and went back to the stove.

"Then it's that huzzy of a Mariella Parmer!" she said to herself. "She's gone an' threw off on him, after all. I don't care, myself. Little peakid, fiddlin' thing! Fine wife she'd make him! I don't believe she could do a day's washin' to save her soul an' all. I don't care — or I wouldn't if it wa'n't for him. But he's been so wrapped up in her all these years I'm afraid it'll kill him. He looked like a corpse. I hope I'll never see her again. It makes me abominate her *above* ground!"

Mahlon went straight to his bed and stretched himself face downward upon it, sinking his face in his arms. He lay there half the day, as he had lain half the night in the forest — on his face, motionless, stunned with the grief that had come upon him. His suffering, as yet, was not acute, but dull and stupefying.

At noon his mother opened the door, and called up the stairway in a frightened voice: "Oh, son! The stock ain't foddered all day. They're sufferin' for water, and I've got the rheumatiz worse in my arm. Your father is just a-goin' around a-stompin' an' a-mutterin'."

Mahlon threw himself heavily to his feet. "I'll come right away," he replied, in quite a loud, steady voice. "I'd clean forgot the foddering."

He shook himself as he went down the stairs, and dashed his hair from his temples with both hands. His mother looked at him with furtive sympathy.

"Come in just as soon as you're through, son, an' have some good hot coffee. I've got your father to go out an' pick some blackberries, so he won't aggravate you."

"All right, mother," said Mahlon, kindly, looking straight ahead of him.

"He's gettin' over it, whatever it is," Mrs. Proudfoot assured herself, with a great relief, as she moved about the kitchen. "I'm mighty glad. But he does look awful; his eyes are fairly glassy. I'm glad I thought o' the fodderin'; if anything 'll make him forget his own troubles, it's seein' an animal suffer — poor dumb brutes that can't ask, he calls 'em."

Foddering the cattle and horses did help Mahlon. When he had finished, he stood beside his favorite mare while she ate, and leaned upon her, drawing her mane through his fingers, yet quite unconscious that he was bestowing his daily caress upon her. She looked around once or twice with oats dripping from her mouth, and rubbed her nose against him in mute affection.

At last he leaned his head down upon her, and a groan of dull agony burst from him. Even that relieved him and gave him speech. "Oh, God! any spy deserves shooting. I've got worse than that — but I did deserve it; and I'll bear it, somehow — I don't know how yet. I could bear it better if I hadn't dishonored myself playing the spy — and yet, if I hadn't, I wouldn't have understood just how they both felt. I'd have married her, and had to see her drag out her life for me, cooking, and raising children, mebbe —" He stopped, and his hands closed convulsively on the mare's mane. That had been the sweetest thought of his life. "I *had* to disgrace myself in my own eyes to help her; it couldn't 'a' been done any other way in the world. If I hadn't heard it all, I never 'd believed how she felt. That's just the reason — the only reason— God put it into that snake to come and tempt me, and then put it into my heart to go. To help her — and if I can help her, I guess I can stand the trouble — and the disgrace. But, oh, God!" cried poor Mahlon Proudfoot, bowing his head in lonely, helpless misery upon the mare. "Only think what it was for a man — even a spy! — to lay and hear! After all these years — to lay and hear!"

When he had swallowed his coffee and eaten a little bread in a silence that even his mother, after one timid glance at his face, dared not break with a complaint, he returned to his attic. He came down at supper-time, and again ate and drank in silence, and again foddered the animals. Then he came in at dark and passed through the kitchen.

Mrs. Proudfoot was bursting with curiosity; she gathered together a little courage. "Oh, son," she faltered; and he turned with his hand on the door and looked at her.

"How?"

She came toward him, putting out her arms; there were tears in her eyes.

"W'y, can't I do anything to help you? I'm your mother." Mahlon shrank as if she had struck him. "If it's about *her* — w'y, she ain't worth all this trouble. Little weakly thing! She couldn't do a day's wash to save her soul. I dare say she can't make bread an' pies fit to eat — she always was spindlin' — an' such a mother! Just think of what lots of nice girls there be who'd be glad to have you. *She'd* ruther set down on the beach an' listen to the wind an' sass people, than to be a studdy wife an' raise childern — "

With a start of pain, Mahlon suddenly put up his hand, as he had in the morning. It silenced her plaintive wailing, and, without speaking, he went on upstairs.

The habit of years led him straight to the window. Mariella's light was shining to him. The sight of it went through him like a knife. It seemed to him that it had never been so clear and bright. With a shaking hand he lighted his own lamp. He stood for a moment straining his eyes across the night; then huddled down upon a chair and, burying his face in his arms, he burst into sobs that shook his strong frame. "Oh, *Mariella, Mariella, Mariella!*" he cried.

CHAPTER XLIV

It was near noon of the following day. Mrs. Palmer was ironing by the kitchen window when she saw Mahlon Proudfoot coming in the gate.

"Well, forever an' a day after!" she gasped out.

She set her iron on the stove, and ran heavily to the foot of the stairs.

"Mariella! You Mariella!"

"Yes, mother," called back Mariella.

"Come here to the head o' the stairs."

Mariella came quickly, and stood looking down at her mother. "What's the matter, mother?"

"Matter? You may shoot me if Mahlon Proudfoot ain't a-coming in the gate!"

Mariella turned pale. She started downstairs, not really knowing what she was doing. Her eyes had a look of dread in them.

"Now see here," said Mrs. Palmer, firmly. "You hold on, can't you? There's no more sense 'n your comin' down than there is in a hen's havin' teeth — not a bit. You stay where you're at. You don't have to see him. I'll see him."

Mariella came on down and stood before her mother; their eyes met — Mrs. Palmer's stern and threatening, Mariella's deep and steady.

"I'll have to see him, mother."

"Why will you? Aigh? Now, see here, Mariella Parmer! Are you a-goin' to make a fool of yourself? I just want to know."

"I'm going to do what's right, mother — hereafter."

"Right!" burst out Mrs. Palmer, passionately. "What is *right*, anyhow? Who knows? It seems as if everything a body wants in this world is wrong, an' everything they don't want is right. Here, you go to teeterin' around, a-thinkin' its *wrong* to dress in di'monds for a man you'd give your eyes for, even if he was as poor as Job's turkey, an' *right* for you to try out drippin's an' fry potatoes all your life for a man you wouldn't love now even if he was rich!"

Poor Mariella! With all her noble resolutions, she was not as yet above shrinking and growing paler at the thought of the drippings and fried potatoes. But her eyes still met her mother's steadily; she moved a little closer to her.

"Mother," she said, in a tone which Mrs. Palmer knew well, "it is useless for you to say any more. Mother," her voice faltered now; she put out a timid, shaking hand and laid it entreatingly on her mother's shoulder, "we have done much that we regret, you and I. Don't let us do any more. I have been weak; deception has been easy for me, and I have yielded to it all my life. It is easy for me still; it will always be my first impulse to get out of a difficult situation by deceiving, but" — her tone gathered firmness as she spoke — "I'm not going to yield any longer — "

"Ain't you?" interrupted her mother, with brief but bitter scorn. "Well, what's marryin' Mahlon Proudfoot without tellin' him the truth, but deceivin'? Just answer up to that."

Mariella uttered a cry of torture. "Couldn't you spare me that? Haven't I gone over that till I was almost mad? Don't you see that we can never escape the results of a sin? We have to bear them and suffer always. But this one deception is my last. I'll marry

Mahlon, and be true to him, and kind; and he shall never know the difference. I must — I must do it; anything else would break his heart. And after a time —"

She stopped with a shudder; she could not picture the future. She threw her arms around her mother's neck. "Oh, help me, mother, help me! Don't make it harder. I'm very, very wretched!"

Her mother's face worked with strong emotion. She pushed the girl's arms away, and stood back on her heels.

"Well," she said, with a sigh, "have your own way. But don't go an' make a loon of yourself, a-cryin' where people 'll see." And then she added, holding up her chin: "If you're sorry, it don't help to let the whole neighborhood know it; they'd only tee-hee behind your back. Keep a stiff upper lip before folks!" — and she did not even know that this was the unwritten motto of her whole life.

When Mariella went into the little parlor, where her mother had taken Mahlon, she felt her whole body trembling and shrinking; but the first look at his face helped her. He was white to his hair, and very grave.

He got up stiffly out of his chair at once and went to meet her, holding out his hand, as if to keep her at arm's length.

"How d' you do, Mariella," he said, taking her hand loosely, and releasing it immediately. Then he stepped back awkwardly and leaned against the organ.

"How do you do, Mahlon," she had said at the same time; and then, gathering courage, she added: "I was not expecting you. Is something wrong?"

His eyes went over her with a kind of ferocious hunger in them. Every line of her sweet face and of her figure was familiar and dear to him. He was unconsciously impressing her beauty upon his heart before taking leave of her.

"I've got the mortgage all paid off," he said hoarsely, still looking at her.

She sat down suddenly, and pressed her hands together in her lap.

"I'm very glad, Mahlon," she said honestly; and then, in a lower tone, she added, "I knew you would never come till it was paid."

"No," he said slowly. "Mebbe I was wrong; I don't know. But I couldn't."

"I understood," she said kindly.

Her tone was so much like the one she had always used to him that his heart swelled suddenly. A kind of blur came before his eyes, and through it he continued to look at her; she seemed so sweet, but so far away — as she had always seemed in his dreams.

He commenced speaking fast and low.

"I guess I've made an awful mistake, Mariella. I don't feel — I don't think — we'd ought to get married, after all — after all these years. I don't feel just the same as I did — "

He could have laughed aloud at that. He broke down. Mariella sat looking fixedly at him, as if not understanding. Her hands were pressed more tightly together in her lap; her eyes were opened very wide.

"I do not understand," she said, at last.

He lifted his voice resolutely; it sounded harsh and rasping.

"I say, my feeling has changed toward you." He turned his eyes away from her now, unable to bear the look of varying emotions on her face. "I don't think we'd ought to get married. I think — I think — we've got kind o' used to gettin' along without each other."

There was a silence. The rich color had gone in a wave across Mariella's face.

"Do you mean," she asked, at last, and her heart was

beating so wildly in her throat that it made her feel faint, "that you do not love me, Mahlon?"

Mahlon's eyelids fluttered and fell.

"I mean — I mean" — he faltered, with his eyes on the floor — "it's been a long time, and I think — we hadn't best — marry — "

Mariella sat there before him, speechless. She was absolutely stunned with unexpected joy. After the days and nights of anguish and despair through which she had recently passed, she was unable to believe in a moment in her happiness. Mahlon gave her one rapid look, and his heart turned cold. Such a light had come to her eyes and such a glow to her face as he had never seen there. He could have groaned aloud; for now, at last, he knew what he had missed — what he had never had.

He felt the necessity of further speech. "I don't think we quite suit each other — any more," he said, speaking with the utmost difficulty, but so slowly that each word was distinct. "You like company and books and — such things; and I don't know anything any more but work and eat and sleep. If I ever had any taste for nice or dainty things, I've slaved it all out of me. My wife 'u'd have to work just that way."

Mariella felt a pang of self-reproach. "I always understood that," she said faintly, but loyally. "I wasn't shrinking from that."

Mahlon could bear no more. He lifted himself and started toward the door.

"I'll have to be going," he said awkwardly. "Mother didn't know I come. I just come to tell you. I thought I'd ought."

He moved slowly. He had reached the door when he felt her hand on his sleeve. He stood still, looking straight ahead of him, white as death. He knew that her face was close to his shoulder, her lips close to his cheek; he felt her sweet breath.

"Mahlon," she said timidly, "after all these years are we to part this way?"

He could not reply. He felt that he could bear anything but her tenderness; he had nerved himself for everything else.

"I want to tell you before you go, Mahlon, that I feel as you do about our marriage. We were very young?" Her voice lifted as if questioning him.

"Yes," he said.

"We did not know what love was?"

"No," said Mahlon Proudfoot.

"We grew into it from children. You have probably come to care for some one else; and I—"

"Well," said Mahlon.

"I, too, Mahlon, love another. I think I ought to tell you, so you will never feel that you have caused me any unhappiness." She pressed his arm gently. "Dear Mahlon, you have made me very happy. I love Mr. Leaming . . . but I refused to marry him because, somehow, I was so sure you loved me. It was very vain of me"—she laughed out, softly and happily—"but I *was* sure of it. I thought you just worshipped me. You know we used to worship each other, Mahlon?"

"Yes," said Mahlon.

"But we were so young?" She laughed again, softly.

"Yes," said Mahlon, "we were young."

"I have been so very, very wretched, dear Mahlon. I could not decide. I have been very wicked too. . . . I believe I have loved him ever since he came; and of course I was really deceiving you every time I lighted my lamp for you. You'll never know how unhappy I was over it—and all the time you were deceiving me in the same way. It has been a tragedy to me for months;

and it turns out to be a comedy." She was so happy that she was heedless of everything else. She felt as if a terrible burden had rolled off her. Mahlon was silent.

"Is it not a comedy?" she persisted.

"Yes," he answered her, "it is a great comedy."

"Oh, I am so glad! I am so happy! — to have it all turn out this way! And yet, Mahlon" — her voice softened again — "I would have been a good wife to you — truly. Not so good, perhaps, as this other who has taken my place — oh, Mahlon," she added coaxingly, "tell me her name. Do I know her?"

"We will not talk about that," said he, very low, "it — it is not all so bright for me as it is for you."

"Oh, Mahlon!" cried she, in quick dismay; "forgive me, do forgive me!" She pressed her cheek against his arm. "But it will be all right, I know. You deserve her, whoever she is; and there is the new house — "

But at that Mahlon Proudfoot groaned aloud.

"Don't talk about *that!*" he cried out, in a voice rough with pain.

"How stupid I am!" said she, with tears of sympathy in her voice. "Of course, if there's any trouble about *her*, it hurts you to speak of the house. But it will be all right!"

"Yes."

"I shall miss your light, Mahlon."

His lips trembled suddenly; he put his hand blindly on the door. But she still held him.

"Wait one minute, Mahlon. We have been so much to each other . . . it has been so many years . . . we mustn't part this way. Kiss me once more, Mahlon; she will not care, will she?"

"No," said Mahlon.

She lifted her sweet lips to his for the last time, and

he bent his head to meet them. She would have put her hand up about his neck in the old way, but he caught her wrist and held it. He could not bear that.

"God bless you, Mahlon," she breathed, with her lips on his.

"God bless *you*, Mariella," said poor Mahlon Proudfoot; and the sob he had been holding in his throat burst from him as he turned blindly away from her.

"I'm a liar and a spy!" he said, between set teeth, as he went stumbling home. "I never had anything but *honor and her* — and I've lost both! But I've made her happy. I set out years ago to love her better 'n myself — and I've done it. I'll do it to the end. But oh, help *me*, now!" cried he, lifting his wretched eyes in a despairing and passionate prayer to God.

When Mariella went into the kitchen, her mother looked up from the ironing table, with a sigh. Then she set the iron down, and stared at the girl's radiant face.

Mariella ran to her mother and threw her arms around her, and kissed her again and again.

"Oh, mother! Kiss me and love me! I am so happy! It's all right, after all. Mahlon doesn't want me!"

Her mother pushed her away, with a kind of fierceness, and stood looking at her.

"Be you gone crazy? A-tellin' me Mahlon Proudfoot don't want you! Don't want *you!*"

"It's the truth, mother; he doesn't. He loves some one else. Oh, I am so happy!"

"Loves some one else, aigh?" mimicked her mother. "Mahlon Proudfoot don't want *you?*"

"No, he doesn't; he told me so himself."

"He told you so hisself! He loves some one else, aigh!" repeated Mrs. Palmer, as if trying to do a villanelle.

"Yes; and I thought it would break his heart if I didn't marry him. Wasn't I vain? Mother, if you were I, would you mind telling Mr. Leaming that Mahlon didn't want you, after all?"

"I wouldn't mind it so terrible much," said Mrs. Palmer, shrewdly.

"But it makes me out so vain! I've been making such a tragedy out of it . . . talking about breaking Mahlon's heart . . . and all the time he was in love with some one else —"

"Was he?"

"And in trouble about *her*, instead of *me!* It seems so vain. *Wouldn't* you mind very much to tell him?"

"I wouldn't mind so terrible much," said Mrs. Palmer. "But the idy o' Mahlon Proudfoot not a-wantin' *you!* I feel just like pinchin' him! After all the trouble we've all been in over it, a-teeterin' around! All is, I'd like to sue him for breach o' promise! An' I would," she added fiercely, "if he had a red cent to his name!"

Mariella did not go down to dinner that night; she could not meet Leaming before her mother. Late in the evening she went out on the porch, where he sat alone, and knelt down by him, trembling with happiness.

"Dearest," she said, very low, "I have been vain and overwrought, but you must not laugh at me, for indeed you do not know the needless anguish it has caused me all these months. Mahlon doesn't want me, after all!"

At her first word Leaming's arm had encircled her almost against his will, and she had not repulsed him. Now it drew her to him powerfully.

"Mariella!"

"It is the truth. He doesn't want me."

"He doesn't want you!"

Like her mother, Leaming could only repeat her words stupidly.

"He doesn't love me; he loves some one else."

Then she told him, sweetly and gravely, how Mahlon had come and released her. Leaming held her close in unbelieving joy; several times he murmured "my own," "my very own," in a voice of controlled but vibrating passion, but nothing more. He allowed her to talk while he kept silence. Not for one moment was he deceived as to his rival's noble renunciation — the more noble in that it had been accomplished in such a way that it could leave no cloud on her happiness. That night he could dwell upon nothing but the passionate joy of holding her as his very own at last; but he knew that later on somewhat of the sweetness must go out of his satisfaction whenever the thought of Mahlon's sacrifice obtruded itself.

"But dearest," said Mariella at last, "I am not sorry for all our doubt and all our suffering. I shall never regret that night in the forest. I know now that the greatest victory is that over great desire. . . . There is only one thing that troubles me now. Mahlon is not happy; he could not bear to have me even mention the house. His eyes had the look that, in my vanity, I have always imagined they would have if he knew I loved you instead of him." Then he felt her soft arm around his neck. "But we will not think about it to-night," she said.

Mariella and Leaming were married and went to England to live — to the envy of Mrs. Mallory and Isaphene, and the jealous rage of Semia, who, planning to confound her rival, had really given her a life happiness.

They urged Mrs. Palmer to accompany them, but she firmly declined.

"I guess I know when I'm well off," she would declare, going about the kitchen, stepping high. "You don't ketch me a-makin' a tom-fool o' myself. Hunh! The very first time a lord or a duke took notice o' me, I'd go an' put my foot right in it, an' make you both ashamed o' me. You just watch women that marry their daughters off to English dukes an' things! I notice they don't go a-visitin' 'em very much in England; they stay at home. They know when they're well off. An' if I *was* raised Out-West an' lived here all my life, I know that much, too."

So she lived alone, eating her Dead-Sea fruit in secret, and finding her only pleasure in going around among her neighbors, boasting of Mariella's association with lords and dukes in England. She never forgave Mahlon Proudfoot for not wanting Mariella; and she never failed to say, when, catching an unexpected glimpse of his house, unfinished and gray, among the trees: "The idy of *him* not a-wantin' Mariella. I feel just like pinchin' him!"

Mariella, in England, was very happy — too happy to be curious concerning the woman who had taken her place in Mahlon's affections. Her deep and constant regret was that he could not have been as happy in his new love as she. In her heart was an abiding thankfulness that she had in some marvellous way been delivered from causing him sorrow and from deceiving him. A vainer woman would have guessed the truth.

Sometimes — many times — her heart ached for her "Sea of Opal," for the red mist of the sunset and the long, cool wash of the waves; for the vast spaces swimming from snow mountain to snow mountain, and the lonely firs with stars shining on their tremulous tips.

Leaming, who never ceased to be her adoring lover, knew and understood the varying lights and shadows of her eloquent face, whose every expression was dear to him.

One day he came upon her unexpectedly, as she stood looking across a field at sunset; and finding a yearning look in her deep eyes, he drew her tenderly to him. "Dearest," he asked, "are you home-lonely?"

"No," she replied quickly, and sweetly as ever; "where you are, my home is. But there will always be hours when I shall want the mountains and the forests, and my own sea. There is nothing here that can ever be to me what they have been; but it is only a vague longing that comes when I am alone, and it is not even a shadow on my happiness."

Mahlon Proudfoot worked harder than ever. As years went by a deeper stoop came to his body; his face took on lines of patient sorrow; he seldom spoke; and even his mother never saw him smile except at some little dark-eyed girl, when his face would grow almost beautiful in its longing tenderness.

Never a night passed that he did not go to his window and look across the dark with the old leap at his heart. He knew that he would never again see a light in her attic window, yet he never missed looking; and he never looked without that brief, swift leap of hope, which always left him trembling. Nor did he ever miss lighting his lamp in the window for her.

He never permitted his mother to enter the attic. He did not live many years; and, although it is said that no one ever dies of a broken heart, when one day he was found dead in his bed, with the little lamp burning brightly on the table by the window, the doctors were at a loss to account for his death.

He had few mourners, for he had made few friends.

The day after his funeral his mother, visiting the attic, saw — dimly through her tears — a narrow path worn threadbare in the rag carpet, leading from the bed to the window, and wondered at it.

OTHER WORKS BY MRS. HIGGINSON

A FOREST ORCHID AND OTHER TALES

New Edition. Cloth. 12mo. $1.50

By *The Outlook*, New York:

"Mrs. Higginson's stories are wonderfully compact, and each has a strong, single situation. . . . There is a freshness of feeling about them and a vividness of style which give them reality."

By *The Independent*, New York:

"Vivid, energetic, and moving, quite beyond the ordinary."

By *The Brooklyn Eagle:*

"It should receive a warm welcome, for it widens our knowledge of, and belief in, our own land. . . . The plots are simple and natural, pathos and humor alternate, and neither seems forced."

WHEN THE BIRDS GO NORTH AGAIN

A VOLUME OF VERSE

New Edition. Cloth. 12mo. $1.25

By *The Boston Transcript:*

"The poetry of the volume is good, and its rare setting, amid the scenes and under the light of a sunset land. will constitute an attractive charm to many readers."

By *The Providence Journal:*

"They have melody to an unusual degree, and, like her stories, show an ardent love of natural beauty. In emotion, they range from the merry to the gravest moods."

THE MACMILLAN COMPANY

66 FIFTH AVENUE, NEW YORK

CPSIA information can be obtained
at www.ICGtesting.com
Printed in the USA
BVHW04s0004020718
520586BV00008B/39/P